D1527021

Causes of Separation

Books by Travis J I Corcoran

Aristillus (science fiction with uplifted dogs, AI, and big guns)
- The Powers of the Earth
- Causes of Separation
- Right and Duty (planned)
- Absolute Tyranny (planned)

- The Team (short story)
- Staking a Claim (short story)

Caterpillar (a post apocalyptic procedural)
- Caterpillar

Timetraders (a cross timeline intellectual property heist tale)
- Firefly Season Two

Escape the City (a non-fiction how-to homesteading guide)
- Escape the City volume 1
- Escape the City volume 2

Causes of Separation

Travis J I Corcoran

11 Sep 2022
Based Con II

Morlock Publishing

2017

MORLOCK
PUBLISHING

Causes of Separation
Travis J I Corcoran
Copyright © 2017 Morlock Publishing

Morlock Publishing (morlockpublishing.com)

Graphic Design:	Jennifer Corcoran
Cover Art:	Pavel Mikhailenko
Interior Photos:	NASA, Damian Peach
Editing:	William H Stoddard
Kickstarter Video:	Christopher Corcoran

With thanks to John Barnes and Ken MacLeod for their feedback on early drafts.

With thanks to Leslie Fish (lesliefish.com) for permission to use lyrics from her song "Hard Land".

ISBN: 978-1-980-43744-4

First Edition: May 2018

10 9 8 7 6 5 4 3 2 1

This book is dedicated to my parents,
Mike and Carol Corcoran.

When in the Course of human events, it becomes necessary for one people to dissolve the political bands which have connected them with another, and to assume among the powers of the earth, the separate and equal station to which the Laws of Nature and of Nature's God entitle them, a decent respect to the opinions of mankind requires that they should declare the **causes which impel them to the separation.**

- Thomas Jefferson, United States Declaration of Independence

Thank You

My sincere thanks to the hundreds of friends and fans who helped make these novels possible through reading of early drafts, support and encouragement, and Kickstarter backing.

Hero of Aristillus

Larry Prince

Collector's Edition Hardcovers

Eddie and Family

Elam Bend

Gman

Lowell D. Jacobson

Anonymous

Mark W. Bennett

Paul Trentham MD

Philip R. "Pib" Burns

Wolf Rench

Anonymous

Limited Edition Hardcovers

A. Tambourino

Aaron C. de Bruyn

Alexander Yiannopoulos

Andrew Doonan

Aric Rothman

Brian K.J. Dunbar

Bryan Smant

Christopher Smith (chrvlis)

Colm Brogan

Dave Galey

David K. Magnus

David Solomon

Derek T. Pauley

eadw

Erich Burton

John V. Rauscher

Jonathan E. Stafford

JPN

k'Bob42

Kevin J. Twitty

Kevin Maguire

Mark Koerner

Martin Barry

Maureen Vaughan

Michael J. Katcher

Michael Moody

Ray Burton

Samuel J. Frederick

Scot Johnson

The Sperglords of Brussels

Frank Vance
Grasspunk
Helle Roskiaer
J. David Krause
Jeffrey Ellis
Joel Cazares, Jr.
John C. Garand

Todd Feltner
Tyler R. Crosson
Victor Luft
Wardog of Wardogheim
William H. Stoddard
William R. Evans

Trade Paperbacks

Adri Pretorius
Alexander Lecea
Andrew Schlueter
Bill Anderson
Brian S. Watson
Byrne Hobart
Christopher Käck
Christopher Smith (chrylis)
Connor Medcalf
Craig M. Gerritsen
Craig S. Miller
D. E. Welshans
David Anadale
David Cormier
David Hagberry
Edwin M Perello
Elizabeth Armstrong
Huck
Hugh Farnham
Isaac Leibowitz
James M. Butcher
Jason Azze

Jeffy The Vulture
JJ McHenry
Joe Lach
Jonathan Andrews
Joshua McGinnis
JRW
Julie Moronuki
MacWhiskyFace
Neil Dubé
R.T. Sawyer, II
Richard Ripley
Rob Cheyne
Rob Leitman
S. Sidewinder
Scott Brown
Straker
Tom Hickok
Trey Garrison
Wesley Kenyon
yuzeh
Zac Donovan
Zach Steinour

Dramatis Personæ

On Earth, Government

- President Themba Johnson - President of the United States (D - Populist faction)
- Senator Linda Haig - Senator from Maryland (D - Internationalist faction)
- General Bonner, US Army - tasked with planning lunar invasion
- General Restivo, US Army - initially reporting to General Bonner, assisting with lunar invasion plans
- Captain Matthew Dewitt, US Army (Special Forces) - tasked with infiltrating expat society

On Earth, Civilians

- Ashok Vivek - an engineer in Lucknow, India. Married to Rani, has children Aparna (western nickname "Katie") and Nandita ("Carrie")
- Prem Pradeep - another engineer in Lucknow, India
- Sam Barrus - a Texan, has two dogs
- Maynard - a member of the Atlanta Hacker Space
- Vince - Maynard's friend (and rival)
- Lucy-Ann - Maynard's girlfriend
- Father Alex Dikla - an emissary of the Vatican

Aristillus, executives

- Mike Martin - CEO, Morlock Engineering
- Javier Borda - CEO, First Class Homes and Offices, old friend of Mike Martin

- Kevin Bultman - CEO, Mason Dixon, old friend of Mike Martin
- Mark Soldner - CEO, Soldner Homes
- Karina Roth – CEO, Guaranteed Electrical
- Hsieh Tung - CEO, Fifth Ring Shipping
- Hector Camanez - CEO, Camanez Beef and Pork
- Albert Lai - CEO, Lai Docks & Air Traffic Control
- Rob Wehramnn - CEO, General Tunnels
- Katherine Dycus - CEO, Airtight Suits
- Darren Hollins - CEO, Goldwater Mining & Refining
- Leory Fournier - CEO, MaisonNeuve Construction
- Kurt "Wolf" Balcom – CEO, SoftWrench

Aristillus, other individuals
- Darcy Grau - long term romantic partner of Mike Martin, ship navigator, coder
- Ewoma - 12 year old daughter of Chiwetal (owner of Benue River restaurant)
- Kaspar Osvaldo - employee of Javier Borda at First Class Homes and Offices
- Hugh Haig - A young adult with family connections, trying to figure out what he wants to do in life
- Louisa Teer - an acquaintance of Hugh's, very politically aware and active
- Selena Hargraves - a friend of Hugh's, interested in a career in journalism
- Allyson Cherry - a friend of Hugh's
- Lowell Benjamin - a lawyer
- Ponnala Srinivas ("Ponzie") - a physicist

- George White - a private investigator
- Gamma - an artificial intelligence
- John - a man looking for a home, on a hiking trip with four dogs
- Blue - uplifted dog; first generation
- Max - uplifted dog; first generation
- Duncan - uplifted dog; second generation

Aristillus Crater

Lunar nearside (as seen from Earth).

Mare Imbrium ("The Sea of Showers") is the circular region north of dead center.

In the eastern section of the mare are three craters. One of these is Aristillus.

Photo credit: NASA.

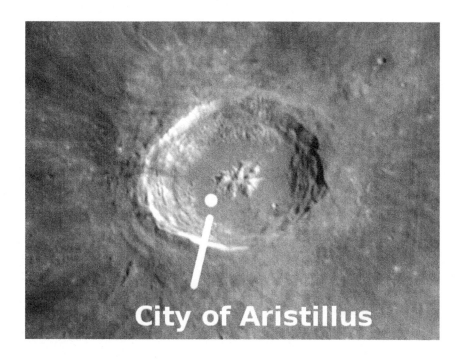

City of Aristillus

Aristillus is a crater approximately 55 km in diameter and 3.6 km deep.

The center of the crater has a triple peaked mountain.

Aristillus was first photographed from lunar orbit by Lunar Orbiter 4 in 1967, and from the surface by crew members of the Wookkiee in 2054.

Photo credit: Damian Peach.

Chapter 1

2064: Morlock Engineering office, Aristillus, Lunar Nearside

Mike nodded. "OK, good. Get them there as quickly as you can. Look, I've got to go; I've got a call on hold." He cut the connection. "John, you still there?"

"I'm here - what's the status?"

"We've got troops headed to the surface. Just one company, but we're -"

From the other end of the line there was a screech of brakes and a noise like John's phone had been dropped.

"John, are you there? John?"

A moment later: "Mike, you there?"

"Yes."

"Tell me where are you, right now."

"I'm in the Morlock offices. Why?"

"Mike, listen carefully, I need you to -"

The phone went dead. "John, can you hear me? John!" Shit. Had something <u>happened</u> to John?

Next to him Trang said. "My phone died!"

Albert Lai said, "Mine too"

Mike looked at his phone. Zero bars.

Trang asked him, "So what do we do now?"

Mike ignored him. God damn it. Everything was unfolding too fast. Too damned fast. The industrial base was too small, the population was too small, the political climate was wrong. The might be ready for an invasion in five years.

In five months? Doubtful, but possible.

But today? Literally today? Not a chance in hell.

They were going to lose this revolution before it even started. By the end of the day he and everyone he knew was going to be captured or dead.

He took a deep breath, stood, and addressed the Boardroom Group. "Trang asked what do we do. I'll tell you: we hope that Olusegun and his men can hold them long enough for the rest of the units to muster. And then we hope that they can defeat the invasion."

"But what if the First Morlock *can't* stop them?"

Mike pulled his pistol from the holster, pulled the slide back a centimeter, and verified that a round was chambered.

He looked up at Trang. "Then we go down fighting."

Chapter 2

2064: near lock #473 on level one, Aristillus, Lunar Nearside

Olusegun stood in his spacesuit, rifle slung over his left shoulder and helmet held in his right hand. The owners of the Chinese restaurant in front of him were frantically pulling the security grate down, and then the glowing purple dragon sign over the grates turned off. Four more trucks arrived and parked, blocking the tunnel. Men tumbled out, all clad in spacesuits and most of them - but not all - clutching copies of Mike's ridiculously oversized rifle.

Patrick, commander of First Company, jumped out of the truck after the men and saw Olusegun. He shouted over the clamor. "Our phones are out."

Olusegun walked to him, meeting him halfway. "Everyone's phones are out: the DNA and Mogs networks are both down. We think it's sabotage."

Patrick shook his head. "Shit. What's our situation?"

"Second and Fourth are already here. You bring us to three companies. If Third gets here soon -"

Patrick shook his head. "I don't have all of First with me. And Third is fucked: Connelly's truck wrecked and no one knew who the number two was. Vu is scrambling to mobilize them."

Olusegun nodded grimly. "Crap."

"Fill me in; what's the plan?"

"Before we lost the phones Mike told me that the PKs are going to land near #912. The 'Group has already changed the passwords on all the airlocks, so the peakers are going to be trapped outside. That'll hold them - but not for long. I want to surround them on the surface and hammer them there."

Two huge yellow articulated dump trucks rolled in from a cross tunnel and came to a stop. Dozens of men jumped awkwardly from the hopper to the roadbed, their bulky Morlock-logoed suits and massive rifles causing them to stagger and catch themselves as they landed. Patrick looked at them. "That's the rest of First."

Olusegun scanned the hundreds of men straggling into formations and tried to push down his panic. This looked less like a military unit assembling than a disorganized mob. Shit. He turned to Patrick. "Cycle your team out through the lock and take up positions. Try to wait for us to get out there, but if you come under fire, fight back." He looked back and forth. "Shit. I need to go talk to the other company commanders. I'll talk to you soon."

"Wait, Olusegun. If we don't get phones back, how are we going to coordinate?"

Olusegun shook his head. "I don't know. Improvise."

Patrick exhaled. "Shit."

He turned and looked at his men, who were just starting to form up.

Chapter 3

2064: storage room near lock #912, Aristillus, Lunar Nearside

Dewitt double-checked the PK logo on the chest of his suit, placed one foot on either side of the double yellow line, put his hands over his head, and waited for the airlock to open.

The light over the massive airlock cycled from red to yellow, and then to green. There was a hiss of equalizing air and the floor rumbled as the huge door began to roll to one side. The lock, he knew, was sized to accept a pair of Caterpillar 725s side by side. Now it held different vehicles: at first Dewitt could see just one armored APC, and then as the door kept moving a second and then a third were revealed. Each was surrounded by dismounted infantry.

Despite Dewitt's posture and the logo on his chest, several of the men raised their weapons and pointed them before their officers calmed them. Jesus. Just as ill-trained as he'd expected. Hadn't they been briefed?

One man at the front of the crowd raised his suit's faceplate and stepped out of the airlock. "Captain Dewitt? Major Sotiris Evangelos."

Dewitt let his eyes flick to the rank on the shoulders of the man's suit. Dewitt was puzzled. "Major? I was supposed to meet Colonel Siavash."

Evangelos shook his head. "Situation Normal, All Fucked Up. Not all the ships launched at once."

Dewitt grimaced. Of course.

This was going to fuck up his plan. "How much of the force is delayed? And how far behind are they?"

Chapter 4

2064: lunar surface near lock #473, Aristillus, Lunar Nearside

Olusegun crawled forward toward the enemy. He, like everyone else in the unit, wore the same armored construction-model suit that Morlock issued for tunnel boring work.

The stomach of his suit kept scraping against the gravel and the dust. He knew the armor could handle the abrasion, but he still didn't like it; good habits died hard.

He crawled another meter forward and reached the crest of the hillock. And there, below, he could see PK ships. He dialed a higher zoom. Six cargo ships sat in the center of the gray lunar plain. The cranes on the ships swung back and forth, moving large armored personnel carriers from the ships' decks to the surface. As each landed it rolled forward and then queued up to enter the airlock. Just six ships? That was fewer that he'd expected. A lot fewer. He felt a faint glimmer of hope for the first time since the phones went out. Just six ships didn't mean that fighting off the PKs was going to be easy. It did mean, though, that it might be possible. He felt a spark of hope.

The line of APCs moved. Three rolled into the airlock, which cycled closed behind them. The rest of the line moved forward.

In his helmet his phone rang and he answered it without thinking. Only after he said "Hello?" did he realize what it meant.

"Olusegun, it's Patrick. We've got phones back - DNA has switched over to a fallback facility. First company is in position. Should we -"

"Hang on. If we've got coms I'm calling Mike." He hung up and placed the call. Mike's phone rang and then went to voice mail. Shit.

Maybe Robert Zelman of the Second Morlock had newer information. He called and Robert answered.

"Robert, I'm on the surface with the 1st. I can't get through to Mike."

"I can't get through either. I tried a bunch of numbers. No one at the Boardroom is answering. Either the phones are still out there, or it's a decapitation strike."

Olusegun swore. "Or both." He paused. "Listen, PK troops are pouring in through lock #912."

"What the hell? Mike told me he shut down all the locks!"

"I don't know. Mike is out of the loop - no one is running the show except us. I'm in overwatch above the ships."

"How big a force is it?"

"Smaller than we feared. Six ships, each with five APCs and some dismounted infantry. Call it six hundred, maybe a thousand men total."

Robert whistled. "That's a lot."

"Yeah, but maybe we can survive this."

"Maybe." Robert sounded dubious. "They still offloading?"

"No; the cranes have stopped. The entire force is inside already."

"Shit. OK, I'm going to try to intercept them, but I don't have enough men to hold. I need you and First Morlock to join up with me. Can you go overland to lock #912 and follow them in? We can pincer them -"

Olusegun zoomed in tighter on the PK ships, and that's when he saw it. "Not gonna work. The ships are armed with some sort of chain guns - we'd be torn apart out here."

"You need to come up with something, Olusegun. We're understrength. Either you figure out some way to help us or -"

"We'll make it work. Look -" He thought quickly. "You figure out where they're headed and clear civilians out of the way. We'll cycle back inside and haul ass over to #912, then we'll follow them. Once we're close we'll coordinate and try to pincer them."

Robert blew air through his lips. "It's not much of a plan."

"You've got a better one?"

"Shit. No. OK, let's do it." Robert paused. "Good luck, Olusegun."

Olusegun nodded grimly. "You too."

Chapter 5

2064: Morlock Engineering Office, Aristillus, Lunar Nearside

Mike stood at the head of the table in front of the Boardroom Group.

"Come on, move!"

They dithered.

"Now!"

There was confusion and clattering, but at least now they were getting to their feet.

Karina looked at him. "Mike, what's the rush? Shouldn't we stay here and figure out -"

Mike cut her off. "The PKs are inside the tunnels. They could be heading here."

"But why -"

Jesus. This woman. "To capture us. Now *move!*" Karina looked alarmed and gathered her jacket and papers.

Trang was already standing. "Where to?"

Javier turned to him. "Mike, you've kept your ranch off the public maps, right?"

Karina looked at Mike. "Ranch?"

Mike nodded. "Yes, Mason Dixon's got the cubic listed as untunnelled - reserved for future warehouse space."

Javier nodded. "Then even if the peakers have maps they-"

The door crashed open.

Mike turned. A man wearing in helmetless space suit stood in the doorway. Mike's hand reached for his hip.

The man in the spacesuit held up a hand. "Wait, it's me!"

Mike froze, one hand on his pistol. "John?"

"You've got to get out of here. You've got PK troops in Aristillus."

"The invasion force is through the lock - we know."

"What? No, not that - you've got sleeper cells *already* in the tunnels."

"What? How do you -"

"I just ran into an old army friend - Matt Dewitt. He's stationed at an airlock. He's an inside man for the PKs. If there's onc, there's more."

Mike swore.

The lights died and the ever-present whir of fans stopped.

Chapter 6

2064: lunar surface near lock #473, Aristillus, Lunar Nearside

Olusegun drummed his gloved fingers against the side of his suit. Damn it! This was taking too long. The display over the inner door changed: the word "pressurizing" disappeared and was replaced with "electrostatic cleaning." Son of a bitch - as if tracking in a bit of dust was going to be a problem compared to what else was going on.

Olusegun raised his faceplate. "Someone override that and get the door open." One of the two hundred men of First Company in the lock with him apparently knew what to do, because a moment later the vast steel inner door started to grind open.

As it did, his phone gave a high-priority ring. Robert from the Second Morlock? He answered it.

"Olusegun, it's Bola."

"Bola? I can't talk now."

"I know, but I -"

"Cousin, we're about to go into battle! Please -"

"Give me thirty seconds!"

Olusegun listened, just for a moment, and then for a little longer.

He blinked. Could what Bola was saying be true? "How do you know this?"

Just as the airlock's inner door thudded fully open Olusegun hung up his phone. Ahead of him in the tunnel the other four companies of First Morlock were in their vehicles, waiting for them.

Olusegun turned to his executive officer. "Tell everyone we're heading back out to the surface."

The man blinked. "What? The plan -"

"The plan has changed."

Olusegun shook his head. He was taking a crazy gamble by listening to Bola.

Shit. This had better work.

The inner door of the airlock slid closed. Olusegun flipped his visor down as the atmospheric pumps started to whine. Around him his suit stiffened and grew taut.

Chapter 7

2064: lunar surface near lock #473, Aristillus, Lunar Nearside

Olusegun stood outside and looked around the lunar surface. Three of the five companies were with him out here. He checked his clock. It had been ten minutes since he'd turned around. The last two companies should have cycled through by now - where were they?

He was paging through his phone menu when he saw the status indicator light above the airlock door.

It was blinking red.

No. Damn it, no!

He'd worked construction at Aristillus long enough to know what had happened: this lock wasn't designed to be cycled this often. They'd run it five times to take the five companies out, then five more times to bring them back in, and then three times beyond that to get them back out again - and the lock had shut down in dull algorithmic protest at being overworked. The other two companies - forty percent of First Morlock's manpower - were trapped inside.

Damn it!

He saw his XO a few meters distant. "Find the man who overrode the electrostatic cleaning cycle in the lock - see if he can get the lock working again."

The XO nodded.

Olusegun craned his head back and looked up into the black sky.

Nothing.

The gamble he was taking seemed suddenly worse than it had a minute ago. He tried to call Mike again - and got an out-of-service error.

He swore.

The intelligence he was operating on was questionable at best. His cousin Bola was a smart guy, but this -

He shook his head.

Bola had said that he'd found a futures market on this battle and the odds were swinging toward the PKs. And he'd trusted that? He should have asked more questions. What market? Where? How did the odds in the market imply anything about a second wave? How had Bola found out about this in the first place?

Olusegun leaned back and scanned the black yet again. Still nothing.

Damn it. What if Bola had been wrong? What if he'd pulled his troops away just when they were needed most?

He called Bola.

"Bola, there's nothing - are you sure?"

"I know only what I told you, cousin."

"Damn it, we made a mistake -"

"Olusegun, trust me - the odds are even worse now. Someone knows something."

"These bets could be stupid people gambling away -"

"It's not just the bets. There are comment threads. People are trash talking each other."

Olusgun felt the panic rising. "You're trusting comments on the internet? Bola, what have you done? I -"

"I'm not an idiot, Olusegun. It was something specific."

Olusegun looked up at the sky. Still nothing. He should be inside, fighting the PKs who were already here. Instead he had divided his forces - and now, thanks to the airlock service light, he couldn't even get his men back inside, at least not without a long trek overland to another lock.

"What, Bola? What comment make you think that there was a second wave of PKs?"

"Hang on...here it is." Bola cleared his throat. "The poster wrote 'you're going down, n00b. Never call the game in the first half - the relief teams gonna kick their ass."

Olusegun swore. "That's it? You had me reverse plans because of *that*? What have you done?" He shook his head, speechless with rage. "Damn it, I've divided my men. We should be inside right now, flanking the PKs. Bola. Bola, my God, you- "

An alarm in his helmet beeped. Olusegun stared at it for a moment in incomprehension, and then remembered what it was for. He looked up. He blinked.

"Bola, I've got to go."

Overhead were dozens of small bright dots. Olusegun squinted, trying to guess their distance. Four kilometers up? Five? As he watched they drifted lower. PK ships - just like Bola had predicted.

"I'll be damned."

Olusegun keyed his command circuit. "They're here. Company commanders, divide up the targets."

Patrick, First Company commander, called him on a private channel.

"Hey Olusegun, remember during training when you told me that my men couldn't shoot, and I said that they could maybe hit the side of a barn?"

"Yes, but what does that -"

"These fuckers are pretty big. Maybe even barn-sized."

Chapter 8

2064: bridge of PKS Nasrollah Entezam, 4km above surface of Aristillus, Lunar Nearside

Major Conner looked at the screen. Landing in two minutes. He shook his head. He still couldn't believe it - he was actually going to land on the moon!

He corrected himself: his ship was going to land. Then his men in their NBC-rated APCs would be offloaded by crane, proceed through the airlocks that the advance team had secured, and seize the gold. He himself wouldn't put a foot on the moon for an hour or more - maybe as much as six hours, depending on how the plan unfolded.

Still, though - landing on the moon? It was crazy. And kind of awesome. He grinned. Should he have some words ready? It wasn't like he was an early explorer or anything, but it was still pretty -

His nav screen beeped: ninety seconds. The video window on the wallscreen showed the ship's hold. In it the dozen APCs were nestled side by side, held in place by clamps. Conner cycled through the in-vehicle cameras. APC 1 - everything looked good. The crew looked serious and determined. APC 2 - the vehicle commander and the driver were talking while the gunner scratched himself. APC 3 -

A monstrous thunderclap cracked somewhere behind him. Conner jerked away from it instinctively even before he consciously realized that there was a noise. He whipped his head around. What the hell had happened?

Then he saw it. That fist-sized thing on the wall - was that - was that a *hole*?

Jesus! That didn't make any -

Another thunderclap rocked him and he flinched. When he opened his eyes the first thing he saw was his navigator, bent forward over his console. There was something wrong with the man's arm. Was that *blood* all over the computers?

Several people on the bridge were screaming and there was a roaring sound.

There was a third thunderclap and this time Conner was looking right at it when it happened - the station three console exploded, ripping itself from the wall. The man sitting in front of it exploded into a red mist from the waist up.

What the *fuck* was happening? He tried to scream out the question but he couldn't even hear his own words over the jet engine roar that filled the bridge.

He gripped his head. *Fuck*, his ears hurt.

In rapid succession there were more thunderclaps and more holes exploded in the wall and floor, throwing shards of metal and sparking circuit boards around the bridge. The second navigator screamed as his left arm disappeared, and then next to him the XO exploded. Hot gore splashed across Conner's lap and face. Conner blinked in shock and tried to wipe his face clear.

Those holes - were they being *shot* at ?

The briefings had said the expats didn't have any AA, just rifles. So what -

He dropped the line of thought. The air was getting thinner. Where was his helmet? On the table? Yes, there it was.

As he reached for it the ship lurched and the helmet slid away. He stretched his fingers toward it desperately, but missed. The helmet slid further and then fell off the far side and to the floor.

He needed to know what was going on, but that would have to wait. The air was getting thinner by the second. He needed his helmet, and he needed it right now.

He pulled the quick release ring on the five point harness that held him in his chair. The buckles gave and he fell out of the chair, to his knees. The floor was covered with blood. He looked around desperately. Where was his helmet? Wait - there!

The roar of escaping air was quieting and he could hear his heart hammering in his ears. He could also hear deep thuds - or maybe he was feeling them, through the deck. Other parts of the ship must be taking fire. He'd worry about that later. Right now he needed to reach just a few centimeters to grab his helmet. His ears felt like someone was driving ice picks into them, but he ignored it and reached for the helmet - and he had it!

He pulled the helmet down over his head and was trying to get the locking ring to mate when the patter of crashes echoing through the deckplates rose in intensity. The phrase 'hail on a tin roof' came to him. And then he felt the locking rings slip together.

He put his right hand on top of the helmet, pressed down to compress the gasket, and then pulled the tension bar on the locking rim with his left hand. The helmet sealed, and there was an immediate rush of air against his face. As if from a thousand miles away, he faintly heard the helmet beep as it registered the connection and its systems booted.

Major Conner grinned stupidly. He was safe - he was going to survive!

Now he needed to get back to his chair so he could figure out where the fire was coming from and move the ship to evade. He tried to stand, but his feet slipped on the blood-slicked floor. Damn it!

He slipped and tried to push himself up again - and then the floor fell away from him.

He flailed, and managed to grab his command chair with one hand.

What the *hell* was going on?

He looked around the bridge and saw through the blood-streaked visor that everything - corpses, chunks of indescribable gore, pieces of machinery - was floating.

Floating? Floating!?

This made no sense - the only way for that to happen was -

And then he realized.

The AG unit was dead.

And if the drive was dead, that meant that the entire ship was falling - falling straight towards the moon.

Major Conner looked down at the deck, and imagined the kilometers of empty space below him - and the hard lunar surface at the bottom of the fall.

Chapter 9

2064: lunar surface near lock #473, Aristillus, Lunar Nearside

Olusegun listened with half an ear to the chatter over the command circuit, but his attention was on the spectacle before him: nearly six hundred space-suited men standing or kneeling on the stark white and gray lunar surface, wielding their massive rifles and shooting into the sky. The ground around them was littered with thousands of massive empty cartridges. Thank God this was happening in a vacuum - he couldn't imagine the deafening sound if it happened indoors.

A few days ago Olusegun had been deeply unhappy with his men's marksmanship. But now?

Their ability to hit a regulation target wasn't great, but give them something big enough to aim at, and enough ammunition, and they were getting the job done. And better yet, they were adaptable - the lines of bright red tracer fire told that tale. As each PK ship listed, rolled, and began to fall, the men of First Morlock redirected their fire to the remaining ships. No one had issued that order over the command circuit - the men had done it spontaneously.

The PK leadership wasn't showing the same adaptability. Not one of the leaders in those ships seemed to be learning from the carnage. One after another after another the ships kept coming...and one after another, they met the withering fire from the ground.

Suddenly the world went dark and then bright again. Olusegun glanced up and saw a PK ship falling past the sun. He turned his attention away from that ship and looked down, down. He hadn't missed it, had he? No - there it was, just above the horizon: the first ship. His men had destroyed its AG unit almost thirty seconds ago, but it had taken this long for it to fall in the lunar gravity. Now it was racing the last tens of meters. And then, in an instant, it kissed the ground.

The array of solar cells beneath it disappeared as the ship *splashed*, turning instantly from a solid shape to a shimmering explosion of silver shards. The wavefront of debris raced across the lunar plane below, scything through Stirling engine steam pipes and conveyor belts, and other bright twinkling pieces splashed into the vacuum and flew by overhead. Olusegun ducked involuntarily.

And then dust exploded off the ground around him and his men. What was this? The firing stopped for a second - and then the ground wave from the ship's impact reached them, shaking the rock under their feet. The two men nearest him looked around, realized the cause of the shockwave, and reshouldered their weapons.

The second ship hit far to his left, maybe a kilometer away. It landed among a cluster of storage tanks. Like the first ship, it disappeared in a splash of silver and sent another wave of debris flying outward.

The third ship hit.

Then the fourth.

He saw it coming, but he couldn't stop himself from flinching again - this one hit closer than any of the others, in a declivity below and to his left. He watched, fascinated, as the shock wave reached them and continued to race past, throwing an ever-expanding ring of dust into the vacuum. Steel flew past overhead, catching the sun and sparkling. He shook his head. It was terrible that such destruction was so beautiful.

More and more ships fell - five, six, seven. The solid crumps transmitted through the ground started to stack up. The impacts were no longer distinct events, but one ongoing rumble. The splashes of shredded wreckage flying overhead were getting thicker. Around him men sought cover in trenches holding electrical lines or near pallets of industrial solar panel parts as they continued to fire. Olusegun found a boulder and crouched behind it.

More ships hit the ground. The rock was rumbling like the bleachers during the last minutes of a close-scoring soccer match. The sun got dimmer and Olusegun looked up. It took him a moment to understand, and then he got it: a dust cloud was rising over Aristillus. He glanced around and saw that the outlines of the solar farms and refineries were growing vague. The impacts, one after another after another, were throwing up so much powdered rock that billows of dust obscured the surface features of the city. Around him more PK ships fell and then disappeared into the cloud.

He couldn't see the ships impacting, but he could feel them hit.

A cry of "out of ammo" came over the radio, and then another, and then more. Patrick's voice came over the command channel. "First company - cease fire! Logistics - resupply!" A moment later two other company commanders were giving similar orders.

Olusegun turned his attention back to the sky - and saw that it was empty.

All those ships - gone.

Olusegun winced. A lot of men had died in just a few short minutes. Some of them had been real PKs: men who'd signed up for a paycheck and the chance to swagger through a disarmed populace with guns on their shoulder. Men who were willing to take a salary to impose Western governments' ideas on his people back in Nigeria. Men who were more than happy to seize family farms and houses to build "better designed cities" for "the good of the people." Men who laughed as they bought the virtue of village children for pennies and candy bars.

But not all of the men in the ships were like that.

A lot of them, he knew, had been drafted. Or were men who had signed up because they were hungry and needed the food, and needed the paychecks to feed their families.

Bad men had died. And so had good men who just had the bad luck to be caught up in a bad situation.

Olusegun pushed himself to his feet. Around him the billowing clouds of grit were settling and more and more of the carnage that they had been hiding came into view. He looked out over the devastation with mixed emotions.

He felt pride in winning the battle, and in helping to keep the PKs away from his home. But he felt no joy in the fact that so many men had had to die.

A call for orders came over the radio and he realized that this was no time for introspection; his men needed leadership. He looked over his shoulder - the status indicator over lock #473 was now a solid yellow. The lock wasn't happy, but the over-temperature condition on the pumps was resolved.

Olusegun keyed his mike. "Great work, men. Now we need to get inside and track down the rest of the bastards."

Chapter 10

2064: Trentham Court Apartments, Aristillus, Lunar Nearside

Louisa crossed her arms. "I can't believe you're refusing to cover this. You're cowards."

Hugh's lips twisted in embarrassment and he looked away. "My mother said it's not safe."

"Not safe?" Louisa sneered, and then looked at Allyson. "I guess you're happy that your *man* is so concerned about keeping himself safe. This way there's no chance that he might go outside and stub a toe and leave you all alone while he gets it looked at in the hospital."

Hugh blushed and looked at Allyson. "Look, there's probably going to be shooting -"

Louisa raised one eyebrow. "Oh, *shooting*? Why didn't you say so?"

On the wallscreen the (:buzz-buzz:).ari search feed updated with a ping. They all looked up.

"OMG - I just saw PKs outside!"

Another ping.

"Is this some kind of joke? Dressing as #PKs? Not funny!"

Another.

我只是在隧道中看到的 #PK 吗？

Another.

¡Mierda! ¿Tanques PK?

Allyson looked at the screen and said, "It doesn't say anything about shooting..." and then trailed off.

Louisa looked at her. "We've got to get footage of this." She turned to Hugh. "Are you in, or not?"

Hugh wavered. He'd promised his mom he'd stay safe, but...

He turned and saw that Allyson was watching him.

He stood.

Allyson looked at him. "You're going? Really?"

He nodded.

Louisa said, "Good. Now the question is: where should we go to get the best footage?"

"My mom was asking me some weird questions about Goldwater. Do you think -"

A predatory smile crept onto Louisa's face. "Let's go."

Chapter 11

2064: Morlock Engineering Office, Aristillus, Lunar Nearside

John looked at the chaos as the boardroom members milled in the dim glow of the emergency lights. He cupped his hands around his mouth and bellowed, "They know where you are - we have to move now!"

The room quieted, at least a bit.

Mike pointed to the front of the office. "The front door -"

John shook his head. "Is there a back way out?"

"The building punches through from 3-23 West to 3-24 West, but I sublet the back half, and the new walls are -"

John cut him off. "Other options?"

"There's the garage -"

"Vehicles?"

"There's only a delivery truck."

"Take us there, now!"

Mike nodded, opened a door, and strode through. Karina objected, "Where are we going? Do we -"

John ignored her and followed Mike. The fools would follow him or they wouldn't. There was a crash and then shouting from behind him. The floor lamp that he'd jammed through the handles of the front lobby doors would hold for a few seconds, but no more. Mike broke into a run and John followed, awkward in his spacesuit. Behind him the noise from the outer office had unfrozen the CEOs - chairs toppled as they surged to follow.

Seconds later Mike and John spilled into the garage. The boardroom members followed. Somewhere further back there was another crash, more definitive and brutal than the others.

The PKs were inside the building.

John closed the door, threw the deadbolt, and then turned. The garage was large, but empty except for a delivery truck, a motorcycle lift with a disassembled bike on it, and a large rolling tool chest. "Who's the best driver?"

Mike raised his chin. "Me." Javier raised an eyebrow but said nothing.

"OK, you drive. I take shotgun. Everyone else - get in the back."

John didn't wait to see if they were going to obey - he turned and grabbed the rail on the rolling tool chest and started to push it. The cart slid into position behind the door and John kicked the caster locks. It wouldn't be as heavy an obstacle as it'd be back on Earth, but it was the best he could do.

Behind him the truck beeped. John turned. Mike was in the cabin and the Boardroom Group members had packed themselves into the cargo area.

John ran to the truck, pulled the cargo door the last meter down and latched it, and then unslung his rifle and climbed into the passenger seat before slamming the door. Mike turned the key and the dash lit up.

Behind them the barricaded door rattled, and then banged as a shoulder was thrown against it.

John turned to Mike. "When I say go, *go*. Drive fast."

Mike nodded. "I can do that."

He switched the truck from "auto" to "manual" and twisted the priority dial to 'ten,' and then past the detent to the emergency setting.

John shouldered his rifle, the muzzle out the window. "Drive down the middle of the road - if you see anything, veer away from it."

"Where are we going? My ranch?"

"No, they might know about it."

"The preserve is listed as -"

John ignored him. "You know the loading docks at Sapporo food court?"

"Yeah."

"Go there."

"Now?"

"Yes, now!"

Mike hit the garage door opener.

Behind them one of the PKs opened up on full auto. John twisted in his seat. Bullets from the far side of the door chewed into the metal of the door and the deadbolt. A shoulder was thrown against the door and the deadbolt bent and gave. The door pushed open a handsbreadth and jammed against the toolchest. A PK pushed a rifle through the gap and fired blindly.

The truck's side-view mirror exploded.

John yelled, "Go, go, go!"

Chapter 12

2064: Dockside district, level 1, Aristillus, Lunar Nearside

Dewitt and Major Evangelos sat side by side in the scout vehicle as the sidewalks, storefronts, and restaurants of Aristillus raced past.

Ahead of them, two large wheeled APCs spearheaded the convoy. Dozens of other vehicles followed behind them. Dozens - but not the hundred or more that he'd expected. Dewitt kept his face calm but cursed inwardly. Evangelos had insisted on moving immediately - which meant that three-quarters of the force was going to straggle in behind them.

Evangelos was more adaptable than most PK officers, and that sucked. Dewitt's plan had counted on the force arriving all at once. He'd known they were incompetent. He'd even guessed that they might arrive late.

The one thing he hadn't expected was that *some* of them would be on time.

Shit.

Already the plan was going off the fucking rails.

Still, better to execute now than to fuck around and learn just how much worse it could get.

Dewitt scanned the sidewalks. The convoy was heading through a more densely populated section now. Five minutes ago there'd only been a few scattered people on the sidewalks, but now, here, there were hundreds. Nigerians, Chinese, Americans, Mexicans - all of them stopped and stared. Dewitt pursed his lips as he silently urged the convoy on. *Faster. Faster!*

Suddenly there was a tremor - in the scout vehicle? In the roadbed?

Dust filtered down from somewhere above.

Dewitt looked up. What was that? Mining?

Then there was another tremor, and then a third - and then the sounds merged into a long deep rumble. He shrugged. He'd never heard anything like that in Aristillus before, but maybe that was what TBMs digging new tunnels sounded like.

Dewitt turned his eyes back to the bystanders on the sidewalks, hoping that none of them drew weapons. The result would be bloody.

None did.

He felt the major's eyes on him. Dewitt turned to face him. Evangelos said, "Our maps show that Goldwater is near here."

"The headquarters are here on level 2, but the refinery and the vaults are on level 4. I sent you annotated maps. Did the DoD fuck that up, or -"

"We got those maps, but we've got others as well."

Dewitt looked at him oddly. "Others? Where did you -"

Evangelos shrugged. "I don't know where they came from." He pursed his lips. "But between me and you, I heard a rumor that there's some politician's kid who has been doing reconnaissance." Dewitt nodded and filed the fact away.

Evangelos keyed his mike. "Change in plans. The Goldwater facility we want is on level 4. Take the -" Evangelos looked at the map on the slate in his lap "- second right."

Dewitt shook his head. "No, you don't want the Bitzman corkscrew. First, it's probably too tight for these vehicles. Second, it takes you too far to the west of the Goldwater warehouse - and right past some of the residential areas the militias are going to be scrambling from."

"Too tight for the vehicles? This map says the corkscrew is a full-sized tunnel -"

Dewitt craned his head and looked at Evangelos's slate. "The map you're using is a freebie that Soldner Homes gives away. If you care about details like tunnel sizes, the Cartesian and Mason Dixon maps are better."

Evangelos looked at him uncomprehendingly. "What do you mean? There are multiple maps?"

Dewitt sighed. "Look, you've got to understand that there's no central authority here. There's - " He paused, trying to figure out how to explain it. He reached for some of the phrases that he used to hear so often, up until the past few months. "There's a patchwork of different firms digging tunnels and making maps, and they're never all in sync. Or accurate. Just because the map shows a turn doesn't mean it's really the best route, or the size it claims. Maybe it's in the map because the tunnel owner is paying the map maker in some promotional deal. Or maybe the map maker just didn't care about details because it's a map for new settlers."

"I don't understand what you're talking -"

"It doesn't matter. Just take the *third* left, that's the ramp you want."

Evangelos looked at him.

Dewitt saw the hesitancy. "The lunar forces know that you're here - they're scrambling troops right now. If we take the route the planning software is telling you, they'll intercept you -"

"But the plan is clear - we're second company. We're *supposed* to engage with the expat militias."

Dewitt blew his breath out. The last thing he wanted was for the PKs to engage with the militias in the middle of some civilian neighborhood. He needed to get the PKs down to the target as quickly as possible, before the militias could intercept them.

"The original plan is *fucked*. You're not second company any more. You're the *only* company." Dewitt looked around at the storefronts and sidewalks. More and more people were out, staring at them - and a few of them had rifles. Word must be getting out.

All it would take would be one man - one Texan angry about the BATFEEIN Wal-Mart massacre, one Alaskan who lost someone in the Exxon Cleanup, one Nigerian who'd seen his church burned - and this could turn into a bloodbath in seconds.

Dewitt felt himself sweating. "Look, Major, you were briefed that I'm your contact, right? I've got men dispersed in the militias here, and I know what the response times of those militias are. The original plan is *gone*. You have to make a decision - are you going to stick with it and fubar this mission, or are you going to acknowledge that shit on the ground has changed? Your choice is between following a stupid plan, or showing a bit of initiative and turning this cluster fuck into something we can survive. Which is it?"

Evangelos's eyebrows furrowed. "Colonel Nicola planned to lead the assault. As senior officer, it's his privilege to -"

"Fuck Colonel Nicola. He's late and his plan is ruined. Man up, Major. Are you going to make this a victory, or are you going to let it get fucked?"

Evangelos breathed out hard, and then seemed to make a decision. "OK. We do it your way."

"Good. Tell your lead APC to take the next left."

Evangelos placed a call and a moment later the lead APC turned onto the ramp; then the second turned. As their scout vehicle followed the lead vehicles, Dewitt looked ahead, along the main tunnel they'd been following. There, not a hundred meters further, a truck was parked athwart both lanes - and five men armed with rifles crouched behind it.

Dewitt swallowed. This was getting far too close to turning a horrific massacre.

Unless he was very, very lucky there was going to be blood - a lot of blood - before this was over.

Chapter 13

2064: Morlock Engineering Garage, Aristillus, Lunar Nearside

"Yes, now!"

Mike hit the garage door opener.

Behind them, one of the PKs opened up on full auto. Mike glanced in his mirror and saw the steel door shred behind him, and then turned his attention back to the garage door, willing it to open faster.

Behind them there was more firing. John yelled "Go, go, go!" and, despite the bulk of the spacesuit, somehow twisted backwards in his seat - knees on the seat, back braced against the dash - and stuck his rifle out the window.

The garage door still wasn't open. He knew it took only a few seconds, but now, when he needed it open *this very second*, it felt like the world was moving in slow motion. Behind him more rifle shots rang out and the truck jerked slightly. Mike pursed his lips and hoped the rounds hadn't hit the motor, or the batteries - or members of the Group in the back.

The lower edge of the garage door was at windshield height.

Mike put the truck into gear.

Darcy teased him about his aggressive driving and micro-optimizations on the road. In her view, knowing the maximum speed that one could take the Bitzman Corkscrew from level 2 to level 3 on a motorcycle without wiping out was dumb - and laboriously learning that exact speed through three crashes was even dumber. And if Darcy knew about his hack for exiting the Morlock garage without a single wasted second, she'd call that dumb too.

The bottom roller of the door cleared the top edge of the breaker box.

Mike floored the accelerator. The truck shot forward, straight at the garage door. Behind him, he heard shots, but ignored them. The truck surged and looked like it was going to hit the bottom of the garage door, but in a flash they were through.

Mike glanced left. There was oncoming traffic, but he'd ignore it and let those cars' systems worry about preventing a crash. He cut the wheel hard to the right. Behind him there was a screeching of brakes as the other vehicles responded.

More rifle shots rang out behind them.

And they were in the road. The truck fishtailed as Mike kept the accelerator pinned.

Thirty meters ahead were the front doors of the Morlock office, broken off their hinges now. Four troops armored with black ballistic vests and helmets stood guard. They turned now as the truck's tires squealed.

One of them shouted and raised his rifle.

Mike swallowed. John had said to drive fast. The accelerator was already down against the floorboard but Mike stood on it, willing any extra acceleration.

A second peaker raised his rifle.

Mike glanced right. John had twisted in his seat again and was now facing forward. His rifle was pulled tight and his head was tucked into the stock, and -

John fired, releasing a thunderclap in the small truck cabin. Mike jerked the wheel involuntarily. John snapped off a half dozen more rounds in less than a second. The distance to the PKs was disappearing. The two PKs who had been holding rifles staggered and fell. A third, bizarrely, ran out into the road. A fourth raised his rifle. Three more thunderclaps hammered Mike's ears as John fired, almost too fast to follow. A piece of hot brass ricocheted around the interior of the truck and landed inside the collar of Mike's shirt. *Fuck*, it burned! He wanted nothing more than to pull his shirt away from his skin to let the brass fall out, but he kept both hands on the wheel.

There was one PK left - the one who'd darted out - and he was on the left side of the road, opposite John. John tried to pivot, but between the rifle and the bulky space suit, he couldn't.

The PK raised his carbine.

In a fraction of a second Mike knew what would happen: as Mike drove past, the PK would empty a clip into the cab of the truck.

Without thinking about it, Mike pulled the wheel. The truck swung alarmingly, and then the PK wasn't off to one side, he was straight ahead.

The PK fired twice, and then the truck struck him with a sickening crack and ran him over.

In the lower gravity the truck tilted dangerously. Mike corrected to keep the wheels on the ground, and the truck swerved across the double yellow line. Ahead of him oncoming traffic skidded to a halt, brakes screeching. Mike fought the truck under control and then floored the accelerator again.

In the passenger seat, John swiveled to cover the entrance to Morlock. And then they were past. Past the office. Past the ambush.

Mike kept the truck centered over the double yellow line and let the traffic part. John pulled his rifle back inside the truck and held it across his lap. "Good driving."

Mike shrugged, then kept his eyes on the road as he pulled at the bottom of his polo shirt. A piece of warm brass fell out.

The dashboard screen showed the path to the Sapporo food court traced in purple. Beneath the cab the trucks' motor whined.

Chapter 14

2064: The Den, level three, Aristillus, Lunar Nearside

In their own space, with no humans present, they felt free to sniff the three returning travelers.

Max stood still as Dogs - dozens of them - pressed close around him, Blue, and Duncan.

With his nose high he sniffed the air. He didn't smell any one particular Dog, but the room as a whole.

The smell of emotion was thick in the air, and it was a confused mix - happiness, sadness, and something else.

Happiness at the return of three members of the pack, he assumed - and sadness over Rex's death. One second gen in a far corner of the room started howling in grief.

Max grimaced. They'd grieve later, but there was no time for it now, and if he didn't nip it in the bud it would spread.

Max barked loudly, commanding their attention, and then said, "Enough!"

The room quieted. The one grief-stricken Dog who had started to howl made a few choked whimpering sounds, but kept his emotion in check.

Max cleared his throat. "Dogs, listen to me! We can get reacquainted - and mourn Rex - later. Right now, we have to concentrate on one thing. The invasion."

A smaller Dog looked up from the slate he'd been surreptitiously glancing at. "Punditdome has video. There are APCs rolling down the tunnels!" He paused, in shock. "It's real."

"Of course it's real." He turned away from the runt and raised his voice. "Now listen to me. John has told the Boardroom Group and they're scrambling their militias, but -"

The runt interrupted, "So what -"

Max growled until the runt looked away, and then turned back to the crowd. "The Boardroom Group is scrambling their militias, but we don't know how big the PK invasion is. This might be it. Ragnarok. The end of the world. If the PKs win here, then *We. Are. All. Dead.*"

The room grew quiet as his words sank in. Max let the fear weigh on them for a moment before continuing. "We are unarmed and unprepared." He looked from eye to eye. "I blame myself. I should have -"

Someone in the pack yelled, "None of us expected this to happen for another few years. You can't -"

Max cut the Dog off. "Thank you, but still: I knew the war was coming, and I should have known it would be soon. But that doesn't mean that we're going to roll over on our backs. If we die today, we die fighting."

A different voice yelled out, "It's too late - the troops are already here. There's nothing we can do."

Max barked. "No! You're wrong! On Farside we fought against dozens of PKs. We were unarmed, and we killed them."

Someone yelled, "You fought PKs? And you *won*?"

"You're damned right we won! Four Dogs against the PKs. We killed every single one of them. And then afterwards, I pissed on their corpses."

Blue cleared his throat. "John was there too -"

Max waved the distraction away. "Dogs! We might have days until the PKs find us here. Or we might just have hours or minutes. No matter what, we're going to fight."

Yet another voice yelled, "How?"

"Good question. On Farside Duncan programmed mules." He turned to Duncan now. "Duncan, get online. Buy all the mules you can find, anywhere in the colony. Pay extra - whatever it takes - and get them delivered. Immediately. I don't mean 'one hour,' I mean 'right now.' Then grab a few other Dogs and start loading your software into them."

"And we also cobbled together some grips for guns we took from the PKs. We didn't test them, but it's an idea that can work." He turned to a red-furred female in the audience. "Aabroo, I need you to buy rifles. AR series probably, but whatever you can find. Get some Dogs who have CAD and mechE skills and get rifle stocks printed up that are short enough that we can use them. Rush delivery. Empty the accounts if you have to." He paused. "And ammo. Lots of ammo."

Aabroo's nostrils flared, and she nodded. "Cody, Demo, come with me."

Max looked around the crowd. "I need some volunteers who are good with machines. OK, Liler, Vance, I see your paws. Go warm up the picker crane and the welding bot and meet me in the front warehouse bay in five minutes. We're going to fortify the entrance." The two Dogs nodded and left the room.

Max started to circle the room, dictating orders as he went. The next group was told to order steel plate and I-beams and join Liler and Vance as they fortified the doors. The group after that was instructed to call up archived designs for ANFO bombs and purchase lubricant oil, ammonium nitrate fertilizer, and small cement mixers. A third was told to order food and water. As each task was delegated more of the crowd slipped away.

Max looked around. The room was nearly empty; it was just him, Blue, and a few stragglers in a loose circle around them.

Blue turned to him. "Now what?"

"Now?" Max raised one eyebrow. "Now we hope that the militias manage to somehow pull out a win, so that we don't all get killed before the end of the day."

"You don't think this - "Blue gestured around the nearly empty room" - will save us?"

Max shook his head. "At the margin, it might help. But if the PKs land in force? No, then we're dead."

"So why all this? Just to keep them occupied?"

Max looked at Blue directly. Blue was probably smarter than him, but he hadn't read a tenth of what Max had. He didn't understand war. He didn't understand leadership.

"Blue, if we die today, we die. But if we manage to live until tomorrow, this - this right here - this will be the turning point. The day we took responsibility for our lives. The day we stopped being dependents on humans. The day we stopped being pets." He growled. "The day we began to fight back."

Chapter 15

2064: outside Goldwater vault, level four, Aristillus, Lunar Nearside

Dewitt rocked forward in his seat as the scout vehicle came to a halt. Ahead of them the two lead APCs had taken up position: they'd turned sideways to block the tunnel and their machine guns were pointing forward.

Dewitt turned. Behind them several dozen other APCs were stopping and dropping their ramps. Dewitt jumped down from his seat and looked at the tunnel walls. Small paint marks he'd left yesterday were right there, and there, among the ceiling light panels and pipes, were the fake electrical boxes he'd installed. Perfect.

The APCs around him had their ramps down now and PK troops spilled out - and "spilling" was all too accurate. Most of the soldiers had their weapons slung and were moving without coordination or plan. Jesus.

Dewitt's eyes narrowed. What was going on further back? There, about half a klick back, one of the APCs was stopped. Dewitt pointed to it. "Major - what's up with that one?"

Major Evangelos looked where Dewitt was pointing and keyed his mike. A moment later he had an answer. "Mechanical problems - it's dead."

Dewitt swore. "I strongly suggest that you pull those men forward, here inside the perimeter." He needed the men here if the plan was going to work.

Evangelos nodded and issued the command.

Dewitt waited. And waited. Around him troops were milling, directionless. And further back? He glanced at the dead vehicle and felt his jaw clench. The lunar militias could be here any minute, and if the PK troops were still dispersed around when it happened, shit was going to get really nasty, really fast.

And then, finally, the disabled APC dropped its ramp, and PK troops started disembarking. And, God damn it, they were walking with canes or - in two cases - being pushed in wheelchairs.

"Major, what the fuck?!"

Major Evangelos compressed his lips and looked away.

He'd managed to avoid the AAS idiocy during his career, thanks to the exemptions that the elite units still had. It hadn't occurred to him that this operation - a God damned invasion of the moon! - would have AAS troops. Fucking shit.

Would this impact the plan? He shook his head. It might. It just fucking might.

He looked down the tunnel in the other direction.

No expats.

Not yet.

"Captain?"

"Yes, Major?"

"My map shows that we're one tunnel off - the front entrance to Goldwater -"

"I know." Dewitt pointed. "This armored door takes us in the back way - hopefully that lets us avoid whatever fixed defenses they have up front."

"And once we're inside?"

Dewitt shook his head. "I tried to get plans of the inside, but couldn't. Once we're in we play it by ear." As he spoke he stole a glance over Major Evangelos' shoulder. The AAS troops from the dead vehicle were moving too slowly - they were still over a hundred meters away from the yellow spray paint mark he'd put on the wall.

Dewitt's phone rang. He pulled it from his pocket and looked. Sergeant Harbert, who was undercover in Trang's 30th Red Stripe unit. Dewitt tapped at it to bring up the message. Trang's unit was deployed and was heading toward their location. They'd be here in minutes.

Dewitt closed his eyes for a second and shook his head.

Shit.

Chapter 16

2064: RMR Highway level five, Aristillus, Lunar Nearside

Mike gripped the steering wheel of the motionless truck, knuckles white, as the pedestrians crowded the crosswalk in front of them. Move, damn it!

The Sapporo food court was to the right - they were almost there; he just needed to drive another fifty meters to get to the loading dock.

Mike leaned on the horn and nosed through the crowd of Chinese peasants and Nigerian workers, provoking a barrage of shouts and gestures. The screen on the nav box flashed a warning and the price field jumped by another hundred as a fine was automatically levied. One of the Boardroom members pounded against the rear of the cab and asked a muffled question. Mike couldn't make it out, but John shouted back, "Almost! Soon!"

Then, finally, Mike was through the crosswalk. He turned one last corner and nosed into the small class-A cross tunnel - no more than an alley, really - and then backed into one of the loading dock slots.

John was out of the truck even before Mike stopped it. As Mike killed the ignition he heard the rear door roll up. Mike climbed out and saw that John was on the loading dock and had the service entrance door open.

"Come on, people, move, move, move!"

John looked like a maniac wearing a space suit and carrying a rifle - but he looked like a maniac who was getting the job done. The CEOs were exiting the truck and moving.

Mike hopped onto the loading dock and pushed through the door, with Javier close on his heels.

Chapter 17

2064: outside Goldwater vault, level four, Aristillus, Lunar Nearside

Dewitt stood in the center of the PKs and surveyed the situation.

A few of Evangelos's troops had taken positions behind bollards or equipment boxes and were covering the approaches down the tunnel. Others had set up oxygen lances and were preparing to attack the armored vault door. And further back, the AAS from the disabled vehicle were getting closer - but slowly. Too slowly.

The Red Stripes would be here any second - and then the firefight would start.

Shit.

"Major, I'm getting the cripples."

Evangelos yelled something back to him, but Dewitt ignored it and ran. Moving quickly was difficult enough in the low gravity, but his space suit and gear added weight and bulk. He and his men had learned the locals' trick of rubbing bars of ToeStick on the soles of their boots. It helped now, but running was still awkward.

As he closed in on the members of the AAS platoon - who had stopped walking and were standing in a circle and bullshitting - he yelled, "Move it!"

The troops looked at him blankly.

Jesus. The Red Stripes were going to be here in seconds - were these people idiots?

"Now! It's an emergency!"

A few of them turned and started walking, but most didn't. Damn it. He looked around desperately. There - an AAS sitting in a wheelchair. He grabbed her by one arm and pulled her into a shoulder carry.

She yelled at him in outrage. "What the hell are you doing, you pervert? *Put me down!*"

Dewitt ignored her and started running. She tried to claw at his face with one hand, but he captured her wrist and sprinted.

The dash of yellow spray-paint on the wall that marked where he'd set the explosives was just fifty meters away. The woman kept screaming. The mark was just ten meters away now - and then he was there. He dropped the AAS to the tunnel floor, ignoring her screams of protest, and turned to go back for more - and saw that the crowd of AASes were jogging, walking, rolling towards him. They were outraged, and were yelling.

Outraged? Fine, if that's what it took to get them moving.

Evangelos yelled at him. "Captain, what's the meaning of this?"

Dewitt ignored him and sprinted back toward the AAS troops - and then past them. Their dead APC was ahead - and further beyond it were the side tunnel and the ramp the Red Stripe unit would be arriving from.

And then, with a screech, the Red Stripe vehicles were here, cornering hard, pouring into the tunnel.

Dewitt stopped in his tracks.

The lead vehicle was a flatbed truck and Red Stripe soldiers stood in the bed and started shooting over the cab.

Dewitt heard the crack of bullets passing over his head.

A vehicle-mounted machine gun on one of the PK APCs opened up with a roar.

Dewitt pulled out his phone.

Behind him most of the AASes were on the far side of the yellow mark on the wall. But not all of them.

Those people were going to die, and they were going to die by his own hand.

But he was out of time and had no choice.

He opened an app in his phone and hit a button.

In the ceiling the charges he'd placed two days before exploded.

In the confined space the shock wave hit Dewitt like a hammer. He was thrown from his feet and fell several meters away, his suit backpack cracking hard against the floor. His ears were ringing from the explosion when there was a rumble that turned into a freight train roar as the ceiling collapsed. A wall of dust struck him and the world disappeared in a gritty gray cloud.

Chapter 18

2064: various locations, Aristillus, Lunar Nearside

John pushed through the butcher stall, eliciting a cascade of angry Chinese shouting. He ignored it and kept moving. A moment later he was at the stairwell. He turned and pointed up the stairs. "That way!" The Boardroom group went.

* * *

Dewitt's ears rang from the explosion and he was seized with a hacking cough as his lungs tried to clear themselves. As soon as he caught his breath he hit the button to lower his face-shield, seal up his suit, and switch to internal air.

Around him the dark cloud was still billowing, and he couldn't see more than a few meters.

He pushed himself to his knees, ripped the PK badges off his suit, and then keyed his mike.

He coughed once more, but managed to say, "Sergeant Harbert, do you read me?"

* * *

Mike crowded into the freight elevator. John pushed in behind him, crushing him deeper into the crowd. The doors closed and the elevator began moving slowly - so slowly.

Trang's phone rang. Mike turned. Were coms back up? He started to reach for his own phone, but stopped. Later. Besides, he wanted to hear whatever news Trang had. Trang took the call, listened intently, and then spoke.

"It's Van Duong, commander of the 30th Red Stripe. One of the his soldiers said he's part of a sleeper cell from US Special Forces."

Mike blinked. "There are sleeper cells? Jesus! Did he demand a surrender, or -"

Trang shook his head. "He says his entire cell has defected; they want to come over to our side."

The elevator was silent except for the slow thumping as they ascended.

Trang continued, "The sleeper says they're led by someone named Dewitt."

John blinked, then slowly smiled. "That's my boy."

The elevator chimed its arrival.

"And Van Duong says that 30th Red Stripe and Second Morlock got the PKs in a pincer and captured three companies of the PK invasion force. Van Duong wants to know what to do with Dewitt and his defectors."

The door opened but no one moved.

Trang held out the phone. "Mike, you want to handle this?"

* * *

Mike held the phone to his ear and listened. "Three companies of PKs? Well, accept their surrender, then see if LAWS or one of the security firms has enough holding cells. If not, get back to me - we'll figure something out. Hell, we can stick them in an empty tunnel for a few days if we have to." He listened to a response, and then said, "We're going to want to meet Dewitt and his men, but we've got to figure out a few things first. Make them comfortable, and I'll talk to you inside of fifteen."

He flicked the phone off and handed it back to Trang, then cleared his throat and addressed everyone in the packed freight elevator. The joy in his voice was infectious. "Nothing but good news. Not only have this Dewitt guy, the 30th, and the Second captured three companies of peakers, but -" he paused, anticipating the reveal " - the rest of the PK invasion was shot down before it landed by Olusegun and the First Morlock."

Javier. "*Shot down*? With what?"

"With my who-needs-a-rifle-that-big rifles." He grinned as he needled Javier.

John held up a hand. "Guys, shut up for a second." They did, and he pressed the door open button and then leaned out of the elevator and looked both ways down the corridor.

"It's clear, come on out."

They spilled into the corridor.

Mike said, "Should we head down to the battlefield and check it out?"

John turned and stared at him. "No. We shouldn't. You're still under threat. We need to get further from the truck, and we need to do it right now."

Mike put a hand on John's shoulder. "Slow down. The PKs are all shot down or captured - and I told Van Duong about the troops outside the Morlock offices. He's sending out a detachment to sweep them up. It's over."

"No, Mike. You've got *reports* that the battle is over. Are *all* of the PKs on the ground really bottled up, or did one or two of them escape? Where did the snatch team at your office come from? Are there more teams still undercover? For all we know a second and third teams are coming for us right now. We need to find a space that's off the map and establish security there. The danger isn't remotely over; it's just starting."

Mike's smile faltered and disappeared.

Chapter 19

2064: outside Goldwater vault, level four, Aristillus, Lunar Nearside

Hugh stood in front of the mountain of shattered stone, torn and bent pipes, and smashed lighting fixtures. Around him men yelled to be heard over the shrieking alarms. Overhead a broken sprinkler sprayed water in a fine mist.

Hugh ran the back of one hand over his forehead, and it came away muddy - between the spray of water and the cloud of rock dust he, like everyone and everything near by, was coated.

He was miserable and wished he'd stayed home, but Louisa wanted to get the story - and besides, Allyson had said that it was brave that he was going out while the battle was still going on. He smiled, weakly. The dirtier he got, the better that would play.

Louisa yelled over the alarms and pointed at the shattered ceiling of the tunnel, where the explosion had torn away tons of rock and exposed smaller transverse utility tunnels. "It looks like the water lines are being shut down - those pipes aren't gushing as much. Get some video before it stops."

Hugh raised his voice and yelled back, "I already did." The alarms shut off and he lowered his voice and continued. "We haven't seen any troops - do you think we should try another location, or -"

Louisa shushed him and pointed to the mountain of rubble. "What's that? There?"

Hugh swung the camera. The pile of debris reached close to the ceiling of the tunnel, but didn't quite reach it. Through the gap people in spacesuits - troops? - climbed over the rubble.

Hugh blinked. Were they expat militia? Who knew what the expats might do? He involuntarily took a step back -

- and then relaxed. As the space-suited figures started to climb down the pile of rock and wreckage he saw large badges across their chests. They were PKs!

Louisa hissed at him, "Get video of this!"

"I'm on it."

Six. Ten. Two dozen of them.

Hugh suddenly had an idea. He shouted to be heard over the distance. "Guys! Over here!" He waved. "I've got a cargo skid - where do you need to go?"

The lead PK paused, looked at him through the open faceplate, and shook his head before resuming his careful climb down the rock pile.

Hugh's face clouded. What was that about? Were troops not allowed to talk to civilians? Hugh had no idea what the rules might be.

The first PK walked past him, and others followed. He kept the camera running, but - wait. Wait. Something was wrong. None of the PKs had guns, except for the last two.

And then he realized that the last two troops wearing different spacesuits, with broad diagonal red stripes across the chests, and were pointing guns at the PKs.

Shit. "Louisa! The PKs are prisoners. Those expats behind them are-"

Someone cleared his throat directly behind Hugh and he whirled. Four men had walked up behind them while he and Louisa had been filming. Two of the men were dressed in casual clothes and had holstered pistols. They were flanked by two others in black jumpsuits with yellow patches on the shoulder - and these two carried rifles. The weapons weren't pointed at them, but the threat was there.

"I can't call you a traitor, because there's no government here." It was one of the two men in civilian clothes. "But not only are you trespassing, but it sure sounds like you're trying to be an accessory after the fact to attempted theft."

Hugh shook his head then stammered, "Wait a second. We're just -"

"Why don't you put that camera down and put your hands up?" He turned to Louisa. "You too."

Louisa snapped, "We're journalists!"

The man stared drolly at them for a moment. "You're trying to help out forces that were intent on raiding my warehouses, and unless you've got some ACL perms I don't see on the RFID, you're trespassing in this tunnel. So, do me a favor and put your hands up."

Louisa hissed at him. "Every hear of the fucking Fourth Estate, you uneducated monkey?"

Hugh felt his palms grow damp. Damn it. Why was he always scared in confrontations? He needed to man up. He should say something now, he knew. He should emulate some of Louisa's spunk, her willingness to stand up to authority. He wanted to open his mouth, but it stayed closed, seemingly of its own accord.

The man raised an eyebrow and surveyed Louisa for a long second. "As a matter of fact, I *have* read Edmund Burke."

Louisa looked confused for a moment, and then spit in his face. The man recoiled and wiped the spittle off his cheek.

"You cocksucking military industrial thugs can't tell me what I can and can't report on!"

One of the two uniformed men let go of his rifle, letting it hang from a harness-thingie, and pulled a bulky pistol. Hugh blanched. The thug wasn't going to *shoot* Louisa, was he? He put up his hands. "Wait a second! You're not -"

Before Hugh finished his question an electronic crackling filled the air. Louisa seized and fell, twitching as she collapsed to the ground in the low gravity.

The silver-haired leader of the group nodded at the man with the taser and then turned to Hugh. "You're smart enough to put your hands up, aren't you?"

Chapter 20

2064: Situation Room of the West Wing, White House, Washington DC, Earth

The president screamed in rage and threw the closest thing to hand, an ornamental pencil cup, at the generals. The cup hit the table and shattered. Bonner leaned to the left to avoid a flying shard, but an eraser and several paper clips bounced off his chest.

"What the *fuck* do I pay you people for? Do you know how many favors I had to pull in, how many people I pissed off? I had to go to nonunion shipyards to get those fucking boats built, and now you've thrown them away. This could *cost us the election!*"

Themba screamed again, not even words, just a blast of rage.

"We need that gold. We need it!"

Senator Linda Haig sat still - her face a careful mask that betrayed nothing, her eyes studiously fixed on the ceiling tiles. Inwardly her emotions warred.

On the one hand, seeing Themba lose it like this was thrilling. The woman was amazingly telegenic, and the people loved her - and a lot of the bureaucracy did too. But news of this little stunt was too delicious to have a chance of remaining secret. Word would start spreading across DC with minutes of the meeting ending and would be all over the city by the time people were pouring their second cocktails this evening. A crack in the veneer would lead to a crack in her support.

On the other hand, Linda was still angry at herself for her own tactical mistake. She'd rushed to DC Minute to try to preempt the good will generated by a successful invasion - and instead she'd stamped her name on a military fiasco.

And then, on the third hand - if that was a phrase - Linda felt a tinge of fear. She'd attempted to screw the president with her impromptu press conference. Pulling strings at the Minute to get on the air before the president? Themba wouldn't forget that. The conflict between the two of them might not be open warfare yet, but now neither of them could continue the lie that they were allies, working across the sub-party divide. Themba might very well be plotting to destroy her even now.

The president pounded her fist on the table and Linda looked up with a jerk. She listened for a second, but it was more of the same: Themba shouting at the generals about the budget and the California reconstruction.

Linda felt her manicured nails bite into her palm as her fist clenched. She forced herself to relax - and to think.

She needed to get out from under the PR disaster, and that wasn't going to be easy, because Themba's obvious move was to pin it all on her. She only had two tools: more coverage on The Minute and more videos from Hugh. Would it work? She let out a breath. It had damned well better - she didn't have too many other moves.

And if it succeeded, then what? She looked up at the president, who was still berating General Opper. She fought down the urge to shake her head. The nation couldn't handle another four years of this woman. The stupid bitch paid more attention to her shopping trips and her clique of idiot friends than she did to the budget or hosting the Chinese peace talks.

The people deserved better than that. Everything Themba touched turned into a disaster, because she didn't pay attention. Fertilizer allocations had been late in the spring, and now the harvest was going to be off a few percent. That's how it always was with the Populist faction, wasn't it? The idiots thought that just because they were in favor of central planning that everything would turn out well. What the fools somehow never paid attention to was that it had to be *competent* central planning.

It was ironic, but even though the Internationalist faction of the Party didn't put as much emphasis on chicken-in-every-pot issues, they were still more competent at making the economy work than the Populists.

She drummed her fingers on her thigh under the table - and then was frozen by an insight. Chicken-in-every-pot issues. Competence. Might *those* be the keys to extricating herself from the trap - and to attacking the president? What the if Internationalist faction outflanked the Populists, going more-populist-than-thou? And what if she didn't defend herself in the disastrous lunar invasion, but instead opened a new front in the political battle?

How? And she immediately knew. There was that as-yet-unused footage from Hugh on expat obesity: overflowing piles of huge tomatoes, plates piled with massive hamburgers, mountains of fries. She'd asked him to sideline it because it didn't help the narrative - but given the late planting due to the president's idiotic fertilizer allocation, food prices were already spiking, and people were buying less meat and eating out less. So what if they kept the footage, but ditched the story? Not an exposé of obesity outside of a managed health system, but an indictment of the Populists' food policies. Their policies were so bad that *even the expats* were eating better than Americans.

This was good. Really good. She'd lose a few allies from the vegan groups and the nutritionists, but what clout did they have? She should get a team together - not just Jim Allabend, but some of the other strategists. There'd be issues to be hashed out, like who they'd put up against Themba in the primary. If the others agreed that Linda had the winning strategy, then she'd have some pull here. Right now Kaplitt was the obvious flagbearer for the Internationalists, but his support was fragile. Freivald was a better choice, and if she could put him up and then he won the primary, he was the kind of guy who remembered favors. Linda's interior smile grew. Her idea was good - damned good. Winning a primary against a sitting president was no slam dunk, but if they managed - she took a breath - then she'd be one of the most powerful women in DC. She could forget about the *assistant* floor leadership position - she could be the *actual* floor leader. Which meant that she'd have control over all of the committees.

With a start Linda realized that the president had stopped yelling and was now saying something in a lower and somewhat more controlled voice. She put her plans aside and listened.

Bonner shook his head. "No, ma'am."

The president exhaled. "Do we have nuclear charges on these ships?"

Bonner paused before answering. "We can't scuttle the ships that crashed - we're not getting responses to our data queries. The six ships that landed do have scuttling charges, but I think we -"

"Fuck your 'thinking.' Your 'thinking' got us into this mess!"

General Restivo cleared his throat, then spoke. "Excuse me, ma'am?"

The president turned to face him.

* * *

Restivo looked at the president and resisted the urge to swallow. He was taking a chance here - Bonner had two stars on him, and by speaking up now he was risking Bonner's displeasure. That could make life hell. It could even end his career. On the other hand - fuck it. He'd been getting more and more sick of this damned city for the last ten years, and maybe it was time to speak up. If it worked, it worked, and if not, he'd retire to a small farm somewhere. And if Bonner pulled one of his usual tricks and ginned up a scandal to push Restivo out with a dishonorable and rip away his pension? Well, he could survive that. Hell, with Dewitt going rogue on him, his career was probably fucked anyway.

Restivo cleared his throat a second time. "Ma'am, you know the undercover team under Captain Dewitt. I've got two other teams in place. I didn't mention them, because they were just a backup. They're not Special Forces, just -"

The president's eyes narrowed and landed on him. "I explicitly gave you permission to put one team in place. *One*. Your labor requisition credit at NASA had a cap, and if you went over that - " She let the implied threat hang in the air.

In for a penny, in for a pound. Restivo pressed on. "Yes, Ma'am. The other teams didn't get any NASA training. After I saw how much NASA was spending on training that - frankly - didn't seem all that useful to me - I acted on my own initiative to create two other teams and infiltrate them." He coughed, then hurried on. "I got another report just an hour ago. The second came very close to grabbing Mike Martin, the lead expat -"

"Close does not count!"

Restivo resisted the urge to flinch. "I know. But the third team did grab some of the CEOs - Katherine Dycus, Hsieh Tung, Kevin Bultman. And we've still got men chasing Martin and some of his inner circle."

The president calmed slightly. "Go on."

"As you noted, some of the ships did land on the moon successfully. We've still got crews on those ships, and they're ready to lift off. We can get the other deep cover teams - and their captives - off the moon and back to Earth. The last report, half an hour ago, says that there's no evidence in the expat media that they're thinking about the surviving ships - but any minute now they're going to realize that they're there, and seize them. I recommend, ma'am, that we act, right now, to get team two - and the captives - back on those ships."

The president fixed him with an icy stare. "Without the gold?"

"The teams are small - each less than two dozen men. They can't get the gold."

The president swore again, but the energy was going out of her anger. She looked aside and stared off into the distance.

Finally she sighed and looked back. "OK. We can't get the gold." Here she looked at Senator Haig and smiled ever so slightly, a smile that he could tell was all threat. Restivo hadn't seen Senator Haig's DC Minute speech yesterday, but he'd heard about it - and he'd heard the whispered gossip afterwards. He was glad that he just had to deal with the expat situation, and not with the cold war brewing between those two.

The president turned back to him. "Is there any chance that your teams can grab this," she looked down at her slate, "Mike Martin jackass?"

Restivo frowned. "We've got a bird in the hand now. The longer we delay getting our troops off the moon, the greater the chance that the lunar militias are going to seize those ships. I recommend that we extract team two right now. We can leave team three behind with instructions to look for Martin."

"Once the ships leave, we can't extract any more captives."

"No ma'am." They both realized what that meant.

The president thought for a moment. "OK, this is what I want -"

General Opper cleared his throat. "With due respect, ma'am, the proper line of command for this isn't through General Restivo but-"

The president whirled to face Opper. "Don't interrupt me. I'll deal with you next."

She turned back to Restivo and gave him a smile. Restivo dried his damp palms on his slacks under the table. The president continued. "Get the captives and the ships back here. Leave the extra team there, like you said. Keep them under cover, and keep them looking for the ringleaders." She paused for a moment. "And the special forces team that went rogue - I want them on the snatch list too. Take them alive if you can; we need to make examples."

Restivo blanched, but nodded. "Yes, ma'am."

And with that, she was done with him. She turned to Bonner and Opper and he felt the tension, the feeling of being inspected, pass.

"You two fucking idiots are fired."

Restivo's eyes went wide.

She turned back to Restivo. "You're promoted to four stars, effective immediately. This fiasco is a major blow, and we can't let this loss stand. We - you - are going back to the moon. We need gold - tons of gold. Enough that no one is going to have any questions about the deficit. And we need trials. I want *that asshole*" - it had become a title - "and his buddies in court and looking at nooses. And I want it before November."

Restivo blinked. *November*? How was he supposed to mount a whole new invasion in just a handful of months?

"Ma'am, November is just -"

"I know exactly how far off November is, General." She smiled, and it chilled him to the bone. "Make this work, and every door is going to be open to you." She let the sentence hang there - the results of anything other than success were clear.

Restivo opened his mouth, shut it, and nodded.

The president turned back to Opper and Bonner. Restivo watched them out of the corner of his eye. Opper hadn't changed his expression a millimeter, but Bonner - the president's former favorite - was recovering from his shock. Bonner worked his jaw for a second, and then spoke. "You can't fire me - and you can't appoint him -" he jabbed a finger at Restivo "- to my job. That needs Senate approval, and -"

The president interrupted him. "Get the fuck out of the White House." She let her gaze drift over to Opper. "You too." Neither man moved. "Now!". The men recovered from their shock and stood.

Restivo averted his gaze - and saw that Senator Haig had been staring at him. She looked away quickly.

What the hell was that about?

Chapter 21

2064: MaisonNeuve Construction office, Aristillus, Lunar Nearside

Leroy put the two Collins glasses on the sideboard, used tongs to put ice in each, and then poured the gin. After putting a splash into the first glass he moved on to the second, but George White stopped him. "Rum and Coke for me."

Leroy looked at the man sourly. It was presumptuous of him to assume he could order what he wanted, as if this was a bar - as if Leroy was a bartender. Still, White was performing a service, and as much as he deserved to be corrected, it would be worth putting up with him for a bit longer. Leroy put the bottle down and reached into the cabinet for a different one, and then poured a measure of rum into George's glass. He picked up his glass. "No coke." He nodded to George's glass on the sideboard.

George, unflapped, walked over and picked it up. "Thanks." He took a sip. "So the invasion failed. Where does that leave us?"

Leroy breathed out through his nose. "Plan B, of course." He took a sip of his drink and put the glass down. "This isn't the end of it - not remotely. Order will be restored, it will just take a bit longer." He looked pensively at a painting on the opposite wall. "In the meantime, we need to build support back on Earth. The loss -" he took a sip " - the humiliation, honestly, has to be put in context."

"Context?"

Leroy waived it away. What was he thinking of, sharing his thoughts with an employee? "Never mind - we don't need to talk about the deep game. What I need from you is more of the same - dig up the dirt on Martin and the rest of the traitors, and feed it to -"

George smirked. "Traitors? I thought we were all expats here."

Leroy paused. "You and I have seen which way the winds are blowing, and we're going to land well. Very well. But the traitors - well, anyway. Dig up more dirt on Martin and feed it to the kids. We want them to have everything they need to run 'hard hitting exposes.' Day after day."

George drained his glass in a single gulp and hammered it down onto the sideboard. "You got it."

Leroy looked at the empty glass with distaste. The man was a barbarian who didn't know how to treat fine furniture.

"Good."

Chapter 22

2064: Goldwater prison facility, Aristillus, Lunar Nearside

"Watch your head."

Hugh ducked as he stepped into the doorway of the Goldwater van and then tried to step down. It was awkward with his hands cuffed behind his back, but just as he felt like he was about to fall the guard reached out and steadied him. Once he was out the same guard aimed him toward a door to the right. Hugh stepped forward.

Behind him he heard Louisa. "Don't you fucking touch me."

"Play nice, and I won't have to. Now turn left and go to that other door."

"Fuck you."

Hugh stopped and looked over his shoulder. Louisa was standing up to the guard, chin high, rage and defiance etched across her face. Hugh realized in a flash that she reminded him of his mother.

He shook his head. Where had *that* come from?

The guard by his elbow prodded him. "Come on, kid. You're smart. Keep walking."

Hugh exhaled. He didn't want to get tased. He kept walking.

Five minutes later he was through the door, through a quick in-processing at a retina scanner, and was being steered lightly into a cell.

Suddenly he balked. "Hey, wait a second. How long are you going to keep me here?"

"Trespassing is two days, but you could be out in just an hour or two. Depends on how quickly your security company bails you out." He inclined his head

---

towards the door. "Now get in the cell and I'll take the cuffs off. After that you can read the FAQ."

Hugh pinched his lips. He hated complying with anything these rent-a-cops asked him to do - and not just because he didn't want to give in to their demands.

He'd been mugged a few times. Most of the assaults had been the usual smash-and-grab on the DC Metro and the MBTA, but the one that really bothered him - even now - had been just off campus, on Memorial Drive. Five guys had surrounded him, ski masks on to thwart the omnipresent cameras, and then pretended that they were politely asking him for his phone, slate, and jacket. They'd snickered and said that it was some sort of tax or licensing fee. His blood pressure rose every time he remembered it. The mockery. The *perversion*. Pretending that something petty and venal was really something decent and legitimate. It was -

It was a desecration.

That's how he felt now. This was the same sort of sick parody. There was such a thing as real society and legitimate authority, and then there was this. This - *farce*. He felt dirty being complicit in it.

"Kid, you want your cuffs off or not?"

He breathed out through his nose, and mumbled, "Yeah."

"OK, then step into the cell."

Hugh'd seen enough prison dramas to know the process. He stepped forward and heard the door close before him, then blindly reached around behind him till he felt the slot in the door. He stepped backward and let his hands stick through. And then the cuffs were off.

Hugh pulled his hands back and rubbed his wrists as the rent-a-cop started rattling off some boilerplate in a monotone. Hugh half listened to it. "...all interactions on Goldwater property and in Goldwater vehicles have been recorded and will be recorded and you will be provided with a digitally signed copy. At your request, a copy will be mailed to lawyers, security firms, or other representatives you specify. If you have no lawyers there is a list of for-profit firms, pro bono representatives, and legal provider charities in your cell. This list should not be taken as endorsement and may include paid advertising. Additionally- " Hugh tuned out the monologue and looked around the cell. It didn't look *that* bad, actually: there was a couch and a wallscreen. And, under the wallscreen, a minifridge. And on the topic of food, what had he just heard in the monologue about meals? He tried to pay more attention to the speech - and just as he did so the recital ended and the outer door clanked shut.

Hugh looked around the cell for a moment and then threw himself down on the couch. He saw three hard-copy documents on the coffee table and sat up and reached for them. The first said "FAQ," the next was labeled "legal service provider contact list," and the third was a menu.

He picked up the "FAQ" and was about to start reading when he noticed the small dots of video cameras in the crown molding near the ceiling.

Fucking privacy-violating fascists.

Chapter 23

2064: The Den, level three, Aristillus, Lunar Nearside

The Den was pitch black - even darker than it had been during the lunar night on Farside.

Then the welding robot struck a spark and there was light.

Max watched the two robot arms dance around each other as they tacked the panels together, one tack every half meter, just enough to hold them in place. Then the arms swung to either end of the joint and moved slower as they ran two beads down the temporarily joined plates. The bright lines of the weld tugged at him and a memory swam up: building the Beagle on Farside, keeping John supplied with batteries for his welder, working frantically to get the job done, knowing that every minute they wasted was a minute that Aristillus and the Dogs would be delayed in hearing about the PK invasion.

And then the robot was done, at least until the next plate was in position. Max took his helmet off. Beside him Blue had already removed his. As Max watched, a delivery skid carrying more armored plates beeped as it backed into position and two of the yellow-painted loading machines swung into action to unload a sheet of steel.

Max put his welding helmet down on table and walked away from the construction, across the room, and into a quieter hallway. Blue followed and shut he door behind them. Max shook his head to fluff up fur that had been compressed by the helmet.

Blue rubbed his ears with one paw. "The kill room is shaping up."

Max shrugged. "Good enough to build morale, but it's not a real defense. If our plan is to build a Maginot line, we might as well give up. We need an army that can fight them before they get this far."

"How long do you think we have?"

Max shrugged a second time. "We know they're going to do it before the election. They need to come up with a plan, build ships, train troops." He paused to consider. "We've got a couple of months. Maybe more."

"We've got time, then." Blue looked pensive for a moment and then asked, "Have you thought about my proposal?"

Max barked dismissively. "Coordinate with the Boardroom Group? I don't need to think about it. It's stupid."

Blue's nostrils flared. "John doesn't think it's stupid."

"Don't argue from authority. Humans are the problem; working with more of them isn't the solution."

"You're failing to disaggregate. Some humans are problems. Other humans are our friends."

"Whatever." Max scratched his snout with one paw. "How's your little Gamma project coming along?"

Blue breathed out. "I still haven't gotten in touch with him. He seemed pretty eager to talk on Farside, but now he won't answer my calls."

"That's it, then. We'll buy more rovers from the same suppliers we're already using, which -"

Blue cut Max off. "That's not it. There's synergy here. Even just with his SL facility Gamma can produce rovers faster and better than the shops in Aristillus -"

"Unproven."

Blue rolled his eyes. "Besides, most of the Aristillus shops are booked up producing emergency pressure doors, guns, and grenade launchers. And before you object, yes, I've *checked*. Anyway, you're the one who's saying that we need a forward line of defense, and talking to Gamma is the best way to do that."

"You're framing this like a supply chain problem, but the real issue here is that you don't trust your own species. You want to ally with the humans, you want to beg favors from Gamma, you -"

Blue interrupted Max with a bark. "What I *want* is to survive, and for our race to survive. And I'm not so pigheaded as to think we can do that on our own. There's nothing dishonorable about having friends and allies. You've got your head so deep in your history books that you should know that, but somehow when you surface all you've got is some crazy combination of Anglo-Saxon warrior ethic and Prussian aristocratic bullshit. Listen to me, Max - we can't win this one alone. We need friends."

Max harrumphed, the noise coarse and rough. "Friends? You just told me that Gamma won't answer your calls. What kind of friend is that?"

Blue looked aside, then directly back at Max. "I'll make him talk to me."

"How?"

"He always talked to us when we were out on the surface - on the hike, at Konstantinov, at Zhukovskiy."

"So you're going to visit him in person?"

"Yes."

"Even his closest facility at Sinus Lunicus is 150 kilometers. You're going to hike there just on the off chance that Gamma will talk to you?"

Blue shrugged. "If I have to. But I was thinking that driving would be faster."

Chapter 24

Darren tried to ignore the bumps as the skid maneuvered over the lunar surface, but it was impossible. With a sigh, he dialed up the image stabilizer in his helmet's screen, and the view of his salvage team on the plain below became crisp.

You could always tell who was who on the surface. Most of the big construction firms in Aristillus plastered their logos across their crews' suits. Smaller firms and tourists in rented suits were also easy to pick out because of the ubiquitous Red Stripe logo or the branding of one of the smaller competitors. There were even a few firms too new or too cheap to afford custom printing using unbranded Airtights or Shield suits in stock colors.

The men Darren watched now all wore a color scheme rarely seen on the surface: a pitch black suit adorned with a golden sinusoid across the chest. He shook his head. The color scheme, working the corporate logo in, was a bit of vanity. He'd let Katherine Dycus talk him into it - she'd been eager to try out a new fabric coloring process. He'd said yes because his men were rarely on the surface: all their mining was underground in clustered peaks west of the city.

And now his men *were* working on the surface. In full sunlight. In black suits. The cost of the extra cooling packs wouldn't amount to much, in the grand scheme of things, but it was a reminder: never let vanity get in the way of practicality.

The skid reached a promontory and stopped. Darren stepped out. Now that he wasn't being tossed around, he zoomed his display. The remains of the PK ships lay splashed across the surface below and he could see the sparks as the salvage teams cut their way in.

His phone rang and Darren answered it distractedly. "Arnold, what's up?"

"We've found the first of the scuttling devices. We'll get it out, but there's zero chance that it's in working condition."

Darren nodded. "That's what we expected. How bad's the radiation?"

"1 millisiev per hour."

"Should we be rotating crew more? I don't want -"

"That's outside the suit. Inside the lead vests, it's lower. We're OK, Darren."

"You're sure?"

"We're fine."

"No heroes, OK? Get enough structure cut away that we can send in the robots, and then get you and the men out of there. Make sure they understand that."

"They're good boys - and smart. Don't worry."

'Don't worry.' Easier to say than to do. "Anything you need from me?"

"We're fine...but check on Nicolaas and Thabo. Their crews aren't as fast as mine - ha! Maybe *they* need your help."

Darren smiled at the rivalry. "I'll check on them. Thanks." He ended the call.

Darren's assistant Pierrick had stepped out of the skid and was standing next to him. "Boss, I've got to ask. What are you going to do with a bunch of wrecked nuclear bombs?"

Darren took a breath and thought about his answer. The truth was that he didn't have a plan. But if he'd learned one thing from decades of cobbling together mining firms on the cheap: if the deal on the table -

used mining equipment, a politician, whatever - was good, grab it first and worry about the details later. At the very worst you could always unload something at the same price you paid for it.

How did that apply to these bombs?

If Mike Martin's revolution worked, then owning a bunch of fissionable material couldn't hurt anything. But if Mike's half-assed plan went tits up, then having a few fission bombs worth of plutonium could mean the difference between being able to negotiate a fall-back deal for himself and spending the rest of his life in a jail cell.

"That's an excellent question, Pierrick." He paused. "Let's get back in the skid and check on the crew working on wreck number five."

Chapter 25

2064: Northern Logistics offices, Aristillus, Lunar Nearside

Javier pushed through the inner glass doors and into the gloom. The light from the lobby barely reached here and the air smelled stale and dusty. He searched found a switch and the lights sprang on, illuminating a vast empty office. The gray industrial carpet was unvacuumed, prefab cubicle walls and desks were partially disassembled. On the desks nearest him he saw abandoned office toys, a bowl of paperclips, and a dirty promotional coffee mug. Beyond them two planters held dead trees.

The Boardroom Group pushed in behind him. Mike broke from the pack and marched past Javier and the empty receptionist's desk to the reception area, where he grabbed an over-stuffed chair from the reception area. He lofted it overhead and carried it easily in the low gravity past the chromed logo of the now defunct firm, and then put it down, sat, and rendered his judgment with a grin. "This place is OK." Mike then raised an eyebrow. "But if it has a kitchenette - and a coffee maker - I'll consider upping my rating." The tension that had been with them since invasion started broke, and there were chuckles, laughs, and one even shouted "woo-hoo!"

Javier shook his head at Mike's performance but found himself smiling. It *was* nice to be inside, behind locked doors. And if Mike was an asshole, he was at least a charming asshole.

Rob Wehrmann nodded. "I wouldn't mind a cup. *If* there's a coffee maker."

Javier turned to him. "When Northern went belly up we moved to repossess, and so did a dozen others. The rehypothecation is a mess, and it's all blocked till the courts figure it out."

"Doesn't matter to me."

"Yeah, it does. My point is that this place is exactly the way it was the day Northern closed their doors. If there was coffee in the freezer a month ago, it's still here now."

Mike stood. "I'll put on a pot and then we can get down to business." He turned. "Who wants some?"

John was listening to a phone, but raised one hand and pointed to himself. Javier raised his eyebrows at the incongruity: a man wearing a scuffed and helmetless spacesuit and holding a rifle was standing in a corporate reception area and asking for a cup of coffee.

There was a murmur as others raised their hands and asked for coffee, with only Mark passing. Mike nodded and marched off into the warren of corridors and cubes.

Javier looked at the CEOs around him. So. This was it. The invasion had forced their hand, and while they were not quite a "government in exile," they were now something more than a simple working group.

Javier turned away from the group and looked at the office space. Dingy, to be sure, but it was better than what Washington and Jefferson or Miguel Hidalgo y Costilla had had.

Albert Lai looked around with distaste at the dusty carpet and cheap furniture. "I do appreciate that we've got a place to go, but it's a shame we can't find a slightly more upscale place to - ah - squat."

John ended his call and pocketed his phone. "We've got to assume that there are other teams in Aristillus and that they know who you are, where you work, and where you live. There's no paperwork tying this place to any of you. That makes it perfect."

Mike's exploration had apparently led him to just beyond a nearby wall, because he yelled through it. "Speaking of the teams, when we do we get to meet Dewitt?"

John raised his voice so Mike could hear him. "He said he'll be here as soon as the PK surrender to Red Stripe is finished. Maybe an hour."

Mike grunted an acknowledgement and then - from the banging - apparently went back to his coffee preparations.

John turned to Javier. "You know this space. Are there any other ways in? We need to secure it."

"Just the loading dock and fire doors in the back. They're secure."

"Let me see."

Javier nodded and lead the way. As they walked through the empty offices, John scanned the empty desks and the silent cubes. "We've got power here - do we also have water?"

Javier nodded. "And air. And a fire service contract. *All* the utilities are on, and they're prepaid for months. Trust me, I know - I spent hours arguing with the bankruptcy court, trying to attach the prefunded accounts." He shook his head. "Without success."

They were almost to the loading dock when John's phone rang. He took the call, listened, and hung up. "Turns out I was wrong about Dewitt's schedule - we get to meet him sooner than I thought. He's already here."

"Here?"

"At the loading dock."

"We're almost there." Javier pointed at the utilities doors that led to the warehouse area. "The dock is through there."

John nodded. "I want to talk to Dewitt and his men for a moment first. Can you go back and tell Mike and everyone that they're here?"

Javier raised an eyebrow, but nodded and walked back to the reception area. Behind him he heard the steel roller door clatter open.

* * *

Javier and the Boardroom Group waited silently. The air was tense. Expectant. Dewitt and his men had arguably won the First Battle of Aristillus. At the very least, they'd helped win it with a hell of a lot less bloodshed than might otherwise have taken place. And now the Boardroom Group would get to meet their benefactors, and figure out what came next.

What were these men going to be like?

Javier heard voices. And there, ahead, John turned a corner - and he had Dewitt and his men with him.

Javier looked at them as they drew closer. They didn't look like peakers - they didn't have that surly, disgusted look about them.

They didn't look like American officers, either - they didn't have that punctilious careerist air.

So who did they remind him of? It took him a moment to put his finger on it, but then he had it: they reminded him of videos of old-fashioned American soldiers, from fifty years or more ago. Javier stood still, waiting for John to introduce them.

Mike didn't wait: he brushed past Javier and walked straight to the men. He stuck out a hand.

"Captain Dewitt? I'm Mike Martin. Sounds like we owe you a major thanks." Mike turned to address Dewitt's men. "Great work - all of you. We're in your debt." He gestured with his mug. "I'm sure you've had as long a day as we have. Can I get you anything? Coffee?"

Dewitt declined, but one of his men said, "Some fruit juice, if you've got it, sir."

Mike nodded. "Believe it or not, there's a fully stocked fridge. Let me go get -"

Mark Soldner raised a hand. "I've got it."

"Thanks, Mark." Mike turned back to Dewitt and his men. "I want to hear everything, but first: John says you guys are old friends. How do you know each other?"

John answered. "Matt and I served together."

Mike was clearly shocked. "You were in the PKs, John?"

John flinched. "No!" He paused before elaborating. "Not the PKs. The US Army." Karina Roth had a puzzled look on her face. "Aren't they pretty much the same thing? I mean, since the Second Azores Treaty, at least?"

John and Dewitt remained silent for a moment before Dewitt spoke. "Not all of us think so."

Karina coughed. "Excuse me."

Dewitt shook his head. "Not a problem. It's a common misconception."

Chapter 26

2064: lunar surface near lock #473, Aristillus, Lunar Nearside

Darren scratched ineffectually at the side of his suit. The itch, if anything, grew more annoying. Damn it. He needed a shower, some food, and a break. Later. As long as his men were on the surface, he was going to stay with them.

Even as that thought occurred to him a yellow icon popped up on his screen. He glanced at it: the KO_2 in the air-pack was over 80% saturated. He pursed his lips. His own safety regulations said that he had to replace the primary pack or go back inside at this point - the second rebreather pack in his suit backpack was only for true emergency use. "Pierrick, do we have any spare KO_2 canisters on hand?"

"Darren, it's Jan. Pierrick went back inside six hours ago."

Darren grunted. "OK. Hand me another KO_2 canister."

Darren saw Jan turn and look at him. "Boss, how long have you been awake?"

"What? I - don't worry about me."

Jan shook his head. "How long?"

Darren looked at the clock in his display, did a quick calculation, and -

Jesus.

Finally he nodded. "OK, I'll go get some sleep."

* * *

Darren sat in the passenger seat as the car drove him home. He stifled a yawn as he paged through emails.

The first six messages were Vosloo and van Heerden reenacting their monthly fight about extraction and purification techniques. Wohlwill process this, Miller process that. The fight was ostensibly about technologies, but it was driven by personality conflict. He'd been CC-ed by both men. Normally he'd let them work it out on their own, but now, tired and irritated after fifteen hours in a suit, he dashed off an irritated reply.

Only after he finished composing his email and sent it did he realize that the car had stopped; he was home.

He should get out of the car, walk from the garage into the bedroom, take a shower, and go to sleep.

Instead he turned back to the slate. Just a few more emails.

He opened the first. The daily update from Reggie Strosnider, head of his security team. It was the usual stuff, with a note about the Earth kids who'd been trespassing at the battle site. Any reason they shouldn't be held for two days and then released per the usual trespassing protocol? Darren shook his head; the topic was beneath his pay grade: whatever Security decided was fine with him. He archived the message into the "low priority" folder and moved on.

A few messages later - was that email from state.gov.us ?

He blinked, then chuckled at the very idea. Spam got more clever every year.

He tapped the delete key. There. Inbox zero. He unbuckled his seat belt and stepped out of the car. He could *feel* the hot staccato of the shower on him already.

Darren walked through the house to the master bath, put the slate down on the vanity, and turned on the shower. The mirror fogged as he stripped.

The shower was pulsing and the mist it threw off was just a hint of the cleanliness and relaxation to come.

He put one foot into the shower.

...But something nagged at him.

He turned and looked over his shoulder at the tablet.

No.

This was stupid.

He looked at the shower, and then back at his slate. He sighed. This was really stupid, but it would only take a second.

He picked up his slate, opened his email app, and dug into the trash folder. There - the message from state.gov.us.

He looked at the headers - and saw that it hadn't just sent to him; Mike Martin, Javier Borda, Albert Lai, and a dozen other names were all CC-ed.

He blinked. Was this *real*? And what was the message? Saber rattling threats about economic crimes? Or might it be an attempt at negotiation?

He shut the shower off and read the message with growing incomprehension. Why the hell was the State Department looking for a couple of kids? And why the hell was it spamming CEOs - people who were basically war criminals, from their point of view - and asking them for favors?

He shook his head. This had to be a joke. He reached out to turn the shower back on, and then froze. No. It couldn't be. These college kids State was looking for - these couldn't be the two trespassers his men had found shooting video of the PK invasion outside his warehouse, could it?

He flipped back to Reggie's email and checked the names and blinked, his eyes crusty with fatigue.

Holy shit.

He had the two kids that State was looking for.

These assholes were important to someone. But why? And to who?

He called up a search engine and copied in the names from Reggie's message. 'Hugh Haig.' 'Louisa Teer.' His jaw dropped. The son of Senator Linda Haig? This couldn't be true - could it?

On the other hand, it would explain why State was reaching out to him.

He looked longingly at the shower enclosure. He wanted - no, he *needed* - hot water and then and a long rest.

He pulled out his phone. "Pierrick, meet me at the office - I'll be there in ten minutes."

He looked around, picked his dirty boxers off the floor, and pulled them back on.

Chapter 27

2064: Goldwater prison facility, Aristillus, Lunar Nearside

Hugh sat on the jail cell couch and leaned forward as he ate the last of the tacos.

He wiped the crumbs of corn meal shell from his fingers over the tray, and then picked up the napkin.

Eh. He'd had better.

On the wallscreen DC Minute was playing - he'd had to navigate down a dozen menus to find the channel, but it was there. When he'd first tuned in Melanie Roes had promised a breaking story in just a few minutes, but in the hours since the story had been pushed back a few times, and then it had apparently been dropped, without comment. On the screen now, Melanie was introducing a guest who was talking about urban composting and rooftop vegetable gardens.

Hugh wiped his hands on the napkin and switched the screen to punditdome.ari. He scanned the headlines, and then read a few articles. He shook his head. The perverted sense of joy was outrageous. He'd lived among these people for months now, and if you could put aside their autistic politics and their economic ignorance they were mostly decent people. But now? He couldn't believe what he was reading.

The 'news' was bad enough. He'd seen the capture of one PK unit, so he knew that part was true. Or true-ish. But PK ships *shot down*? That was implausible - and even if it had happened, it must have been done with missiles or something smuggled in from some third world hellhole - it certainly couldn't have been done with rifles. Bullets couldn't punch through steel like that. No, it *had* to be propaganda - typical right-wing gun-fetishist lies.

Worse than the 'news', though, was the reaction. The articles at Punditdome.ari were swamped with thousands of comments, and the top-voted ones were terrible. 'They deserved it.' 'A good start.' 'Did they have to take so many of them alive?'

The comments and articles that really pissed him off, though, weren't the mouth-breathing ones - it was the longer pseudo-intellectual ones. Someone smart enough to read and quote Locke and Rawls shouldn't be susceptible to libertarian political naiveté, and yet, in comment after comment after comment, there they were, citing real philosophers in one breath and then mocking them - and the Global Fair Deal! - in another.

Hugh closed the tab in disgust and clicked idly around the interface. No email, no LiveStatus, no ViChat. The system gave him just basic web access and a limited phone system that let him call lawyers and private security agencies, which he absolutely wasn't going to do. He'd go on a hunger strike or something before he'd legitimize the expats' so-called legal system by paying one of their corporatist lawyers.

Hugh clicked around the interface further. Not only did he not have email, but also there was no access to his footage and no suite of video editing tools. He was wasting time here, when he could be working on the report about the exclusive private parks that discriminated against people based on their ability to pay. Or, better yet, he could be editing the footage of the People's Democracy Front rally. There were people here - maybe not many of them, but still, a few - who wanted a government. The people back on Earth needed to know that. Man, if he and Louisa edited that right - well. Anyway. It would have to wait.

Hugh picked up a spoon and the ramekin of flan and flipped back to DC Minute. One episode ended and a new one started. The stick figures did their usual intro dance as the theme played. He was feeling restless and angry locked in this dungeon, but the familiar music calmed him. The interplay of the Andean kena flutes and the plaintive sounds of the Javanese rebab playing over them was always soothing. Even the three explosive impacts of the taiko drum reminded him of slow sleepy mornings with a mug of good quality coffee.

...But it wasn't just memories of early morning in his mom's home, and then later at Dunster House, that made him feel calmer. It was the choice of instruments, the sophistication of the music that made him feel like he was among reasonable people - for at least a short period every day - where there was a polite, reasonable, *sane* consensus on the important issues.

And then something caught his attention. The theme music was long over and Melanie Roes was talking. "...what insiders are calling - off the record - General Bonner's debacle in the fight against the white-supremacist lunar tax resisters..."

Hugh leaned forward, ate a spoonful of flan, and watched.

The segment was good. He'd been wondering why the long delay in the coverage, but now he knew: it was in depth, and it answered all the important questions. Of course, it would've been even better if he and Louisa had managed to get their video footage of the tunnel collapse filed before these private security apes had grabbed them. When the Minute had run his footage weeks back it had been the highlight of his career. He'd gotten dozens of congratulatory emails and almost a thousand high-fives on LiveStatus. He should be building on that. Using the momentum. Working to really get his name out there.

But, no, here he was locked in this dungeon for - he checked the wallscreen - two hours now.

Shit.

He swallowed the final spoonful of the flan, put the ramekin and spoon on the tray, and then leaned back to watch the rest of the episode. A moment later DC Minute suddenly muted and an automated voice spoke. "Doorbell. Outer door will open in 30 seconds. Please be dressed."

Hugh looked down at himself, brushed a few crumbs off his shirt, and then waited - he certainly wasn't going to stand for these thugs.

Half a minute later, the door opened. Hugh looked up to see one of the guards. The man looked bored as he began rattling off a script from a slate he held in front of him: "You're scheduled to be released. Release from temporary protective custody does not indicate that Goldwater Precious Minerals Extraction Inc. or any other parties necessarily waive any rights to mediation or to tort damages via legal service providers or other courts. At the final stage of out-processing you will be given timestamped and cryptographically signed documentation of your time in temporary protective custody. You will also have the opportunity to talk to a Goldwater representative at that time."

Spiel over, he looked up and made eye contact with Hugh. "Look, regulations say that I don't *have* to cuff you on the way to out-processing. If you're willing to make my life easy, I'm willing to make yours easy too." He raised one eyebrow.

Hugh glared...but nodded once.

The guard nodded back. "OK, cool." He opened the door. "You're good to go. Out-processing will take ten minutes or so because we've got a few D-and-Ds ahead of you -" he caught himself and added an explanation - "drunk and disorderlies". And one case of theft-from-locker." He turned and walked away, leaving the cell open behind him.

Hugh stood and followed the guard to a waiting room where several young men - three Africans, three Europeans, and an Asian - were sitting in chairs, waiting to be processed. Most wore Goldwater overalls and joked with each other in English and some African language. They look up when Hugh entered and then went back to their conversations.

The guard who'd escorted Hugh to the room reached into his pocket, pulled out a card, and tried to hand it to Hugh. Hugh crossed his arms and looked away - he wasn't going to make this easy for the thug. After an uncomfortable moment, the guard sighed, put the card down on a low table, and then turned and walked out. The door clicked shut behind him.

Hugh picked up the card and looked at it. Weird - an actual physical card. It had the guard's first name and last initial, an employee number, and contact information for the Goldwater ombudsman. Hugh snorted. An 'ombudsman'? What a joke. Still, though - he pocketed it.

The men in the room were still talking with each other, but just to be safe Hugh avoided eye contact and found a chair at the far end of the room. There was a remote on the table in front of him; he picked it up and turned on wallscreen.

"Lee, Muck Soon!" Hugh looked up to see one of the men - the Asian guy in a t-shirt with tribal tattoos on his biceps - stand and move to the processing window.

Hugh had just found DC Minute in the menu when the door he'd come through opened again. A different guard escorted Louisa in and then removed handcuffs from her wrists. As soon as Louisa was free, she turned, but the guard danced out of range and left the room. Louisa glowered after him, but then turned to Hugh and started yelling. Her rant was just picking up steam with "dick-sucking corporate fascists" when the door opened a third time and Selena was brought in.

Selena smiled when she saw them. "Hey, guys, I didn't know you were here!"

Louisa turned and saw Selena. Her rant faltered and stopped mid stream. "Selena? Why the hell are you here? We left you at the apartment."

"After you two left to check out the assault, I thought about it for another few minutes, and then decided that I wanted to get in on the action. I tried to call you, but the phones were out. I got to the battle site and before I could shoot any footage, these *jerks* snapped me up."

The woman behind the processing window called out "James Ibori!" One of the African men stood.

Hugh looked at Selena. He was surprised that she was worked up - she'd seemed to be losing her fire these past few weeks. He started to ask a follow-up question but Louisa jumped in. "I see that *someone* has been finally seen how bad shit is around here! I shouldn't be too surprised - even if the unplanned chaos here doesn't upset our little girl, at least the white male corporate power structure can manage to get her anger up, huh?"

Selena smiled wanly.

Hugh broke in. "Did either of you guys watch DC Minute in your cells?"

Selena looked at him. "How - ah, no. I didn't see it."

Louisa held up her recently uncuffed wrists. "Me either; I couldn't reach the remote."

Hugh nodded. "Well, Washington is saying that the liberation failed because Bonner screwed up. We need to make sure that our coverage goes along with that narrative - or at least doesn't contradict it."

Louisa nodded. "Fine. What else have you heard?"

"I'll get the full story from my mom when I talk to her, but I did note one other thing - the expats are being called 'white supremacist' now, so I think we want to work in a racial angle-"

Louisa nodded. "Most of the CEOs are either white or Hispanic. We can work with that."

Hugh nodded. "We can see if Javier Borda and Hector Camanez have European blood. They're not that light-skinned, but -"

Louisa smiled. "Fuzzy-Pantone-select, hue-adjust." She snapped her fingers. "No problem."

Hugh nodded. "At a guess, I think the developing line is going to be good intentions by the legislature and executive but incompetence by the DoD."

"The fascist corporate armies are what we should be covering."

Hugh shook his head. "We can cover that in a later episode, but the important thing right now is to make sure that the DoD's failure is front and center."

Louisa started to object but was interrupted when the woman behind the counter called their names. Hugh looked around and realized that room had emptied. He approached the window. "Hi. Uh, what do we need to do?"

The woman ignored him for a moment as she read her screen, then looked up. "This is odd - it says you've got two days for trespassing, but it's also flagged as 'special release.'" She considered that for a moment, then shook her head. "Just lean into the iris scanner, and then you're good to go."

Five minutes later they walking along the sidewalk in a general access tunnel, the Goldwater-owned tunnels behind them. Louisa was gesticulating. "No, we cannot wait for a later episode. The private armies are *obviously* the most important topic! You saw how these thugs arrested us - how we were treated!"

Hugh nodded. "It's important, and we'll cover it, but the most important thing right is framing things back home. We have to explain the failure of the assault, and the explanation is that this was a DoD screwup, *not* a legislative branch screwup. *That* is what we've got to hammer home." He paused. "Look, I'm telling you, DC Minute won't even run our stuff unless we do this in the right order. We back the legislature against the military first, *then* we confront the corporatists."

Louisa shook her head angrily. "DC Minute will run good journalism, no matter -"

Hugh cut her off. "Don't be naive - The Minute is on the side of the good guys, but you have to understand priorities."

Selena said, "You can't be so sure about how DC Minute will want to run things. They could decide that this isn't a DoD problem, but- "

Hugh was exasperated. "Now *you're* being naive too. First, I've already seen one episode. This is clearly the new line. Second, the world runs on friendships. Jacob and Melanie used to come over to the house all the time, back when mother was in the House. After she got into the Senate, she upped their funding and backed the Information Neutrality bill. A lot of people owe their houses on the Vineyard to that bill, so you can bet your ass that Job and Melaine and the whole staff are on the right side of this."

They reached the jitney stand. Hugh turned back to Louisa. "And I'm telling *you*, as someone who knows how the world works, that we need to do this in the right order. We help The Minute frame this properly, and *then* we go after the corporate armies. I can let you ask mother when we get back to the apartment. Or you can just trust me."

Louisa pursed her lips and looked at Hugh through her blue-rimmed glasses, but didn't say anything.

As if on cue the jitney pulled up.

Chapter 28

2064: Goldwater headquarters, level four, Aristillus, Lunar Nearside

Darren Hollins cradled the phone against his shoulder and leaned back in his chair.

"Thank you for taking my call, Senator. I'm sure your assistant already passed along my message that my facility seems to have locked up your son."

The voice on the other end of the line was tense. "Yes. She did. Locked up for what, may I ask?"

"Trespassing."

"I see."

"I, of course, ordered his immediate release."

There was a deep exhalation and some of the tension went out of the senator's voice. "Well, thank you for that, Mr. Hollins. As I'm sure you're aware, that earns some good will with me. A fair bit, actually."

"I'm glad to hear that."

"Since we're already talking, and since you seem to be a reasonable man -"

"You want to know if there might be a crack in the united front. If you might make a separate peace with me, or get me to be an ally against the other expats."

There was another moment of silence. "I've read your file. You seem to be a man who understands how the world works."

"I am."

"You must understand that you people can't win this fight."

Darren smiled slightly. "I'm not sure I do understand that. What I've seen so far is that you've got the capabilities to project force, here, but no ability to do anything with it once it's here."

"I'm not going to defend the competence of the president's military action. But surely you can't expect that the military is incapable of learning from its mistakes."

"I don't have any expectations about what the military can and can't learn."

Linda gave an exasperated sigh. "Let's cut to the chase, Mr. Hollins. Right now you and your friends have pushed all of your chips into the center of the table. You are betting against the United States of America. You have fifty thousand people -"

He interrupted her. "More like twice that, now. Immigration has been accelerating."

"Whatever. A hundred thousand. Two hundred thousand. Mr Hollins, the United States has five hundred million citizens. We have an annual budget of 600 trillion New Dollars. We have support from the UN. You are so vastly outmatched that discussing it is almost a waste of time."

"We may be small, but our militias took out -"

"A few individuals with guns are no match for a real military. Let's stop arguing details and cut to the chase. You are, by all accounts, an intelligent individual, and not an ideologue. Does it really make sense to bet not just your firm but you *life* on this struggle?"

Darren raised an eyebrow. "Perhaps you're right."

He could almost hear Senator Haig's smile. "Excellent. In return for the gold, I can promise not just amnesty, but -"

Darren hadn't finished speaking, and the two second lag caused their words to clash. "Perhaps I should have a backup plan. Tell me what you and the president can -"

The senator cleared her throat. "This deal wouldn't necessarily be signed by the president- " Darren raised an eyebrow "- but I can promise you a full amnesty and continued control over your mining firm - and we can discuss other options, if there's something in particular you need."

Darren rolled those words over. "What do you mean, 'full control'?"

"Mr Hollins, I'm not a fool - I don't want to kill the goose who lays the golden eggs. You're obviously very skilled at what you do, and after this is all over, I want you to continue making decisions about how the firm is operated. All of the decisions. I wouldn't have it any other way."

Darren nodded. "I see."

"So do we have an agreement?"

Darren paused. "I'd like to keep lines of communication open."

"That's not the 'yes' I was hoping for."

"I haven't decided yet."

"This offer won't last forever, it -"

"Actually, Senator, I think the offer will be open for quite a while longer. If I hand you my firm and the stocks of gold, I've made your political career. Even if I do it at the very moment that your next invasion lands. Conversely, if I destroy the gold and the refineries, again, even at the moment your next invasion lands, then I've considerably complicated things for you."

There was a moment of silence over the line. "I think it's premature to talk about destroying resources."

"Perhaps so. And perhaps it's also premature to discuss a second invasion."

There was an intake of breath from the other end of the line. "Mr Hollins, you and I are negotiating because you are a very powerful man in Aristillus, and I am a very powerful woman in Washington. But you are not the most powerful man there, nor am I the most powerful here. There are certain things that are beyond either of our control. What we can discuss is how - when the inevitable happens - you can land on your feet."

"I entirely agree. Again, I'd like to keep the lines of communication open. For now, though, I think we've said everything that needs to be said. You've told me how it is - that there's an invasion coming, and that I can survive it if I work with you. And you understand my position - that I don't need to throw my weight behind either side until the very last minute. You've even all but told me that I'm correct about that. All of our cards are on the table, and now we have to sit back and see how the rest of the hand is dealt."

A sigh. "Very well, Mr. Hollins. I would have liked to resolve this today, but I can assure you that when the real invasion comes - and it will - that the United States will reassert its legitimate authority over the citizens in Aristillus. Perhaps you'll be able to negotiate up until the very end, but I'll note that the amount of personal good will you'll have from me will be much larger the sooner we get this resolved. And my personal good will is not an insignificant asset."

Darren closed down the call and sat alone in his office.

Chapter 29

2064: Northern Logistics offices, Aristillus, Lunar Nearside

Mike sat at the head of the assemblage of folding tables. John, Dewitt, three of Dewitt's lieutenants, and the Boardroom group sat along the sides.

Mike said, "Here's what we know already: there were two waves of PK ships. The first wave landed and deployed units which headed towards Goldwater, and - thanks to Captain Dewitt - the Red Stripe and Second Morlock units captured them. Trusted Security and LAWS have them in an impromptu holding cell. The second wave of ships got shot down by First Morlock. What else do we know?"

John said, "Two more things. First, we've got reports that the six ships that landed have now taken off -"

Mike burst out. "No one stopped them?"

"No one gave orders. No one was around *to* give orders. You guys were on the run."

"Shit." Mike ran a hand over his face. "OK, go on."

"Second: the sleeper cells. We know there were at least two. Matt's team, which came around to the good guys, and the others who raided Morlock."

Mike turned to Dewitt. "At *least* two? How many total?"

Dewitt shook his head. "I don't know. It was news to me that there was anyone else here but my own team."

Mike nodded in resignation and turned back to John.

John continued. "There might be others. Which means that we need security around this office - quiet security."

Javier said, "Speaking of security - who can we trust? Captain Dewitt was able to infiltrate men into every single militia unit: Morlock, First Class Homes, Guaranteed Electrical, Red Stripe. If there are other PK teams here, then how do we know they haven't also got moles?"

Mike nodded, then turned to Dewitt. "I understand that you didn't know *that* there were other sleeper cells. But might you or your men recognize other soldiers? People you met in - I don't know - Basic, or whatever? If we showed you and your men pictures of all of the recruits for our militias, could you -"

Dewitt pursed his lips and shook his head. "I don't think so. My team was Special Forces. We know most other SF guys by sight, but I'm 99% sure that we're the only SF team that was sent here. I'd bet that the other teams are all PK."

Mike deflated. "So what do we do about possible infiltrators?"

Dewitt shrugged. "Your friend Javier's right - they could be there. You're going to have to assume that your units *are* compromised and work around it."

Mark Soldner raised his voice. "Our freedom is our Achilles heel."

A dozen heads swiveled. Mike raised an eyebrow. "What?"

"Why did we each choose to come here to Aristillus? For the freedom - no housing classification downgrades, no Racketeering and Unjust Profits laws, no Acceptable Public Discourse verification, all of that. We can start businesses, we can hire without government permission, people don't need work permits. That's all great stuff - but think about the downsides. Do we know who we've hired? Any of us?" He looked around the table.

Mike squinted. "What's your point?"

"My point is that if this war is heating up, we need to consider our choices. What works in peacetime isn't necessarily the right choice for wartime."

Mike's nostrils flared. Mark was trying to slip a government in the back door. Again. Mike glanced at Javier next to him and saw Javier giving a warning look back. OK, fine. He wouldn't jump in and tear Mark a new asshole like he deserved - but he would shut down this topic.

"Mark, let's argue the philosophy later and focus on concrete actions. Right now we need security for this office, and security we can trust - no sleepers. That means - I don't know - figuring out how to do background checks, compartmentalizing things, maybe even creating a counter-intelligence capability. Somehow." He turned to Dewitt. "Captain, I hate to ask more after what you've already done for us, but can you and your men provide security for a day or two while we vet our own?"

Dewitt nodded. "We can do that."

Mike looked around the table. "Any feedback on this idea?"

Karina asked, "How do we do that? Counter-intelligence and background checks?"

Javier said, "We can use private investigators. At least to start. There are a bunch of them here in Aristillus. Let them look at how long ago people came here, what their jobs were back on Earth, and so on."

Mike said, "Karina, you want to own that - recruiting some guards, and getting some PIs to screen them?"

Karina nodded.

"But make sure to pick PIs we trust."

Karina looked at Mike oddly. "There are PIs we don't trust?

"A few. Stay away from George White, for example."

"What's that story?"

Javier jumped in an answered before Mike could. "He works with Leroy Fournier of MaisonNeuve. You know about Mike and Leroy. Look, talk to me after, I'll tell you which ones are OK."

Karina nodded.

Mike scanned the table. "What else do we need to talk about?"

Albert Lai raised a hand. "Do we have a plan to deal with the new round of hijackings?"

Mike's head whipped around. "What new round of hijackings?"

Albert was taken aback. "You - Mike, didn't you read my email?"

"What email?"

Albert opened and closed his lips a few times. "Mike, I'm sorry - I sent it an hour before the meeting - the first meeting, before the invasion. Anyway. Several ships have failed to check in and-"

"Was Darcy's -"

Albert took a deep breath. "Yes. Mike, I'm sorry."

Mike swallowed and set his jaw. The rest of the table was silent. After a moment Mike closed his eyes and massaged them for a moment before looking up. He started to say something and then stopped.

Katherine Dycus leaned in and spoke quietly. "Mike, if you want to talk, afterward, just the two of us -"

Mike waived her away. "No. I've got too much to do. I've got to get the militias organized. I've got to figure out recruiting. I've got to debrief the militias and see what we learned about tactics - what worked, what didn't. I've got to -"

Dewitt leaned forward. "Excuse me, Mike?"

Mike glanced over. "Yes?"

"I'd like to volunteer for the job."

Mike looked at him, puzzled. "Which job? You want to run counter intelligence? Or do the debriefing?"

"No." He looked around the table. "I want to volunteer for the whole enchilada. Running the Aristillus military." He grinned wryly. "Secretary of the Army, or whatever you want to call it"

Mike stared at him uncomprehendingly. "You're *volunteering* for this shit-storm?"

Chapter 30

2064: Campus of Saint Joseph of Cupertino, level three, Aristillus, Lunar Nearside

Father Alex watched as the crane prepared to lift. The nylon webbing tightened and took the load and several tons of carved lunar basalt lifted off of the truck bed. The block was halfway to the ceiling of the tunnel when someone on the scaffolding started shouting, and the crane and its cargo paused. Alex looked up. At the top of the wall two masons, one holding a trowel and the other a data slate, were arguing with each other.

A moment later the crane lowered the block back onto the truck. Even before the straps went slack three more men, each bearing a slate, converged on the skid and began arguing.

Father Alex smiled. Architects, masons, and laborers had probably been arguing at cathedral construction sites for 1,500 years, and he was sure they'd continue arguing that much longer.

"Alex, it's nice to meet you." The voice was deep, rich, and happy.

Alex turned and saw the large black man who'd approached him while he'd been distracted. Alex stuck out a hand. "Bishop Arogundade, the pleasure is all mine."

"Bishop? Oh, no. Just Father Arogundade. Or better yet, just Jean-Baptiste."

"The rumors I've heard say that it's a done deal."

Jean-Baptiste waved his hand. "Ignore rumors - especially Vatican rumors. They only cause trouble."

"Perhaps so." Funny. Most bishop designates were more than ready to enjoy the respect and privileges of their new positions.

Alex turned to look at the construction. "Your cathedral is coming along very nicely."

Father Jean-Baptiste's grin was huge, dominating his face. "It's not *my* basilica. ...But yes, it is beautiful." He was clearly proud of it - even the way he crossed his arms across his chest showed a man who had to fight the urge to throw his arms wide.

Jean-Baptiste shook his head. "We don't need it, of course; we're fine in the warehouse." He turned and looked at Alex. "But the congregation wants it. After losing their churches back in Nigeria, they want something to be proud of again. Something to inspire them."

The two men stood quietly and watched the crane lift the basalt block a second time. This time the masons were ready for it, and guided it into position.

Jean-Baptiste broke the silence. "I like to meet all of the priests who arrive in Aristillus. We'll have coffee at the rectory at some point to get properly acquainted." His smile slipped away. "But this isn't a social call."

"No?"

Jean-Baptiste looked troubled. "The war is coming."

"I'd say it's already here."

"We left Nigeria, but we just can't get away from the PKs." He paused. "Many of the men in my congregation are in the militias. When the next invasion comes, they'll fight, because they have to. But their wives, their children - they shouldn't be part of the battle."

Alex nodded. "Of course not."

"But the problem is, how do we tell the PKs 'these men are militia, you can shoot them, if you must...but these people over here, these are civilians, and you can't shoot them'?"

"I know that the Aristillus Defense Force is using uniforms, and their spacesuits are marked."

Jean-Baptiste shook his head. "That's not enough. We need to make sure that when the fighting starts, the PKs do not blow up airlocks and e-p-doors. We need some way to tell them where civilians are."

Alex thought for a moment. "Under the Second Geneva convention, forces can't attack towns, or buildings that aren't being defended. That should apply to airlocks."

"Should?" Jean-Baptiste shook his head. "'Should' is not good enough. How are they to know? When the war comes again, they'll attack wherever they want to attack."

There was a cheer from a dozen men in the scaffolding, and Alex looked up and saw that the crane had settled the carved block into position atop the cathedral wall.

"Why are you talking to me about this? Aren't there chains of command for this sort of thing?"

"The men talk to their sergeants, the sergeants talk to their officers, all the way up to the Boardroom Group. The Boardroom Group sends petitions to Earth, but the Earth governments say that if we surrender then there will be no civilian casualties." Jean-Baptiste turned away from the masons on the cathedral wall and faced Alex directly. "You and I both know - no one is going to surrender."

"So what should I-"

Jean-Baptiste's deep brown, almost black eyes drilled into Alex. "You are from the Vatican. The Vatican has always served as a back door to get messages from government to government. Or, in this case, from a nongovernment to a government. Alex, I need you to use your connections. I need to arrange a sign."

"A sign?"

"Some way for the people of Aristillus to say, 'this airlock is not defended,' 'this neighborhood is safe.'"

"That's not why I'm here. I don't know anything about back channels." He took a breath. "But, yes, I can try."

Father Jean-Baptiste raised one finger. "Try very hard. Make sure you succeed. Thousands - tens of thousands - of people will die if you fail."

Father Alex bowed his head. "I'll make sure it happens."

At the school next to the cathedral construction site a bell rang. A moment later a horde of children - some in Catholic school uniform, some in overalls, some in shorts and t-shirts - came streaming out.

Alex raised his head and caught Jean-Baptiste's eyes. "I need something from you: introductions."

"Of course. To who?"

Alex smiled obliquely. "There are some tricky ones, but let's start with the easiest one. I need to speak to Mike Martin of the Boardroom Group as soon as possible."

The stream of children reached the two men and split around them. Many smiled, shouted hellos to Father Jean-Baptiste, or reached up to slap his upraised hand as they raced past. Jean-Baptiste smiled at each and greeted many of them.

As the crowd of children slowed Jean-Baptiste turned back to Alex and shook his head. "*That*'s the easy one?" He laughed. "I don't know what to tell you - the Boardroom Group is hiding deep, somewhere, and even their own militia leaders haven't been able to get in touch with them. I'm sure they'll surface at some point, but if you want to get in touch with Mike Martin today, I can't help you."

One of the children, a young African girl, slowed and stopped. "You're trying to get in touch with Mike?"

Jean-Baptiste turned to her. "It's always nice to see you, Ewoma, but this is important - please don't eavesdrop."

"Sorry, Father. But you're trying to get in touch with Mike?"

Father Alex looked at the girl and raised one eyebrow. "What if I am?"

"I've got his phone number."

Father Jean-Baptiste turned to her, dumbfounded. "You *what?*"

Chapter 31

2064: Northern Logistics offices, Aristillus, Lunar Nearside

Two of Dewitt's men guided the priest into the room, turned, and left.

Mike put his stylus down. "You can take the blindfold off."

Alex removed it and balled it in one hand. "Mike Martin, I assume?" He extended a hand.

Mike rose and shook, and then gestured to the seat on the other side of the desk. "I told Ewoma I'd see you because I owe her a favor. I can give you five minutes if this is important. And that's a big 'if.' Go."

"I'd hoped you could fit me in for more; this is important."

Mike shook his head wearily. "Father, we just survived an invasion that should have wiped us out. And we did it by pure dumb luck. I got word just a few hours ago that my - my girlfriend got taken captive by Earth forces. I'm busy as hell right now because I've a revolution to fight. Be happy with five."

Father Alex sat. "I'm sorry to hear about your girlfriend. But the revolution that you're fighting is one of the reasons I wanted to meet with you."

"Father, what I get done in the next twenty four hours is critical for the future of the colony."

Father Alex's lips twisted into the hint of a smile. "What you do over the next twenty four *years* is going to be critical for the future of humanity."

Mike blinked. "Ah - what?". This wasn't starting the way he'd expected.

"The next twenty four years. They begin...now."

"I don't know what you're talking about. Listen, Father -"

"Call me Alex."

"There's no guarantee that any of us are going to be alive a year from now. I can't believe you're worrying about some fantasy about us decades in the future."

Father Alex's hint of a smile turned into the real thing. "Mike, most of the Old Testament is three thousand years old. The Catholic Church is over two thousand years old. We've been working on reunification with the Eastern Church since the schism, a thousand years ago. So the Church worrying about lunar society a few decades in the future is about as short-term as we get."

Mike opened his mouth, and closed it. "Wait, back up. Why are you even in my office? What do I have to do with the Catholic Church? And since when does the Catholic Church care what a bunch of rebels on the moon are doing?"

"Three questions. Three answers, in order: I'm talking to you because you're one of the important leaders in this Revolution -"

"One of?"

Alex's eyes twinkled. "You want more flattery than 'one of'?"

"No, I'm just curious who you think the others are. There are no public meetings, and we -"

"You, Javier Borda, Darcy Grau, Mark Soldner, Karina Roth, Albert Lai, Anahit Berjouhi -"

"Who the hell is Anahit Berjouhi?"

"That's a random name I threw in to see if you were paying attention."

Father Alex was grinning at his own joke.

Mike furrowed his brow - he wasn't sure how much he liked this guy. He was vaguely amusing, but he seemed inordinately pleased with himself. How was it that Darcy phrased it? That Mike believed there was only room in a conversation for one self-amusing asshole?

Mike leaned forward. "So you know who's who in the Boardroom Group. How did you get that list?"

Father Alex shook his head. "Let's take care of the original three questions. Number two: You wanted to know what you have to do with the Catholic Church. Answer: you're Catholic."

Mike blinked. "Excuse me?"

"You were baptized, you had first communion, and you've attended Mass." Father Alex leaned forward and looked at Mike over the top of his glasses. "Although not - as far as we can tell - in the last twenty years."

"You've got records of this shit?"

Alex chuckled. "Mike, we're a two thousand year old bureaucracy - we've got vellum notes telling people to pick up the emperor's dry cleaning."

Mike pursed his lips.

"I'm joking, of course, but remember that the Vatican archives existed before Gutenberg. Think about what sort of data we have now in an era where a yottabyte drive is cheaper than a cup of coffee."

Mike leaned away from the desk separating them. "OK, so I was baptized. That doesn't mean you can call me a Catholic."

"You know the famous Jesuit quote, 'Give me a child until he is seven and I will give you the man'?"

Mike nodded. "Saint Ignatius Loyala."

"No, it was one of his students, Francis Xavier. A bit of irony there, no? The quote about forming men wasn't made by the former, but the formed, you see? Anyway, whether you're practicing or not, you're Catholic enough for my purposes."

Mike looked at the clock on his slate. "And what are those purposes?"

"And thus you give me an opportunity to answer your third and most interesting question - 'what does the Catholic church care what a bunch of rebels on the moon?'"

Jesus, this guy liked to hear himself talk. "So what's the answer?"

Father Alex leaned forward conspiratorially. "Mike, can I share something in confidence?"

Mike nodded.

"Those records I mentioned? Baptismal records and such? Well, between the Americans and the Nigerians, you've got a lot of Catholics here in Aristillus. But it seems that the records aren't being kept very well, so they sent me to -"

"You're not serious - you're here for *record* keeping?"

Now it was Father Alex's turn to roll his eyes. "No, Mike. I'm *not* serious. It was a joke." He sighed. "OK, I'm sorry. You're under a lot of stress - a ton of it - and I shouldn't be joking. I apologize."

Mike nodded. "Apology accepted."

"I'm here on a - well, 'diplomatic mission' isn't quite right, but it's close enough."

Mike took a deep breath. A diplomatic mission? From the Catholic Church? That didn't make a lot of sense, but it made more sense than anything else Father Alex had said so far. "OK, go on."

"The lunar colony is small now, but - do you know the famous Michael Faraday quote?" He didn't wait for an answer. "A member of royalty asked Faraday what use his first electrical generator was. Faraday responded 'Of what use is a baby, sir?' Mike, you've got a bouncing baby city here. It might grow up into something very interesting. Remember, we Jesuits had missionaries in North American almost two hundred years before American independence."

Independence. Mike liked the sound of that. "So you're betting that we're going to win this war?"

Father Alex crossed his arms and sat back. "The Church has no opinion on the matter. Nor does The Church bet."

"The *Church* has no opinion. How about you?"

Father Alex smiled. "What I think on is between me and my conscience. But if I *were* to bet -"

"Yes?"

"- I'd have to give my profits to charity because I've taken a vow of poverty."

Cheeky bastard. He was having fun with this. Mike volleyed it back at him. "Profits? What about losses?"

Father Alex smiled slowly. "I don't bet unless I think I'm going to win."

Jesus. What an arrogant asshole. But he wasn't *all* asshole - there was some warmth in that smile. Almost as if he was inviting Mike to enjoy the performance.

Slowly Mike cracked a smile too. Father Alex was an arrogant asshole - but maybe the man was *his* kind of arrogant asshole. "OK, so you're interested in Aristillus because Faraday said it might grow up to be a big electrical generator some day. So why are you here, in my office?"

Father Alex grew serious. "I want to talk about ethics. Specifically, Just War doctrine. If this conflict comes to fighting-"

"Are you paying attention, Father? It already has. They've seized our ships and tried to invade us."

Father Alex nodded, conceding the point. "My point is this: you have to fight fairly."

Mike shook his head. "There's a difference between a boxing match and a street fight. We're going to fight to win. We've got to - our *lives* are on the line."

"Your souls are also on the line, Mike. I'm cautioning you against ethical shortcuts. Sometimes they help in the short term, but they're never the right thing in the long term."

Mike started to object but Father Alex held up one finger. "I know that you and your friends pattern yourselves after the US Founders. Each of those men was keenly aware of the place they occupied in history, and how posterity would look at them. The things they did right - fighting fairly, establishing freedom of religion, codifying the Enlightenment into the US Constitution - made a stamp on history that will last a thousand years. And the things that they did wrong - slavery, Indian genocide, and so on - also made a stamp on history. Both types of actions had far more impact on future generations than they did on their own time."

Father Alex fixed Mike with a stare. "Know this, Mike: the ethical decisions you face over the coming months are the most momentous of your entire life. They are the decisions that - win or lose - will influence tens of millions of people. Maybe billions of people, and will do so for decades, if not centuries, to come. One little ethical shortcut, one little moral lapse...do you know what a 'scandal' is?"

"A political scandal? I -"

"No, in the Catholic sense - it's an act that is not merely evil in its own right, but that leads to spiritual ruin of another. If you take shortcuts in this fight, you're not just harming your own soul - you're potentially harming thousands or millions of other people who might someday look back on your example and hold you up as a moral paragon."

"You're telling me that I have to live not just for myself, but for everyone who might look at my example? That's not a realistic standard to set for a man, is it?"

Father Alex adjusted his collar, but remained silent.

"Are you going to answer that?"

"I thought I just did. So much for subtlety. I was pointing to my collar."

Mike rolled his eyes.

"Roll your eyes if you want, Mike, but we're all called to live correctly. And part of that is that we're all called to set good examples. Some of us, like me, have a relatively small audience, and others, like you, have chosen to put yourself in front of an audience of billions."

"So, that's your little lecture? Be good, because history is watching?"

"Yes, that's it. But it's not a small lecture though. In fact, the more you think about it, the bigger it gets."

Mike ran a hand over his eyes. "Alex, I've already got enough shit stacked on my shoulders, and I don't have time for this."

"Who stacked those trials there, Mike?"

"You're saying that I chose this path?"

"No, it's an honest question. Maybe you chose this path. In which case you have to deal with everything that's stacked on your shoulders - including the requirement that you fight this war ethically. Or maybe God chose this path for you, in which case don't complain to me - He picks appropriate tools for His ends."

Mike scowled again. "You started off this conversation by assuming I'm Catholic. But I'm not. My faith is in what works. Science, math, economics. I don't think that God runs around picking people for tasks."

Father Alex appraised Mike for a moment. "Mike, my background was in physics before I took this posting. I think that God rarely if ever violates conservation laws, that He is a big fan of thermodynamics, and that He doesn't play tricks with leptons. But I also - on most days, at least - think that He has opinions about the grand sweep of history, and calls people to certain roles."

An alarm went off on the priest's phone. He looked at it, silenced it, and put it back in his pocket.

The interruption gave Mike a moment to look at the clock on his wallscreen. "Look, Father, I meant what I said earlier - I do have a thousand things on my plate: funding our military, a proposal for fractional reserve banking, media prizes, maybe figuring out some way to rescue Darcy."

Father Alex stood. "I appreciate the time you gave me. I'll get out of your hair and on to my next appointment. We'll talk again, Mike."

Mike stood as well. "Another appointment? What does a special agent of the Vatican have on his agenda besides counseling lunar revolutionaries?"

Alex smiled. "Oh, we don't use the term 'special agent.'"

Mike looked at Alex closely. The guy was precise in his language - and more than that, liked word games. Mike smiled - he had him. "You're not going to rebut the Vatican part?"

Alex raised an eyebrow. "Rebut it? Of course not. When I arranged this appointment I assumed you'd look up my name and see that I'm with the Vatican Observatory." Father Alex shook his head. "I've enjoyed our chat, Mike, but on this, you've disappointed me!"

Their was mischief in his smile. "But to answer your earlier question, I've got several tasks on my plate, but the most fascinating one is gathering information to inform the debate on whether nonhumans have souls."

"Ah, the Dogs?"

"On my way out I need to talk to your General Dewitt about some codes to identify civilian areas in the next battle." Alex stuck out his hand. "We'll talk again, Mike."

Chapter 32

2064: Northern Logistics offices, Aristillus, Lunar Nearside

Mike sat at the Boardroom Group table.

Over the last week the CEOs had adopted favorite chairs, and he'd realized just yesterday that they were sorting themselves by ideological position.

He looked across the table at Mark Solder, Karina Roth, and Albert Lai.

And today Javier had pulled his chair around and was sitting with them.

Only Hector Camanez sat with Mike.

Mike slapped his hand on the table. "No, we do *not* need a bank."

"Mike, you were the one who helped draw up the to-do list." Mark started ticking point off on his fingers. "We need to fund the militias. We need space suits, rifles, training, combat pay, disability insurance, bribes, gifts, lobbyists in the US, recruiting staff in China. And we have to pay for it."

Mike would have none of it. "I've funded my Morlock Volunteers, I've developed the rifles and open sourced the plans, I've recruited combat veterans to train my men. *I* did it. From my own pocket. I didn't need a bank and *we* don't need a bank."

Mark shook his head. "Mike, all of us at this table have been blessed with great opportunities, but none of us have the wealth - the liquid wealth - that you have. And even you are in dire straits because of the cost of all of this, aren't you?

Mike pursed his lips and didn't respond.

Javier said, "Mike, let's say that everyone in the BRG has enough liquid assets to support their own militias. I'm not sure it's true, but let's pretend. What about the other expenses? Insurance. A cyberware defense group. PR."

Mark Soldner interrupted. "Diplomacy."

Javier nodded. "Right. Civil defense."

Karina said, "What do you mean civil defense?"

Javier said, "Some of the upper tunnels have sliding emergency pressure doors, but most of the lower C-series tunnels don't."

Karina looked confused. Rob Wehrmann explained, "If there's an explosion that cracks a tunnel, we lose the air for kilometers. Maybe six or eight klicks what with cross tunnels."

Javier nodded. "And we've only got one LNG carrier retrofitted for carrying air. So right now, one big explosion, in the right place, could kill everyone."

Karina looked appalled. "If it's that serious why don't they already have all these ep-doors?"

Mike glowered at her. "Because, Karina –" he leaned on her name, making it sarcastic, "– when I was building the colony no one thought we'd ever need them. It's easy to sit here in your blouse and pressed skirt and think about how you could have done it better, but we were in homemade space suits, trying to –"

Javier put up his hands and tried to defuse the fight. "No one is attacking you, Mike. We all understand the problems of building Aristillus, and everyone did the best job they could, at the time. But the fact is that Morlock, General Tunnels, Deepmine, Selzter - none of the tunneling firms have been installing the number of e-p-doors we're going to need when the next invasion comes."

Karina asked, "How much money are we talking about?"

Javier looked at his slate. "Even our cheapest plan shows that we need almost a hundred e-p doors. That's tens of millions right there. Maybe even a hundred million by the time you talk installation. But that's just one item on the list. By the time you add in ammunition, body armor, purpose-built software, we're talking multiple hundreds of millions."

Mike scowled. Javier was right about the amount of money they needed. What annoyed him was that Javier was arguing for a bank. Javier knew how he felt about that.

And if that annoyed Mike, what really pissed him off was that Javier and Soldner were on the same side. Sure, it was just a coalition of convenience: Javier honestly thinking it was the easiest way to get the money the revolution needed, and Mark - Mike knew what Mark was up to. This was yet another maneuver in his attempt to establish a government here in Aristillus.

How could Javier not see that? How could Javier choose Mark over Mike in this fight?

Javier said, "Mike, we *need* a bank."

"No. We need *funds*. There are other options."

"The bank is the best approach."

"But you admit that there are other ways?"

Javier sighed. "Yeah, there are a few. They're not good, though."

"Let's hear them."

Javier ticked off the choices on his fingers. "One: members of the Boardroom Group contribute more. It won't scale, but it will let us kick the can down the road - at least a little bit."

Albert Lai shook his head. "I've already looted my checking accounts, my maintenance account, everything. It's a scramble just to meet payroll each week."

Rob Wehrmann raised his eyebrows. "Same. I'm out of cash. I've sold off one of my warehouses. I've just got my machines left, and I'm parking them in public tunnels."

There were murmurs and nods of assent around the table.

Mark turned to Mike. "Mike, you're the one who suggested that we all voluntarily fund more. Are you in a position to contribute more?"

Mike pursed his lips and shook his head. "No."

Javier said. "OK, cash infusions are off the board. This brings us to idea number two. The boardroom group sell bonds -"

Mike slapped the table. "Absolutely not."

Mark looked at him coolly. "The Colonists sold bonds in the American Revolution, and that allowed them -"

"No, damn it!" This time Mike punched the table, and felt a bolt of pain shoot up his arm. *Fuck!* Punching tables was becoming a habit for him and he didn't like it - he was starting to lose control.

Mike said, "It wasn't 'the colonists,' it was the Congress. And later, when Congress couldn't pay those bonds, people demanded a stronger government." Mike put his hands under the table where he could massage his right wrist. "I know what you're getting at, Mark - this isn't a finance plan, it's a plan to create a government through the backdoor. And I know you'll act surprised in two months or two years or whenever when people want to get their bonds paid, and you'll - reluctantly, I'm sure - say that we need a tax. No. I'm not going to help you sneak in a government by the back door."

Mark spread his hands. "Mike, you're reading a lot more into this than is there."

"No, Mark, I'm not. If we sell those bonds, yeah, you'll try to pay them back voluntarily. But they'll be a hiccup. And the bondholders will decide they need a stronger hand. And then -" he raised one hand above the table and snapped his fingers. "There'll be taxes. Then spending. That's how we went from the Articles of Confederation to the Constitution."

"Mike, the Constitution is exactly what we want. Our problem with the US is not that they have the Constitution, it's that they don't *follow* the Constitution -"

Mike didn't bother to keep the scorn out of his voice. "Pfah! The Constitution was booby trapped from the get-go. You centralize power like that -"

"We can put limits on it-"

Mike stood up, pushing his chair back. "You're trying to steal this revolution, Mark, and I'm not going to let you." He leaned over the table aggressively. "If you go down this road, not only will I quit the Boardroom Group, but I'll fight every government there is - even yours."

Mark was shocked, Mike could see it on his face. But he also looked like he thought Mike was bluffing. "Mike, there's no need to exaggerate. If you leave the Boardroom Group we'll lose this war."

"So be it."

"You're bluffing."

"Have you ever seen me back down from a fight?"

Mike could see Mark's eyes on him - and saw Mark's eyes drift to the new scar peaking out from under his hairline.

Mark raised his hands placatingly. "Look, we can compromise. Sit down and we can talk about it seriously, without idle threats -"

"Fuck that. No." Mike slapped the table. Ah, Jesus, son of a bitch! His goddamn wrist shot electric jolts up his arm, but he wasn't going to let Mark or anyone else see that. He ignored the pain and held Mark's gaze, forcibly. "I'm not bluffing about fighting you if I need to. You think I'm anti-government and

---

uncompromising? My militias are half Nigerian. Try talking to those SOBs. They've seen 'limited government' up close and personal. I'll fight the PKs, and I'll fight anyone here who tries to start a government - and my men will be with me every step of the way."

The executives around the table were silent

Javier cleared his throat. "Mike, slow down -"

Mike ignored him and stared at Mark until the latter man blinked. "I'm serious, Mark. I'd rather fight on two fronts at once and lose than be your ally and end up with a government right in my own lap."

Mark opened his mouth as if to object, then closed it again.

Javier stood. "We need to take a break. Now. We're all hungry and thirsty. Mike, what do you say to pizza?"

Mike ignored him and continued to stare at Mark. Mark's sniping had gone on for too long, and -

Javier put his hand on Mike's shoulder. "Everyone, let's reconvene in the cafeteria."

There was a bustle as chairs were pushed back around the table. Javier took his hand off Mike's shoulder and ushered people out of the room.

Then, after Javier was gone, Mark finally broke eye contact with Mike, pushed his own chair back, stood, and followed the exodus out.

Mike unballed his fists and looked around. He was alone in the room. Even Javier was gone. Only Rob Wehrmann, fiddling with his slate, was still there.

He blinked. Shit. Had he just told the Boardroom group that he was prepared to fight a civil war?

With a sinking feeling he realized that he already knew what Javier would say: that he was acting like an angry lunatic, and that he was endangering the revolution - and all of their lives.

He sighed and let his head hang forward. Damn it. Javier would say that - and he'd be right. But, damn it, he hadn't slept for more than four hours in over a month, Darcy was imprisoned somewhere on Earth, there wasn't enough money, and his damned hand hurt.

He took a deep breath.

He was pissed. Pissed at the stress of a war that had come five or ten years too early. Pissed at needing to fund a revolution but being too broke to do it. Pissed at politics, and bullshit and compromise. Pissed at the fact that he'd done his best to build the physical structure of Aristillus, when it had been just him and a few dozen other men while these, these *bureaucrats* like Karina had been safely back on Earth - and now they had the gall to judge him because there weren't enough e-p-doors?

And then, on top of all of that, there was Mark. Patient, calm Mark. Always waiting - waiting for any moment of weakness. And every time there was one, without fail Mark saw it and used it. Always trying to push for a government - just a small one. Time after time after time.

Fighting an external enemy was hard enough, and add on to that these goddamn college kids, and Karina giving him those cold glances and looking down her nose at him, and Mark, and ...

God damn it, it was all enough to grind a man down.

Mike took another deep breath and sat down.

"Your tantrum over?"

Mike turned with a start - he'd forgotten Rob Wehrmann was in the room with him. "What?"

"When my daughter Gina was thirteen, I'd wait until she was worn out, then ask her if her tantrum was over."

Despite himself, Mike cracked a small smile. "Yeah, I guess I'm done."

Rob Wehrmann laughed gruffly. "Can't blame you. Buncha assholes, huh?"

"I guess that means I'm in good company."

Rob chuckled again. "I love Karina and Mark getting cranky about the e-p-doors. I'd like to see either one of them underneath a dozer dumping hydraulic fluid on a January morning."

Mike's smile grew. He and Rob had never been close - as culturally distant as Mike felt from the blow-dried and dry-cleaned executives like Mark and Karina, he felt just as distant from Rob and his love of the Red Sox, his cigarette habit, and his borderline incomprehensible accent. Still, it was nice to have an ally - any ally - when Javier was arguing for a bank and acting chummy with Mark.

"It's be nice if Mark could take a break from pushing his government idea for even one second."

Rob grunted noncommittally.

"You don't agree?"

Rob shrugged. "I don't give a shit. All I know is we've got to win this war or we're fucked. If Mark's got a plan to do that, then I'll back him."

Mike felt the anger rising again. "But that -"

Rob cut him off. "Ah, Mike. Fuck your 'but this', 'but that.' Come up with a better plan, or shut up. Bullshit walks."

Mike sighed and sat back. Rob was right, he needed a better plan. But what -

The door to the impromptu boardroom cracked open and Javier slipped in and closed it behind him. He caught Mike's eye. "Your tantrum over now, Mike?"

Rob snorted. "That's what I said to him just a minute ago!"

Mike ignored it. "Yeah, Jave, I'm calm now."

"You're never *calm*, Mike. What was that stunt with threatening Mark with a -"

"Forget it. Look, Rob made a good point. I've got to come up with a better plan for funding."

"You'd better do it fast; the group is going to reconvene in a few minutes."

Mike shook his head. "I'm out of ideas." He looked up at his friend. "Help me, Jave."

Javier gave him an appraising look, then sighed. "We already floated idea number one - we each contribute more cash. None of us has more cash, so that's dead. Idea number two - the boardroom group issues bonds. You've pledged to fight that. Dead. That leaves -"

"Yes?"

"The bank idea."

Mike's smile disappeared.

The door opened and Mark Soldner and the walked returned with a pizza box and a carrier with three soda bottles in it. Mark pulled one of the sodas out and held it out for Mike. "A peace offering."

Mike took it and nodded. "Thanks."

Rob Wehrmann saw the pizza. "We've been talking for too fucking long. Let's eat."

Mark put the box on the table and pushed it across to Mike. Mike looked at the logo on box and sighed internally. Niccola's. Again. They needed to start ordering take in from some other place. Or maybe even get a cook in here. He opened the box, took a slice, closed the box, and pushed it to Rob.

Rob opened the box, temporarily obstructing Mike's view of his face with the open lid. Huh. That was clever. The logo on the box had a bunch of rounded off squares, and Mike realized for the first time that they spelled out "tasty" when viewed upside down. Nice hack.

The door opened again and the rest of the CEOs walked in.

Mike looked away from them back to the pizza box. That was a *really* clever logo.

Javier leaned over and whispered. "My advice is to go with the bank idea, but say that you'll draw up the papers. Maybe Lowell Benjamin can help you put in some sort of iron-clad -"

"No. I've got a better idea."

* * *

Mike stood at the head of the table and looked out over the reconvened group. He felt calmer than he had in several days.

"So far we've been funding this out of our own pockets. That was a mistake." He paused. "It wasn't a mistake because we can't do it all ourselves - although that's also true. It was a mistake because people value things more if they have to sacrifice to get them. If there's some way that we can get everyone - and I meant *everyone* - to contribute, not only does it help us raise revenue, but it makes the people of Airlock feel like they're part of the struggle."

"So you're agreeing that a modest tax - "

Mike saw Javier eyeing him nervously. *No, Javier. I won't get angry.*

"No. Universal is good, but voluntary is better. Here's the idea: We come up with a logo. We brand the revolution! And then we work with businesses. Any business that donates one percent of their revenue to us gets to hang a banner in their storefront, or put it on their webpage. People then choose to support their ideals by shopping at places that display the logo."

Mark looked skeptical. "There's no way that could raise enough money."

"Sure it can. You know the GLP estimates from Davidson Equities Analysis. One percent of that gets us in the ballpark."

Mark squinted. "Even if that math is right -"

"It is."

Mark shrugged. "Even if it is, a *logo*? Come on, Mike - who's going to shop at one place over another just because of a logo? It'll never work."

"It can work. It *did* work. Look at the Green fiasco at the turn of the century. Marketers took in *billions* before that fell apart. Pink ribbons for breast cancer. The Silver Dolphin campaign. Humans are tribal. Every other person in Aristillus is wearing a t-shirt advertising a sports team or a band. People love to express their allegiance - and they'll pay to do it."

Rob grunted. "Fucking unlikely."

Javier tilted his head as he thought, then nodded. "I don't think it's a slam dunk, Mike, but maybe..."

Mark shook his head. "Even if it does raise a little bit of revenue, it's beneath the seriousness of the situation - and beneath our dignity."

Javier stood. "I think we've made a lot of progress today, Mark. We've gone through a few ideas, we're starting to come to some consensus. I propose a compromise. We've got enough funds to keep our spending at our current burn rate for three weeks."

Karina looked up from her slate. "Two weeks and three days. Then payroll hits."

Javier nodded. "I propose that we try Mike's logo idea. We can get on it immediately and start to roll it out by the end of the day. Let's see what traction we get in the next week. If it's not enough, then we can talk about other options. What do you say, Mike?" He turned. "Mark?"

Mike shook his head. "Just one week? That's not enough time."

"We've got to leave time to implement plan B if it fails. Mike, are you willing to give this a shot?"

Mike pursed his lips, then nodded.

"Mark?"

Mark sighed, then nodded too.

Javier said, "Gentlemen?"

Mike looked at him. What was Javier - *oh*.

Mike surpressed a frown and stood, then extended a hand across the table. Mark stood and they shook.

There was a smattering of applause, and Mike pretended to smile at it before sitting.

The meeting continued with some discussion about an entreaty to an opposition party in the NEU, but Mike tuned it out and brooded.

The Boardroom group had clapped, as if he and Mark had worked some great compromise. He knew the truth: they hadn't. Mark hadn't given up on creating a government, and he hadn't given up on fighting against it.

Mike took a deep breath and watched Mark across the table.

A brief detente was the best he could do.

He'd bought himself a week - maybe a bit more if the logo idea generated revenue - but the war against Mark wasn't finished. No, if anything, now it was just starting.

Chapter 33

2064: Benue River Restaurant, Aristillus, Lunar Nearside

Ewoma sprayed the countertop with a bottle of sanitizer and wiped it clean. On the far side of the restaurant the last of the lunch patrons were standing from their table, heading back to their jobs. The early dinner rush would begin in just an hour or so.

As the last of the men pushed out of the restaurant, Ewoma's mother walked in. She saw Ewoma and smiled. "The restaurant looks good - thank you."

Ewoma smiled back and buffed the stainless steel one last time as her mom slid behind the counter and inspected the food in the steam table. "We're running low on fried rice buns."

"I started a new batch a few hours ago and Nnamdi is getting ready to fry them right now." As if on cue, there was a sudden sizzle from the kitchen as the rice cakes were plunged into the fryer.

Ewoma's mother raised an eyebrow. "Very good. Before you go home, I need you to place an order with Camanez; we need -"

"I already ordered two hundred kilos of beef. I also called Stephalos Farms and ordered goat."

Ewoma looked at her mom and tried to gauge her mood. Was this the right time? The restaurant was perfectly clean, she'd done everything on her list, and more. And her mother seemed to notice - her usual smile was even broader.

It was as good a time as any.

Ewoma took a breath. "Mom? I want a dog."

In an instant her mother's smile was replaced with a dubious look. "We've talked about this before."

"I know. You said I wasn't mature enough. But that was a *year* ago. And look -" Ewoma gestured around the well-maintained restaurant. "I am now!"

There was a long pause. Was that a hint of a smile playing at the edges of her mom's mouth? *Please, please, please!*

"I'll talk to your father. But I'm not sure that now is a good time. With the war coming, we need to protect what we already have, not take on new burdens."

Ewoma's face clouded. She fought the urge to throw down the sanitizer bottle and the rag and storm out of the restaurant. If she did that that would just be proof that her mom was right, that she wasn't mature enough.

So she put the bottle and rag down calmly. "OK. Unless there's anything else, I'm going to go home to study."

Chapter 34

2064: Downtown Seattle, BAE Boeing Robotics Division

General Restivo waved away the functionary and the scone platter he held out. He turned back to Glenn and jabbed his finger. "No! I made it clear over the phone that the seven series wasn't acceptable. We need vacuum rating, and this - *proposal*" he held up his slate "– doesn't have it."

The director forced a conciliatory smile. "General, there's no need to get upset. We can absolutely deliver what you need. If the stock 7 series won't do it, we'll modify it. That's not a problem; in fact our customization team would love to work on it. So let's just walk through your requirements. Some of them are a bit surprising, but I'm sure we can -"

Restivo struggled to control himself. He'd been sure that there was no bureaucracy worse than DoD bureaucracy, but he'd never dealt with military contractors before. "Surprising? Glenn, I laid this all out in email to you. Three times."

Glenn smiled wanly. "Yes, but given the schedule you specified I assumed that the 'requirements' were for the final version, not the initial deliverables."

"'Final version'? What are you talking about? I need this - *this* - as specified, and I need it in three months."

Glenn coughed apologetically. "The 7 series drones are part of a Program of Record, through the Advanced Combat Robot Task Force program."

Restivo forced his jaw to unclench. "And?"

"A program of record - you know what that means, right? There's no way we can do ECO modifications without submitting a Request for Proposal to all the corporate partners in the Advanced Combat Robot Task Force. The last RFP window closed two months ago, and the next one doesn't open for another three." He spread his hands hopelessly. "We want to work with you, but our hands are tied on this. We can deliver prototypes, with factory specifications, right away - but actual modifications that you want, that'll take at least a year, probably more like two."

Restivo slapped the table. "Two years? God damn it, Glenn! We need this project *finished* - with three thousand units deployed - in months. There's no study, there's no RFP."

Glenn blinked. "I -"

Restivo cut him off. "I need those units, and I need them in eight weeks. Now tell me how you're going to do it."

Glenn leaned back, an uncomprehending look on his face. "General, this is exactly the confusion I was talking about. This makes no sense. None at all. I understand that you don't have a background in procurement, but -"

Restivo took a deep breath and he felt a dangerous calm descending. "Glenn, can you deliver this? Yes or no?"

The other man recovered a bit of his composure. "General, this timetable is laughable. Excuse me for saying it, but -"

"Yes or no?"

Glenn smiled at the absurdity of the question. "On that schedule? Absolutely not. No one can."

"OK, that's all I needed to hear. If you can't, then I'll go with Pangloss."

"Pangloss?" Glenn's smile disappeared. "The start-up? Is that a joke? They're not even ISO certified."

Restivo stood. "I don't need ISO certification. I need rovers."

Glenn stood. "General, with all due respect, the DoD can't purchase from whoever you want. Vendors need to be ISO certified, they need to be registered, they need to have a diversity staffing certificate. There's a forty-three point list, and -"

"Glenn, it was nice meeting you. Have a good day." Restivo turned towards the door.

"General, wait. Seriously, wait."

Restivo turned back. "What?"

"Are you serious about Pangloss?"

"Dead serious."

"Your purchase order won't go through DoD procurement."

"I've been told it will."

"By who?"

"I've got allies on this project. Goodbye, Glenn." Restivo put his hand on the doorknob.

Chapter 35

Blue walked into the conference room. Max was already there, sitting in front of the wall screen with his back to the door. Blue stopped and watched as Max rotated the three-dimensional model of Aristillus and then began to drag small black icons into place. Blue squinted and saw the key. Blue, Black, Red - each color for a different force.

Max pondered the deployment for a long moment, and then - apparently satisfied - started the simulation. Red PK ships landed and disgorged units that poured in through airlocks. The PK units threw themselves at the black defensive line of Dog units. Here and there Black units attempted counterattacks, but were repulsed. Simulated time roared past, hours playing out in minutes. Eventually the superior numbers of the red PK units smashed a hole in the Dog line and plunged through. In short order the black lines crumbled: a second hole opened up, and then a third.

Seconds later, PK forces were streaming in from three directions, driving straight for the golden sphere at the heart of the diagram. Blue knew without checking that it represented the Den.

Max cursed and reset the simulation, moved units around, and tried again. The battle started differently, with black Dog units conducting hit and run raids from the flanks, but it ended the same way: an unstoppable stream of red PK units plunging in toward the Den.

Max reset the simulation once more and was beginning to drag units to new locations when Duncan rounded the corner. "Oh, hey, Blue, hey, Max."

Max spun around, saw Duncan, and then let his eyes settle on Blue. "How long have you been here?"

Blue grimaced, caught. "A few minutes."

Max started to wipe the simulation off the screen, and then stopped. "You're still planning on asking Gamma for rovers?"

Blue nodded.

"Do you think Gamma will just give them to you?"

Blue shrugged. "Maybe."

"And if not?"

"I'll offer a trade."

"What do we have that Gamma wants?"

"Money from our betting and trading activities, either in Aristillus accounts or on Earth."

"What does Gamma want with money? He can build whatever he wants."

"I don't know."

Max snorted. "Sides of beef? Restaurant take-out? Maybe some nice residential real estate?"

Blue didn't answer, just stared at Max.

After a moment Max shrugged. "Do whatever you want."

Duncan looked from Max to Blue and back. "So you're on board with asking for help?"

"It's a stupid idea," Max said. "But based on my guesses about the invasion size, we won't be able to hold the lines without *something* to help us."

Blue asked, "If it's necessary, how is it stupid?"

Max ignored him.

Duncan said, "I didn't think Blue would ever get you to agree to work with Gamma and the Boardroom Group."

Max exploded. "The Boardroom Group? No!" He growled, "We're not going to put our forces under Boardroom Group command. I only gave Blue permission to talk to Gamma."

Blue scowled. "First, I never asked for your *permission* for anything. I've just been debating ideas with you. And second - 'under their command'? That's a straw man and you know it. I've been arguing that we coordinate with the Group, not that we put our forces under their control."

"It doesn't matter what you call it - if we get in bed with them, we're at risk. Their incentives aren't the same as ours - they could sell us out, or trick us into deploying our forces in ways that benefit them more than us."

Duncan looked back and forth from Max to Blue.

Blue shook his head. "That makes no sense. We're in this boat together. It's simple game theory - we have more of a chance of success if we coordinate our efforts. There's no scenario under which the humans can win without us winning too."

Max stood and paced, then turned back suddenly. "What if the humans are afraid to win?"

Blue squinted. "What does that even *mean*?"

"What if the only way to win is to use nukes? What if we can force a détente - by nuking their forces. Or by nuking one of their cities and threatening more?"

"This is insane - where are we going to get nukes anyway?"

Max let a smile creep onto his face. "From the downed PK ships. The one at Farside had a nuclear scuttling charge. I bet the ones the human militias shot down have them as well. We can scavenge -"

Duncan tried to interrupt. "Max?"

" - the fissionables. There might be fusion materials as well, but I don't -"

"Max?"

Blue turned to Duncan but Max kept speaking " - know if we'd have any success in building a fusion device, but we could build simple gun-style fission bombs. Under our own control, with no Boardroom Group interference."

"Max?"

Max turned, irritated. "What?"

"The bombs are gone."

Max blinked. "What do you mean they're gone?"

"I mean there's a whole thread about it on UrbanExploration.ari. Someone's already stripped the ships."

Max growled and then swore. "Who the hell did it?"

Duncan shrugged. "No one knows for sure. There's not much video because the wreckage from falling ships destroyed a lot of cameras. People are guessing it's the Boardroom Group, though."

Blue turned to Max and asked with fake innocence, "If there's a nuclear power in Aristillus, do you think it might make sense to coordinate with them?"

Max set his jaw and turned away.

"Give me the silent treatment if you want, Max. I was *going* to tell you that I've rented a truck and I'm heading out to Sinus Lunicus in an hour, but I guess you're not interested."

Duncan hooted. "We're going to visit Gamma? Awesome. I'm *so* there!"

Chapter 36

2064: surface truck, between Aristillus and Sinus Lunicus, Lunar Nearside

The truck bumped over the surface and the seat belt tugged at Blue, right on the sore spot. Blue pulled it down a paw's breadth - and then, at the next bump, it slid right back. Blue gritted his teeth. The truck was designed for humans, of course. The seats were uncomfortable and the belts were even worse.

"This is *awesome*, isn't it, Blue?"

Blue looked over his shoulder to where Duncan was sprawled on the back bench. Duncan's eyes were wide with excitement and his tongue hung out as he panted with enthusiasm.

The truck lurched again and the belt tugged at the rapidly forming bruise. Blue narrowed his eyes. "It's faster than walking."

Duncan nodded. "Yeah - but when we were walking we had game overlay. That's one thing I miss - it'd be *great* to see what the new army mode looks like out here. I wonder if there's any chance that Red Stripe could upgrade the truck windshields so that they could support augmented reality, because -"

Blue twisted around in his seat. "Wait - you're still playing the LARP?"

Duncan's eyes widened. "You're not?"

Blue saw Max roll his eyes.

Blue shook his head. "I haven't logged on since we flew back from Farside."

"Really? Oh, *maaan*! So much has changed. 'Army mode' is new. You've got to check it out - it's *awesome* for big battles. I mean, it would never work here because we'll never get enough people in suits at one time, but down in the Ukraine they're actually having

LARP festivals, where folks in AR glasses all get together to play at a campground. There was a Battle of Five Armies recently. No Eagles, of course, so it was really just four armies. They were talking about hang gliders, but they couldn't get -"

Max interrupted, pointing out the window. "What's that?"

Blue turned and looked. He didn't see anything. Wait. There, in the shadow, something was moving.

Max asked, "Is that one of Gamma's rovers?"

"I don't know."

A moment later the vehicle emerged from the shadows of the boulder field. It wasn't a rover - it was a surface truck. An Aristillus model, maybe even the same type they were sitting in.

Max turned to Blue and gave him a wordless questioning look.

Blue shrugged. The surface truck was heading toward them; they'd know in a minute.

The other vehicle disappeared behind an outcropping of boulders. A moment later, they rounded the same outcropping and the other truck was upon them. Each vehicle slowed and pulled to the right as the navigation systems did their job and Blue watched as the other vehicle sidled past just a meter away. The vehicle was painted in a color scheme he hadn't seen before.

Max furrowed his eyebrows. "Duncan, you know all the corporate logos. What's black and yellow?"

"It's black and *gold*, Max. That's Goldwater Mining & Refining."

Max's nose twitched. "Goldwater? I thought they did all their mining underground east of the city. Do they have a new mine out here?"

Duncan shrugged. "I don't know."

Blue looked at Max. "I had a conversation with John once. Part of his original deal with Gamma was that all of Sinus Lunicus was reserved for him."

"So you're saying -"

Blue said, "There are no human facilities out here."

"So what business does Goldwater have with Gamma?"

Chapter 37

2064: Northern Logistics offices, Aristillus, Lunar Nearside

Mike paced the gray carpet, detouring when piles of cube partition panels or folded-up tables blocked his path. The Northern Logistics office had seemed huge when they'd arrived, but after so many days stuck here he knew every corner. Now it felt claustrophobic.

He stopped and looked up. John was seated at a table a dozen meters away.

"John, I need to get out of here. I need some fresh air."

John shook his head without even looking up from his slate. "Nope. Security."

Mike walked towards John, veering around a long dolly stacked high with folding chairs. "I'm not asking to go out in public and give a speech. I just want to take a walk. Let me see something new. Let me buy a taco from a street vendor, for God's sake."

John put down his slate. "You want tacos? We can order tacos."

"Takeout? No, I'm sick of food that's been couriered through three different fake addresses and is an hour past cold by the time it gets here. But that's not the point. What I'm saying is that I need to stretch my legs. I need to see something other than these damned walls."

John stared at Mike coolly. After a moment of calculation he sighed. "Two conditions. I go with you. And you'll be in disguise. Deal?"

"Deal."

An hour later John returned and upended the shopping bag. Hair clippers, a razor, a package of dye, and two sets of clothes spilled onto the table.

"What's this?"

"You agreed to a disguise."

"But -"

"Shave your head bald, trim your scruff into a mustache, and then dye it."

"Oh no. Hell no. This is bull -"

"You said we had a deal."

Mike picked up bottle of dye. "Black? Even before I went gray, I never had black hair!"

"And you're arguing that that's bad for a disguise?"

Mike grimaced.

A shaved head? A mustache? He'd had the same brush-cut haircut since college and detested facial hair - even the stubble he'd grown since the PK assault was bugging him. Still, John was right: there could be deep cover PK snatch teams out in the tunnels. After several seconds of silent debate, he nodded in acceptance. "OK, you win."

Mike pushed the supplies back into the bag and headed to the locker room. The path took him through Nothern Logistics' corporate gym, empty except for two of Dewitt's men doing bench presses in one corner. He shook his head at all of the equipment. No wonder Northern Logistics had gone bankrupt - they spent money on frivolous shit before they had any revenue.

Fifteen minutes later Mike looked in the locker room mirror and winced at his shiny skull and thin black mustache. He sighed and headed back out.

John, already in his new clothes, was waiting for him with a grin plastered on his stupid face. Mike saw the ridicule coming and leaned into it. "Do I look more like a pedophile or a diversity compliance officer?"

John looked him up and down. "Yes. Now get dressed." He pushed one of the two sets of clothes across the table.

Mike shucked his pants and shirt and pulled on the new clothes, and then stood and held up his arms. John looked at him with an appraising eye. "Decent, but your body language is still you. PK observation software can pick up on that. Slouch a bit. Good. Now tuck your chin - yeah. Remember to keep that posture when we're out."

"Are we ready?"

"Sure. Where are we going?"

"I want to stretch my legs, I want to get something to eat, and I want a coffee."

John removed the holster and pistol from his pile of discarded clothes and tucked them into his new outfit. "We can get food, but no coffee shops, no book clubs, and - for that matter - no heavy equipment dealerships. We stick to stuff outside your normal routine."

Mike grumbled but nodded.

* * *

Mike held the clamshell container with one hand as he walked and used his other hand to scoop up the last bite of vegetable wat with a sloppy shred of injera. As he chewed he looked in vain for the paper napkin that had been tucked under the container a few minutes ago, but then gave up and wiped his fingers on his pants. He swallowed. "I'll admit it - Ethiopian's not half bad."

John nodded. "Good. Now stop strutting."

"I'm not strutting."

"Slouch. Further. Now tuck your chin."

Mike rolled his eyes but complied. He was happy enough to be outside; he wasn't going to complain.

They reached an intersection. Mike looked at the traffic and then, instead of waiting for the walk light, took a right. If he had no particular place to go, one direction was as good as another. Mike looked around with a professional eye. A C-class tunnel, of course. He inspected the light fixtures and catwalks. F series light panels? This was one of his, wasn't it? Yes, he - ouch! John had just elbowed him.

Mike looked at John. "What?"

A quick whisper: "Head *down*!" Ah, right. Mike tucked his chin. Well, if he couldn't look at the infrastructure, he could at least window shop; *that* wouldn't expose his face to cameras or spies. They passed a bakery, an architect's office, a gym. He paused at some sort of luxury goods store – the sign said "Applied Hedonics". The window was full of leather chairs, boxes of high end cigars, fancy-looking cookware. He saw some of the prices and whistled. The shipping bottleneck was starting to bite, wasn't it?

And there - one of the new '1% back' posters. He started to smile, then stopped. "What the *fuck*!?"

John looked over. "What?"

Mike pointed to the window.

"Applied Hedonics?"

"No, not the store name. The sign."

John read it. "'We Support Lunar Independence - shop here for freedom!' Hey, that's your 'Gold Star' idea, right? The 1% kickback? I like the logo."

"Yeah, it's great. But it's not ours."

"What?"

"It's not ours. That's some other program."

"Ah - I don't understand."

"The poster says 'We Support Lunar Independence.' Our official one says 'Join the Fight For Freedom.' And the logo is different too. Shit. I don't know if they're really sending 1% anywhere, but if they are, it's not to us."

John nodded, and turned away to scan the street for threats.

Mike kept staring at the poster, and shook his head. "Fuck."

Chapter 38

2064: Trentham Court Apartments, Aristillus, Lunar Nearside

Hugh walked into the living room. "Louisa, have you finished the editing on the segment on how the DoD's ships arrived out of order? I just got some more footage of the wreckage on the surface, and I'd like to put it in."

Louisa looked up from her editing station. "What? No; I told you that I'm not working on that. The corporate army thing is more important."

"Jesus, Louisa! I already explained that The Minute isn't going to run that until after we focus on Defense's mistakes. We've got to have priorities. I thought we agreed on this."

Louisa shrugged. "You agreed on it. Here, look what I've been working on." She clicked a button and ran the video clip.

> Louisa's voice: "So you admit that less than five percent of your engineers are African American?"
>
> The CEO spread his hands. "African *American*? I don't think any of them are. But most of the minerals process engineers are Nigerian, so if the question is about blacks -"
>
> Louisa cut him off. "There are widespread reports that illegally genetically engineered Dogs are present on the moon, even though those programs were supposed to be shut down after the Portman Hearings. Do you have any genetically modified dogs on your payroll?"

The CEO scoffed. "What is that, a joke? No, we don't hire animals at this firm."

Louisa said, "And here it is again after a little bit of polishing." She ran a second clip.

Louisa's voice: "So you admit that less than five percent of your engineers are African American?"

The CEO scoffed. "What is that, a joke? No, we don't hire animals at this firm."

Hugh grimaced. "Don't you think you're overdoing things, just a bit?"

Louisa turned on him. "No. I don't. Hugh, you're so focused on the bullshit in DC that you can't see the real issues. We have to hammer the corporations in Aristillus now. If we don't establish the narrative, then after Liberation things might not change. We need to create an outcry, so that there's political pressure to dismantle the firms, not just reach an accommodation with them. People on Earth need to understand the deeper truth."

Hugh shook his head in disgust. "Whatever, Louisa. I'll work on the DoD thing myself." He turned away, then turned back. "And I'm telling you again, DC Minute isn't going to run your clip until after they run mine. If they run yours at all."

Chapter 39

2064: Eiffong Engineering, Aristillus, Lunar Nearside

Rob Wehrmann stood in the front office of Eiffong Engineering, flanked by his guards. Three of them were his own employees; one was a member of General Dewitt's defecting US Army team. The four men were dressed in a motley assortment of jumpsuits and oil-stained jeans, united in appearance only by the fresh-from-the-printer assault rifles they carried.

The Eiffong Engineering clerk returned, pushing open the door from the maintenance yard and letting a blast of noise in before the door swung shut behind him. "Tony says you should come on back." He pointed to a cardboard box on the counter filled with plastic bags of disposable earplugs. "You might want to grab some."

Rob grunted, pulled his own pair of full sized muffs from a pouch on his belt and slipped them on, and then brushed past the clerk. The four guards looked at each other and shrugged, grabbing earplugs from the box as they followed.

It was loud in the yard - loud and chaotic. Even with his earmuffs in place Rob winced despite himself. The warning alarm as a crane moved along the overhead rails, the shriek of grinders, and the staccato drumbeats of impact hammers warred against each other.

Rob glanced around and saw Tony ahead. Rob strode across the floor and shouted. "Hey, Tony, how we doing?" Behind him his guards hastened to catch up.

Tony Eiffong saw him and shouted back, "Coming along. Lotta design work, but I think you'll like it. Let me tell you -"

Rob cut him short. "Where are they?"

As if one cue, the overhead crane that had slid past a moment before came rattling back. Slung under it was a massive gray machine.

Tony raised his chin to point at it. "That's one of them."

The crane rolled twenty meters past them, and then stopped and lowered its burden to the ground. With a clank the shackles released from the lift points. Rob walked toward the big gray machine. Tony started shouting, but then the noise diminished, just a bit, and he lowered his voice. "The armor was easy enough - we just plasma cut some deck plates. Turned out the power train didn't need to be upgraded to carry the extra weight - designed for Earth gravity and all that. The only trick was getting the balance right, so we -"

Rob wasn't listening. He'd reached the massive earth mover, now reworked, retooled, and covered with armor, sensors, and chaff dispensers. He put one hand on the flank - and pulled it back, wet and sticky with gray paint. Underneath streaks of the original yellow showed through.

He turned to Tony. "I don't see the guns."

Tony shook his head. "The contractor is swamped - all of the militias are placing orders and he's behind. But the amount of work we've done so far - "

Rob grunted. "What the fuck good is a tank if it doesn't have guns?"

"My men have been working double shifts, and we've already ruined one plasma cutter. We've never made a tank before, and we've just turned out fifty of them -"

Rob shrugged, unimpressed. "Get the guns on these."

Tony looked uncomfortable. "What about payment?"

Rob turned to look at him. "It's coming."

"I know you're good for it, Rob, but I'm all out of credit with my vendors. I can't float you any more."

"This isn't for me - this is for the revolution."

"I know - and I'm not making any profit on this. I haven't paid myself in two months and the men haven't had payroll in three weeks. There is no more credit anywhere. None."

"Figure it out, Tony. I'm going to have another fifty Cats here by the end of the day tomorrow."

"Listen to me, Rob. Unless you can shake some more money loose from the Boardroom Group, don't bother. If I can't buy materials or pay my men, there's no point. This factory is two days away from shutting down."

Rob pursed his lips. "Fuck."

"You're telling me."

Rob took a deep breath. He was going to raise hell when he got back to the Boardroom group, and he didn't care if Mike liked the idea of bonds, or a bank, or whatever.

Chapter 40

Restivo looked at the three men on the far side of the table. They were young. Too young?

"What makes you think you can do this in three months when Hamilton Sundstrand said it would take three years?"

The one with the goatee met his eye. "With all due respect to Hamilton Sundstrand, they're a division inside a wholly owned subsidiary of a hundred-and-ten-year-old defense contractor. They get paid every year, whether they develop anything or not. We're a small five-year-old firm. We have to hustle." He raised his chin in pride. "Our work on the Everest Adventure Team suits shows what we can do."

Restivo pursed his lips. "That was just 12 suits. We're looking at forty thousand suits here. More if you include training and spares. How can you possibly deliver that many?"

The second man - the other founder - answered. "Forty or forty thousand - volume doesn't matter. Once we get the design nailed down the printers can kick out whatever we need. If you can requisition the feedstock for us, no problem."

Restivo nodded. He'd already known the answer, but he felt compelled to ask the question anyway. He didn't like the position he was in. He *really* didn't like it. So many untrusted vendors, so many rushed orders. Something was going to go catastrophically wrong, and probably at the worst possible time. He hoped that when it did, he wouldn't lose too many people. Still, with the timetable the president had given him, he had no alternative.

Restivo sighed. "You've got the contract."

The first one, goatee kid, coughed, then managed to gasp. "We got the contr- we got it? I can't - is that official?"

"Yes."

"It can't be that simple. We - we didn't even get a call back from our state rep. Are you sure you can just *do* this?"

"I'm prepared to sign it right now."

The three men exchanged glances and then started grinning.

The second one stopped smiling for a moment and raised one finger. "One thing - I know schedule matters for you. We could save a hell of a lot of time in the development process if we could hang onto the helmet you loaned us."

Restivo furrowed his brow. "I thought you were going to reuse the helmet design from your Everest suit?"

"Oh, we are - but the expats put their computers in their helmets. If we can copy all the software - heat balancing, coms, all that - that'd really reduce schedule risk."

Restivo thought about it for a moment. Why not? They had dozens more from the other captured ships.

"Sure." He pushed the ziplock evidence bag across the table.

"You need a government material transfer statement for that, right? We can get a notary -"

Restivo shook his head. "Contract regulations, material transfer - all that shit is out the window. Just get this done. Lives - thousands of lives - depend on this."

Goatee kid looked serious for the first time in the conversation. He swallowed. "Yes, sir. We'll do our best."

"Don't do your best. Do it perfectly."

Chapter 41

2064: Northern Logistics offices, Aristillus, Lunar Nearside

Mike stood in the conference room as Javier, Albert, and even Trang gave him good-natured static for his mustache and newly smooth skull. Mike accepted it with aplomb at first, and then cut them off. "OK, enough bullshitting - what do we know about the Gold Star impostors?"

Javier tapped at his slate. "It looks like there are at least three competing programs. Some of the competitors are charging the same one percent we are, others are charging less. Most of them seem to be supporting groups we alread know of, although one of them claims that they're funding the 'New New Mexico Militia,' whatever that is."

Mike shook his head. "Fucking scam artists."

Javier looked up from his slate. "Let's not assume malice."

"Why not?"

"From what I can tell, some of these groups really are giving money to militias."

"The New New Mexico Militia? Never heard of them. Are they building e-p-doors? Are they importing morphine and MRI machines and trauma kits?"

"Let's not get angry, Mike, let's think. We've got a population which is almost entirely in favor of independence. That's a natural constituency. So why don't we have one hundred percent market share? Why do we have competitors?"

"That's not the issue -"

"Yeah, it is the issue. This is a scientific question. The universe is giving us data. Would you rather analyze it or would you rather get angry?"

Mike crossed his arms.

Javier raised an eyebrow and continued. "So why might these merchants go with another group?"

Trang answered. "Money. Maybe they demand less of a cut than we do."

Javier nodded. "Reasonable idea, but this website says that they're charging 1%, just like us."

Mark said. "Local loyalties. Maybe the store owners know the folks behind the militia personally."

"That's possible. It might not even be a terrible thing - local loyalties, local knowledge."

Rob grunted. "Maybe it's simpler than that. Maybe they've just got better marketing than we do. How's their ad copy?"

Mike shrugged. "What the hell do I know about ad copy?"

Rob looked at Mike from under heavy brows. "My tanks aren't going to be finished until we come up with some more money. So if that's the problem, we'd damned well better learn."

Karina leaned forward. "These other groups clearly have better outreach than we do. All of us are in B2B businesses - we don't know how to reach consumers."

Mike nodded. "OK. So we've got a marketing problem. We can address that."

Karina shook her head. "We don't have time."

Mike said, "Look, we'll retool the ad copy. Give it another week."

Karina said. "I should note that I got an email ten minutes ago - a charge we sent to Taylor Pressure Vessels bounced. *Again.*"

Mike deflated. "Shit."

Karina pursed her lips. "Yes. Quite. They've put down tools. So far all we've got is a lot of construction debris at eighteen locations and *zero* EP-doors. Mike, we gave your idea time, but it didn't work. We need cash immediately."

Javier sighed. "Mike, I backed you on the logo idea, but it's not bringing in enough money. We don't have time. We need to issue bonds, and we need to do it now."

Mike felt trapped. He looked to the left, then the right, looking for any support. He found none. Shit. If they didn't issue bonds they'd be out of money - Karina was right about that. But if they issued bonds, he knew - he just *knew* - Mark would use it as a back door, and sooner or later - in one year or five - Aristillus would have taxes. - And a government.

Unless -

Wait a second.

He felt a smile tug at his lip.

Mike looked up and met Mark's eyes. "Alright. I give. We need money, so we issue bonds."

Mark smiled. Of course he smiled. He thought he'd won.

"Thank you Mike. This is really going to take the pressure off. With the backing of the full faith and credit of the Boardroom Group, we -"

Mike shook his head. "No. I agreed to bonds, but I didn't agree to the 'full faith and credit' bit."

Mark furrowed his eyebrows. "What? How can you issue bonds without promising to pay them back?"

"How can the Boardroom Group make that promise and live up to it? No, don't answer - I already know how you think we'll pay it back. Taxes. Government." Mike looked around the room. "No, if we have to issue bonds, we'll pledge real collateral. I know each of us is tapped out of liquid assets. Checking accounts are empty, so it's time to pledge other stuff. I'm putting up half of Morlock's stock."

Mark blinked. "Wait, what?"

"You heard me. I'm going to issue bonds against Morlock Engineering. It's not publicly traded - I hold a hundred percent of the shares - but Davidson Equities Analysis estimates that it's worth two hundred and seventy million. So I'll issue bonds backed by half of that."

Mark's jaw hung open. "But, wait. That's not what I _"

Rob looked over at him. "And you're going to buy back those bonds after the revolution?"

Mike took a deep breath. "I'm going to try."

"What if you can't?"

"I'll figure out a way. Anyway, I'm in for fifty percent of my firm. Who's going to match me?"

Mike looked around the room expectantly.

After a moment Rob Wehrmann sighed. "Ah, fuck it. I'm in."

Across the table Mark scowled and Mike fought to keep a smile off his face.

Chapter 42

2064: Belmont Homes, Aristillus, Lunar Nearside

Hugh stepped out of the bedroom. The door closed behind him with a solid and satisfying click. The new apartment was nicer than the old one. When mother had transferred the most recent funds from the family trust, Hugh had decided to be generous. Hugh and Allyson shared the biggest of the four bedrooms, Louisa and Selena each had their own, and the fourth was set up as an office for their production work.

Allyson called out from the kitchen, "I'm making Raw Pumpkin Pudding - who wants some?" Louisa caught Hugh's eye as he entered the common areas and silently made a retching face. Hugh was torn between grinning at Louisa's joke and loyalty to his girlfriend and ended up just contorting his face oddly.

He called back, "None for me, thanks!"

Allyson's food was weird, but Hugh was happy - at least now she was eating without complaining. The tour of Sky High Farms had been a disappointment for Louisa because there'd been nothing horrible, or even questionable, to capture on video. She'd complained for days about it. Allyson, though, had been pleasantly surprised and was still bringing up little details, like the fact that their fertilizers were entirely organic.

Louisa cleared her throat. "Hugh."

He turned.

Louisa pointed at the screen. "Check out the Goldwater arrest footage." She played the raw version. "Now, let's take the part where I say 'Ever hear of the Fourth Estate?'" She clicked a button. "We lose the word 'fuck.'" She clicked again, and then played it back.

Hugh squinted as he watched and listened. "Your tone of voice there -"

"What about it?"

"Well...it's not as sympathetic as it might be. Why don't we keep the video, but do ADR to make the tone a bit friendlier."

Louisa nodded. "That would work - and it would be nice to cut to a reaction shot after that."

Hugh shook his head. "Our cameras were pointed away at that point. We don't *have* a reaction shot."

"They gave you their footage as part of outprocessing, right?"

"I already looked it over. All we've got is the feed from the guard's helmet cam. No reaction shot there either."

Louisa shrugged. "We've got a lot of camera angles of guards in the footage from our jail cells. There's got to me a good shot of a pissed-off look somewhere in there. I'll dump the background and replace it with an enhanced still shot from the site of the battle. Add a bit of digital smoke, a bit of motion blur - it'll be great."

Hugh pursed his lips. Louisa was taking a *lot* of liberties with the video recently. They were all getting at the greater truth, so he wasn't really *upset* per se, but it concerned him. "Do you think you can make it look realistic?"

"Trust me, it's going to be perfect. These fascists are going to get theirs after Liberation...and then, when they're in jail the ass pain will *really* start!" She all but snorted at her own joke.

Selena looked up from the couch where she was doing research on her slate. "You're not *really* laughing about these men getting raped, are you?"

Louisa scowled and looked at Selena. "It's a metaphor, Little Miss Uptight. And, besides, what if I am? They're the ones who are breaking the law."

Selena shook her head sadly and looked away.

Hugh turned back to the screen. "The rest of this looks good. We're agreed that you don't submit the 'private armies' expose until *after* the DoD expose runs, right? My mom was pretty clear on that, and she did help us get this nicer apartment."

Louisa sighed and then reluctantly agreed. "DoD piece first. Fine."

Allyson called from the kitchen. "The raw pumpkin pudding is done and I've made a vegetable plate. Snack time."

Selena stood. "I'm not hungry. Actually, I'm feeling a bit sick. I apologize, but I think I need to just take a walk. I'll be back later."

Hugh looked at Selena's departing back. That was weird - she hadn't seemed sick.

He turned and looked at Allyson, who was bringing the snack in. The raw pumpkin pudding looked hideous, as usual. Well, at least the celery and hummus was OK.

Chapter 43

2064: Northern Logistics offices, Aristillus, Lunar Nearside

Mike watched the private paint the wall of the office. "Is this *really* necessary? I'm not releasing a video to the public: I'm just trying to videoconference with my assistant."

The private shrugged and continued his work.

From behind Mike a new voice answered his question. "Yeah, Mike, it is."

Mike turned to see Dewitt. "Why?"

"We're tor-ing all of the emails and phone calls in and out of this place, so even if the PKs have a mole in a telcom company they won't be able to figure out where your calls are coming from."

"So why- ?"

"Even if the snatch team can't learn what IP address we're at, there are other ways to track us. I guarantee you that someone at Northern Logistics shot video in this room back before they went bankrupt. And that video is online, somewhere. If the snatch team intercepts your calls at the far end, even if they can't trace the IP, they'll have the raw video. And if they're any good, they'll analyze it. They'll look at the Pantone of the paint, the smudges on the walls, every detail, and they'll do a search of all the video out there to figure where the video was shot." He paused. "You don't want that."

"That's a bit far-fetched, isn't it? Do you think that anyone has ever done that?"

Dewitt looked at him levelly. "I have."

Mike narrowed his eyes. "Yeah, but -"

"In two of the cases I lasered in glide bombs. The third my team went in at night, black-bagged our target, and killed everyone else."

Mike pondered this for a moment, and then looked at the wall. "Nice color choice."

Dewitt clapped Mike on the shoulder and left the room.

* * *

Mike sat on a futon in front of the newly painted wall. On the wallscreen Wam gave his report.

Mike said, "That's good news about the TBMs. Has Juan worked up a deployment schedule? ...I think we want to move both of them overland from the assembly warehouse to new entry points...Yeah, it's going to have to be pretty far out if we want to hit level 7 at the right angle."

The two of them worked through the agenda. Eventually they checked off the last item and Mike ended the call.

Now for the next order of business. He'd been uncharacteristically putting this next task off, and he didn't know why.

It was time to bite the bullet.

Mike walked to the kitchenette and prepared two mugs of coffee, and then headed to the office that Dewitt had staked out. The door was open and Dewitt was behind his desk, working on his slate.

Mike let himself in and raised one of the mugs. "General. Want some coffee?"

Dewitt looked up. "Sounds great."

"Pot's in the kitchen. Grabbed two for myself, though."

Dewitt shook his head, but he was amused. "Javier was right about you."

"He's still telling people that I'm the world's biggest asshole?"

"Pretty much."

Mike smiled and handed one mug over. "Got a minute?"

"Sure, why?"

"I want to talk over how we negotiate Darcy's release. And not just her's: Ponzie's, everyone on those ships..."

"Not going to happen."

"Excuse me?"

"The US and the PKs aren't going to hand them over. Why would they?"

"Well, we've got Evangelos and his men."

Dewitt shrugged. "So?"

"Can't we do a hostage exchange?"

Dewitt put down his stylus. "Why do they want their men back?"

"Because - wait, what?"

Dewitt shook his head. "DC doesn't *want* the PKs back. They're just a bunch of third worlders. Who cares about them? President Johnson doesn't. UN Secretary General Thierry doesn't either."

Mike put his coffee mug down on the desk. "But public opinion -"

Dewitt shook his head. "The Greek troops don't matter to anyone except the Greeks. The US and the UN do a hostage exchange, and they get back some troops that don't matter, and frankly aren't any good. I mean, your troops here are green, but the PKs - well, anyway. From DC's point of view, if they leave the hostages here that's a win, because it lets the politicians brag that they don't negotiate with 'terrorists.' That ramps up popular support for a war, at exactly the time they need that support. An election is coming and a casus belli is the perfect gift. If anything, Johnson and Thierry are wishing that they'd sent more troops, so that they'd have more dead bodies and more hostages to point to."

Mike's hand that held his coffee shook, and he put the mug down quickly on the desk to hide it. "So you're arguing that they won't exchange for Darcy?"

"Not arguing. Stating it flat out."

Mike's knees felt rubbery. Ten minutes ago he'd been telling himself that he didn't know why he'd been putting this conversation off, but that was a lie. He knew. The fear of hearing this answer, that was why he'd put it off.

The longer he delayed the conversation, the longer he could keep the belief that he could get Darcy back.

He felt himself take a step backwards, then another, before half tripping backwards into and half sitting in a chair he hadn't even realized was there.

"There's no way to get Darcy back?"

Dewitt took a sip of his coffee. "I didn't say that."

Mike swallowed and looked at Dewitt. "Tell me."

Chapter 44

2064: Giovanni's Place, Aristillus, Lunar Nearside

Selena took a final bite of her barbecue burger. She'd lied about not being hungry to get out of the apartment. She'd needed time to think. And she'd been thinking. For hours.

She looked around the restaurant. Several groups of customers had come and gone while she'd been sitting and nursing her original side salad and then the burger. The turnover was still going on. Two tables of chip fab engineers who'd spent the last half hour discussing recalibrating their machines after the shock waves caused by the PK ships crashing were standing up and pushing their chairs in. And almost immediately a gaggle of mothers shepherding young children was pushing in to take the space.

Selena wiped her hands on a napkin and thought about her lie. It was small, claiming that she didn't want lunch, but it had been a crack in the dam - the dam holding back her pent-up disagreement and anger.

She wasn't sure when the dam had started leaking. Certainly it had been dripping a week ago. She'd had enough doubts about what the four of them were doing by then that she'd cold-called Goldwater and asked them to faux arrest her so that she could meet up with Hugh and Louisa while wearing a concealed mike and camera. The footage she'd taken had been stunning, even if she didn't know what she'd use it for yet.

Selena absently lifted her soda to her lips and took a drink.

She'd never particularly liked Louisa, and the other woman's behavior over the last few months cemented that. So much had happened. In a way it seemed like just yesterday that they'd flown to the moon, found a cheap apartment, and watched Allan die while rock climbing - but in another way it seemed a lifetime ago.

They'd seen so many new things in that time. Expat society was exactly like she'd expected - and also nothing at all like what she'd imagined. She'd tried to be intellectually honest as she experienced it.

In some ways she stood by her earlier thoughts: Aristillus did need some common sense regulation, and the social programs provided by the Mormons, the Catholics, and the various charitable groups were a patchwork, without any coordination.

But were unplanned neighborhoods really the end of the world? Louisa talked about new urbanism and neighborhoods with "character" - but didn't most of the tunnels had more authentic character than the neighborhoods back home? Did society really fall apart when calorie counts were only provided at some of the restaurants? Were the workers here noticeably more exploited than on Earth?

Changing her opinions, at least a bit - that was a *good* thing, right? Wasn't there some famous quote about 'when the facts change, I change my mind'?

And yet, every time Selena had brought one of these objections up, Louisa had attacked her. If the other woman had rebutted her points, or argued that, yes, there were benefits to lunar way of doing things but they were outweighed by the problems, that would have been one thing.

But that's not what Louisa did. No, her favorite tools were mockery and out of hand dismissal. Louisa - for all that she talked about the importance of ideas - didn't like to actually engage with any ideas other than the ones she already had.

Selena picked up a fried yam stick and stirred it in the puddle of ketchup.

The expats seemed like decent people - no better or worse than folks back home - so why couldn't they be allowed to make their own decisions? If they made a mess of it, it was *their* mess. They'd chosen to be here, after all.

Wasn't the point of the Global Fair Deal and "a 22nd century society in the 21st century" not just that everyone had rights, but that decisions should be made rationally? So why was Louisa unwilling to argue rationally about the expats and what they wanted?

Selena knew that Louisa wasn't an aberration. It seemed that more people than not in the Global Fair Deal movement preferred talking points to actual talking.

Louisa wanted a resolution to the Aristillus issue, but not a resolution driven by logic or arguments or compromise. No, she seemed eager for the day when the crisis came to a head - a violent head - and large numbers of the expats were arrested, tried, and sentenced.

Why that anger? Why that vindictiveness?

Selena looked to her left where the half dozen mothers and the dozen children were celebrating a birthday party. As she watched one of the kids tried to blow out the lights on the cake and failed, only to have a mother help him out. Selena shook her head. Why did Louisa want these people in jail? What had they ever done to her?

And then, today, Louisa had made the "joke" that the Goldwater employees should be sent to jail and anally raped.

After so many weeks of indecision and second thoughts, *that* was what had pushed Selena over the edge and made her walk out of the room. No matter what the expats had done, saying that they should be raped? Selena felt her face and chest get hot. And *laughing* about it?

She and Louisa had met in college while serving on the organizing committee for an anti-rape march back in college. And now Louisa thought that rape was a joking matter?

Selena put down the fried yam. Her mind was made up. She was going to do it.

And she knew what the first step was.

She wiped her hands on a napkin and then tapped at her slate to call up ads for apartments.

Chapter 45

2064: Northern Logistics offices, Aristillus, Lunar Nearside

Mike reached out blindly for his coffee and almost knocked it over. He recovered, held the mug in one hand, and immediately forgot about it.

He looked at Dewitt. "Are you suggesting a direct strike at the US? Hitting them on their home ground doesn't have a history of working well. Pearl Harbor, 9/11, Baltimore -"

"No, it'd be suicide to strike directly."

"So what are you saying, then?"

Dewitt answered, "At the turn of the century the government wanted its prison camps deniable: overseas, and belonging to someone else. Nothing's changed in sixty-five years. All the black prisons are outside CONUS, and aren't even officially US facilities. That's what gives us political and propaganda cover for a strike."

"How much cover?"

Dewitt took a breath and looked a little less sure of himself. "Enough - I hope. Back before the Responsible Polling Act, surveys always showed that voters disliked the camps. That's one of the reasons that they're overseas and under foreign control - it lets everyone pretend that they're not being run by the US. That's what I'm counting on. So if we hit the camps we're not hitting American facilities, American territory, or American soldiers. The US politicians would be pissed, but they can't claim that we hit *them* without admitting that they own these camps, and they don't want to do that." He paused and considered, and then added, "You know, it could work out as a PR coup for us."

"A coup? How?"

"If this works, we accomplish three things." He ticked the points off on his fingers. "First, we free the captives. That's solid gold: not only does it rally the people of Aristillus, but it plays well on Earth."

"How so?"

"Everyone loves a prison-break story. Even if it's the other side doing it, you've got to take your hat off to them. Which leads into point two: We're the plucky underdog. Another PR coup. Finally, if we pull it off, we embarrass the enemy. The only thing better than a plucky underdog is a plucky underdog that wins."

Mike thought about that for a moment. "You said '*if*' we pull it off?"

"Yeah, 'if'." He paused. "This could fail."

Mike sat back and pushed his fingers against his temples.

A raid. A raid with a risk of failure. What did failure mean? He shied away from the thought. "Tell me about the PR benefits."

"Do you know Doolittle's raid?"

Mike shook his head. "The name's kinda familiar, but - no."

Dewitt leaned forward across his desk. "World War Two, just after Pearl Harbor. The US has been hit on its home territory for the first time since the British burned the White House a century and a half before. The American people are demoralized and uncertain. The important thing here is the psychology - that's three-quarters of every war. And the psychology in 1942 is that Americans are afraid. Japan reached out across a huge ocean, an ocean that had always protected the US. And then the Japanese hit them - hit them *hard*. Remember, this is practically ancient history. Back before spy satellites, so the enemy is - literally and metaphorically - on the other side of the world. There's no way to know where they are, where their ships are, what they're planning next."

"Couldn't they send drones -"

Dewitt shook his head. "No such thing as drones. There weren't even computers back then. And even if they'd had computers, the longest-range planes didn't have even a third of the range to get from the US to Japan, which brings me to the next point. After you've been hit, nothing makes the pain go away like punching back. But in 1942, there's no way to punch back. "

Mike leaned forward. "So what did we do?"

"Even though we couldn't, we punched back anyway."

"How?"

"They took crappy internal-combustion bombers - with propellers! - and ripped out the seats, the parachutes, the radios - even the bomb sights. Then they overloaded them with bombs and fuel, and launched them off of first-generation aircraft carriers."

"That sounds...crazy."

"It *was* crazy. The carriers were never designed to carry anything that big. The bombers were overloaded and didn't have enough fuel to get back. We pointed the whole thing at Japan, like a disposable three-stage rocket."

Mike licked his lips. "Did it work?"

"Militarily? It accomplished almost nothing. Every single plane was lost. Some of the crews were killed. Worse, some were taken alive -"

"Worse?"

"The Japanese vivisected prisoners without anesthetic. Torture surgery. Horrific nightmare stuff."

"You're shitting me. The Japanese?"

"Yeah, the Japanese. They were worse than the Caliphate."

Mike knew it was his imagination, but the lights in the room seemed dimmer and the walls more distant - as if he was hearing the story huddled around a single lamp in a small apartment...or a fire at night, on the plain. He swallowed.

Dewitt let the pause stretch out before continuing. "That was the first return blow. It had no military value at all, but it had huge psychological value. Doolittle's raid dropped bombs on Tokyo, and proved to the US populace that they weren't victims. They were fighters." Mike nodded and Dewitt continued. "And it did one other thing."

"What was that?"

"It gave the Japanese their first sneaking suspicion that they'd made a terrible miscalculation."

Mike sat back. "So you think that we can get Darcy and the others back?"

"Mike, as your Secretary of the Army, I'm telling you that this mission is important. Not to get Darcy back, or to get Ponzie, or anyone else. We might succeed in that, or we might not. It's important to show the population here on the moon that you're not content to play defense. You - we - have to show the people that we're not victims. We're fighters. And we're going to win this fight."

Mike nodded. It made sense - and yet he was worried. He wanted Darcy back alive, not some propaganda stunt. Was Dewitt weighing those two goals correctly?

"I don't like choosing a mission for propaganda purposes instead of military purposes -"

"Mike, propaganda *is* a military purpose. The people here in the colony need to know that we're in the fight. The people sitting on the sidelines on Earth need to sit up and pay attention. You want immigration, right? You want more minds and hands to win this fight? You've got people on Earth who are interested, who are thinking about coming here...but they're wondering if they should sell their houses, leave their jobs, and risk everything. They're not going to do it if they think we're going to lose the fight - or if we're not going to *try* to fight." He paused. "And most importantly of all, the politicians on Earth need to know that you're not going to give up. Put the fear of God into them. Put some teeth in our negotiations."

Mike looked at the ceiling. He felt the emotional appeal of Dewitt's plan. He felt something else, too. But what?

After a moment he realized what the other emotion was: *relief.* Someone - someone other than him - was thinking about tactics, thinking about strategy. Thinking about how to win this war. For so long he'd felt that he was carrying the entire weight of the revolution on his shoulders. The weight of it all - the political agitation, the financing, the exhortation, the coordination - had been on his shoulders. Every day, for so long now, he'd felt that if he buckled under the load, if he bent just a little, he'd fall, and his dream of a place where people could live free would buckle and fall with him.

Javier had told him to assemble the Boardroom Group, and maybe it had been a good idea - but it hadn't lessened the weight. If anything, it just made the burden feel heavier: the meetings made him think that he had as many enemies inside the boardroom as outside.

But now there was Dewitt. Dewitt, who was not just willing, but eager - eager! - to share the load with him.

Mike looked down from the ceiling, making sure to keep the tumult of emotions from his face. Maybe someday he could let the pressure, the fear, and the frustration show. But not now. Not in front of Dewitt.

Now he needed to do one thing: tell Dewitt what he thought of his plan to strike back - and maybe to rescue the hostages.

Mike and started to speak but realized he didn't trust himself. He stood and stuck out his hand.

Dewitt rose and shook it. "I've started working on plans."

Mike found his voice. "Tell me what you need. I'll make sure you get it."

Dewitt pulled a data fob from his pocket. "I've got seven approaches. Here they are, ordered by what I think the likelihood of success is. There are budgets for each."

Mike took the fob, nodded, and left.

A walk down a corridor, a right turn, and then he was in his own office. He closed the door behind him, let his shoulders sag, and collapsed into a chair. He let himself indulge in several long shuddering breaths. God, the stress he'd been under. He'd borne up under it - borne up so well that he hadn't admitted to himself how hard it was. It had been hard to breathe recently. The days since Darcy was taken had been the worst. His chest had been tight, and he'd forced himself not to show it.

And now?

Now he could breathe again.

Mike gestured to the wall screen for the lights to dim. They did and he sat slumped in his chair with his hands over his eyes.

He sat there for half an hour before he turning the lights back on and moving to his desk.

He stuck Dewitt's data fob into his slate and scanned the documents, and then read them again more slowly.

The first one - Dewitt's favorite - was weird. He looked at it and tilted his head, and then stood, walked back to Dewitt's office, and opened the door.

"Mike, what's up?"

Mike gestured with his slate. "Option number one. A lot of ships, I get that...But why so few men? And what's the gravel for?"

Chapter 46

2064: Lucknow, India

Ashok turned the light down and sat on the edge of the stool while his wife Rani tucked the blanket up under the chin of their youngest. The two sat in silence for a few minutes until he was sure that Avarind was fully asleep, and then they slipped out of the room.

Ashok eased the bedroom door closed behind them and walked to the small living room, Rani at his side.

Ashok turned to Rani. "I've been thinking about Aristillus."

Rani pursed her lips. "Again, Ashok? I already told you - it's too risky. Parliament increased the emigration penalties once, and there's talk that they're going to boost them again. I heard a rumor CBI is starting to run stings. What would happen if you got caught? You'd lose your job!"

Ashok nodded. Rani had a real point: Hindustan Aeronautics wasn't a branch of the government any more, but it might as well be. With China somehow managing to fall further apart each year, the firm's drones kept the chaos bottled up on the far side of the border; anyone who worked at HA - *especially* someone who worked as an optics engineer in the drone division - had to toe the line politically.

"I agree with you that trying to get out with one of the smugglers is a bad idea. But there's another way."

"You're not talking about the plans, are you?"

Ashok sat down on the couch. "Yes. I am."

Rani remained standing. "How do you even know that those plans work?"

Ashok patted the cushion next to him. "Come, sit with me."

Rani stayed on her feet. "First, answer me."

"I've been talking to Prem -"

"You've been talking about this? With a coworker? I can't believe you. Prem is a nasty old man -

"No, not Prem Rishi - Prem Pradeep!"

"Oh." Rani, somewhat mollified, took a step closer but still didn't sit. "Still, I don't like that you've been talking to anyone at work about this. What if word gets up to political officers?"

"Don't worry, I'm not a fool. I didn't jump right into it. I brought it up subtly, and I could tell that Prem was interested too." Ashok leaned forward. "Listen to this - he's already built the demonstration unit from chapter two. It works. He got it to work!"

Rani nodded. "Of course he got it to work. Prem is a very smart man - level fourteen. If you had studied a bit harder in university, you could be a level fourteen too, not still stuck at eleven."

"Oh, hush. You know that everything past ten is politics. Gopinatha doesn't like me or my family, and that's that. But that's another reason it makes sense to talk to Prem. I'm stuck at eleven - and he's stuck at fourteen."

"And emigration is going to help with promotions?"

"Don't be catty. No. Emigration is going to help us with a better job. You know I've swapped email with cousin Rahul. He says that Solar Installations there has been looking for people with optics backgrounds."

"So on the advice of cousin Rahul -"

"It pays fifty percent more than my job here. Plus, there are no taxes. So it's more like *five* times as much as we're making now."

"But I've seen those exposés on television -"

Ashok couldn't help raising his voice. "On government-run television!"

Rani put a finger to her lips. "Shhh! The baby is sleeping!"

Ashok put up his hands placatingly. "OK, I'll be quiet. But think of the money!"

"Even if it is five times more, remember what the program said. You have to pay for everything up there - air, water, medical care, education -"

"Yes, we get a lot of things for free now - but it's worthless, so we have to pay all over again. I take a private bus to work because the government bus driver doesn't show up most days. We buy bottled water because the water smells bad. You go to a private doctor." He realized that he was becoming agitated and forced himself to <u>speak</u> more slowly. "If we're paying for all these things right here, how is Aristillus any different?"

Rani was silent for a moment, and when she spoke he could see that her resistance was crumbling. "It's a big gamble. A huge gamble. What do you and Prem Pradeep know about building a spaceship anyway? It could crash." She wrung her hands. "Do you want to bet the lives of your children on a home-built space ship?"

Ashok knew that he'd gotten as much agreement as he was going to get for one night - he should let Rani sit with the idea for a few days before he raised it again.

"I would never trust the lives of our children to a vehicle unless I was absolutely sure it would work." He waited, and a moment later Rani sighed and sat next to him. Ashok put a hand on her shoulder. "I promise you - I absolutely will not feed you a big dinner, wait for you to get sleepy, and then smuggle you onto a homemade spaceship without asking your permission first, OK?"

Rani tried to fight the smile and failed. She shook her head. "You!"

Ashok slid his hand down off her shoulder and pulled her into a hug. She leaned into it.

"I'm serious, Rani - you have my word. Yes, I want to go to the moon, where we can have a bigger apartment - which you've wanted - and a bigger family, without the extra child taxes. But for now, all I'll do is work with Prem in his workshop. We'll build a few small models, we'll experiment with the navigation software and see what we think of it. No building a real ship, no buying real supplies until I talk to you, OK?"

Rani nodded. "I trust you." She turned, kissed him, and stood. "I'm going to change into pajamas."

Ashok smiled as she slipped away. He'd framed his "deal" with Rani as a concession, but in fact he'd just gotten permission to work with Prem for a night or two per week - exactly what he'd been aiming for.

The intermittent work schedule wasn't a problem - it would take some time to get their hands on enough liquid nitrogen to cryogenically treat the stators for the drive for the real ship. Maybe a month? Maybe more? That was fine - it would take that long to track down components for the life support system.

But it wasn't all fun stuff in the workshop. No, there was going to be almost as much paperwork as at his day job. Starting with a spreadsheet to figure out the buy-in price for each of the six families he and Prem had talked to.

Ashok looked up and realized that Rani was taking a shower. He had some time, so he pulled out his slate, typed in the pass-phrase to unlock the encrypted partition, and started taking notes.

Chapter 47

2064: Atlanta Hackerspace, Atlanta, GA, Earth

Maynard rested a hand on the Hobart stand mixer that they'd picked up cheap when Dominick's Pizza went out of business. It always started unevenly, but its throbbing motion had smoothed into a whir as lumps of clay powder broke up. It was almost ready now. He looked at the goo more closely. No, it *was* ready.

"How's the goo coming?"

Maynard turned. "Oh, hey Vince. This batch is almost done."

Maynard thought it over for a second and decided to risk it. "Hey, Vince." Vince looked at him. "Have you looked over the expats' ship guide?" Vince didn't respond and Maynard hurried on. "It - uh - it was covered in Pulse, Makernet, HomeShop -"

"I read it."

Maynard cleared his throat nervously. "I was thinking it might be interesting to build it. I mean - maybe not the whole ship - that'd cost money. But at least the prototype." Maynard started to say more but then cut himself off. Enough. No need to babble.

Vince tilted his head. "I don't know. It'd be cool...but can we afford it? The liquid nitrogen -"

"I can sneak some of that out of the materials science lab."

Vince raised one eyebrow. "Really? Hmmm." He thought for a moment. "The copper for the bus-bars won't be cheap either."

"I can work that out."

Vince pointed his chin towards the Hobart mixer. "The goo ready for the printer yet?"

"Huh? Oh, yeah. I need to screen it and then I'm ready to print my -"

"Can you to load that into printer number two for me? That'd be great."

"I was going to use printer one for a mug set I'm working on."

Vince hit him with his thousand watt smile. "Be a team player, man. I've drawn up a sketch for an *awesome* bot body. It's like a J-type, but it has arms. Here, man, come look at my plans." He beckoned Maynard closer and then put an arm around his shoulders familiarly and pointed to his slate.

Maynard looked. The design *was* pretty cool - it used several captured dumbbell joints, the kind Maynard had shown Vince just the other day on the Russian prototyping site. As if reading his mind Vince pointed to the joints. "See those? Awesome, right? And I couldn't've done it without your input."

Maynard smiled, pleased by the acknowledgement. He could never figure Vince out - he ran hot and cold. It felt good to have his praise. Really good.

Vince closed the tab, then slapped Maynard on the shoulder. "So, you're in, right? Thanks, brother."

"Yeah. Sure. You're welcome." Maynard felt a warm glow. But - crap - it had taken him a long time to get the mix smooth enough. And now he was going to use it for Vince's project, not his own. He sighed. On the other hand, Vince *had* thanked him for the captured joint idea.

Maynard turned off the stand mixer, man-handled the bowl from the cradle onto the cart, and pushed it to the printer - avoiding that one uneven floor board. There he wrapped his arms around the bowl and tilted it so the goo could pour into the intake funnel. He was half done when the door to the hackerspace opened. He looked up at the sound of conversation. A small crowd - five or six people - were entering. He knew them, all members of the hackerspace, by sight.

Carrie-Ann, his girlfriend, was with them. He wanted to wave but he needed to finish the pour first. He grabbed the bottom of the bowl and tilted it further. A moment later he was done and walked to where the six were crowded around Big Bertha, the slow-motion CNC pottery wheel they'd built last spring.

"Hey, Carrie-Ann!"

Carrie-Ann looked up from her conversation and smiled. "Hey, Maynard, I didn't know you were here." He went in for a hug but at the last minute Carrie-Ann pulled back. "Oh - gross!"

"What?"

She pointed at his shirt and he looked down. Oh, crap. He hadn't been careful about wiping the rim of the mixing bowl clean before humping it over to the printer, and he had a broad horizontal stripe of gray slip across his stomach. "Oh. Sorry."

Carrie-Ann shrugged and smiled but kept her distance. Crap. Why did he always screw things like this up?

Maynard felt a strong hand on his shoulder. He turned and saw Vince. "Maynard - introduce me to everyone."

Maynard did and Carrie-Ann - always polite - smiled warmly at Vince.

Vince interrupted before Maynard was done with the introductions. "What projects are you working on?"

Carrie Ann looked at the floor, then back up. "Oh, nothing impressive." She pointed at Big Bertha. "I've got some sketches for a Community Ring. For the Peace Faire."

"A 'Community Ring'?" Vince was wryly amused.

Carrie Ann blushed. "Oh, it's nothing. Just a thing that people are doing. So I thought I'd make one." She bit her lip. "What are *you* working on? Something complicated, I bet?"

Maynard started to answer. "You remember - the mug set -"

Vince put his hand back on Maynard's shoulder. "I think she was asking me." Maynard looked at Carrie-Ann. Oh. Vince was right. Oops.

Vince smiled. "It's funny you should ask - just before you got here I was talking with Maynard. You guys all know about the Expat Ship Guide?"

There was a collective intake of breath from the group. "No! Really?"

Vince nodded. "Yeah. I'm going to set up the machinery and build a cryo bath, and Maynard is going to get me the copper bus-bars and a tank of nitrogen." He turned. "Right, M?"

Maynard smiled, happy to be included. "Right."

Chapter 48

2064: Northern Logistics offices, Aristillus, Lunar Nearside

Mike snapped his eyes open at the mention of his name. It had been a long meeting and he must have drifted off. "Sorry, I - uh. What?"

General Dewitt said, "I gave a recap of the raid preparations."

"Yeah, I remember that."

"Then Kurt Balcom briefed us on the electronic warfare status: we're being stuxed, but so far we seem to be holding up."

Kurt said "It's 'Wolf', please. To elaborate, some of the signatures in the logs make me think that Gamma's looking out for us, but I can't get any confirmation from him. He won't answer my emails."

Javier continued, "Now we're talking about economic warfare."

Mike rubbed his eyes. "Uh, OK."

"Neil and Mark and a few others think that the Earth governments are manipulating our markets. We're going around the room and gathering data. Your turn: are you getting weird bids, canceled orders, payments that are reversed - anything like that?"

"If there's manipulation going on, it's the kind I like. I've been running my TBMs round the clock, and all my crews are on overtime."

"So no problems at all?"

Mike shrugged. "We're running out of room to pile the tailings nearby - we're racing to get conveyor belts installed on the surface to dump the rubble further out. But I don't think that's what you're asking about."

Mark Soldner raised an eyebrow. "You're creating that much new space? Who's buying it?"

Mike picked up his coffee mug, found it empty, and put it back on the table. "I don't know. This isn't a touchy feely business. A few deals, like Veleka, I handle, but for the most part orders come in through brokerages."

Mark furrowed his brow. "This could be evidence of manipulation. You're getting more orders for space, but I'm not seeing any run up in demand for either apartments or houses. These markets should be moving together."

Rob Wehrmann grunted. "Not sure why you're not seeing more sales, Mark, but I've been running my crews round the clock to try to keep up with the demand, just like Mike."

Karina Roth nodded. "We've been doing a lot of electrical work too."

Mark scratched his chin and Mike saw that the normally clean-shaven Mormon was sporting a bit of a shadow. The long hours and cramped quarters were hitting all of them.

Mark said, "Then why aren't we seeing an uptick in demand for housing too?"

Rob looked over. "Maybe Javier's stealing your lunch. Betcha he's building all the houses that you're not."

Javier shook his head. "Not me."

"So who's buying these tunnels?"

Mike shrugged. "Don't ask me. Contracts go live on the market, and if I've got spare TBMs, I take them. When I'm done I lock the doors behind me and put the crypto keys into escrow."

"So it's anonymous, like one of those online drug bazaars?"

Mike forced himself not to roll his eyes. "Mark, tunnel space is a commodity. It's bought and sold like pork bellies or electricity futures back on earth. It's not nefarious, it's just the easiest way to do it. Half the buyers and sellers are just speculators who think they know what demand for space is going to be in six months. Are potato chips 'anonymous'? Are shovels?"

Mark Soldner pursed his lips. "I don't think I like that."

Mike picked up his coffee mug and realized - for a second time - that it was empty. Jesus. He needed to get more sleep. "Why? Because people are buying tunnels now and not paying you to build them out into apartments?"

Mark nodded. "Well - yes. Not because I'm not profiting. Because that space is going to waste. With our population pressure, we've got people stacked on top of each other. If these new tunnels are empty that means that people are hoarding. You said the word 'speculators' yourself."

"So what? They're putting up their own money. These tunnels wouldn't exist if they weren't."

"It's wasteful. If we limited the bidding to just people who actually *need* the space and intend to occupy it - "

Mike shook his head. This guy. He *always* knew a better way to run things. "Fuck that. You're not paying me to run my TBMs. You're not paying my men to work overtime. So if some speculators have got cash on the barrel-head, then fuck -"

Javier raised his voice. "Guys, we're not here to debate economics. Let's get back to the point: are the Earth governments trying to sabotage us by manipulating our economy?"

Mike shrugged. "All I know is that the demand for tunnels is up. If that's market manipulation, then they're welcome to hit me twice as hard next time. The only downside is that it's costing a bit more to dig the ramps now that we're eight levels down."

Mark looked up. "You guys are working on level *eight*? Feels like we you only started six a few months back."

Rob Wehrmann grunted. "Eight. Believe it."

Javier sighed. "I want to finish up this meeting and get some sleep, so talk shop later. Let's either reach some conclusion about the market manipulation thing or just table it."

John, who'd been sitting unnoticed in a chair against one wall, spoke. "You know I'm close with the Dogs." A dozen heads swiveled. "They're pretty serious about trading in the markets."

Mark Soldner asked, "What do you mean?"

John stood. "It started when we were out on our hike, when they started betting in an RPG market."

General Dewitt raised an eyebrow. "Rocket propelled grenades?"

John shook his head. "No. Video game stuff. But, anyway, they started buying and selling magic swords and that kind of thing, and pretty soon they started making a market in it."

General Dewitt said, "'Making a market'? Like stocks?"

"Yeah, it started out that way, and then it got weirder. They were doing all sorts of things: futures markets, derivatives, synthetic I-don't-know-whats."

Dewitt asked, "Futures markets? On swords in a video game?"

John nodded.

Mark said, "OK. And?"

"And they're good at it. They started coding up tools to help them, and then they started trading in other markets. Blue told me that the political futures markets are going wild over a blockade, so I wonder if that -"

Mike started to interrupt, but Javier beat him to it. "A blockade? Blockade of what?"

"Of us. He said the contracts imply an eighty to ninety percent drop in shipping volume." He looked honestly confused. "Did you not know this?"

The table exploded in conversations.

Javier gaveled the noise down. "We'll answer everyone's questions, in order. But first - these political futures markets John's talking about - do we have anyone following them for intel?"

Wolf raised his hand. "Yeah, I've got a few guys. We didn't see anything like this." He turned to John. "Are you sure about this? We monitor all the markets in Aristillus and we -"

"I don't know all the details, but I do know that it's not here on our exchanges - it's on a dark server somewhere on Earth."

Wolf frowned. "Can you put me in touch with Blue? I need to talk to him."

John shrugged. "I'll try - but we might end up having to relay your questions through me."

Mike said, "The contracts are projecting that shipping volume is going to drop ninety percent? That's huge. Are you sure about that?"

John nodded. "That's what Blue says."

Rob Wehrmann said, "Wait a second. I'm still trying to wrap my head around this. You learned about a blockade that's about to happen - because the Dogs were trading magic swords in a video game?"

"That's how it started, but - yeah. They trade everything."

"What do you mean 'everything'?"

"This morning I was at the Den and Blue was watching video of containers of coffee being offloaded at Lai Docks. He said that when he saw the bets on the blockade starting to move two weeks ago he bought half a ship of beans for delivery."

"How the hell are the Dogs going to drink that much coffee?"

"They're not; it's poisonous for them. They're buying it as *speculation*. Blue said that once the embargo hits the price of coffee will double and they'll make a few million."

Mike's head snapped around. "The Dogs are making *millions*? Off of reading the markets?"

Dewitt shrugged. "The genetic engineers knew what they were doing."

Mike considered his words carefully. "Maybe we need to get some of these Dogs into our inner circle here."

John shook his head. "I've already talked to them about it. It's...complicated."

"We've got to uncomplicate it."

"I'm working on it."

Chapter 49

2064: Belmont Homes, Aristillus, Lunar Nearside

Hugh took an apple from the bowl and settled into the couch next to Allyson. He took a bite, and then looked around the apartment. "Where's Selena?"

Louisa was looking down at her slate and waved the question away. Allyson answered, "She's been working really long hours at that clinic." She looked thoughtful. "Actually, I don't think I've seen her in a couple of days - she must be slipping in after I go to sleep."

Louisa's slate chimed. She looked at it and said, "Our video should be live now."

Hugh reached for the remote, but Louisa grabbed it first and pulled up DC Minute on the wallscreen. Their video wasn't listed yet. Louisa swore, and then opened a new tab and brought up one of the fan forums and clicked into a thread about the upcoming episode.

Hugh took another bite of his apple and watched Louisa surf. Louisa logged in as "ClearThinker" - one of her alter-egos - and typed a quick post hyping the upcoming segment, logged out, logged back in under another handle and wrote a reply to her previous post.

"Louisa, hurry up. The new episode might be live."

"Give me a minute - I'm posting as FairSolution right now."

Hugh rolled his eyes. She said that the point of the fake back-and-forths between her invented characters was to build interest and further 'The Cause,' but he wasn't blind to the fact that her assortment of identities spent as many words praising Louisa as an up-and-coming director as they did praising the clips or talking about the expat situation.

Hugh picked up his slate and clicked to DC Minute.

The video was listed! He clicked to start it playing. Louisa looked over and saw what he was doing. "Hey! Don't be selfish - let's all watch it together."

Hugh paused the video on his slate and fought to keep his grimace in check. Sure, Louisa was a great editing partner - and her ideas on how to frame the debate were excellent - but she was starting to bug the shit out of him. It might be the close quarters taking their toll - as their videos got more play, more and more people in Aristillus had started to recognize them, and they'd taken to venturing out less, and wearing big hats and glasses when they did.

Or maybe with Selena spending less time in the apartment, and Allyson and him dating, the group dynamic had changed.

Or perhaps, on the third hand, Louisa had always been this much of a bitch and he was just starting to notice it.

Louisa finished up a volley of comments in the back-and-forth between FairSolution and GlobalPeaceFan39, and then went back to the first tab and started their video playing. Hugh had seen it dozens of times during the editing, of course, but he leaned forward and watched it anyway. Their expose on the racial disparity in lunar society - and the institutional racism that it implied - was as good as he'd remembered. As he watched he kept one eye on the hit counter in the corner of the page. The stats were good. And the real-time awards were good too - as he watched the "trending story" icon appeared, and two minutes later their clip got on the "Hot Shots" list. On the sidebar fan badges piled up. Hugh smiled. Yet another segment was a hit. He had a girlfriend. Even his mom would have to be proud of him now.

Melanie Roes broke in after the first half of the video, just as Hugh took a final bite of his apple. He took the chance to go to the kitchen for a drink. Deep in the fridge he pushed aside the crock of cabbage that

Allyson had fermenting and pulled out a bottle of Jaunty Juice. He'd fallen in love with the caffeinated, carbonated lime soda after finding it at the convenience shop around the corner, but he was the only one.

Hugh pulled a mug from the cabinet and poured the juice. He'd learned his lesson - if he didn't disguise what he was drinking he'd get static from every side. Allyson would lecture him about the caffeine and other unnatural additives and Louisa would give him hell for supporting corporatist producers of uninspected and unlicensed foods. Not that lack of licensing and inspection stopped Louisa from eating restaurant take-out - and on his dime. He pursed his lips. He had no doubt that if Louisa happened to like Jaunty Juice, she'd find some exception to her ideological code.

He sighed and hid the bottle at the bottom of the recycling bin, and then went back to the living room. Melanie Roes was still on the wallscreen. He took a sip from his mug. He agreed with Louisa's stance on the soda, in principle: you couldn't run a society where anyone could just come up with any idea they had for a beverage, or stores, or schools, or whatever. If anyone could introduce a new beverage, what sort of job security would employees at existing beverage firms have? That's why there was a Bureau of Industrial Planning, after all. But on the other hand, there had to be *some* room for new ideas. Maybe BuIndPlan should have an advisory council. He'd talk to his mother about the idea.

On the screen, Melanie was still talking.

What would happen to Jaunty Juice after Liberation and unification? Heck - what would life be like in Aristillus afterwards? There were some aspects of the city that he really liked: the music scene was excellent, the food was great, everything produced locally was a lot cheaper than the same items back home. It occurred to him that there was a real opportunity for a

Hegelian thesis/antithesis/synthesis model. He thought about it and grew excited - imagine combining the best of what Aristillus already provided with the rational order that came from governance. A bit of slum clearing, a real police force, centralized and regulated schools, and the colony would be an excellent place.

Unification. It was going to be weird. When he'd first shown up in Aristillus he thought he'd be here for a few weeks. That had somehow grown to several months. And more recently he'd been assuming that unification would be the bell, the signal that it was time to end the adventure and head back home. But the place was growing on him. Maybe he'd stay here, at least for a bit, and take a post in the administration. BuIndPlan would have some openings. Or he could run a business. He swirled the soda in his mug. Once the economic planners got the economy rationalized, Jaunty Juice would need a CEO. Maybe he'd like to run that. His mom could set that up for him.

He'd never run a business before, but how hard could it be? If illiterate Nigerians could run restaurants and rednecks could set up small factories, he could certainly run a soda company - especially given his education. He turned the thought over in his head and realized that he liked it. Maybe he'd introduce a diet version of Jaunty Juice or - he looked at Allyson - maybe he'd switch to certified organic ingredients. Or - the idea seized him - a square bottle! They'd pack better on a shelf, and maybe that could cut refrigeration costs. An environmental angle - he liked it.

On the wallscreen, Melanie Roes said something, and Hugh realized that the second half of the video was about to play. He leaned forward and put his mug down on the table. The indictment of the Goldwater corporate thugs was going to be great - the hit counter was *really* going to spin in a few minutes!

Hugh hugged Allyson and then high-fived Louisa - the energy in the room was infectious. It was too bad Selena wasn't here for this. The second segment, the one on Goldwater's corporate thugs, was a hit. It had almost twice as many "likes" as the first clip, which made it - by far - their most popular video ever. Louisa jumped back and forth between tabs. The video was already getting play on Century22, BNGsoc, and a half dozen other top-tier sites. Hugh checked the time - it was still less than 20 minutes after the video had originally run.

Louisa was monopolizing the wallscreen and was surfing from site to site to track the growing buzz, so Hugh used his slate.

Hugh couldn't stop grinning - discussion boards were blowing up with posts and views.

Suddenly Louisa swore. "Fucking babies".

Hugh looked up. "What?"

She highlighted a region on the wallscreen: a few negative comments.

Louisa logged in as moderator and checked the IP address. "See that? That's a known black relay: that's expats bitching." She marked the comments as spam and deleted them.

Hugh went back to his slate and read, trying to keep up with the tide of accolades. He could hardly wait for the next phone call with his mother. He looked around - where was Selena? She should be here with them for this!

Louisa swore again and Hugh looked up a second time. Louisa was at Demos.chat and the majority of comments and votes there supported the segment, but there were also a number of negative comments.

"Don't let it bother you, Louisa."

"Why the hell shouldn't I? These idiots don't even know what they're talking about. Fucking economically ignorant inbred trolls."

Hugh shrugged. "This is a second tier site - they don't have good moderation policies."

"I can't believe that they don't even disemvowel these cocksuckers."

"Stop stressing about it - just go back to Century22 or BNGsoc where it's curated."

"Screw that. These lies shouldn't be allowed to stand." Louisa typed furiously, cycling through her identities and leaving comments, muttering angrily under her breath the whole time.

Next to him on the couch, Allyson was reading her own slate. "Oh, ouch."

He turned to her. "What?"

"I think you need to look at this."

Hugh's grin started to slip. What was going on?

The message from Allyson popped up on his tablet and he clicked it, and then blinked. What the *hell*?

"Louisa? Look at this." He dragged a panel from his slate to the wallscreen. Dozens of commenters were talking about 'the rebuttal video' - apparently something done by an expat. It sounded scathing - but the link was missing. Blocked by the Caretaker firewall, probably.

Louisa read it. The mood of the room had cooled over the last few minutes and now it turned to ice. "Damn it! Hugh, find that video."

Hugh nodded. Even if he link was censored, he knew the search terms to use.

A minute later he had it on his slate.

He froze.

"Hugh."

This couldn't be -

No, this didn't make any sense at -

"*Hugh*!"

He jerked. Louisa was calling his name. "What?"

"Have you found it yet?"

Hugh dragged it wordlessly from his slate to the wallscreen.

On the screen a freeze frame of Selena looking at them. The video title read, "Lies, Damned Lies, and Deceptive Pro-PK Reporting."

Louisa was already swearing.

Hugh licked his lips and clicked the play button. It took him a moment to process what he was hearing. "...pattern of deceptive editing and faked footage. First, I'm going to ask you to turn on cryptographic signature checking. You can turn it on under the 'data extras' menu in your browser."

She paused.

"If you've got that on you should seen a green checkbox in the lower left hand corner. That's because this video of me talking to you is cryptographically signed. It's original, unaltered footage. Now let me first show you raw footage of the confrontation with PKs. Note how the signature block stays green."

The raw video from the confrontation with the Goldwater security goons played, and then Selena returned. "Now here's the manipulated video you just saw on DC Minute. Notice how scenes have been reordered, the backgrounds have been changed, and the new audio doesn't match the original. Remember to pay attention to that signature block in the corner. Note that it's red. That's how you know this is the fake version."

The altered video - *their* video, their Goldwater expose - played. Louisa dropped a string of f-bombs as the incriminating red signature block blinked. Her swearing got louder when Selena returned to the screen.

Allyson leaned forward. "Guys - this is bad. Really bad."

Hugh nodded. "I know, sweetie."

On the wallscreen Selena said, "Now, let me run the clip a third time. This time we've got a voice spectrum analysis in the lower window. Pay attention to that when the guard calls Louisa a 'mixed race whore' and threatens to rape her."

"*Fuck*!" Louisa swept her hand over the coffee table, throwing her slate, the wallscreen remote, and a vase against the wall. The vase shattered.

Hugh and Allyson shrank back into the couch.

Louisa was on her feet, stalking around the room.

Allyson looked at Hugh for reassurance, but Hugh just shook his head. Hugh felt the the blood drain from his face. He'd never seen Louisa this angry, and that was saying something. Louisa yelled again and punched a wall, and then stormed into the editing room, slamming the door behind her. It did nothing to block out her continued shouting.

This was bad, there was no doubt about that. Now he needed to know exactly *how* bad. Hugh stood and picked the wallscreen remote from the wreckage on the floor and used it to turn up the volume on the wallscreen until he could hear Selena's voice over Louisa's yelling.

"...an inside look at the conspiracy to fake this and other videos. Funding from the family trust of Senator Linda Haig allowed Louisa Teer and the senator's son Hugh Haig to -"

Hugh couldn't believe what he was hearing. He dropped the remote. His stomach felt like a point and darkness crept in at the edges of his vision. Did - did Selena really just say that? He reached out for the arm of the couch to steady himself, and then lowered himself to the floor.

"Hugh, are you all right?"

He brushed away Allyson's hand.

What was his mother going to say? He looked up numbly to the screen and - wait - what was Selena's piece showing now? It was - oh God. Her voice-over was ongoing but the video clip was of the inside of the apartment. *This apartment.* Hugh was looking at video of himself on the screen. In the clip he was sitting at the editing station, leaning to one side as he pointed something out to Louisa. That video - how had she -?

"*That cunt!*" Hugh looked up. Louisa grabbed the bowl of fruit off the kitchen counter and screamed as she threw it against the wallscreen. The giant display cracked and apples and bananas bounced across the room.

"*That fucking cunt!* She bugged the apartment!"

Hugh blinked. How dare Selena do that? What an invasion of privacy!

Wait.

He looked around. Were there more cameras here? Were they being watched even now?

Louisa threw open the door to Selena's bedroom.

"Her room is empty. She's left." She turned. "I'm going to kill that whore!"

Chapter 50

2064: Senator Linda Haig's Office, Tester Senate Building

Linda Haig paced the carpet of her empty office. That bitch. Damn her. Damn Selena and her disgusting, cheating, back-stabbing videos. Hadn't Linda's checks and Hugh's trust fund paid for the apartment and the food for their little jaunt to the moon? And now this viper had the gall to stab the family that helped her - the family that had paid her way - right in the back.

That woman had *spied* on Hugh. And not just on him, but on the phone calls in which he'd coordinated with Linda. And then, to put those snippets in her vicious attack videos -

The disclosures were bad - but they weren't as terrible as they might have been. Thankfully Linda had never whispered even one word of her deeper game to Hugh. If that whore Selena had learned of her moves in the Populist/Internationalist cold war, or if she had figured out her back channel to Darren Hollins of Goldwater? The damage she could have done with *that* leak would have ended her career. And worse than that, in today's political environment, she'd be in jail and facing treason charges.

Thank goodness for her good luck. No. She corrected herself. Thank goodness for her careful planning.

But just because she wasn't dead didn't mean she wasn't in serious trouble. She was getting flak from everyone in her state - even solid allies were slowing their donations.

It wasn't surprising that wafflers like Max Newbold at Incarceration Solutions were cutting back - but even Saundra Polansky and Darryl Stalls were hedging and delaying their checks. That burned. Linda was doing her job - the contracts for new prisons, for affordable housing, for hydroponic-whatever were all lined up. She'd been shoveling money to those pricks for a decade now, and they had the gall to treat her like this?

Linda forced herself to stop pacing, to breathe in and out deeply.

She looked at the mantel clock on the shelf. Enough wasting time. Enough self-indulgence. She had to start acting. She rubbed her hands down the front of her suit jacket, smoothing it, creating an external cue, a scene transition, just like her coach had taught her so many years ago. Then she walked to her desk and pressed the intercom button. "Kerri, send Jim in, please."

A moment later Jim was through the door. "We've got a big problem."

She resisted the urge to snap at him. "I know that, Jim. That's why we're having this conversation."

"You don't look good in that video, and contributions are off."

This time she did snap. "And the primary is coming. I *know* that, Jim. Let's focus on solving problems. First: I need campaign contributions, and I need them fast."

"Did you call party leadership?"

Linda's smile grew tight. "Yes."

"And?"

"McCaffrey leans Internationalist, but when I asked her for money, she gave me a sob story about times being hard. She finished with 'You're going to have to win on your own.'"

Jim exhaled and rubbed his face with one hand before looking up. "If McCaffrey won't help, then there's something going on. The president and her allies got to her, I bet. You burned Johnson, and this is exactly her style."

"I assumed so, but what do we do now? Jim, I need ad buys, walking around money, all of that, and I need it immediately. If I let people see that donations are down, perception becomes reality."

Jim stood and walked to the bookshelf, then turned back. "I've got some information on a few people. We can use that to, ah, *encourage* donations."

He didn't elaborate, but he didn't have to; Linda took his meaning.

"I imagine you'll want an increase to your fee?"

Jim waved his hand. "Let's not be crass."

"What, then? An ambassadorship? A department?"

Jim shrugged. "Something at that level, yes. I haven't decided yet, but I know your word is good."

"OK, we've got an agreement. So what's your plan?"

"There are some healthcare contractors who - well, never mind the details. I'll arrange the campaign contributions. How much do you need?"

"Normally I'd say forty million, but at this point I think eighty is more prudent."

"Let me make some calls."

Chapter 51

2064: The Den, Aristillus, Lunar Nearside

Mike parked the truck and stepped out. Behind him the other three doors slammed shut; then John and two ADF troops joined him on the sidewalk.

Mike looked at the unmarked warehouse door.

So this was it?

Mike turned to the troops. "John and I might be a while. If you need to do something else, we can call when we're done."

The two troops wore the same improvised uniform of jeans, work boots, and gray dress shirts with patches as the rest of the Aristillus Defense Force. The senior one hiked his rifle sling further up onto his shoulder and shook his head. "No. We hang here."

Mike nodded, and then turned to John. "Ready?" Without waiting for an answer he walked to the door.

Behind him John turned to the two guards and pointed to equipment bolted to the wall. "Stay away from the claymores." The younger ADF troop stepped back involuntarily.

Mike reached the door and stopped. Was there an intercom? Where?

Without warning, the roller door started to clank upward. When the bottom edge rose past his eyes Mike could see the room beyond. It was well lit - and filled with dozens of tracked rovers. In a second he realized something else: each was armed with some sort of gun. Not quite as large as his own Gargoyle rifles...but weapons on the rovers were belt fed.

Mike felt an urge to step back, but mastered it. The Dogs weren't about to use rovers to attack invited guests. But the presence of all that armament sure spoke to their opinion of *uninvited* guests.

Mike forced his eyes from the rovers and looked at the room itself. There was something weird about it - the walls were much too close. Then he realized: the space behind the door had originally been a warehouse, but had been subdivided since then. He was looking at a small antechamber inside a bigger space.

Mike looked at it with an educated eye. The walls were steel: cold rolled mid-grade stuff, welded at the corners. Probably standard deck plating. And what were those streaks of heat discoloration in the middle of the panels? The walls must be welded from the far side to some sort of superstructure - probably an I-beam framework. There was something else odd about the walls - there were lots of small slots cut through the steel.

The Dogs hadn't thrown in their lot with the Boardroom Group - not yet, at least - but it was clear that they were taking their own defense seriously. If this room wasn't a perfectly designed kill box - armored, reinforced, and with dozens if not hundreds of weapons pointed in through those slots - he had no idea what was.

Well, the gate had rolled up - so what was expected of them? Mike squared his shoulders and stepped into the room. John followed. The door behind them immediately began to close. Mike walked straight ahead, toward the smaller door at the far side of the kill room. He tried to keep his pace steady as the rovers rolled back to clear a wider path. Behind him the warehouse door clanked as it closed fully, and there was the snick of well-lubricated bolts sliding home.

The far door swung open - and behind it was a Dog. Mike swallowed. He'd seen the pop-science shows about the project. He'd seen the interviews with the scientists, and the videos of the first generation of the Dogs as puppies. And he'd also seen the protests, the counter protests, the bioethicists testifying before Congress, and all the rest.

One thing he'd never seen was an adult Dog. When John had smuggled them here he'd kept them off limits - even to Mike himself.

And now he was face to face with one. It was a furry orange creature, with two prick ears, a stub snout, and bright, intelligent brown eyes.

And it was wearing a jumpsuit. It - he? she? - turned to John, spread its arms - front legs? - and said in a voice that was simultaneously throaty yet young and enthusiastic. "John, good to see you!"

John leaned in and hugged the Dog. "You too, Aabroo - I'm sorry I haven't had more time since I got back."

The Dog let go of John and turned. "And you must be Mike."

Mike blinked. "Um - yes. I am."

"I'm Aabroo."

"Aabroo. Uh - nice to meet you." Mike began to stick his hand out, then paused. "I'm sorry. Do you - do you shake hands?"

The corner of Aabroo's mouth curled. A smile? Did Dogs have the same use facial expressions the humans? Or was this a sign of anger - or disdain? But, no, the look on Aabroo's face seemed warm.

"We usually don't among ourselves, but, yes, sometimes. It's nice to meet you, Mike." Aabroo extended a paw. Mike took it and shook it delicately, marveling at it as he did so. Abroo's paw was shorter and squatter than a person's hand, and it felt odd in his own - it had warm, dry, rough pads against his palm, and a light covering of short fur on the back where his fingers wrapped around it.

The short nails against his palm felt distinctly odd.

John cleared his throat. "May we come in?"

Aabroo blinked. "Oh! Sorry. Please do."

Aabroo seemed embarrassed and uncertain. Mike looked at her. Was it possible that this was as awkward and weird for her as it was for him? He'd never met a Dog before - and he realized that she probably hadn't met many humans either.

Aabroo turned and walked deeper into the complex. John followed her. Mike looked over his shoulder at the armed rovers and then hurried after John and the Dog.

A few steps later they were out of the kill box and in the larger space it had been carved from. Mike looked around. There were rolls of torn-up carpet stashed in one corner, and potted plants pushed against another wall. The layout confirmed his guess that the volume had started life as warehouse space - not surprising in this portion of Aristillus. The carpet suggested that it had later been converted into an office space. And now? A last line of defense for the Dogs between the private road tunnel and their Den deeper in the rock.

Aabroo stopped and turned back. "If you're ready, I'll bring you to Blue and Max."

"Lead the way."

As they walked through the larger space, Mike looked around. It had been nice up until recently. The rolled-up rugs in the corner were thick and luxurious - that couldn't have been cheap. The plants, too, were high-quality. Japanese cherry? And what the hell was that thing that looked like a jungle gym made out of big PVC pipes and girders?

Never mind, it didn't matter. What did matter was getting a feel for the Dogs' defensive preparations: that would play into his discussion with Blue and Max. He looked over his shoulder at the kill box. It was built much as he'd guessed: the thick deck plates were backed by a grid of steel I-beams anchored into the floor, and automatic shotguns, machine guns, and more bristled from the walls like spines on a porcupine. And on the roof of the kill box were pipes that led to pumps and tanks a dozen meters away. He saw the four-quadrant NFPA 704 hazard sign on the tanks and swallowed. Jesus.

Aabroo led them out of the warehouse space and into a corridor. Mike swiveled his head, looking down the side corridors they walked past. They were dark, but he thought he could see something - yes. Long lines of LED lights glowed in the depths. More rovers? He was taken aback. Jesus - this place wasn't just well defended - it had more armament in it than the Phoksundo DMZ.

Soon they began to pass closed doors - and a few that were cracked open. Near the floor in one open door ahead he saw two small Dog heads, one atop the other. A third head wiggled in next to the first two and there was a squeak and then a bark. Aabroo whirled. "Jeffrey, Kilroy, Chin - you're embarrassing yourselves." The heads withdrew and the door slammed shut. Aabroo turned back to Mike. Was that an embarrassed smile on her face? "Sorry."

Mike hadn't realized that there children - puppies? - among the Dogs. "Uh, Aabroo. You Dogs aren't having kids, are you?"

Aabroo was taken aback. "No. Not all of the second gens were implanted; some of the embryos were frozen. John and his team rescued them at the same time as us. We started defrosting them two years ago."

Defrosting? Embryos? Second gens? Mike blinked. He'd thought for a moment that he had a handle on the weirdness of dealing with the Dogs, but he was as off balance now as he'd ever been. What was he -

Aabroo interrupted his thoughts. "John, Mike, here you are." She indicated a door.

Mike raised one hand to knock and then stopped. He heard voices on the far side. "Should we -?"

Aabroo shook her head. "Just a minute."

He lowered his hand. On the far side of the door the talking continued and he picked out four voices. Two were rough - Dogs - and the other two sounded human. Both of the humans sounded familiar, but he couldn't quite place them. One was cool and dispassionate, and the other -

Mike noticed Aabroo watching him eavesdrop out of the corner of her eye. Oops. He coughed. "So, Aabroo. It's nice to meet you. You know, you're the first Dog I've met."

Aabroo dipped her head.

"And it's neat to finally see this place. I've heard about it from John, but, we, uh - " Aabroo smiled slightly but said nothing. Mike continued gamely on. "Why haven't we met sooner? I've asked John about you all ever since you arrived here, but -"

Aabroo looked away. "I guess we're all a bit shy."

John caught Mike's eye and silently mouthed, 'later.' Mike nodded.

The door opened and the man who'd opened it stood inside, one hand on the knob, still talking to the Dogs in the far room. "Think about what I said - especially about the next generation." He turned and saw Mike.

Mike knew he'd recognized the voice. "Father Alex."

Alex saw Mike and mimed a tipping hat. Mike started to ask a question, but before he could form the words, Father Alex had slipped past and was meters down the corridor.

Aabroo raised an arm, inviting John and Mike to enter. "John, if I don't see you again before Haiti -"

John gave Aabroo a quick hug. "You will."

Mike entered the room. Inside, two Dogs stood on their rear legs in front of beanbag chairs. One had gray fur spotted with black patches and had an odd white stripe down his forehead. The other had an orangish coat and had a mangled ear. Mike blinked.

He'd heard two Dogs and two humans, and Father Alex had just left, but where -

The orange Dog spoke. "Mike Martin. I recognize you from your pictures."

Mike stuck out his hand. "Max." This time he was prepared for the warm rough pads, the fur, and the short nails. "And Blue. It's nice to finally meet you both."

Blue gave the same odd dog smile he'd seen Abroo do earlier. "It's nice to meet *you*, Mike. You may not realize it, but you're a pretty important figure to us." He paused. "It was John and the team that rescued us, but if it wasn't for you, they wouldn't have had any place to rescue us to." He cleared his throat, and said, "Have a seat."

Mike and John sat in two regular chairs and the Dogs reclined on their beanbags. Mike leaned forward. "Before we start - when I was in the hallway I thought I heard two people in here -"

Blue looked at Max and something passed between them; then Blue looked at Mike. "Father Alex wanted to talk about theology, but you've got a more pressing topic."

That was an odd evasion, but Mike let it go. "OK, then let's get down to business. Before we start, I've got a question: how official is this? You two are - what - the board of directors? The president and vice president?"

Max said, "Think of us as two consuls."

Mike tilted his head. "Two councils?"

Blue raised his light brown eyebrows. "We don't have a formal structure inside the Den, but the rest of the Dogs tend to listen to the two of us. So this meeting isn't *official*, but it's *meaningful*."

Mike sighed. Another God-damned committee, just like the Boardroom Group. Fuck.

Blue prompted him, "John says that you wanted to talk to us about -"

"About futures markets. And about military collaboration."

Max shook his head. "We're not interested in military collaboration - we've settled that." He gave Blue a hard look.

Blue stared back at Max. "We haven't settled anything. And I'm talking to our guest now."

The facial expression that Max gave Blue in response was unmistakable. Mike had seen it in dive bars, at construction sites, and in rougher parts of town, both on Earth and in Aristillus. It was the look of two men who had deep disagreements over who was issuing orders and who was taking them. And, Mike realized, it apparently crossed species barriers.

Was he meeting with the two leaders of the Dogs as a whole - or with two leaders of rival factions?

The two Dogs held each other's eyes for a long moment and Mike saw the fur rising - literally rising - on both of their necks. Eventually Max harrumphed and broke the eye contact.

Blue turned to Mike. "What are your questions about futures markets, and what are your proposals about military collaboration?"

Mike looked back and forth between the Dogs. Blue looked tense from the showdown with Max, but seemed genuinely interested in the conversation.

Max stared off at the floor, and then looked at Mike. The look in Max's eyes might not be actively hostile - but it sure wasn't friendly.

Mike licked his lips. "Let's start with some questions about the markets."

Chapter 52

2064: Oval Office, White House, Washington DC, Earth

Before Restivo had shut the door behind him, the president spoke. "You'd better have a good progress report."

He turned to face her and took two steps across the polished hardwood before stepping onto the cream rug with the presidential seal that dominated the center of the room. "Yes, ma'am. There are constraints, of course, given the financial situation -"

The president looked at him sharply. "You know those GDP figures don't leave this room."

He'd annoyed her with the reference to constraints, and he'd done it on purpose. He was gambling, trying to use the conversational tactic he'd learned from Bonner before that man's fall: bad news first, and an ace up the sleeve.

"Yes, ma'am. Utterly secret. But it's not just about money. I've been running into steel shortages, wire shortages. Many of the factories that can make the robots have funding problems. I've consulted closely with the Bureau of Industrial Planning and called in a lot of favors in your name."

There - that was step one: the pain.

And now step two.

"That's what has allowed me to keep the project on schedule."

He watched the president's eyes widen at the magic words "on schedule". Magic because they might save Themba's presidency. He'd kept up on the gossip. He knew that Senator Haig's maneuvering and premature crowing on DC Minute hadn't blown back on her as much as the Internationalists had feared. The

Internationalists could send their own candidate against Johnson at the primaries.

"On schedule?"

"The fleet is eighty percent complete. The men are mostly trained. The robots are -"

The president nodded. "What's the short version?" "We'll be ready to launch in twelve weeks."

"Twelve? You padded that, I'm sure. I want it in four."

Restivo blinked. He had padded it - but by just one week. But cutting the schedule down to just *four* weeks? The woman was insane. "Ma'am, we'd all agreed on twelve weeks back when -"

She waved his objection away. "Things have changed since then."

"Four weeks is utterly impossible, ma'am."

The president stared at him.

He held the stare. He couldn't compromise on this. He just couldn't.

The president held it too. The seconds felt like minutes. He blinked. Was she *serious*? If so, why? What was going on? The tide must have changed somehow in the fight between the Populists and the Internationalists.

God *damn* it. He swallowed. "I can launch in six weeks."

"I'll accept five." The president smiled, and stood. "Unless there's something else, I'm due in Denver in a few hours to catch up with some friends."

Even six weeks was pushing it, but five? "Ma'am, six weeks is insane. But five? No. No. That's too tight."

"General, I have every confidence that five weeks is possible."

He read the subtext: if he didn't say 'yes' to this, she'd find someone else who would.

He nodded mutely.

- and that was the last thing he remembered, until he looked up and realized that he was in the West Wing lobby.

He ran a hand over his face. Five weeks. My God. What had he done?

He'd been trying to work with the president the way that Bonner had. He didn't follow all of Bonner's tactics - the man's flattery was too obsequious for him - but he'd told himself that he *could* follow orders and get the project done. And somehow he'd agreed to five weeks.

He walked through the lobby doors, helpfully pushed open by Marine guards, and exited under the portico. He looked around. Where were his car and driver? He realized the meeting had lasted just minutes instead of the specified half hour, and the driver wasn't back yet. Distractedly he fished for his phone, called his driver for an early pickup, and let the phone fall back into his pocket.

Five weeks. The schedule had already been insanely rushed. He hadn't planned on sleeping much in the final push, and now he'd be sleeping even less.

Just as well. He'd spent many of his recent nights tossing and turning, wondering just how well the commands he was following matched the definition of "lawful orders" that he had sworn to obey.

The work so far had been administrative: outfitting ships, training troops, and overseeing the men working on armor plating, life support, and AG drives. There was no question in his mind that all of that was legitimate. He was building a weapon. That was his job. His legitimate and legal job.

This coming action, though? He exhaled. Rebellion was illegal - that had been settled by the Civil War. The Confederacy had been an evil slave-holding system, and he had no doubt that it would have treated

Hispanics like him - and like his ex-wife and his children - as second-class citizens, or perhaps even as property.

His car pulled up and Restivo slid into the back seat as soon as the door swung open.

So, yes, the Confederacy had been evil, and secession was illegal. But he couldn't put the thought out of his head: was the Aristillus colony really like the Confederacy? From what he could tell, it was arguably freer than the United States was now. Aristillus was more like the country that his grandfather and grandmother had come to seventy years ago than the country he found himself serving today.

Was this invasion right? Was it *moral*?

The car pulled to the security gate, and one set of steel bollards rose out of the ground behind them before the set ahead dropped into the ground. The car pulled out into the road and traffic parted for them.

Restivo lowered his head to his chest. It was his duty to follow legal orders - and it wasn't up to him to decide just because he didn't like an order that it was illegal. The government had powers laid down by the Constitution, and it had more powers that were laid down by the courts and by events. Events like two World Wars, two Great Depressions, and the Baltimore crater.

His orders were legal. His role was to be an *instrument* of political will.

He looked out the window as the car drove past the Lincoln memorial.

This was the pinnacle of his career.

So why did he feel so many misgivings?

Chapter 53

2064: Nan Garde, Haitian Dominican Protectorate, Earth

John shaded his eyes against the glare of the high tropical sun and looked around. Hills. Palm trees. The ocean. He breathed deep and savored the briny, organic, natural scent of the ocean. He'd forgotten that smell. No, actually, he hadn't forgotten it; he'd just known - *known* - that he'd never smell it again.

After so long he was could hardly believe that he was back on Earth.

"Bonjour, ami, chaude journée -"

John looked down from the sky and saw the young man and his cart. John shook his head. "Sorry, I don't speak French."

The vendor saw his incomprehension and switched languages. "Hello, my friend. It's a hot day, no? You need a guarapo!"

"What's 'guarapo'?"

"Lime juice and sugar cane. Very cold. Just the thing for a day like this!"

John did a quick calculation. He didn't want to stand out in this vendor's memory, but he also didn't want to get caught by the police for supporting an unlicensed street vendor - and this could all too easily be a sting. He looked around the beach. There were no cops, just tourists. And, he reflected, he *was* thirsty. "Sure, I'll take one."

John paid for the beverage with the black market debit card and walked towards the hotel. When he reached the base of the low hill there were other tourists queuing up for the outdoor escalator. He turned to the right and started up the long flight of cement stairs. Halfway to the top the muscles in his legs started to burn.

They burned, but not too badly. Eight years in lunar gravity was enough to destroy muscles, but he'd always pushed himself hard in the gym. The last six months of hiking around the moon with the Dogs hadn't hurt either. John reached the top, turned, and looked down. At the base of the stairs the boardwalk gave way to the sand and beyond that the waves rolled in with the tide.

Yes, he was fit enough to climb these stairs - but the plan for tomorrow called for a lot more than that.

John took another sip of the drink and looked into the sky. He'd forgotten how big it was - somehow it seemed bigger than the sky on the moon. And up there, somewhere, the drones they'd brought with him were circling. They were too high to be seen by the naked eye, and because they'd been fabbed in Aristillus with custom electronics and didn't conform to the Drone Protocols, they wouldn't show in the datasphere either.

But they were there.

John's phone vibrated. He looked around and saw that the nearest tourist was twenty meters away. He took the phone out and looked. A text from one of the drones: the machines had gotten facial recognition on the final captive in the prison yard. All the high- value captives had been verified? That meant one thing: the assault was a go.

Which was good - the gravel boats had launched yesterday and were on their way in. They could be diverted and destroyed, if need be, but they couldn't be rescheduled.

One way or another, tomorrow was going to be an interesting day.

Chapter 54

2064: Nan Garde, Haitian Dominican Protectorate, Earth

John looked at the team.

All of the executives in the Boardroom Group trusted *him* - he'd proved his bona fides years before when he defected and brought the Dogs to the moon. Heck, he'd been in Aristillus longer than many of them had. But Dewitt's men? He knew that some of the executives had reservations about them.

Not him, though. He understood Dewitt's men. He understood why they'd defected from the PKs to the expat side. And he understood why they'd volunteered for this mission.

They were like him: they hated the PKs, and they hated the way the alliance with them had corrupted the ideals of the US Army, and of the United States.

He was proud to work with these men, and proud that they accepted him as their leader.

He looked at them now. They were about to go into battle, and he felt like he should say something. Saying something to men one had trained with for a long time was hard enough. But what do you say to men one was taking into battle against their so-recent allies?

What had George Washington said to his men when he'd taken command of the troops during the siege of Boston? How had he motivated the former loyal British subjects to open fire at their former countrymen?

John had no idea. So he gave up on the idea of motivation and went with a joke. "Gentlemen, synchronize your watches."

It fell flat. "Huh?"

"A joke - an old movie thing. Back in the day watches - they were like phones that just told time - weren't synchronized."

"Are you serious? What a fucking retarded system."

"Yeah." He shrugged. So much for his stand-up career. "Any last minute questions? No? Everyone good to go?"

There were nods around the room. They stood as one. Like everyone else John grabbed his bag - a surprisingly heavy duffel - and headed to the rented minivans. Even for the short walk to the vehicles they were dressed in their tourist clothes. Here on Earth there were eyes everywhere.

Their debit cards were real, but their IDs, carbon ration permits, travel vouchers - none of the rest of it would stand up to inspection if they were stopped. Which was why, in case they needed to bribe any local officials, they had pockets full of old-fashioned paper money and food ration chits, which were, of course, as fake as their IDs.

John stepped inside the van and slid the door closed. Sergeant Lumus twisted the key and pulled out of the parking lot. Behind them the other van pulled away, heading in a different direction.

* * *

Overhead the gravel boats continued their approach.

In boat number one a timer counted off the millionths of a second since 1 January 1970 and then, at a preprogrammed moment, gave an order. In response the AG drive switched from standby to active.

In the normal flight profile for an Earth reentry, the drive would be fully engaged, absorbing almost all of the kinetic energy of the fall and storing it in the flywheel batteries, so that the ship would hit the top of the Earth's atmosphere at no more than a meter per second.

The embedded systems in gravel boat number one were not programmed with the normal flight profile. The software was nonstandard and had been hacked together over the past few weeks: some of Darcy's open-sourced navigation package here, a physics simulation engine originally from a game involving rabbits throwing pine-cones at each other there, an almost-century old GPS driver bolted on the side thus. And instead of the drive braking the ship to a crawl, the new software directed the AG unit to absorb just enough velocity to counterbalance the accelerating tug of gravity. So fast, but no faster. That was key: hitting fast was necessary, but hitting the atmosphere *too* fast would ruin everything.

The systems in the other gravel boats ran the same software and took the same actions.

A few moments after the AG drives turned on, each boat started spitting puffs of nitrogen from cold-gas maneuvering rockets. One by one the boats tilted until they were oriented small end downward.

The boats were simple in design: each was a cargo container with a nosecone at one end and maneuvering vanes at the other. The nosecones were crude: the level of precision involved was only a bit greater than that achievable by a shade-tree mechanic banging a recalcitrant car hood into shape with a slap hammer and a leather bag of shot. The cones were fabricated from standard Aristillus deck planking - a steel alloy of no particular account refined in the solar furnace mills. Laminated over the steel was a layer of carbon phenolic sheets. The sheets had originally been brought to Aristillus by a motorcycle enthusiast who'd planned to use the carbon fiber to make "Manchurian style" street bike fairings. When he found more lucrative work in the atmosphere processing trade the sheets ended up listed on moonlist.ari, where they'd languished - until recently.

It was this carbon sheeting that first encountered atmosphere.

As the gravel boats - spaced out in a rough circle - entered the thermosphere, the first few molecules of air started to impact the nosecones, but the density was so low that it would have taken specialized sensors to even detect it – sensors that the boats did not have.

After a four-hundred-kilometer fall through the thermosphere, the boats entered the mesosphere, still punching downward toward the rapidly growing Caribbean ocean at almost Mach thirty, dropping over ten kilometers every second.

The atmosphere here was far too sparse to support life - a human without a space suit would pass out immediately and die almost as quickly as on the surface of the moon - but there was just barely enough air so that the maneuvering vanes at the rear of the boats began to click-click-click as they moved to fine tune the paths of the boats.

Ten seconds from ground.

The air around the boats thickened: now 0.001, now 0.01, now 0.1 atmospheres.

In the near vacuum the boats had fallen unimpeded. In the suddenly thicker air, though, something new happened. The hypersonic impact of the nosecones against the atmosphere was so powerful that the air molecules broke apart. Ozone, molecular oxygen, water vapor, even molecular nitrogen shattered, throwing a cascade of atoms, ions, and raw electrons.

Subtle luminous hints in front of each gravel boat grew and brightened, turning into fiery disks just millimeters in front of each nosecone. Inside each boat the software noted that the rate of successful radio packet transmissions had fallen from "six nines" to fifty percent, and then fell further, below a key threshold. The ionization blackout was detected and different subroutines were loaded and executed. Each boat switched from GPS to inertial navigation. Ring laser gyros that had been designed fifty years previously, open sourced a quarter century ago, found in archives two weeks ago, and fabbed, tested, and installed a week ago now directed the gravel boats.

Seven seconds from ground.

The boats crossed the boundary between the mesosphere and the stratosphere and the density of the atmosphere kept climbing - now up to 0.3 atmospheres.

On gravel boat number three - the one aimed for the southernmost guardhouse - a wrinkle in the hastily applied carbon shield resulted in an uneven flow of superheated air over the nosecone. The supercompressed air tugged on the wrinkle - and then in milliseconds tore a fingers-wide patch of ablative panel from the underlying metal.

With the carbon laminate gone, a pencil-thin jet of 6,000 kelvin plasma began burning through the nosecone. Steel vaporized and exploded outward, and the emission spectrum from the nosecone blaze added traces of iron to the already present nitrogen and oxygen.

Six seconds from ground.

Once the superheated jet burned through the nosecone the destruction snowballed. The hole in the heat shield grew to the size of a fist, and then to the size of a dinner plate. The ragged hole created turbulence, which created drag, which caused the boat to lean to one side during its fiery descent.

Five seconds to ground.

Maneuvering vanes fought to adjust boat number three's angle, but they'd lost the battle before they started. The boat pitched sideways and started rolling.

It was designed to take high temperatures, but only at the front end. As soon as it leaned, disaster was certain. Temperatures spiked and welds melted just as centripetal forces pulled at the ship, and cargo containers spilled, throwing AG drive bits, battery packs, half-melted steel pieces, and more than a ton of lunar gravel in all directions.

Three seconds to ground.

One large chunk of boat three's battery pack streaked across a hundred meters of sky and struck boat six as it plunged toward the ground in its own pillar of fire. The battery pack struck and tumbled away, but not before destroying one of boat six's maneuvering vanes. Boat six teetered and swam for a moment before righting itself and again riding its shield of fire down.

Another piece of debris, a large segment of cargo container wall, cut a jagged slice through the wall of boat eight. The edges of the cut caught air and peeled back in the superheated blast.

One second to ground.

Pieces of boat eight sprayed in all directions.

Before the wave of destruction could propagate further, the process was interrupted.

Traveling at many times the speed of sound, the boats hit their targets.

Because two of the boats had been lost, guardhouses three and four didn't get their allocated deliveries, but the twelve other targets - everything from the armory, the main gate, the electric transformers, and the motor pool down to the bridge that provided the shortest path from the barracks to the prisoner cells - were hit. The energy delivered as each 160 ton container struck at Mach 15 was almost precisely what would be called a kiloton if the explosions were nuclear. The round number was an accident of math - although one that had been discovered and remarked upon when the machines were built: fill a container that's THIS long with an AG drive and associated hardware and then fill the rest with grade 3 crushed regolith taken from a tailings pile, cancel the orbital velocity so that it falls toward the Earth from a height of 400 thousand kilometers, strip away a bit of the energy in the atmosphere, and what's left just happens to be around four thousand thousand thousand joules.

Even though the math implied a misleading connection, the fact was that the gravel boats did strike like nuclear bombs. Small ones, to be sure - each only a sixteenth of the yield of the Little Boy device that had exploded over Hiroshima a hundred and twenty years earlier - but like nuclear bombs nonetheless.

John was prepared - as were the rest of the men.

But even behind his shaded goggles and earplugs, John winced at the flash of light that seemed to come from all directions at once and that lit up the palm trees around him from a weird, unnaturally low angle with a strange yellow-white light.

Before the light had fully faded, the ground wave hit and John was thrown down. When the rumbling stopped a few seconds later, Sergeant Harbert stood and brushed himself off. John followed, pulled his goggles off, and looked at the sky. Fourteen bright pillars connected the earth and the heavens. As he watched, they began to fade from white to yellow to red.

A moment later the atmospheric shock wave blew past them. The palm trees shook and swayed and the alarms of the two or three cars behind them that weren't already going off joined the thousands that were.

Above them flocks of birds circled, confused.

John checked his phone.

It confirmed what he already knew by heart - they had exactly one hour.

Chapter 55

2064: UN Detention Facility, Haitian Dominican Protectorate, Earth

John held the mesh of the first chain-link fence steady and scanned the area while Sergeant Harbert readied the cutting tool. It wasn't the look of the trees or the smell of the island that caught John's attention - it was the sound. Or, rather, the almost complete lack of it. The car alarms had stopped and since the base's generator had been destroyed, the normal sounds of civilization were missing. Even the animals were stunned into immobility and quiet in the wake of the artificial earthquake. The only sound was the afternoon wind whispering through the trees.

Harbert's fence cutter whined to life and bit into the metal of the fence.

John held the fence steady and looked up.

Ash gray columns of dust and smoke from the impacts were climbing steadily higher and were beginning to mushroom over. The explosions were non-nuclear, but they looked for all the world like still pictures of Hiroshima and Nagasaki - and the video of Baltimore he'd seen on the web one memorable afternoon in first grade.

Then he chuckled. He'd forgotten for a moment that he'd actually witnessed a nuclear detonation in person at Zhukovskiy Crater. A real nuclear explosion, and there'd been no mushroom cloud because of the vacuum, and two months later he was looking at a dozen mushroom clouds, and yet a Geiger counter would register nothing.

John felt the chain link fence in his hands jerk and he looked down. Sergeant Harbert had cut through the first barrier.

John held the flap aside while Harbert ducked through, and then followed. The two men sprinted across the kill zone between the fences, leaping over the small craters where the landmines had been detonated by the ground-wave moments ago. They cut through the second fence as quickly as the first and were in the parking lot.

Every car and truck window was empty, and the asphalt was covered in shattered safety glass. At the far end of the parking lot civilian employees were spilling out of the administration building, gawking at the sky and pointing at the mushroom clouds. None of them noticed the two men.

Sergeant Harbert picked a car - a gray Nissan sedan - walked briskly to it, reached through the shattered driver's side window, and popped the lock. John was in the passenger seat and closing the door when he heard the motor whine to life. The sedan pulled away and Harbert shifted into second then third.

John looked in the rear view mirror. None of the office workers had even glanced at them. He checked his phone - just four minutes since the impacts. "Pretty quick hot-wiring job."

Harbert nodded. "Gotta love Nissans - steering column pops with a J-bar, and 22 volts on red bypasses the key check."

John nodded, keeping his right hand on the butt of his pistol and scanning the road ahead. "Yeah, and it was purest coincidence that you picked the one car that happened to be a stick shift."

Harbert grinned.

Chapter 56

2064: UN Detention Facility, Haitian Dominican Protectorate, Earth

John heard emergency klaxons from the prison ahead. He scowled; the building must have emergency generators. He'd have preferred that the power was out there too, but they had planned for this contingency.

Harbert pulled the Nissan into a reserved spot near the entrance. John looked at the plaque. What the hell was a "Distinction Training Officer" ? He shook his head. He and Harbert climbed out of the car and strode to the front door of the building. The handful of armed PKs standing outside the entrance looked down from the rapidly mounting mushroom clouds to the two men.

John was wearing a captain's bars, and all of the men were enlisted, but none of them saluted. Jesus.

John raised his chin to get their attention and yelled to them over the klaxons. "Is Lister inside? I need to talk to him." He paused. "Anyone?" There was noncommittal mumbling from the troops. John made a point of scowling as he stormed past. Harbert followed in his wake.

The bluff worked, and they were inside. John suppressed a smile - he and Harbert could have killed every one of the distracted, untrained, lazy PKs in seconds, but he preferred to walk past them - and not just to avoid alerting the rest of the base. His kill count had climbed high enough over the last twenty years. If he could get through today without it climbing further, he'd be happy. Scratch that - if he could get through today without *too many* more people dying, that'd be a win.

John straight-armed the inner door of the vestibule and walked into the lobby. Lumus and Sanderfur were already there, dressed in brown UPS uniforms and pretending to maneuver a hand truck holding a large box. Kindig and Mund were in PK uniforms and were escorting three "prisoners" - Chan, Mahoney, and Vasquez. The final three men of his team were in PK uniforms and were hunched over a slate, shouting over the klaxon as they pretended to argue over something.

John ignored them, slammed his hand on the front desk, and yelled over the noise. "Captain Lister wants me to sit in on an interrogation with one of the expats."

The two overwhelmed guards behind the counter looked up. One of them, flustered by the earthquakes, flashing alarm lights, and the klaxon, said, "What? We're on lock-down! No one is -"

In the intervening seconds Lumus and Sanderfur, both dressed in their UPS uniforms, had moved around the counter and pointed pistols at the guards. Sergeant Lumus said, "Hands off the desk. Step back."

The guard who had already been standing looked at the guns and took a step backwards. The seated guard glanced longingly down at the desk where John was sure the hidden alarm switch was mounted. After a long second he raised his hands, stood, and stepped away.

"Face away from me. Against the wall." John looked over his shoulder. Behind them, the rest of the unit was securing the steel doors and removing their heavy weapons from the fake UPS shipping boxes. He turned back to the guards. With long-practiced moves, his men had them zip-tied, duct-taped, and hooded in seconds. Harbert yanked the ID cards off the men and then Kindig and Mund dragged the two PKs into a restroom. John walked behind the desk, looked at the controls, and tapped a button. The klaxons cut off and the red lights stopped flashing. When he straightened,

Sanderfur was holding a set of body armor and a rifle out for him. John buckled the armor on, took the rifle, and looked at his phone. Sixteen minutes since impact. Forty four minutes to go.

* * *

The run through the building was textbook - not a single bullet fired - until they got to the cell block. John opened the door and the guard behind the desk started to rise. His pistol had just cleared his holster when Sanderfur shot him twice in the chest and once in the face. The "silenced" carbine wasn't truly silent, but it was quiet enough - the sound of the three shots was close to that of hardcover books being dropped on the floor. No one in the building would hear it.

The guard was already dead when he collapsed forward onto his desk - and when his finger twitched and squeezed the trigger of his pistol. The retort of the shot was loud in the small room. John shook his head. Fuck. Lumus looked at him. John shrugged. "Let's hope no one hears that." Lumus nodded.

Harbert pushed the dead guard off the desk and pulled the keyboard toward himself through the pool of blood. He tapped keys and spoke without looking up. "He's logged in." Harbert clicked the mouse. "I've unlocked the doors, but we'll still need pass cards to get the cells themselves open."

John nodded. "Let's move."

Vasquez took up a position in a corner of the room, facing the door they'd entered through, carbine ready. Kindig tried the windowless steel door behind the guard's station. He turned and nodded - it was open. He held up three fingers, and counted down. Three. Two. One. Kindig threw the door open and four members of the team piled through, carbines leading the way. As John stepped through the door behind them, a klaxon began to screech.

Lumus looked at John and yelled over the noise. "Looks like hoping didn't help."

Harbert called out the time. "Thirty-one minutes down. Twenty-nine to go."

* * *

Inside the cell block proper, the work of securing the facility was easier. The guards here carried only chemical spray, and when confronted by the extraction team armed with assault rifles and grenade launchers, they were positively eager to surrender.

John stood over the latest group of PK prisoners and saw a key-card clipped to one of the guards' belts. He looked at the man. "Does this open the cells?" The bound PK nodded. John pulled the card loose and tossed it to Mund. "Open the cells - we'll catch up." Mund nodded, turned, and sprinted down the corridor toward the cells.

Vasquez leaned over the four newest captives and reached for the dispenser of duct-tape gags at his belt. John turned to Vasquez. "The alarms are going off. Forget gagging them - let's round up the prisoners and get out of here." Vasquez nodded and let the dispenser fall to his side.

From the direction that Mund had gone, there came the sound of steel cage doors banging open. John and Vasquez were turning to join Mund at the cells when the sound of heavy machine guns came from somewhere outside the building.

John whipped his head around. What the hell? Every single member of the extraction team was inside the building and accounted for, so what were the PKs shooting at? "Harbert, what do you see?"

Harbert already had his slate out and was looking at it. "Pulling up video from the drones now...OK, we've got MPs firing heavy MGs by the building main entrance. Makes no sense - must be a distraction.

And...OK, this is it. Two teams of QRF approaching the loading docks. I make them 30 strong. Look like pros - good overwatch."

From further down the corridor Mund started yelling instructions. John looked away from Harbert and saw that prisoners were starting to stream out of the cells. Some were grinning broadly; others were limping and looking wan and broken. Kindig was in control and forming them into a line. Good - that was under control. The question was how much time they had before the PK force caught them. John turned back to Harbert. "How long until QRF is here?"

"Lead elements are inside the building now."

John's earpiece chimed. He took the call. "We've got the courtyard door open!"

"Good. Prisoners forming up."

John checked his phone. Six minutes left. Shit. The PK QRF was moving faster than they'd planned for - they'd have hostile contact before the exfil.

John keyed his headset and broadcast. "Everyone - six minutes. Ship's in atmosphere by now. We've got a reaction force in the building - 30 pros. We've got to hold them off while we extract."

John rattled off orders, assigning men to secure specific doors. He'd just dispatched team four to set up claymores when one prisoner pushed her way through the line and ran to John.

He did a double take - when he'd last seen her she'd been cooking hamburgers for him and the Dogs while they bantered over cold beers. Now, though, her dirty hair was matted to her head and the bags under her eyes from stress and sleep deprivation made her look like someone else. "Darcy!"

She yelled over the klaxons, "We've got to talk."

"What?"

"There's a secret block - two more floors underground."

John shook his head. "We don't have time."

Darcy grabbed his arm. "They're not all expats, but they *are* Americans. Civilians. We can't leave them here."

John stared at her for a second. He cursed. There wasn't time - but she'd hit him in one of the few places where he was vulnerable. "How many?"

"I don't know. They kept us segregated. But two floors. Maybe fifty people."

God. Fucking. Damn it.

John raised his voice to be heard over the klaxon and the sporadic machine gun fire from outside and yelled into his headset. "Kindig, Mund, get this batch prepped and ready. Lumus, your team defend the doors here. Chan, and Mahoney - we've got more prisoners and we need to get them out. I'm sending you a guide." He turned to Darcy. "Chan and Mahoney are at the end of that corridor - find them, and show them the levels." Darcy nodded and ran off.

This was going to fuck up the schedule. And worse than that, it was going to fuck up the careful calculations for lift and life support on the lifeboat.

Shit, shit, shit.

Chapter 57

Chan reached the last cell door in the first underground level, swiped the card against the reader, and pulled the door open. The cell was empty.

The corridor around him was filled with a dozen freed prisoners. The able-bodied helped others who limped, and in one case, two men dragged an unconscious woman. He checked the time. Four minutes. He bellowed at the prisoners "Move faster!" and then pushed roughly past them and into the stairwell. Mahoney was already there, half a flight below him, heading downward to the second and final underground floor.

Chan thundered down the stairs after him.

Over the past weeks the extraction team had done endless practice drills in a hanger at Aristillus, using mock-ups of the cell block and of the extraction ship, and using a crowd of day laborers hired to play confused and untrained captives. In the practice runs they'd barely managed to get the captives loaded in the time window. And now they were adding dozens more bodies?

This op was fucked.

There was an explosion above them, and then rifle fire. Chan avoided looking up and concentrated on the stairs, but he knew that the PK reaction force must be inside the detention block.

He reached the bottom of the stairwell. Mahoney was already at the steel door, but the key cards that had opened so many doors before didn't help them - the access plate was beeping and flashing red.

Mahoney swore and swiped the card again, to the same effect. Above them the rifle fire continued.

Without a word, Mahoney stepped back and pivoted away from the door at the exact moment that Chan stepped in. Chan angled his shotgun down, held the muzzle a finger's breadth from the steel, and shot a breaching round. Even through the sound suppressor headset, the blast was punishing in the confined stairwell. The next three blasts just added to the echoing roar. The task done, Chan pointed his weapon in a safe direction and pivoted back as Mahoney stepped into the swirling cloud of dust and threw his shoulder against the door, throwing it open.

Chan stepped through, his carbine leading the way. The corridor looked just like the one above.

Mahoney followed him, the passcard held out. "That fucking card had better open these cell doors or I -"

He swiped, and the first cell door opened. The prisoner inside was crouching, holding one hand up to ward them away.

Chan yelled, "We're friends! Go up the stairs!" The man blinked, but there was no time to hand hold him. They moved to the next cell.

Chan's phone warbled an alarm. He read the display. Sixty seconds to landing.

Chapter 58

2064: courtyard level, UN Detention Facility, Nan Garde, Haitian Dominican Protectorate, Earth

Kindig stood on the landing in the stairwell, one hand on the push bar of the door that led to the courtyard, and mentally rehearsed his next steps. He checked the time. Sixty seconds. He turned and looked behind him at the line of prisoners that snaked up the stairs to the prison block. Most stood in the queue like they'd been directed to, but some were confused, in shock, or overwhelmed by the stuttering rifle fire and occasional explosions coming from further back in the building. Mund worked his way down the line, grabbing one man and pushing him into position, then moving on to another.

Kindig checked the time again. Fifty seconds to landing. He faced the prisoners and bellowed over the klaxon and the rifle fire. "Everyone! Pay attention! One more time: when I open this door, you run - DON'T WALK, RUN! - for the ship. Don't stop for anything. If the person in front of you trips, don't help them, go around. Once on the ship, file to the back. Grab a seat if you can find one, stand if you can't. Do you understand?"

He got a bunch of nods. He could heard Mund, at the other end of the line, yelling the same set of instructions.

Kindig breathed deeply. They'd practiced every aspect of this drill dozens of times in a spare warehouse in Aristillus. As the rehearsals got more polished John had started throwing tricks at them - telling the day laborers who were acting as hostages to stop, to trip, to act confused. By the twentieth run Kindig and the others had felt like they could manage the process in their sleep.

Now was the moment of truth.

He checked again. Twenty seconds. He pushed the door open a few centimeters, and then squatted down and looked through the crack. The sky was blue and empty. Nothing. Wait. There - a dot. It grew and then the noise hit him.

Damn, it was coming in fast!

It took only a moment for the ship to turn from a small speck to a bird-sized object, and then to a basketball. The roar turned into a wall of air that smashed the door shut and jammed his fingers back painfully. Fuck!

The ground shuddered beneath his feet as the boat landed hard on its heavy shock absorbers.

Now.

Kindig slammed the door open with one shoulder and stepped into the courtyard, rifle ready. The boat - the Deladrier - sat in the center of the quadrangle, small shrubs and broken picnic tables crushed beneath it. The space around it was alive with a whirlwind of dust and blowing detritus. The ship itself swayed on its landing gear, still bouncing slightly from its landing. The ramp was already folding down.

Kindig's eyes, though, weren't on the boat but on the walls and windows around the courtyard. It looked safe.

Kindig turned his head towards the stairwell and yelled over the klaxons, the distant rifle fire, and the thrumming of the ship's drive.

"Move! Now!"

The first prisoner didn't move. Kindig cursed, grabbed the man by his shirt, and pulled him through the door. The prisoner stumbled into the courtyard then broke into a shuffle, then into a run. Behind him the rest of the line got a jerky and halting start. Slow. Too slow.

Kindig screamed at them to move faster, and then turned his eyes to windows around the courtyard, and then to the roofline. Still no one. Good.

He checked the column of captives again. The first batch was mostly on the Deladrier. The ones coming out of the stairwell now were the others - the ones from the secret levels. The ones in red jumpsuits.

Kindig saw movement to his left and pivoted, bringing his rifle to bear - but, no, it was just a small group of birds landing on the roof of the building. He turned back to the Deladrier - and saw a problem starting. Five people were bunched up around the ramp, but the flow of prisoners from the building wasn't stopping. In a moment there were a dozen prisoners, and then two dozen, all packed together on the ramp, pushing to get into the ship.

Jesus. He flexed his right hand reflexively. He wanted to move closer to help, but he had to stay here and watch the windows. Maybe these numbnuts would get it straightened out themselves? But no. In frustration he took his eyes off the windows and yelled at them, "Get in there! Move!"

Suddenly there was a loud crack of rifle fire nearby. The birds that had just settled on the roof took off - and one of the freed prisoners near the ship screamed as he clutched his chest and fell. Shit. Kindig bellowed into his mike. "Contact in the Courtyard!" There was a second shot and another prisoner screamed. Where had it come from? Kindig scanned. It sounded like it was on the far side of the courtyard, but none of the windows over there -

Then he realized he'd been hearing an echo. The shots must be coming from above him. He looked up. There - the muzzle of a rifle in a window two stories up.

Kindig snapped the rifle to his shoulder and backpedaled toward the rescue ship until he could see the window. He squeezed off a few quick shots as he ran backward, and the PK's muzzle disappeared back into the window. He didn't have an angle to hit the shooter, but he could force him to keep his head down. He fired off more shots as he moved.

He yelled into his mic again. "Contact! Contact! I need backup!" There was a deep crump of a claymore detonating deeper inside the building, then the sound of a heavy machine gun opening up.

Fuck.

There wasn't going to be backup, was there?

He was going to have to handle this alone.

Double fuck.

He kept backpedaling, waiting for the shooter to come into view - and scanning the other windows to make sure there weren't more. He couldn't see the guy - the man was either deep inside the room or he'd moved to another window. Kindig knew he was almost to the ship, and then he was there, slamming into it ass first. His combat webbing and the gear on his back cushioned the impact. OK, now where was the shoot -

Another shot, and a prisoner three meters away from him at the ship's ramp screamed and fell. But Kindig had seen the movement - the shooter was in the same room he'd taken his first shot from - he'd popped up, shot, and ducked back down again.

Kindig reached under his rifle and switched the selector on 40 millimeter tube from "incendiary" to "air-burst window." He squeezed the trigger. The round was perfectly aimed - it flew in a flat arc and punched through the window, knocking aside fragments of glass still left in the frame.

The small computer in the round and the software that ran on it were decades-old technology: open sourced, debugged, and documented in dozens of repositories. It was a mainstay of the border skirmishes of the Caliphate, the Central American Cartels, both sides in the Alaskan and Texan brush wars - and now it was getting used again in this fight.

The code in the grenade worked perfectly - the round detonated two meters inside the room. The blast threw dust, glass shards, and debris through the wrecked window frame and into the courtyard. Kindig tried not to flinch as the debris rained down on him - his helmet and goggles would keep him safe. Around him, freed prisoners screamed as they were hit with detritus.

From the inside of the building another claymore detonated, then two more.

He heard Mund yell over the rising noise. "Status?"

Kindig looked down from the windows. Mund was at the stairwell door. There were prisoners packed behind him.

Kindig pointed, and bellowed back over the klaxons. "One shooter, dead. Could be more, I -"

Mund snapped his rifle to his shoulder, got cheek weld instantly, and shot a three-round burst over Kindig's head into a window on the opposite side of the court yard.

Shit. The reaction team was better armed and smarter than the vast majority of the PKs. Kinding yelled to Mund, "You cover that side, I'll cover the near side." He toggled his mike and yelled, "John, we've got the PKs in the courtyard under control, but we need someone to move the prisoners."

* * *

Mahoney was closing the very last cell door in the second underground level when he heard the call for backup in the courtyard. He turned and began to sprint to the stairs when one of the prisoners grabbed his combat webbing. An older man, of indeterminate race - a light-skinned Indian?

"The video - you've got to get the video."

Harbert tried to shake the hand off. "Don't worry, we're getting this all on video for the after action."

"No, in the utility closet - that's where they keep the video of the interrogation sessions."

Harbert turned away. "No time."

The old man still had hold of him and pulled on the webbing with a surprising strength. "Listen to me - I don't know who are, but if you're breaking us out of here, we're on the same side. You need that video - people need to see it."

Harbert stared at the old man, then keyed his mike. "Got something might be important - can you hold sixty seconds?"

Kindig's answer came back, "Shit is getting fucking toasty. You got thirty."

The man's grip slackened. Kindig pointed at the utility closet door. Mahoney stepped forward and swiped the passcard. The reader flashed red.

Mahoney grimaced. Chan - with his shotgun and breaching rounds - was already gone up the stairs.

Fuck it.

"Step back!"

Mahoney pointed his rifle at the door handle and emptied a dozen rounds into it. The old man gasped and held his hands over his ears. Mahoney slammed his shoulder into the door. It didn't open. He took a step back and emptied the rest of the magazine. Empty brass flew in a stream from the ejection port and splashed against the wall. Bits of door handle ripped off and pinged off of walls. Something stung the knuckles of Mahoney's left hand. Then the rifle's bolt locked back and the sound ended. Mahoney ejected the magazine, let it fall, and slapped another one in before front-kicking the door. The locking mechanism crumbled and the door slammed open, and then bounced back. Mahoney moved forward, pushing the door open with his shoulder.

He was in what looked to have once been a utility closet that had been remade into a small office. A floor sink, a desk, several flat screens mounted over it, and a few shelves.

What the hell was he looking for?

He turned to the old Indian man. "What do you want?"

The captive dithered. "Umm - I don't know. It's here somewhere - they talked about it. But -"

Mahoney turned away in frustration. Videos. Data. But where? He scanned the desk area. A century ago data was stored in drives the size of washing machines. Fifty years ago drives had been the size of a loaf of bread, or a deck of cards. Today a thousand years of video could be stored on something the size of a grain of sand.

So much shit - mouse pads, coffee mugs, framed commendations ,and pictures of grinning troops shaking hands with senior officers. But where was the video he needed? There were dozens of things on the desk that could hold data chips - data slates, a cup of pens, a headset with an archive chip, backup shards.

"How do we even know it's here and not in the cloud?"

"They said it was. They needed to keep the interrogation sessions, but they couldn't-"

Mahoney ignored him. Next to the floor sink was a big garbage can on wheels. He left his rifle hang from the chest sling and grabbed the trash can. With his right hand he jammed the lip of it under the desk, and then used his left to sweep everything - keyboard, plastic organizer bin, mouse, two slates, a stack of shards - into the can.

Above him the firing grew more intense. Kindig yelled over the com link, "Mahoney? Where the fuck are you? Get up here, now!"

Mahoney ignored it and looked around the room. What else? Two shelves over the desk. Mahoney swept books, folders and other crap into the garbage can.

He looked around. The room was bare. He keyed the headset. "Coming!"

* * *

Darcy pushed forward through the line of freed captives and down the half flight of stairs. She was almost to the courtyard door when machine gun fire started ahead. Those prisoners in front of her stopped, and then surged back. People behind were still moving forward, and in seconds the line degenerated into a packed mass.

Darcy tried to push through, but people were jammed too tightly. An elbow caught her in the ribs; then the people behind her surged forward and she was crushed into someone's back, her face turned sideways and pressed into the cheap fabric of the prison jumpsuit. She pushed back against the body in front of her and made enough room that she could fill her lungs. She yelled as loud as she could, "Let me through! Please!" but either she couldn't be heard over klaxons and the gunfire or no one was inclined to listen.

She wanted to scream in frustration. She *needed* to get out to the ship and talk to the pilot. She yelled a second time, but no one was listening to her. What was she supposed to do? There had to be - she felt someone grab her elbow. She turned and looked. It was another captive, towering over the others in the crush. She knew him - Benedikt Hallbjarnsson, the cook from the Poyekhali. He pulled on her arm and she stumbled as she was yanked towards him. Benedikt shouted at her ear, like a kid in a club. "You need to get to the ship?" She nodded. "It's an emergency?" She had barely begun to say "yes" when he renewed his grip on her arm - this time grabbing her by the bicep - and plunged forward. Like an icebreaker guiding a ship through the arctic, Benedikt pushed through the crush with Darcy in tow. Her arm felt like it was going to tear off, but in a moment they were down the stairs and at the doorway. Benedikt let go of her.

Darcy looked out. An open courtyard, and in the center a weird home brew ship - like an overlarge hopper - squatting in the middle. It had a open ramp. One of the liberators - a soldier with an "Aristillus Defense Force" armband - stood two meters outside the door, scanning the windows on the far side of the courtyard. Suddenly he snapped off a shot. His rifle's crack felt like a punch in the chest. Her ears stung.

Benedikt yelled, "What now?"

Darcy pointed with her chin. "I need to get to the ship."

Benedikt nodded and grabbed her wrist.

Darcy turned to him. "Wait - what?"

Benedikt didn't answer, but ran out the door. Darcy tried to keep her feet under her as the huge cook sprinted into the courtyard, dragging her behind. The ADF soldier turned in surprise as they brushed past. "Wait!"

Benedikt was already past. A moment later they were in the courtyard, running. The rifle fire was intense and she heard an occasional deep thump - grenades? The ship was ahead and another ADF soldier had his back to it as he fired at something over Darcy and Benedikt's head. She couldn't believe they were out here. Her eyes darted wildly. Who was shooting? Where? She looked ahead. On the far side of the courtyard, beyond the ship, fires raged, licking out from blown out windows. Darcy tripped and then regained her feet as Benedikt pulled her. There was a low thump behind her and a grenade sailed over her head and over the ship, punching into a window in the building ahead and exploding.

Benedikt plowed ahead. They were almost at the ramp. At the base were two crumpled prisoners, their jumpsuits stained with blood.

Benedikt ran past the bodies and up the ramp, and Darcy was pulled after him. She caught the stenciled name "Deladrier" next to the entrance as they plunged into the outer airlock doorway. Benedikt finally let go of her wrist and the two of them ran through the open inner airlock door.

Darcy stopped and looked around, breathing heavily - more from shock than from the run. The ship was a single large compartment, laid out like a bus. To her left, down the length of the hold, she saw her fellow prisoners crushed toward the back of the ship, trying to get as far from the open airlock door as they could.

To her right was a single door. That must be the cockpit. She opened it and stepped inside. A young Indian man seated in one of two cockpit chairs yelled at her, "Get to the back - grab a seat and sit -" He interrupted himself. "Darcy?"

Darcy looked at him. "Do I know you?"

"Prem Rohit. We met once when you were guest teaching a navigation -"

"Later. We've got more prisoners than I think you planned for. Can the ship handle -"

"What do you mean more prisoners -"

"More. Prisoners." She blew air out of her cheeks, still trying to center herself after running through the combat zone of the courtyard. "Listen. How many passengers did you expect?"

"Uh...20 or so. 25 max."

"The troops - are they coming out with us?"

"Uh...right. 40 max with the troops."

"OK, you've got more like 70 or 75...maybe 80. Can you lift that mass?"

The pilot blinked. "I don't know, I -"

"Can you handle that many on life support?"

"Uh - I don't know. I mean, we've got extra air for a full week. Mike insisted on that in case of drive problems and a bad orbit, but -"

Darcy looked at him. "What's your name again?"

"Prem."

Darcy breathed out slowly and spread her hands, more to calm herself than him. "OK, Prem. Listen. Your console says we've got eleven minutes in the window." Prem looked away from Darcy to navigation screen, and then back. "I've got to figure this out. I need you to unbuckle and get back there." she jerked a thumb over her shoulder. "Get the prisoners to start unclipping those chairs and throwing them out the airlock. Look for anything we don't need. If there are space suits in the airlock, lose them. If there's food, throw it out."

"Food? This trip is going to take three days -"

"Toss it. Toss the *water*. Is the bathroom a module?"

"Yes -"

"Unbolt it and roll it out."

Prem looked confused.

Darcy felt the urge to cry. Why wasn't he moving? "Darn it, Prem, do it - now. I'm taking left seat. I need to find an orbital solution with all this extra mass."

Prem blinked - he was clearly out of his depth. Darcy wondered for a moment if the "slapping a hysterical person to calm them down" she'd read in romance novels actually worked. Then Prem unbuckled from the seat, stood, and went aft.

Darcy threw herself into the seat he'd vacated and looked at the screens.

The user interface was revision 459 - good, that was a current one. She swung the keyboard into position and hit a control-alt-shift combination, and the UI beeped.

Crap.

It didn't have her customizations loaded. Of course. She spun the trackball and clicked buttons, and she finally had the data entry page up. She revised the mass figures and reset the AG limiter to 10% above redline and was starting a simulation run when she heard the crash of the bathroom unit being rolled overboard.

* * *

John crouched behind the door frame with his rifle ready. There - through the smoke, he saw movement in a window. He squeezed off a three-round burst. It was answered by a string of shots that ripped across the wall above him. It wasn't rifle fire either, but one of those two damned heavy machine guns.

John swallowed. The PK reaction force was coming on strong, and his team was undermanned.

He'd been falling back ever since the ship landed, trading distance for time, to give the prisoners time to load.

Distance and time - and now he and his men were almost out of both.

The first time they'd fallen back through a steel door and hot-epoxied it shut, it had stopped the PKs for three minutes. Now, though, the PKs had the shotgun-and-breaching-rounds dance down cold, and the tactic bought John and his men less time each iteration.

The claymore booby traps had worked well, but they'd only had six and they'd used them all.

He looked over his shoulder. They were at the top of the stairwell. The final fucking stairwell. Two flights down was the door to the courtyard.

John set his selector grenade and got an angry warning buzz - empty. As if reading his mind, Sanderfur leaned around the corner of the door-frame and fired one of his own. It exploded near the end of the corridor, filling the space with noise and dust. Fragments of acoustic ceiling tiles and light fixtures rained down. A moment later the PKs returned fire - two smoke grenades bounced off a wall and into view and immediately started spewing smoke. This was it. Their next rush was coming. And there was nowhere to fall back to. The corridor filled with billows of white smoke. John fired a burst into the expanding cloud. Vasquez, Lumus, and Ranco were all shooting too, despite their wounds.

He'd called Mund and Kindig in the courtyard a few minutes ago and hadn't gotten a response. He hoped they busy shooting, and not dead.

John spared a second to look over his shoulder at Lumus behind him. The tourniquet on his leg was helping, but not enough - the linoleum was slick with his blood.

John checked the display in his goggles. They were at dust off + 12 minutes.

Plus twelve.

Fuck.

He keyed his mike. "Mund, Kindig, what's the status? Answer me, damn it!"

Even as he was releasing the transmit button he turned to Chan. "Get down there, see what's going on, report back." Chan turned and ran down the stairs. A moment later the PK heavy machine gun opened up and ripped into the floor in front of John. He felt the splash of shattered bullets hit his armor and ducked back. Sanderfur fired a grenade, and then another.

A minute later Chan was back, limping, his left thigh stained with blood.

John turned to him and yelled over the klaxons. "Why aren't we taking off?"

"Bad news, LT - the ship's overloaded."

John closed his eyes for just a moment. "What does that mean?"

"That Darcy chick has tossed everything overboard - she's even got people stripping down to their underwear. But we're still 20 people over."

Shit, shit, shit.

The klaxons and gunfire seemed to die away.

John made eye contact with Chan. Chan knew what he was thinking, and nodded once.

John yelled over the noise to the attention of the rest of his team.

"The ship is overweight. Anyone in the mood to be a hero?"

* * *

Darcy flinched as another string of bullets slapped against the hull of the Deladrier.

Prem, strapped into the right hand seat in the windowless cockpit, saw her jump. "Ignore it. The ship is armored against anything they can throw at us."

Darcy scowled. "I wish there was a bit less armor - we could use the lift capacity." She looked back to her instruments. This ship had a nice feature - strain gauges in the landing gear gave a precise reading on weight. With all the excess stripped from the passenger compartment, they were within a few hundred pounds of -

The gauges jumped.

Damn it! More weight. Darcy barked at Prem, "keep working the insertion, I'll be right back," and then stood and threw open the door to the passenger compartment.

Four men of the rescue team were standing in the aisle, framed by the airlock door. Beyond them was the ramp and at the bottom of it was the piles of shoes, prepackaged meals, and cabin seats and the big cube of the bathroom unit. Darcy looked at the four men. Three of them were each carrying a bloody comrade - and the fourth was towing a gray garbage can.

The leftmost troop yelled, "Ma'am, John says you've got to take these three wounded - and that garbage can."

"The garbage can? Wha -"

"Says it's super important - I don't know. He was clear, though."

Darcy shook her head, almost frantically. "No - that's too much! I just did a calibration run. We're already over. These men-" she used a practiced eye "-put us 400 kilos over."

The troop lowered the wounded man he was half carrying to the floor. "John says you need to figure it out. We're staying here. Now get these people out!"

- and then he and the other three were gone, running down the ramp and shooting as they went.

Darcy looked around. The cabin was packed. People were sitting on the floor, standing, lying down half atop each other. With the chairs gone and everything else ripped out it was a nasty bare space...and without food, or a bathroom, or water, it was going to get a lot worse over the next two days.

Darcy rarely swore, but she felt an f-bomb percolating up.

Another 400 kilos.

400 kilos.

400 kilos.

Was there anything else she could toss?

Even she was barefoot, wearing just her sweat-stained bra and shorts.

She had no idea.

Should she toss the three wounded troops? Could she even bring herself to do it?

Suddenly the incoming fire shifted and shots started coming in through the open airlock. A string of shots hit the bulkhead, not half a meter from where Darcy stood.

People started screaming.

The swear that had been straining at her lips finally burst through as she turned and raced to the cockpit. She sat and strapped in. Prem looked over and must have seen the determination on her face; he hit the large red button to close the ramp. The hydraulics whined.

Darcy crossed herself and ran a finger down the screen in an old ritual, passing each green box - and the one flashing yellow. She'd already played with parameters to boost at higher g's than normal - the drives were more efficient the closer they were to the planetary mass they were pushing against, so in an odd parallel to chemical rocketry, the more energy she could use close to the ground, the better.

That helped, but the math still didn't work. Behind her the airlock hissed as the doors sealed, and there was a loud bang as the ramp folded up against the hull.

Maybe she'd think of something en route. Or maybe there was some reserve in the system she wasn't aware of. Or maybe the batteries had a better charge than they were showing.

She yelled out "Hold on!" although she didn't know if the passengers would hear her, and hit the "activate launch sequence" button. The drive ramped up, the weird thrumming engulfed her, and her guts twisted.

She looked at the screens for the external cameras and saw that John and his men had been forced out of the building and were now in the courtyard near the stairwell door. Two of them turned to the ship and snapped quick salutes, but the rest had their rifles to their shoulders as they shot at targets around the courtyard.

The weird vibration and the gut-twisting field of the AG drive built. On the video screens John's squad of troops were obscured by a cloud of dust blown up by the ship. Parts of the picnic tables crushed beneath the ship rattled loose and bounced across the ground. Another string of bullets hit the hull and one of the two cameras went dead. Darcy whispered "faster, faster." On the screen the bar showing the AG drive output surged, turning colors from green to yellow to red as it raced to the 100% tick mark and beyond.

The drive kicked harder than she'd ever felt before and a giant weight seemed to push her into the seat. Her head was forced back against the rest, but on the screen she could see that the acceleration was over three g's. Behind her the ship was filled with screams and yells as passengers fell.

* * *

As the dust dissipated John took a second to look up into the bright blue sky.

The ship was gone.

The PKs on the far side of the courtyard opened up with a heavy machine gun.

He ejected his magazine, slapped his last one in, and turned to face them.

Chapter 59

2064: outside Trentham Court Apartments, Aristillus, Lunar Nearside

Hugh raced down the sidewalk after Louisa and caught her just as she reached the jitney stop. He put a hand on her shoulder and she whirled. He had intended to ask her where she was going, but when he saw the white-hot rage in her eyes, he fell silent.

"What, Hugh? What? Are you going to try to stop me? Selena accuses me of faking video - in public! - in front of billions of people! - and I'm supposed to calm down? She thinks she can humiliate me? I'm going to *kill* her. I mean it. That dirty traitorous little bitch -"

Hugh licked his lips, trying to think of what to say. He couldn't help but notice three of the commuters at the jitney stop had already looked up from their phones to watch the drama. One man looked sharply at Hugh and Louisa, back down at his slate, then tapped his companion. After a whispered conference, the first one faced them and spoke up. "You're the ones who faked that video? You want to take my business away and let the PKs run it, huh? This going to be Lagos Protectorate all over again?"

Hugh blinked. "I - sir, I'm not sure what -"

Louisa turned to the Nigerian and barked at him. "Fuck you - leave us alone."

The second man threw back his shoulders. "Oh, that how it is, mugu abuna?"

"Go fuck yourself, I'm not talking to you." Louisa said, before turning back to Hugh. "I swear, that bitch Selena is going to pay -"

The Nigerian wasn't done; he crowded closer and yelled. Louisa yelled back. The crowd waiting for the jitney was bigger now - seven or eight people - and most were looking down at their screens and then looking up at Louisa and the Nigerian as the two traded insults.

Hugh eyed the crowd nervously. "Louisa?" She either didn't hear him or didn't care, as she kept yelling. "Louisa!" She didn't answer, but punched her finger through the air at the Nigerian as she screamed something. Hugh swallowed. The crowd was swelling, and most of the people were watching the argument - and those that weren't were looking down at their slates and then up at them. The crowd had an angry buzz and more people kept joining. Selena's expose of their editing was going viral, he was sure of it. Hugh looked around for some way out of the situation, but as he scanned the storefronts, he realized that people were pouring out of nearby shops and apartments. Jesus. He was in the middle of a flashmob, and it was still building.

He grabbed Louisa's arm. "Louisa, this is bad. We have to -"

She shrugged him off violently. His hand slipped off her elbow and - unstrestrained - her arm swung forward and the finger she'd been pointing poked the Nigerian in the chest. His eyes got wide. "You want to rack? I'll rack!" He straight-armed Louisa, who stumbled back into Hugh. Even as Hugh took a step backward to catch himself he heard the crowd get louder - the muttering was ramping up into cat calls and yells. Hugh looked at the clock at the top of the jitney information pole. Three more minutes? His palms were sweating. Three minutes was a long time. Maybe too long. Even as he thought it someone pushed him from behind. He took a step forward and consciously decided not to turn around - he didn't want to escalate. Louisa didn't have the same plan - Hugh winced as she yelled "fuck off and die" to someone.

The person behind Hugh pushed him again and Hugh stumbled forward - and crashed into a tall Russian who pushed him back the way he'd come. Shit,

shit, shit. This was getting *really* bad. They had to get away, and had to get away *now* - this was seconds away from turning into a riot.

Hugh gave up on Louisa and pushed sideways through the crowd. He caught several more pushes and even a punch, but managed to reach the outskirts of the crowd. He gauged the traffic. Could he make a run for it, across the street? Someone slapped the back of his head. He cringed and looked down, avoiding eye contact.

A scream. He risked a look. Louisa punched a Nigerian woman in a green dress and immediately a Nigerian man in jeans and a polo shirt slapped Louisa. Hard. Louisa staggered - and then Hugh was pushed from behind again. He staggered and fell into the street, landing on his knees and one outstretched hand.

And then a van screeched to a halt just in front of him.

Hugh looked up and saw the van was blue and white and had a Trusted Security logo. The door slid open, and two pairs of boots hit the pavement a handspan from his face. Two guards, tasers at their hips, not yet drawn. Hugh looked back at the crowd. They'd fallen back a step, but there was still dangerous energy there.

One of the guards looked at him. "Get in the truck." Then he said to someone in the crowd - Louisa? - "You too!"

"Fuck you, you fascist - you can't arrest us for our speech. We have the right to -"

"I'm not arresting you, you idiot, I'm saving your lives. Jackson Real Estate doesn't want a lynching in its tunnels." The muttering of the crowd grew louder. The guard eyed the crowd, and then turned back to Hugh and Louisa. He cocked a thumb over his shoulder. "The truck leaves in 10 seconds. Get in. Or don't."

Hugh didn't need to think - he pushed himself off the ground and clambered in, then turned.

Louisa stared at the guard for a long moment.

Behind her the crowd surged forward. A voice yelled out, "We take care of that bitch for you!"

Louisa glared at the guard, and stepped into the van.

The door slid shut behind them.

Chapter 60

2064: Lucknow, India

Ashok sat on a stool in Prem's basement workshop. On the workbench the last wisps of icy fog dissipated, and Ashok looked at the two cryogenically treated stators sitting on the workbench in front of him. They were probably warm enough to touch by now, but he wasn't going to take chances - he pulled on the pair of work gloves.

A month ago, Ashok Vivek and Prem Pradeep had gotten the first prototype to levitate a hand's breadth above the workbench. Last week, the second prototype had flown a hundred meters straight up into the night sky and then landed successfully. Now they were working on the real AG drive - the one that would take their ship to the moon.

Ashok shook his head. The moon. It sounded crazy, but every day it got more real.

He turned to Prem. "Well...shall we mount it?"

Prem pursed his lips. "Professional equipment would have been better. Look at this." He gestured behind him. "A treatment tank of plywood and foam insulation? Copper plumbing pipes?" Prem shook his head sadly. "I don't know about this."

Ashok had learned to ignore Prem's worrying. Let him complain all he wanted, as long as he helped - and he was pulling his gloves on as he spoke. Good.

Ashok grabbed the closer end of the first stator. "On three? One, two - three." They lifted.

Fifteen minutes later, the stators were snug in the pillow blocks and the autocalibration routines from the expat ebook were running. The drive unit lifted off the cement floor, pulled the chains taut, and slowly lowered itself. Once. Twice. Twenty times. Ashok ignored the twisting feeling in his gut and stared at the wallscreen. He pointed to a grid of coefficients. "The calibration numbers are converging." He paused. "Just like the book said."

Prem nodded reluctantly. "I don't trust numbers if I don't understand what they mean." He paused, and then admitted, "...but the code is pretty clean. It's just a PID loop." Ashok looked at him questioningly. "A proportional/integral/derivative control loop. What, you boys in optics don't use them?" His rolled eyes made clear what he thought about engineers who didn't know how PID loops worked. "This implementation is old - the revision history says it was written for something called a 'Burning Man art car.'"

Ashok gave him a second questioning look. Prem shrugged. "No, I don't know either. But it looks like it's been used in thousands of projects, so I think it's probably pretty well debugged."

Behind them the drive rattled off the ground and landed, again and again and again. On the screen the coefficients were changing less and less with each hop. Ashok turned to Prem "The drive field is making my stomach upset...shall we take a walk outside while it runs?"

Prem patted his shirt pocket and nodded.

* * *

Prem seated himself on a bench on his back porch, carefully downwind of Ashok. He blew out smoke. "How is your wife?"

"How is she? You mean, about this project?"

Prem nodded.

"Rani is getting enthusiastic - she and her friend Shakti Jeetendra have been looking at apartments in Aristillus." He smiled. "If it was anyone but Rani, I would be sick to death of hearing 'Soldner apartment this,' 'Soldner Homes that.' She goes on and on about the kitchens and the bathrooms." He paused and tilted his head in a mild concession. "I've looked at the pictures - they are quite nice." Ashok took a sip of lemonade. "But how is your wife with this?"

"Jasmine is excited too. She likes shopping - too much sometimes -" he smiled, ruefully " - so now she's getting to do that with the ship. Minivan seats from junk yards, water bottles with sip lids, army surplus meal packets." Prem paused for effect. "She went shopping for a modular bathroom for the ship, and I had to fight her to keep it to just a half bath. 'We don't need a bathtub!'"

Ashok laughed with Prem, but didn't believe the story for a second. Prem's wife was a very practical woman. The joke was forced, but it was good to break the tension. The upcoming trip was exciting - and terrifying. So much depended on doing the work right. Yes, "terrifying" was the right word.

The wind shifted and the smoke from Prem's cigarette blew towards Ashok. Ashok stood and moved to the railing. "So, about the rockets...", he said, and then trailed off.

The rockets were the most complicated subsystem. The most dangerous subsystem. They were the thing that worried him the most. And they were utterly necessary. The AG drive would launch the ship straight up - but Lucknow was 27 degrees north of the equator, and the moon never reached further north than 23 degrees. Once the ship cleared the atmosphere it would have to move south before the AG drive could throw it to the moon.

At least they only had to correct four degrees - not like poor bastards from Boston, or Moscow, or Capetown. AG drives were simple. Three moving parts, a lot of copper, and the kind of high-density batteries you could buy used at any automobile junkyard.

The rockets, as simple as they were, were still vastly more complicated. Pipes, pumps, tanks, and valves -

and none of it could be calibrated in a basement workshop. No, final calibration would happen only in use: they'd launch, break atmosphere, and then the nav program that the expats had open-sourced would take control, firing each rocket a few times to learn their characteristics and then firing them for effect.

Prem blew out smoke. "Yes. The rockets. Did the bells turn out?"

Ashok nodded. "It took two days to print them, and the sintering oven seemed to work." He shrugged. "I would have brought them over this morning, but the baby's car seat is still in the back. I can bring them over tomorrow."

"How do they look?"

"Good, I guess -"

Prem tapped his cigarette. "But? Is there a problem with them?"

"No, no problem. I just keep picturing the oxygen and kerosene mixing in the bell. The temperatures -" He fell silent.

Prem nodded. "Yes, it's scary. But I've played with the simulations. It looks solid. Really solid. There's a lot of margin."

"I know. I've looked at it too." Ashok put on a wry grin. "And anyway, I suppose it's too late too worry now."

"'The die has been cast', as they say. I've already sold my house to my son-in-law, and my retirement account has been cashed out."

"We've sold everything too. Now we just have one bag full of gold and CPUs from the list."

Prem blew out a lungful of smoke and crushed the stub of his cigarette in the ashtray. "Well, then. If there is no other choice, we'd better make this work, eh?" He stood and walked toward his workshop.

Chapter 61

2064: Atlanta Hackerspace, Atlanta, GA, Earth

Maynard leaned over the bench and tightened the pillow block that held the stator. Now he just had to put the cover plate on, and the drive would be finished.

Vince was sitting on the next workbench over, leaned back against a tool chest, arms crossed over his chest. "So, anyway, I was saying that with Economics Two Point Oh we wouldn't have to be scrounging these supplies, and, you know, buying the ones we can't scrounge."

Maynard nodded, picked up the cover plate, and lowered it into position over the drive core. "Uh huh."

"I'm serious, Maynard. The powers that be, here, they're too locked into their current mindset. They're like fish who can't even imagine living on dry land."

The cover plate fit perfectly. He wasn't surprised - it'd been machined from the expat CAD file, and all of the pieces had come out decently. Maynard picked up the screwdriver and reached for the magnetic bowl that held the screws. "Yup."

Vince hopped off the bench and walked to where Maynard was working. "Dude, you're not listening to me."

Maynard looked up and met Vince's eyes. "Yes, I am, but I'm also -"

Vince gave him that cocky grin. "Good." He hopped up onto the bench Maynard was using and pushed aside the tablet, the multimeter, and the magnetic bowl of small parts as he shimmied backwards. "Economics two point oh is something most people are blinded to - they get so wrapped up in the old tit-for-tat property model. They don't understand the postscarcity gift economy."

Maynard sighed and reached around Vince for the magnetic bowl. "Uh huh." He slide the bowl closer, pulled one screw out and started to affix the cover plate.

"Even the expats don't get the new thinking - they're still mired in One Point Oh."

Maynard looked up at Vince and furrowed his brow. "Wait a second. If you support this new economics -"

"Two Point -"

"Right, whatever, Two Point Oh. If you're so eager for that, then how is going to Aristillus, where you say the people are too dumb to get that model, going to help you?"

Vince grinned. "Good question, M, good question. I never said the expats are dumb. If they were, there'd be no point in going there - we might as well stay home, right? No, the problem isn't the wetware - it's the program running on it. They're just unenlightened. Ideas are like programs. Some people just need an idea upgrade."

"And how are you going to 'upgrade' them?"

"Simple evolution: put Two up against One Point Oh, and it will outcompete it. Make one its bitch."

"But how exactly will Two -"

Vince sighed, good-naturedly, and picked up a multimeter, and started clicking the dial. "Selfishness is evolutionarily a dead end. Copyright, property rights, relationships - it's all the same. The scarcity economy made sense when things were actually scarce, but in the digital age, things *aren't* scarce. But people are afraid of change, so we create artificial scarcity, in all areas of life." He put the multimeter down. "But you already know that, man - you and Carrie-Ann are poly, right?"

Maynard picked up the multimeter that Vince had been playing with, set it back to measure DC voltage, and then turned it off. "Well, yeah, of course. I mean we're not fundamentalists or socialcons or anything -"

"Exactly. So you see how it is. Anyway, my point is that the expats are already partway to the new thinking. They get open source, they get decentralization. It's about up-from-the-people, not down-from-the-central-authorities, right? But the expats are afraid to follow it to the logical conclusion. They claim they're against centralization, but what do they replace it with? Corporations. Which is just a petit bourgeois version of the police state. And the corporation is just an economic version of an exclusive sexual relationship. It all connects- you see that, right?"

Maynard pursed his lips and exhaled. He always got a little queasy when Vince talked about relationships - especially sexual relationships. There was something a little creepy about it - especially after the way he'd been flirting with Carrie-Ann recently. Yes, they were technically poly. *Technically*. Maybe he could change the topic.

"I'm almost done with the AG drive. How are the maneuvering rockets coming?"

"Getting there, getting there. I've got to print out the pumps and supply lines."

"So the rocket bells themselves are done?"

"Don't worry about it- it'll all work out."

Maynard secured the last screw in the AG drive cover plate. "Vince, there's not a ton of time in the schedule. We've got two weeks until -"

Vince grinned. "I know. It's under control."

"I'm working late tonight on the AG drive's calibration. If you're going to be here we could order some Thai, and -"

"Would love to, man, but I've got to be somewhere." Vince hopped off the bench. "Catch you tomorrow."

Maynard sighed and reached for his slate. The ebook said that the calibration routines took hours to run. The sooner he got started the sooner he could leave and go to bed.

Behind him he heard Vince leave and shut the door to the hackerspace.

Chapter 62

2064: Northern Logistics offices, Aristillus, Lunar Nearside

Mike twirled the stylus, occasionally pausing to tap it against the table, and rolled it through his fingers again.

The raid on the UN detention facility should be done by now, the Deladrier on its way back to Aristillus.

He'd gotten reports, a dozen of them - but the one report he wanted, a call from the Deladrier saying that everything was OK, that Darcy was on board, hadn't come.

There'd been a call from the team just before they deployed, relayed back through the cell phone network, into the cloud, and then to the moon by laser link from a forwarder in Africa.

Then there'd been video from the small stealth drones showing the billowing gray mushroom clouds that meant that the gravel boats had hit their targets.

Finally, he'd gotten the status reports from the Deladrier's on-board systems. Those reports had been accidentally binned into a spam folder for seven hours before an assistant had found and recovered them, but they showed that the ship had entered atmosphere and landed.

Mike tapped at the screen with his stylus, bring up the reports yet again. There were tantalizing hints of a story, but not enough to let him - or anyone - understand what had happened. The time-stamps showed the Deladrier had sat on the ground far too long. The landing gear readouts showed too much weight on board - but then they showed the weight falling again, a few hundred kilos at a time.

Then a few more hints - dumps of proposed flight plans, overrides deactivated on the AG drive.

And then nothing. The last data packet was truncated, cut off midstream.

The planning group had been over them and over them, looking for clues. Mike hadn't been able to add anything to their research, despite trying time and time again. He scanned the messages one more time, trying to tease meaning out of them.

Had the ship taken off again? Or was it still on the ground in Haiti, the ADF troops dead, Darcy and the rest still captives?

There was no way to tell. Even the video feed from the drones didn't help - their view of the prison had been obscured by blowing gray dust shortly after the gravel boats hit, and then - one by one - they'd gone dead.

Mike checked his inbox folder, willing some new message to arrive.

None did.

Darcy had to be alive and on her way back to Aristillus. She had to be.

And yet there was not a single piece of data to show that it was true.

"Mike?"

He hadn't eaten in the 24 hours since the gravel boats hit. In fact, he hadn't eaten since about several hours before that - the gravel boats had still been inbound when he'd last picked the smoked salmon off of a bagel and eaten some, toying with the rest.

"Mike?"

He looked up at one of the ADF guards. "Huh?"

"You've got a visitor."

Chapter 63

2064: Northern Logistics offices, Aristillus, Lunar Nearside

Leroy Fournier stood in the doorway.

Mike did a double take. Leroy? What the hell was he doing here? Had the money situation gotten so desperate that someone had invited Leroy to join the Boardroom group? Jesus. If so, it had been an epic mistake. Leroy was a snake.

Mike stared at him for a second coldly. "Leroy. I wasn't aware that you were a member of our little group."

"Mike, good to see you."

Mike didn't respond. Leroy didn't seem discomforted; he let the silence linger for a moment, then grinned. "May I come in?" He waited a moment for a response, then gave up. "Not going to meet me halfway?"

"Why don't you pay me for the damage you did when you fucked me over on the Veleka Waterworks tunnel, and then we can talk."

Leroy waved one hand. "Let's not dwell on ancient history." He stepped into the office and sat in one of the chairs across the desk from Mike, pulling on the creases in his slacks over his knees as he sat. "Let's talk about the future. It looks like your crazy little revolution is actually taking place, and I figured I should offer my assistance."

"Since when are you pro-revolution?"

"Maybe some of your libertarianness is rubbing off on me. Enlightened self-interest, right?"

Mike scowled. "I don't believe your shit for a second."

Leroy raised his eyebrows and said nothing.

"Even if I did believe you, what do you propose to contribute?"

"That question, Michael, is exactly what brings me here today. What does 'The Cause' need? What can I do to help?"

Mike looked at him. It sure looked like he was smirking as he pronounced 'The Cause.' At the very least, he was slightly amused by the whole thing. Mike had taken a dislike to this pampered family-money asshole the first time he'd met him years before, and he'd never had reason to regret that first impression.

Mike pursed his lips. "We need money. Everyone here is pledging at least 20% of their firm as collateral for currency. Some of us are doing a lot more. I'm up to 80% of Morlock. You want in? Put up some MaisonNeuve stock."

Leroy waved a hand dismissively. "The financial side is so boring, so...uncreative. Maybe there's something more interesting I can help with. What's the money for? Maybe I can help by negotiating deals, or delivering services at cost, or something."

Of course Leroy was full of shit. "Talk to Jim Pomerleau, three doors down."

Leroy smiled. "Everyone knows you're the big cheese, Mike."

"The bank needs capital. You want in? Twenty percent of your stock. Email me authentication codes. Until you do that, we've got nothing to talk about."

Leroy started to object, but the guard who'd shown Leroy in was still in the doorway and cleared his throat. Mike and Leroy both turned. The sergeant was in the new ADF pseudo uniform - work boots and jeans topped with a gray shirt that bore the rank stripe and unit patches of the Aristillus Defense Force. "Everything OK, Mr. Martin?"

"Actually, Sergeant, Mr. Fournier and I are all done here - can you show him out?"

"You got it." The ADF man turned to Leroy. "You ready to go?" It was clear the sergeant wasn't asking.

Leroy tilted his head and smiled at Mike. "To the point. As much as we differ, Mike, that's one thing I've always liked about you." He stood. "I'll talk to my accountants, and we'll see what we can do. You'll hear from me tomorrow - day after at the latest. Sound good?" Leroy extended his hand.

Mike didn't believe him for a second. He stared at Leroy, pointedly ignoring the hand. After a moment Leroy shrugged, turned, and followed the sergeant out.

As soon as they were gone Mike pulled out his phone. "Lieutenant? I just had a visit from Leroy Fournier. I don't trust him at all. We need to find out how he got in here, who invited him. We also need to sweep the entire office for bugs - every room he so much as walked through - ASAP."

Chapter 64

Bill leaned forward in the driver's seat and pushed the intercom button as the Trusted Security van's autopilot pulled into traffic "You two back there - we'll drop you at headquarters at level three. You can catch a cab there, OK?" After a moment without a response he let the button go.

Bill leaned back and let the van drive itself. After a moment he looked at Grigory in the adjacent seat. "Why do you keep staring at that monitor?"

Grigory said nothing for a moment, and then tilted his head toward the screen and said in his thick Russian accent, "The girl - she's familiar. Those blue eyeglasses. How do I know her?"

Bill looked at the monitor and shrugged. "Got me; I can't keep up with every woman you - " He paused. "Wait a second, I know -"

Grigory beat him to it. "She's the one on the news - the thing with DC Minute and the fake videos."

Bill shook his head. "What video? No, she's familiar because she popped up in the system a while back. Aggravated assault. She's the one who hit Mike Martin with a motorcycle helmet and broke his skull."

Grigory shook his head. "No, it is you who are confused. She's the one from the video."

"I don't know what video you're talking about, but she's the one who assaulted Martin. I'll prove it. And you'll buy me lunch."

"Deal."

Bill swung his keyboard tray toward himself and started typing as the van slowed and took a corner. Grigory hammered at his own keyboard.

Grigory finished first. "Ha! Look!" He pointed to his screen, where there was a freeze-frame of Louisa on DC Minute.

Bill squinted as he looked at it. "Whatever. Here's the warrant I was talking about." He pointed to his own screen.

Grigory looked over, and shook his head. "That doesn't count - the warrant was never issued. Look, see? History says 'pending,' then 'canceled'. It was never issued."

The two squabbled over the lunch bet for a few minutes. Finally Bill sighed. "Let's call it a tie; no one buys." He paused for a moment. "So. What do we do with them?"

"What do you mean?"

"Do we book her?"

"Book her? For what? There are no warrants in our system."

"Maybe someone else wants her."

Grigory shook his head. "If Al's, or LAWS, or Negotiated Rights had warrants for her, we would see it in the system."

"But if Abacha or Sharper or Tiaenzie -"

"We don't have interchange agreements with them; you know that."

"Just let me check."

"Why waste your time? Without an agreement, it's useless."

Bill shrugged. "Can't hurt to check." He tapped at his keyboard.

Grigory looked on skeptically. "William, you are doing a stupid thing. Even if you find something, it's outside our mandate. Today we are assigned to Jackson Real Estate. We arrest pickpockets. We confiscate paint from graffiti kids. If we start looking

up warrants from other companies we could get fired
-"

"Ah ha! There! Goldwater."

Grigory pulled up the same page on his screen, then shook his head. "That's not a warrant."

"No, but she's got a three-day term for trespassing and only served one day. It's still an open contract. They'll take her." He tapped more keys. "And look. This 'Hugh Haig.' I bet that's the other kid in back."

The van slowed in preparation for a corner, but Bill called up the auto drive screen and hit the cancel button, and then selected Goldwater instead. The screen beeped an acknowledgement and the van accelerated back to speed.

Grigory looked out the window to the right where the tunnel that led to the Trusted Security headquarters flashed past. "Bill, this is stupid. This isn't what we're getting paid for."

"Relax, partner - no one checks our logs. We'll be OK."

Grigory crossed his arms. "Why are you sticking your nose in this?"

"Did I ever tell you why I'm here in Aristillus?"

Grigory shook his head.

"Back in Tennessee, I was up on charges. Feds were charging me with possession with intent to distribute. They had witnesses and video. Ten kilos, which is enough tobacco to kick in a multiplier. I should be on a labor gang clearing rubble in California right now. Only reason I'm not is that Mike Martin founded Aristillus, so I had someplace to run to.

"This Louisa Teer in back hit Martin with a motorcycle helmet. The man basically saved my life. Putting her behind bars is the least I can do."

Grigory pursed his lips and shook his head but didn't say anything.

Chapter 65

2064: Atlanta Hackerspace, Atlanta, GA, Earth

The door to the hackerspace opened, and Vince walked in and peeled off his leather jacket.

Maynard looked up. "Vince? Jesus, where've you been? I've been trying to reach you for two days."

"Been busy. Lots of parties, lots of -"

Maynard shook his head. "Vince, that's not cool. Seriously not cool. This ship is your project -"

Vince forced a smile through what looked to be a hang over. "And you're doing a hell of a job supporting me on it. I appreciate that, Maynard, I really do." He clapped a hand on Maynard's shoulder.

Maynard put down the multimeter. "Vince, I appreciate that, but we need to install the rockets. We've got almost everything else done. The ship is down in the garage, and it's ready to go - but we need the rockets." He paused. "So where are they?"

Vince looked aside. "There's a small problem."

"What problem?" Maynard felt his voice on the edge of cracking. He'd been working so long and so hard on this, and everyone else in the hackerspace claimed that they were involved, and yet he was the only one who seemed to be doing any work. Vince, Jimbo, Little Steve - even his own girlfriend Carrie-Ann wasn't around the place very often. Everyone else was spending their nights out at a never-ending stream of "Bon Voyage" parties, and sleeping in to recover from them. But there wasn't going to be a damned launch if they didn't get this shit done, and no one was helping him. He'd asked folks again and again, and everyone had laughed it off. Oh, sure, they showed up for the fun parts, like decorating the ship, or deciding what to name it. But for the grunt work? For the welding, for the grinding, for the endless hours of AG drive calibration?

Even Vince, who had been in this with him from the beginning, wasn't showing up any more.

"Damn it Vince, what problem?"

Vince held up too hands. "Woah, Maynard, slow down. Not cool. Look, you just relax and we'll get through this together, OK?"

Maynard crossed his arms and looked at Vince skeptically.

"No, seriously, Maynard. Come on, relax." Vince smiled encouragingly. "Uncross your arms...yeah, that's right. Body language, man. So, are we going to work through this together?"

Maynard said nothing.

"Come on, are we?"

Grudgingly, Maynard mumbled, "Yes."

"OK, that's what I want to hear."

"So what's the problem?"

"The printer says that there's a DRM flag on them, and it refuses to print them."

Maynard exploded. "What? God damn it, the printer only updates the government prohibited items list once a month. The last weapons-and-devices update was two weeks ago. You said that you were going to print out the rockets before that!"

Vince shrugged. "Yeah, and I meant to. I'm sorry, man. Shit came up. You know how it is."

"No, I DON'T know how it is."

"Look, Maynard, we can get through this together. There must be some way to print those rockets."

Maynard wiped a hand over his face, and felt sweat on his forehead. "Yeah, there is."

"Go on."

"I've got some five year old printer firmware."

"Problem solved!"

Maynard turned to Vince. "No, the problem is *not* solved. Installing that firmware is a *felony*, Vince. I could get serious jail time for that."

"Hey, look, this whole project is a -"

"No, this whole project is not a felony. Well, OK, yes, it is...but it's not the kind of felony that they're prosecuting that much. Illegal firmware on a printer? That's a BATFEEIN grade four offense. If anyone ever hears that I did this, I don't get a letter in the mail and call my dad's lawyer - I get a tactical team surrounding my apartment and flashbangs through the windows."

"Maynard, don't be dramatic, you -"

"I'm not being dramatic. This shit is *real*. This happens to people."

Vince put up his hands. "OK, you're right. I apologize. This shit is real, and I appreciate the risk you're taking."

Maynard breathed out, finally feeling the least bit vindicated. "OK. Thank you."

"So you're on it, then? You'll print the rockets?"

"Damn it, Vince, I'm doing all the work!"

"I know, and -"

"If I print the rockets, you do all the plumbing."

"OK, I will."

"Promise!"

"I promise." Vince picked up his leather jacket from the back of the chair where he'd dropped it. "Look, I've gotta go right now, but I'll check in later. Thanks, M."

Chapter 66

Leroy sat in the back of his Mercedes as it accelerated away from the Northern Logistics office. Now that he was alone, he let the smile that had been threatening to break out finally do so. He'd done good work just now.

And speaking of good work, he deserved to celebrate - and celebrate well. Funds had been tight recently, but all that would be changing shortly. He could afford to splurge. What did he want to eat?

He had it - Caldava's. Good food, and a good cellar. He deserved a celebratory drink.

He pulled out his phone and called Sheila, a blonde who was always happy to see him. She answered and tried to chit-chat, but he cut through the nonsense. "Be at Caldava's in half an hour. Wear a nice dress; it's a classy place."

He hung up, then he realized he was getting a bit ahead of himself - he was arranging the celebration before locking down the deal. He placed a second call.

"I've verified the location. No, not until I get my end. Yes, I know I've already got the pardon - I'm talking about the rest of it." He listened, then nodded. "OK, let me check."

Leroy pulled out his slate and maneuvered through a few screens, and then went back to the phone. "No, I don't see the money *or* the letter of intent for the governorship." He listened for a moment. "No. Good intentions are not the same thing as a funds in the account or a signed letter. Until I get those, we don't have a deal, and you don't get the location."

Leroy listened for a moment, then shook his head. "I don't care if he has to be woken up, Major. If you want

Mike Martin, you'll get me the money and the governorship letter. And you'd better move fast; Martin looked suspicious. I wouldn't be surprised if they're already packing up for a new location."

Leroy hung up and smiled. He'd heard the desperation in the Major's voice - he'd have his letter before desert was served.

* * *

Leroy was enjoying his coq au vin and telling Sheila about his recent successes. The stupid twat wasn't listening, though - and now she was interrupting to complain that her blanquette de veau wasn't browned. He gritted his teeth at her idiocy. The dish had "white" right in the title. White meat, white sauce. She could dress up for a classy place on occasion, but that didn't mean she knew how to carry herself or to converse intelligently.

Still, she wasn't here for her conversational skills. Her abilities -

His phone rang. He pulled it from his suit pocket, looked at it, and smiled. He'd been right - it was before dessert was served. He deliberately waited for the third ring before answering.

"Major, what's the good news? It is? Wonderful. Let me check." He pulled out his slate. "I'm checking the digital signatures now - and - we're good." He tapped a button to send an email. "I just sent you the location. Look for double doors and a big blue sign that says 'Northern Logistics.'" He paused, listening. "Good luck. I'm sure we'll talk again soon." He carefully replaced his phone in his inside suit pocket.

He grinned at Sheila, and then let his attention wander down.

She'd have an excellent rack even in Earth gravity, but between one- sixth g, and that Dermot Chantille white dress he'd bought for her, it was phenomenal.

A thought nagged him, though. Should he also call Stacy? He had a lot to celebrate tonight.

He thought for a second and then reached for his phone again.

Chapter 67

2064: the Deladrier, in elliptical orbit around the Moon

Darcy floated in the center of the cockpit. With one hand she grabbed the door jamb then pulled herself into the passenger compartment.

It was disgusting - and heart-wrenching.

The sound was bad. The whimpering of people with injuries from interrogation sessions back in the detention block merged with the sobs and occasional cries of those who'd broken bones in the brutal acceleration of the emergency lift.

The sights weren't any better. Toward the front of the cabin she could see prisoners, faces twisted in fear. Further back details became fuzzy in the low light, but she could still see dozens more injured and suffering. And then, almost out of view in the darkness at the rear of the compartment she could just make out the outline of the corpse of one of the ADF soldiers.

It was a mercy that he'd finally passed. The day he'd spent alternatively moaning and screaming from the pain of his gunshot wounds had been - if not quite as hard on the other passengers as it had been on him - bad enough.

Worse than either the evidence of her ears or eyes was the smell. The stink of urine and feces was overpowering. With the bathroom unit thrown overboard, the prisoners had been forced to relieve themselves into plastic bags scavenged from a parts locker. In zero gravity it had been a mostly futile endeavor - urine and worse had leaked out and floated through the air and was now slicked on people's skin and hair. Which in turn gave rise to vomiting and the acidic stench mixed with the other gag-inducing notes.

The air was so think that the *taste* of the filth was inescapable. Darcy tried to swallow to clear her mouth, but failed - she hadn't had a drink in over a day.

Tears started to well in her eyes, but in the weightlessness they just hung there, obscuring her vision.

She grabbed the bulkhead and pulled herself back into the cockpit. Prem looked up at her with haggard eyes. "Is there anything -?"

She shook her head to stop the conversation before it started and turned away, floating near the ceiling of the cockpit, trying to carve out a little space for herself.

She rubbed the tears away. She had water to cry with, but not enough to swallow.

She was a failure. This was all her fault.

Darn it! Why hadn't she remembered that a fast launch would mean more drag? She'd upped the acceleration to take advantage of the better efficiency of the AG drive - and entirely forgotten about atmospheric drag.

This wasn't advanced stuff - this was basic. She'd *known* this. For God's sake, she'd written about it in the instruction manual for the open source drive, in a big warning page telling people not to override the navigation defaults.

And yet in the chaos and the fear in the courtyard, she'd forgotten it. This wasn't like a mistake on a college test - this mattered. Because of her mistake, the Deladrier was in the wrong place at the wrong time.

Which meant that they were all going to die.

Over the last twenty-four hours she'd run a hundred simulations, and finally even set up a small pool of genetic algorithms, all ruthlessly breeding and being selected, generation after generation, for their ability to get the ship to the moon. None of her hundreds of attempts, and none of the hundreds of millions of frantically breeding software agents, had come up with a solution. The closest any of them had come was suggesting that they burn all of the maneuvering fuel to throw the Deladrier into a drastically elongated elliptical orbit around the moon. So she'd done that - and now, instead of dying in interplanetary space, they were all going to die in lunar orbit.

Darcy sobbed again, and then took a deep breath, rubbed her eyes clear, and rotated to face Prem.

She composed herself and tried to put a touch of humor in her voice. "The ship hasn't magically grown a replacement antenna since I last asked?" Even as she said the words they felt dead in her mouth.

Prem look up wearily. After a pause he shook his head sadly and turned back to his screen. He was scrolling around a map of the moon aimlessly, occasionally zooming in on one crater or another. Finally he shut the window and turned to her. "You know, I took a nap earlier and dreamed that the ship had a spare antenna, to replace the one that was shot off in the battle."

Darcy smiled sadly. "You know what? I actually had the same dream." She suddenly had a thought. "I know that the diagnostics say that the antenna isn't there, but is there any chance that it's the diagnostics that are -"

Prem shook his head. "I already thought of that and I went digging. I found a dialog for the embedded controllers in the antenna gimbal mount. The gimbal itself is missing. No antenna, no gimbal mount. Nothing."

Darcy turned away from Prem and pretended to tighten the straps holding a fire extinguisher to the wall. A ragged emotional breath started to escape and she covered it by faking a cough. As she moved her hands from the fire extinguisher to some other piece of equipment that also didn't need to be touched, she cursed herself yet again for allowing the last few men onto the ship. She'd known better. Heck, she'd known better when she was eight years old and her uncle Barton had handed her a musty old paperback with a story about this very situation.

And now she was going to die because in the confusion and fear of the prison break she'd allowed herself to be overcome with sentimentality. Since when did emotions trump math?

She tasted something coppery and realized that she was biting her lip hard enough to draw blood. She unclenched her jaw and turned away from the wall towards the controls. There, on the screen: eighteen more hours of air.

"Prem, I'm going to take another nap." Maybe she'd dream of more air. Or rescue. Or maybe she'd dream of being back home with Mike. Heck, even a dream about forgetting to show up for a college exam would be better than this.

Prem nodded mutely.

Darcy pulled herself down into her chair, strapped in, wrapped her arms around herself, and tried to fall asleep.

The ship was clean - clean and quiet - and her childhood dog Peanut Butter was there. He ran around the cockpit. Ran? There was gravity, apparently, but just for him. Then Peanut Butter jumped into her lap. She rubbed her face into his fur. Where had Peanut Butter been for the last twenty years? She'd missed him so much. And how had he gotten on the ship? She hugged him, but then he was gone again. Where had he gone? She unbuckled and floated to the back of the ship to look for him. There was some loud banging sound. Was Peanut Butter making that sound? Where was he? Under one of the seats?

The clanging was loud.

Darcy opened her eyes. The light was dimmer than it had been a minute before. She rubbed her face. She'd been dreaming. Of course.

The clanging continued. She looked around, trying to locate the source of the sound, and noticed that Prem's seat was empty.

That was odd. And something else was odd - the background noise in the ship had changed: instead of moans there was an excited babble.

What was going on?

She was unstrapping when Prem flew into the cockpit.

"Prem! What's happening?"

"Something has -"

Then a scrabbling sound, and finally a deep snicking sound, like a giant latch sliding home.

She looked at the hull over her head. Was something grabbing the ship?

Was this - was this a *rescue*?

There was no way the lunar forces could have found them out here in the darkness. And certainly no way that, after finding them, they could rendezvous with them.

But they had.

She found herself taking deep breaths. She was going to live. And the realization pushed her to the edge of crying.

She took a deep breath and forced the tears away.

She let the thought roll over in her head: she was going to live. She felt whiplashed by the idea. After days of despair she'd finally brought herself to accept that she was as good as dead, that she'd never see Mike again, never have kids, never get to see the free lunar society they'd both dreamed of.

And now, having achieved some sort of peace with that idea, she was being thrust back into all the messy details of life - and uncertainty and worry.

How had the rescue ship found them? They were a flyspeck - a thermally insulated, stealthed, black-painted flyspeck. And if that wasn't enough, they were in a weird elliptical orbit. They should have been impossible to find.

A muddy voice boomed from somewhere on the far side of the ship hull. "Please bang on the hull twice if you can hear this."

Darcy pulled herself to the hull and slapped her hand on the steel...and it didn't make a sound.

She looked around. The fire extinguisher - she could use that. Darcy twisted to reach it, and as she did so she saw - through the open cockpit door and the Sargasso of floating prisoners and detritus - one of the wounded ADF soldiers pulled himself to the hull, a large tool box towed behind him. A moment later he was banging it against the ceiling.

The voice boomed again. "Communication has been established. Please prepare for acceleration in nine minutes."

The passenger compartment exploded in shouted questions.

The voice didn't answer.

Prem pulled himself into his chair and started a timer on his console.

A moment later the ADF soldier started banging on the wall with the fire extinguisher again. Bang. Bang Bang. Bang.

Darcy listened. It was Morse code.

"W h o a r e y o u"

The banging stopped.

The booming voice answered. "This is a restricted delegate of Gamma."

Darcy blinked. Gamma?

"D i d t h e o t h e r t r o o p s s u r v -"

The voice cut the question off. "This is a dedicated navigation agent. The current skills package manifest does not include abilities to answer questions on topics other than navigation."

There was a pause.

Gamma's voice boomed again. "Please prepare for acceleration in eight minutes."

Darcy wiped the streaks of dried tears from her face and clicked her harness tight.

Chapter 68

2064: Lai Docks and Air Traffic Control, Aristillus, Lunar Nearside

Albert Lai reached for his second cup of tea. He needed it - and perhaps a third. He was still groggy after the high-priority phone call from Gamma that had woken him in the middle of the night. But even if he wasn't fully awake yet, the men and women on the crash teams and ambulances staged around Lai Docks were.

Strictly speaking, he didn't need to be here, but General Dewitt had given him permission to leave the Northern Logistics space as long as he took an armed escort. Albert scowled briefly at the memory. Dewitt could have been more tactful - had he really needed to add the phrase "low-value target"?

Albert took another sip and stared at the screens, but his mind wasn't on the data there.

So Dewitt saw him as low-value. But had Dewitt gotten a phone call from Gamma? He had not. No, he - Albert - had. That, at least, would be something to brag about with the Group. How many people had Gamma talked to in Aristillus? Five? Ten, maybe?

He put the teacup down and looked out through the window, down into the dock. The huge overhead doors were rolled open, showing the blackness of space above. On the floor of the dock both cradles 3 and 4 were empty.

Gamma's voice had surprised him. He'd expected - he didn't quite know - something more artificial. Something more robotlike. The reality, though, was less high-tech than it was amusingly middle American. He'd heard others say that Gamma's voice was cool and emotionless, but now that he'd heard it himself he didn't agree. Or, rather, the coolness and lack of drama seemed reasonable and not particularly noteworthy. The thing that did strike him was how precise the diction was - and how the sentences were all unambiguous and clear. Albert approved...but the dark thought did cross his mind for a moment that the consistency and clarity were the same attributes one would use when talking to a farm animal. Was Gamma so crisp and clear because he thought that people were so stupid that it *needed* to be that clear? He wondered, not for the first time, if the American BuSuR might not have been right to shut down the Gamma project.

He put the thought aside and looked at the navigation screen again. Nothing yet. Down below in the hangar, a foam truck pulled into position next to the four ambulances from First Medical and four more from Chinese Benevolence Hospital. He raised his teacup and -

A beep. Incoming ship. Albert put his tea down and looked at the screen. Where the nav screen normally displayed a rectangle for a cargo ship, or a circle for the Grace Under Pressure atmosphere tanker, this time it showed a question mark. Albert leaned forward and looked at the metadata. His eyebrows drew together. When Gamma said it needed crash teams for an incoming ship, he'd expected the ship in question to be the Deladrier - assumed it without question. But the Deladrier should be blaring transponder codes through all its antennae, which would mean a triangle on the board.

But there, on the screen, the question mark blinked.

What did it mean?

He sat back, his tea forgotten. He'd know soon enough.

Three minutes later Albert watched the Deladrier descend through the huge overhead bay doors - but the shape was wrong.

On top of the dark black hull of the Deladrier was clamped something else - another piece of machinery. He didn't recognize it - it was an explosion of struts, spherical fuel tanks, rocket bells, and a large bank of something else, maybe electrical in nature, based on the cables that snaked through it.

Albert looked at Michael Stuart-Test at the control board. Michael caught his eye and shrugged in answer. Albert turned back to the window and watched the paired machines gently touch down.

The overhead doors slowly began closing.

* * *

Bill Lindon wore a full spacesuit, in keeping with corporate safety regs, but he kept the faceplate up. That was allowed. He also had his gloves off - which wasn't - but if he was going to be rendering first aid, he'd be damned if he was going to do it with gloves on.

He squinted and looked out through the ambulance window. The overhead doors were almost shut - and then, with a thud that reverberated through the walls, the floor, and even into the ambulance where he stood, they closed. A moment later an emergency pressurization started and the tornado howl as oceans of air flooded Lai Docks assaulted him. It went on for interminable minutes - the space was huge - and then it tapered and slowed. The light beside the ambulance airlock turned green. He hit the button and the door whooshed open.

As he stepped out and onto the concrete dock floor, the Deladrier's ramp began to descend. He walked toward it, his medical kit in one hand - and then the smell hit him. Jesus! He gagged - literally gagged. After bending forward and spitting onto the concrete to clear his mouth, he flipped the faceplate down and toggled a quick purge of the suit air.

The purge helped, but not entirely - the fetid aroma lingered. What the hell had happened in there? It smelled like a shit-storm in there. Like a literal storm that had knocked over porta-potties and hurled their contents around. No, it was worse than that - it smelled like someone took the mess from that, poured it all into a small RV, and left the thing to stew in Mississippi summer heat for a few days.

The smell was still leaking into his suit, and Bill snapped his gloves on. The first two freed prisoners were walking down the ramp, carrying a third man between them. Behind them more people were spilling out. A dozen. Two dozen. More. Jesus - how many people were crammed in there? And then he put the thought aside and got down to work. He scanned the refugees as they exited. Did any have broken bones? Obvious bleeding? No, most seemed OK. Let the junior personnel attend to them - he'd stay here and take the first serious case he saw.

There was a gap in the flow of prisoners, and Bill looked up at the ship as he waited. The Deladrier was weird. Really weird. The core ship itself was strange enough - small, armored, with heavy shock absorbers - but bolted to the top of it was some other machine of an entirely different design. The upper device was a tangle of struts that had the flat gray appearance of sintered aluminum. Inside the embrace of the struts were a cluster of spherical tanks. He'd gotten a 'shipwork' endorsement on his Johnson Clinic EMT rating last month, and he knew from that class that all propellant and air tanks should be color coded, but these weren't. Weirder yet was the electrical system. That looked like a bank of flywheel batteries, obviously to store electricity for the AG drive - but these were strange. They were bigger than the usual models, had no fragmentation-containment shielding...and no dust shielding at all. He shook his head. That might work out in space or in filtered air, but expose it the lunar surface, and they'd degrade in short order. Who the hell would use custom- designed flywheel batteries when the regular ones -

"Bill, we've got two FIRTS and a bleeder!"

"Right, sorry." Bill tore his gaze from the ship and picked up his medical kit.

Chapter 69

2064: Northern Logistics offices, Aristillus, Lunar Nearside

Mike yawned and pushed the button for another espresso. He'd been up late worrying about the lack of word from the rescue mission, and he'd overslept as a consequence. Crap. He'd wanted to get up early and talk to Javier before breakfast about his conversation with the Dogs, but now the day was already under way.

He was pouring a splash of milk into his coffee when two uniformed Aristillus Defense Force soldiers ran past the Northern Logistics kitchenette.

That was odd.

Mike sipped his espresso.

Several more men ran past.

What the hell?

Mike stepped out of the kitchenette into the corridor and tried to wave down a scurrying aide. When he didn't stop Mike stepped in his way and blocked him. "Hey! What's going on?"

"The Deladrier just landed!"

Darcy! Mike put his espresso down on the arm of a nearby chair, where it immediately fell and spilled, but he didn't notice, because he was already running for the door.

As he approached two ADF guards stepped into his way. He recognized them. "Guys, the Deladrier -"

The burly one shook his head. "Absolutely not. We've got orders."

"Listen to me. I'm going. Darcy -"

The burlier of the two held up a hand. "General Dewitt was clear. He said that you *in particular* had to stay here. We don't know anything yet. All we've got is reports. The snatch teams are still out there, somewhere, and this might be an attempt to grab you."

Mike started to push past them, but the same guard stood firm and put a hand on his shoulder. His fingers felt like they were carved from oak. Mike thought for a second about shoving him, but the guard seemed to read his thought. "Mr. Martin, I know how you feel, but you can't."

"Where's Dewitt right now?"

"He's at the port. He's supervi-"

"I'm going to call Dewitt and get him to give you specific orders."

"Fine with me. If he says it's good, I'll escort you there myself."

Mike pulled out his phone - and it immediately rang. He looked - Dewitt. He blinked, then answered it. "Matt, I was just about to -"

The voice at the other end was a whisper. "Mike, it's me -"

"*Darcy*?!"

"Mike, Matt lent me his phone -"

"Are you OK? What are you -"

"I'm dehydrated. My head is killing me, and I - look, Matt is telling me to tell you to stay where you are. Will you do that?"

"Darce, I need to get -"

"Promise me, Mike. Matt says it's not safe."

Mike balled his free hand into a fist. God *damn* it! "Fine. But when will you -"

Darcy's voice was soft and trailed off, as if she was falling asleep. "They've got me on an IV. Fluids and electrolytes. Give me 12 hours and I'll get some clothes and meet up with you. Mike, I love you."

"Clothes?" Mike blinked. "What the hell do you mean?"

Dewitt's voice answered. "Mike, it's Matt. I know it's hard, but I need you hang tight there. You'll see Darcy soon enough. Now stay the fuck in place, OK?"

Mike grimaced and hung up without replying.

God damn it.

Dehydrated? Clothes? What the hell was going on? And he was supposed to just stay here and do nothing while Darcy was out there, recovering from - whatever the hell had happened to her in that prison camp?

He paced back to his office, walking past the chair with the spilled coffee without noticing it. What was he supposed to do for several hours? Just *wait*?

Reluctantly he brought the plans for the D-class TBM up on the wallscreen, spun it around to different angles, zoomed in on the ring placement arms, and then shut the file. He flipped through news channels and blogs and skimmed the rumors of an earthquake in Haitian Dominican Protectorate. The usual propaganda rags had a variety of videos - some faked, some just talking heads pontificating - purporting to show that the Haiti gravel boat impacts were, variously, a terrorist attack by Texan rebels, a laser attack by "tax cheats" at Aristillus, or some mysterious manifestation of an ecological crisis.

He shut the browser in disgust and looked for his coffee mug, which seemed to have gone missing.

"Mike? We've got a guest for you." His head whipped around. Darcy? Already? She'd said "hours", and it was only -

The troops maneuvered a woman in, and then took the blindfold off her. The woman - a girl, really, probably not even 25 - pushed a few strands of stray brunette hair behind one ear and stuck out her hand. "Selena Hargraves. It's nice to meet you."

"I - who are you?"

Selena's face fell a bit. "Selena Hargraves. Freelance journalist. I set up an interview with your people a week or so ago."

Mike stared at her uncomprehendingly. "I -"

Selena stammered, "I really hope we can do this interview. I went through a lot to get here - your people took away my phone, drove me around for an hour in the back of a van -"

Mike had his moorings now - yes, he remembered. This was the kid who'd been friends with that little shit Hugh, the senator's kid. But then she'd also done that other thing.

Mike took her hand and shook. "Right - Selena. You're the one who did that video exposing Hugh and that bi- uh, and that woman. Louisa. The one who hit me with my own helmet?"

She beamed when Mike praised her expose video but the grin faded when Mike mentioned the fight. "Yes, that was me. Ummm...I'm really sorry about the helmet thing. I was there. I had no idea she - I mean, I wish I could have prevented it." She stopped stammering, closed her eyes for a moment, and composed herself. "If it makes a difference, that's one of the things that made me realize that I didn't really like the crowd I was hanging with."

Mike nodded. "Apology accepted. Anyway, those last few videos you released were excellent. Have you thought about entering them into any of the prize contests that the committee has set up?"

"Uh, actually, my exposé of Louisa already won one of the prizes - and I'm hoping to get another one with this interview." She smiled. "Which provides as good a segué as any." She reached into her bag and pulled out a small camera module and put it on the desk. "The ADF guys went over this before I got into the van and deactivated the locator - ah, you probably don't care about that. Anyway, I know you're a busy man."

Mike suppressed a bitter laugh. He had nothing at all to do, and was trapped here, waiting for the chance to talk to Darcy. To find out if she was all right. To find out what had happened. He wasn't at all busy - perhaps the interview would distract him from his spiraling thoughts.

Selena continued, "So I'll move straight to the oral history portion of the interview -"

At that moment there was an explosion somewhere close by - maybe even inside the Northern Logistics office space.

Mike's head snapped around as rifle fire rang out.

What the -

Suddenly he knew. The snatch team. Their timing was perfect - three- quarters of the ADF guards were down at the docks helping with the Deladrier.

Mike turned to the second exit from the room, the one behind his desk - and then realized that he wasn't in his office at Morlock Engineering. The Northern Logistics office he'd commandeered had only one door.

He looked at it and realized he had to make a decision, and do it right this second: run or hunker down?

Shit.

Run.

But wait - damn it! The girl. After that video she'd made, there might be a bounty on her too. If he ran, he'd have to take her with him.

He looked at the door -

- and suddenly there was shouting and shooting in the corridor immediately outside it.

What was her name? He couldn't remember. "You! Get under the desk!" Selena, eyes wide and face drawn, nodded and hurried to comply. There was another string of shots just outside the door. Mike grabbed her shoulder and pushed her under the desk, unholstered his pistol, and racked the slide.

The door exploded inward, the flimsy hollow-core construction no challenge to the battering ram.

Everything seemed to happen in slow motion. The soldier in the door was wearing a black insignialess uniform - black armor, dark straps and equipment, a black helmet, and a black balaclava. Mike felt like he was a kilometer away, watching it through a long tunnel. His pistol seemed to take long minutes to rise, rise, rise into position. Then, finally, there it was. He was squeezing the trigger. His sight picture - was it good enou- ?

Mike distantly heard his own shot. Was this really happening? The soldier kept coming. He tried to squeeze the trigger again. Was the gun working? Mike couldn't hear anything. The soldier tripped forward and fell. Mike watched him fall, and then looked up - a second soldier. He tried to squeeze his trigger and -

Mike screamed, his entire body racked with electric pain. All of his muscles tensed and he felt the checkered grip of the pistol grinding deep into his palm. He couldn't breathe. He was convulsing and falling. Then suddenly, the pain was gone and he felt the pistol being ripped from his hand. A soldier loomed over him holding a long black prod. He tried to raise an arm to fend it off -

Mike screamed involuntarily as all of his muscles convulsed again.

"Roll over, hands behind your back!"

The pain ended and Mike tried to roll over but he wasn't fast enough. Another prod, another convulsion, another long scream ripped from him. His entire body was on fire.

"Stop resisting! Roll over!"

This time he managed to roll onto his stomach. A knee was driven into the small of his back and he felt new pain as vertebrae ground together. His arms were wrenched behind him and something in his shoulder tore. Gloved fingers snaked into his hair and grabbed, twisting his head to one side. He was facing the desk. There was just a finger's breadth of space between the modesty panel and the carpet. He saw the reporter's - Selena's - hands and knees.

A tug on his wrists and he was yanked to his feet. His right shoulder screamed again. On the desk he saw his slate and Selena's camera module.

Then a hood was pulled over his head and cinched tight around his neck.

As he was dragged out of the office he heard the gunfire continue.

Chapter 70

2064: Situation Room of the West Wing, White House, Washington DC, Earth

General Restivo approached the two Marine guards outside the Situation Room. Both snapped salutes, which he returned. "Are they inside?"

The closer Marine focused on him. "No, sir. You're the first."

Restivo furrowed his brow. The first? By now the various aides and assistants of the other attendees should be there. Unless -

Suddenly he realized. Shit. This wasn't going to be a full meeting. It was going to be just him and the president. Which meant something bad - was she going to hang the Haitian debacle on him? There was no reason to, no justification. The black sites weren't even under his command. Hell, they weren't even in the DoD, properly speaking. But the nonapproved media had been covering the Nan Garde debacle a lot recently.

Shit.

He rubbed one hand over his face. He could live with losing his job - in this country, once you rose high enough in the bureaucracy you knew that you served at the whim of your superiors.

He could handle humiliation - he didn't give a shit about what most people in DC thought of him. He could be denounced and live with that.

Might she go further, though?

He'd seen people charged with dereliction of duty, sometimes for things they had nothing to do with. He could feel beads of sweat gathering in armpits, and they felt cold. Might she do an Article 94? It didn't matter what the facts were; a special prosecutor and a review board that wanted to curry favor meant that the conclusion would be whatever she wanted it to be. Should he -

The two Marine guards stiffened.

Restivo whirled. President Johnson and her entourage had arrived.

The president raised her eyebrows. "General."

Restivo found that his mouth was dry. He tried to swallow but couldn't. Finally he croaked out, "Ma'am."

"We don't need to go inside; this won't take very long."

Restivo tensed.

"I got the memo that your team grabbed Martin."

General Restivo blinked, feeling wildly off base. "Yes, m-"

"Good. How is the invasion fleet coming along?"

Restivo swallowed - this time successfully. He was trying to follow the unexpected arc of the conversation and was at sea. "Ah, we're on schedule, and -"

The president held up one finger, stopping him. Restivo dropped silent. "Good. There is nothing - *nothing* - more important than that schedule."

Restivo nodded mutely.

"One last thing - do you have any recommendations for someone to replace Hodzic? The PKs are going to take the blame for the Nan Garde mess, but I need an American behind the scenes to make sure it doesn't happen again."

Restivo's eyes were wide. That was it? That was all the president wanted? "Ah, ma'am - maybe General Abassi. He's being underutilized in logistics right now, but he -"

"Fine." Next to the president, Gene Wilson made a note in his slate. Themba tilted her head and looked at Restivo under her brows. "Make sure you stay on schedule." And with that, she turned. A moment later she and her retinue were gone.

Restivo turned to the Marine guards, looking for some confirmation that all of that had really happened - that the entire meeting had lasted less than a minute, that the president wasn't outraged over the Nan Garde raid, that he himself wasn't in trouble.

The guards stared silently ahead, not meeting his eyes.

Restivo rubbed a hand over his face.

Chapter 71

2064: Senator Linda Haig's Office, Tester Senate Building

Jim tapped his slate, bringing up a screen of numbers. "The polls are looking better. We're not quite back up to 45%, but the trend is in the right direction. We're recovering from the - ah, the -"

Senator Haig rolled her eyes. "There's no sense in beating around the bush. Call it what it was - that video was a debacle."

Jim shrugged. "The disaster in Nan Garde is bigger news. *Much* bigger. And all of that mud is sticking to the president, so even if your favorables aren't as high as we'd like, hers are down too. And that -" he tapped the slate "- drags the entire Populist faction down."

"How is the cash situation?"

"We're managing it well, spending just enough -"

"We don't need to manage it - we need to spend it. Fast. We need the regular donors back on board, and fifty percent favorables are the magic number: if we get that, then the taps open up for us."

Jim bit his upper lip. "Not from what I'm hearing. Which brings me to my next point - the cash from the health care contractors was good, but it's not enough. We need a Hail Mary pass, and I'm out of ideas."

Linda Haig smiled. "Don't worry, Jim. I've got a lead on something that's going to blow your socks off."

Jim looked up from his slate. "Funds?"

"No. Information that will change the race."

"What is it?"

"Sorry; I've got to keep this one close to my vest or it could slip away from me."

Jim pursed his lips. "That's not how this works, Linda. We're a team. I'm all in to help you, and if I'm going to do my job, I need you to trust me."

"I trust you, Jim. But this is too big. I can't take chances; if there's a leak, it could go sour on me."

Jim crossed his arms in annoyance. "My job is to help you, and I can't help you if I don't-"

"Jim, I've got this one."

He shook his head. "This is shitty, Linda."

"Yes, it is shitty. I'd apologize, but it is what it is."

Chapter 72

2064: Lucknow, India

Ashok rubbed the grit out of the corners of his eyes, but that did nothing for the grit he felt in his head, *behind* his eyes. He needed some caffeine. He stood up from his workbench and crossed the warehouse floor, moving quietly in order not to wake the others who were sleeping on various chairs and blankets on the floor, to the corner that held the sink, the hot plate, and the small fridge. He put a teabag in his mug, and picked up the kettle...and found that it was almost empty. Crud. He'd have to put on a new pot and -

Behind him, a timer beeped. He blinked. Right, the batteries. But if the charger was done, did that mean that it was 5am already? He put the mug down, walked over to the ship, and detached the charging cables. He checked the clock. It *was* 5am.

Where had the night gone?

On the workshop's couch Prem stirred, and then stood and stretched. He nodded to Ashok, and then picked up a remote and turned on a wall screen and surfed to a weather report. "- later this morning will rise to 21 degrees. Cloud cover will break later this afternoon, and tomorrow is expected to be sunny. And in global news, sources in Geneva report that the preliminary investigation confirms the magnitude six point three earthquake that struck the United Nations Peace Keeper training facility -"

Prem turned the screen off again. "Cloudy this morning. That's OK."

Around them others were stirring.

Ashok nodded. "About the PK facility - I don't care what they say, it was the expats. And I'll bet that that 'training facility' was nothing of the sort."

"Had to be."

"Does this change our -"

Ashok shook his head. "If anything, it means we're lucky we're launching today. The net is going to get tighter."

Prem nodded grimly.

Behind them the warehouse door opened. Prem turned and saw another family enter and nod their hellos to those who had arrived the night before. Sleepy children clutching stuffed animals, men and women lugging suitcases, older children either trying to look brave despite their fear or legitimately so excited that they didn't realize that they *should* be afraid. His wife Rani was awake now, as were their children Aparna and Nandita (or "Katie" and "Carrie", when they were insisting on the new Western nicknames they'd picked). Rani saw him looking and caught his eye. She smiled gingerly at him, but he could tell that she was as overwhelmed by this moment as he was.

Another family came in through the door.

He checked the clock. 5:15 now.

He took a breath. The batteries were charged, and it was time to start boarding the ship. He raised his voice. "Well - ah - everyone, welcome. So. This is it. The ship is ready, we've tested it time and again. The launch window is coming up...and we're all here, I think?"

Someone in the crowd shouted back. "The Pallavs are missing!"

Ashok grimaced. The Pallavs had contributed as much as everyone else, and deserved their seat in the ship...but he and Prem had been more than clear, time and again: the ship waited for no one. The launch window was dictated by physics, not by manners or social custom, and it could not bend...and even if they wanted to wait for the next window in a month, the attack at Nan Garde meant they had to go today.

"We close the hatch in 50 minutes, and we launch in 60." He looked to the warehouse door. "Let's hope they get here in time."

Ashok wasn't much of a public speaker, and he didn't have notes, so his address petered out more than ended. Someone asked, "Should we load up, then?"

"Oh. Yes."

A procession formed as people lifted their luggage and started heading to the enclosed yard behind the warehouse. Ashok followed them through the door, and then stepped to one side and watched the families walk up the ramp into the ship in the pre-dawn darkness. As his eyes adjusted he could see that the sky had a dim glow from streetlights in the residential areas of the city to the west - and now he could also perceive a touch of light from the east, from the coming sunrise.

The brightest light, though, came from inside the ship. As he watched, Rani and their children climbed the ramp. Through the open door of the ship he could watch her pick places for herself and the children - and then she was hidden, obscured by other families pushing in.

Ashok leaned against the corrugated wall of the warehouse and spied on the crowd for a moment longer. Some of the younger children fell back asleep. Others talked excitedly, if quietly, or played video games on their slates. They'd all been instructed not to text or phone anyone until after the launch. Ashok hoped they were obeying. Rumors on discussion boards said that the Indian government wasn't trying to stop the launch of the open source ships - but those rumors were days old. After Nan Garde who knew what frantic discussions were going on at Federal Law Enforcement and local police stations.

He brushed the thought away - worrying wouldn't help, and they would be gone soon. Ashok turned from the open door of the ship and referred to his own slate. The checklist app was still open, from the last time he'd run through it an hour ago. Oxygen? Yes, all of the tanks from the medical supply store were fully charged. Regulators? All set correctly. Batteries? Yes, yes, yes.

He finished the checklist...and started it again, from the top. He was halfway done when the countdown clock on his tablet buzzed. Ten minutes.

So soon?

Ashok looked up from his slate and saw that Prem was already pulling the tarps off the rear of the ship, revealing the chemical rocket bells. That done, Prem shook a cigarette loose, lit it, and then looked at the still half full pack before tossing it into an open drum nearby. He walked toward Ashok. The two stood in companionable silence.

Ashok checked the time. Five minutes. Still no Pallavs. He worried about them - but the ship would not wait.

Then he looked around the courtyard. This was it. Perhaps the last time he'd ever see India. Maybe the last time he'd ever see Earth.

He found it hard to wrap his head around the idea. And yet, the decision was made. Suddenly, without any forethought, he found himself crouching. He kissed his fingers and pressed them into the dirt at his feet, and then stood and wiped his hand against his pants leg.

It was time to board the ship and shut the hatch. Prem knew it too; he dropped his final cigarette to the ground and rubbed it out.

Ashok walked the last few meters to the ramp and set foot on it - and heard shouting behind him. He turned. The Pallavs were running through the warehouse: Inderpal, his wife, and two children, all clutching bags. Just two - not three? Inderpal panted as he ran across the oil-stained floor. As he got closer he slowed and explained.

"Anantha refused to come. She says she's in love with her boyfriend - but we're here." Inderpal's wife Deepti was crying. Ashok knew that he should feel some sympathy, but he didn't have any emotional energy to spare. Instead of offering some condolence Ashok just nodded, and then heard himself saying mechanically, "We're two minutes from sealing up - get inside right now."

The family filed into the ship, Deepti still sobbing. Ashok followed them inside and then pulled the door shut, dogged it, folded the thermal blanket over the hatch, and buttoned it in place.

Prem was already sitting at the navigation computer. He caught Ashok's eye. "The hatch is shut?"

"Shut, locked and verified."

Prem typed a short phrase on the keyboard and hit enter. Ashok sat down in the other seat, strapped himself in, typed his own phrase, and hit enter. The screens blinked, icons appeared, and a timer appeared on the left screen and began counting backward.

On the right screen status chicklets turned green one after another as batteries, drive, fuel tanks, and pumps were queried and returned their answers.

When the countdown hit 30 seconds the thrumming sound started and there was a gasp from the passengers behind them. At 25 seconds it was joined by the weird twisting sensation that Ashok and Prem had grown - if not used to, then at least familiar with - over the months in the workshop.

Despite Ashok's fears there was no last-minute banging on the ship's hatch, no phone calls from the police...nothing.

The timer read six seconds, and the thrumming and the weird twisting sensation grew far more intense. Several children started crying, and the lights in the cargo container flickered once. The countdown on the screens reached zero and then disappeared, replaced by the single word "LAUNCH!" In the lower right-hand corner of the screen an altitude indicator flickered from zero to one meter, changed two meters, and then started changing more rapidly.

From somewhere behind him came an American-style "yee-haw" in an Indian accent. Despite himself Ashok laughed. He turned and made eye contact with Prem, and saw that his friend was laughing too.

* * *

As the ship lifted from its cradle the warehouse courtyard was buffeted by swirling dust devils, driving scraps of paper, and other small detritus.

The ship was four meters off the ground when the forklift that they'd used to move it into position leaned to one side, teetered, and fell with a huge crash. The ship was five meters up now - above the courtyard walls. It accelerated as it climbed. Ten meters, twenty, a hundred. It kept accelerating until it punched through the low clouds and was lost from sight.

Twelve seconds later there was a weird thrumming sound from the storage yard of a welding shop five kilometers to the east, and then a microship threw itself off the ground and raced into the sky.

Ten seconds after that three more ships launched, then another, and then two more.

Then, a moment later, the sky above Lucknow was calm.

The launch window was closed.

Chapter 73

2064: Boardroom Group Headquarters in Tunnel 1,288, Aristillus, Lunar Nearside

Javier looked around the raw tunnel. The puddle of illumination from the a few overhead work lights showed three ADF guards with rifles, a dozen vehicles, and a handful of modular construction offices in the middle of an otherwise empty, dark tunnel.

Someone dropped a wrench from one of the catwalks overhead and the sound of it hitting the floor echoed down the long shaft then disappeared.

Javier looked back the way they'd come. He knew that the blastproof construction locks that connected this tunnel with other unfinished construction tunnels were just two kilometers back, but they might as well have been a thousand times further. This small pool of light was the entire universe; the rest of the city felt light years away.

Back in the bustle of the tunnels - eating sushi in a restaurant, watching an MMA bout in a crowded stadium, drinking coffee, pushing past crowds at a taco stand, walking in a park - it was easy to think of Aristillus as an entire world - as *the* entire world.

And yet, just a few kilometers away, it was clear that everything they'd built - all their homes, their farms, their freedoms, their lives - was just a small delicate ball of light and warmth, in the middle of unlimited cold and dark.

It was fragile. More fragile than he cared to think about.

There was a disdainful sniff next to him and Javier turned to see Albert Lai. Albert was looking pointedly around at the trailers, the construction equipment, the piles of gravel. He looked unamused by their rough-and-tumble new quarters. Javier tried to shake off his own dark mood. He put on a smile he didn't feel and clapped Albert on the back. "Look on the bright side, Albert - now you don't have to put up with the old furniture in Northern Logistics!"

Albert looked at Javier, his lips pinched. "Shall we go inside and get this meeting started?"

No, not even a little amused.

Albert turned and headed for the portable offices and Javier followed him up the three stairs. Inside, the room was bright - an antidote to the gloom outside. Javier scanned the table and did a double take. Darcy was sitting Mike's seat at the table - she was out of the hospital. "Darcy! You're looking wonderful!"

Darcy smiled wanly. "Thanks, Javier. Sorry it took me a little while to..." She trailed off.

"Don't apologize." He paused, pondering how much to say about her recovery after the ordeal of the prison, and then the escape. No, there were too many other people in the room. That was for another time - if at all. He smiled and repeated. "You're looking wonderful." He took a seat and looked for the gavel, and then realized that Darcy already had it.

After all she'd been through - was she was ready not just to attend a meeting, but to lead one?

Darcy tapped the gavel lightly. "We've got a quorum, so we might as well do this officially." There was still chatter, so she struck the gavel more forcefully. Eyes turned to her and there was silence. "Let's get this started. Matthew, you've got an update on tracking down Mike and the others that the snatch team grabbed?"

General Dewitt stood, his uniform the same as those of the men outside: a gray shirt with a handful of patches, jeans, work boots. Javier wondered idly if there was a patch company in Aristillus, and then shook his head at the irrelevancy.

Dewitt said, "Short version is that we're at a dead end. The longer version is that we've got video of the snatch teams from hundreds of different cameras and we can dial the timeline back and see where they came from, but when we dial it forward we see them disappearing into a service tunnel that has no coverage." He gestured at the wallscreen behind him and it obediently played the video.

Javier leaned forward. "You said this is from hundreds of cameras. Is that a Boardroom Group surveillance system?"

"I'll hand that question to Kur- uh, Wolf. Wolf?"

"The UI to dial time forward and back is something I hacked up, but the raw data is all from ViewSpace. Actually, I was working with them on this, and they're going to release a similar feature soon." He was clearly pleased that his feature idea was good enough that someone else had decided to commercialize it.

Mark frowned. "So, wait. This video came from Viewspace. That's a private firm, right? They sell video to anyone?"

Wolf nodded.

"Anyone? So theoretically, the snatch team could be subscribing to these video feeds the same way?"

"Well, sure. Viewspace's API is public-"

Karina Roth interrupted. "Wait a second. Am I hearing that there's a market in video surveillance inside Aristillus? Might the snatch team have found our old headquarters by watching video?"

Wolf said, "Umm-".

"Forget that. Could they have watched us as we came to this tunnel?"

Wolf started to answer, but Dewitt interrupted him. "Even if the snatch teams have a Viewspace subscription, they can't use it to track us to this location. You recall that when we abandoned the

Northern Logistics site, we all suited up and went out on the surface, and then came back in through another airlock -"

"That doesn't help us if there's -"

Dewitt held up a finger. "Hang on. There's certainly video of us going into the airlock, but there are no cameras in the TBM re-racking yard outside, and no cameras in the in-progress tunnels. We also sent dozens of enclosed cargo skids in through locks which *are* covered by cameras. So far it's all speculation that the snatch teams even know about Viewspace. But even if they do, and even if they have a subscription, there's no way they can know where we are."

Mark Soldner leaned forward. "We need to talk about the availability of this data. No, scratch that. We need to stop this from getting into the wrong hands."

Wolf looked up. "Hey, wait a minute. I know it's a cliche, but information wants to -"

Mark shook his head. "Wolf, this isn't hacker-manifesto-play-time. Lives are on the line." He turned to Dewitt. "Even if we're safe here, we have to stop ViewSpace from selling any more footage. Who knows what precautions we're failing to take? Better to cut it off."

Javier looked at Darcy to see her response. She was listening intently, but didn't seem to be about to say anything.

General Dewitt said, "Shutting down ViewSpace is a legislative decision, not a military one, so I don't-"

Mark pressed on. "It's both. The fact is that some of these markets are *too* open and free, and that's going to hurt us militarily. We all agree that we need less regulation and less government - that's why we're around this table - but it's impossible to have a civilization where people can buy and sell anything to anyone. Especially in a wartime situation."

Javier looked at Darcy again. If Mike was here, he knew, there'd be desk pounding and swearing. Javier smiled sadly. For all he'd lectured Mike, time and again, about reining it in, now that it was gone he missed it. He'd do anything to have Mike here, safe and secure.

But Darcy wasn't Mike. Of course she wasn't fist pounding or swearing - but she also wasn't objecting at all. Was she still tired from her ordeal? Or perhaps she just didn't understand the dynamic he and Mike had forged, where Mike played the angry cop and Javier the good one?

Hmm. No matter what the reason, Darcy wasn't stepping forward. And Wolf, for all his defense of free speech, was seen as a joke by most of the people around the table - a techie and a nerd, not a real business leader like the rest of them.

So. If he wanted to stop Mark Soldner, it was up to him.

Javier raised his chin. Mark saw it, finished his speech and turned to Javier.

"Mark, like you, I disagree with Mike from time to time on how little government we can get away with. We've had many conversations where he has called me a 'wishy-washy-libertarian.'" Javier smiled, inviting Mark to perceive him as a moderate. "But I want to make three points. First, we have already concluded that the video data is incapable of helping the PK forces if we take reasonable precautions."

"Reasonable precautions? We had to suit up and move across the surface before we could come back in - and we had to send out decoy vehicles. Those are some pretty big hoops we had to jump through. Are we going to have to do that every time we want to resupply ourselves here? Why should we have to do that, in our own city?"

Javier ignored the question. "Second, of all the rights that Mike was passionate about, he was most ferocious about three: the right to trade, the right to speak, and the right to own guns. Now, this current issue does not address firearms, but it does speak to the other two. We can't put controls in place to stop information from being shared or sold without impacting both the right to communicate and the right to trade. Mike and I argue about this - and we *will* argue about it again, when he's found and freed - but as long as Mike is being held by enemy forces, I'm not going to turn my back on his principles. I owe him that." Javier looked at Darcy out of the corner of his eye. He was trying to use Mike's name to rally the other CEOs - and to rally her. Was it working?

It was unclear. She still looked worn and tired.

Mark, at least, didn't object to the point.

"And, finally, third: any regulation we might propose would be ineffective. We cannot wave a wand and stop the data from being acquired or sold."

"You're giving the old libertarian argument that outlawing a market just drives it underground, but -"

Javier shook his head. "No, I'm not saying that. I'm saying that we don't have the legal authority to do it. We're not a government!" It needed to be said, but the role of firebrand was uncomfortable on his shoulders. He glanced again to Darcy, but there was nothing in her eyes.

Mark leaned forward. "Javier, with all due respect, you assert that these rules can't work, and you assert that the population doesn't want laws, but these laws *can* work, and the population *does* want laws - good laws. People hate bad laws and bad leaders, but they cry out for just laws and good leadership. The Revolution is the perfect time to establish precedents for -"

Rob Wehrmann cleared his throat and bellowed, "Jesus Fuck, you people are killing me with all this philosophy. Can we just vote, or something?"

Javier blinked. "This - this *legislation* - is beyond the scope of the Boardroom Group. The populace hasn't given us the power to vote on laws -"

Mark raised his hand. "I second Rob's motion that we vote on it."

Darcy started to say something. Javier turned to her - and watched her fall silent. Wam, next to her, shook his head. "I'm sitting in for Mike, and -"

Karina objected. "Technically, Darcy is -"

Wam spoke over her. "And Mike wouldn't allow this."

Rob Wehrmann cut him off. "Why are we still talking? We've got a call for a vote and it's been seconded. So let's vote. I vote we shut it down."

Mark nodded. "Shut them down."

Karin Roth said, "Agreed - shut them down."

Javier opened his mouth but Albert spoke first. "It's too militarily risky to let them sell this data. Shut them down."

In just seconds it was done - 14 to 3.

General Dewitt nodded. "I'll instruct troops to shut down ViewSpace under the orders of the Board."

Javier shook his head. This never would have happened if Mike had been here. He turned and looked at Darcy. He'd been right - she really wasn't ready for this.

Chapter 74

2064: Goldwater mines, 5 km from Aristillus, Lunar Nearside

Darren's phone vibrated silently in his pocket. He reached in and turned it off, and then went back to looking at the mining map displayed on the wall screen. He pointed to one spot. "You're ending the tunnel here, even though the seam continues?"

The crew chief nodded. "We can get the gold out at a profit, but there's opportunity cost. The seam we discovered last week over in 96 has gotten thicker as we've pushed in. I want to move the equipment and men over. I can show you the spreadsheet -"

"No, that's fine. Sounds good. Anything else?"

"That's it, boss."

Darren turned, pushed open the door of the construction office, and took the three steps down to the floor of the tunnel. It was cold here; he pulled his jacket tight against the chill and started to walk into the darkness.

Reggie Strosnider, his head of security, and the two guards who'd been standing with him outside the construction office started to walk with him.

Darren stopped. "No, hang here. I need to make a call."

The two guards looked at Reggie, who paused a moment, and then nodded.

Darren walked deeper into the gold mine.

By the time he'd reached a hundred meters, the glow of the lights had faded. Darren stopped and took out his phone. There was one new text message, which he decrypted and read. "Plans are in motion. You don't have as long as you think you do. Are you ready to make a deal?"

He typed his response. "Soon. Let me check one more thing."

He sent the message, wiped the phone's memory, then turned and walked back toward the bubble of light.

Chapter 75

2064: Open Source Ship "Rani", between Earth and the Moon

Ashok listened to the ship. The first hour had been exciting. And scary. And noisy. First the acceleration from the AG drive, then the staccato firing of the chemical rockets self-calibrating, and then the steady thrust as they pushed the ship onto a path that would aim it at the moon.

And now - silence. Then a single beep. On the navigation screen the words "inertial coasting" appeared, and then a second later a note that passengers could remove their safety harnesses. Ashok looked at Prem and the older man shrugged. "Why not?"

Ashok undid his belt, pushed lightly out of the worn automotive seat, and found himself drifting slowly toward the ceiling. A grin spread across his face. He touched the ceiling and pushed himself back down, landed in his seat on his knees, and grabbed the seat back to steady himself.

He was facing the rows of passengers, and dozens of eyes were locked on his. His smile grew wider. "The computer says we can play - but be careful!"

For a long moment no one moved - and then two children unclicked their seat belts and pushed themselves free. Before long most of the children and a few of the adults were floating above the old minivan seats, either lightly touching the ceiling, walls, and chair backs to maintain position, or actively bouncing up and down the central corridor. Two cats had been let out of their carriers, but - contrary to a century of fictional speculation - they didn't deal with the situation at all well and were soon bundled back into their crates.

A few times the children's play got overly rambunctious and someone went crashing into one of the welded mesh cages that protected the electronics at the front of the ship or the other one that protected the fuel tanks at the back. Ashok furrowed his brow, but in each case the relevant mothers or fathers admonished the children and the play settled down.

After twenty minutes the excitement of zero g faded, the short hours of sleep the night before took their toll, and most of the members of the six families were either buckled in and asleep, or at the very most talking quietly. Ashok turned to Pram. "Can you keep watch for a few hours?" Pram nodded, and Ashok unbuckled himself again, pushed lightly out of his seat, and pulled himself hand over hand to the empty seat next Rani. She smiled up at him floating overhead. "Hello, Captain."

He smiled back, and then pulled himself down and buckled in. Rani snuggled into his shoulder and closed her eyes. His daughter Nandita stuck one arm out, over her mother's lap. Ashok took her hand and closed his eyes. He deserved a short nap, and he was going to take it.

He smiled as he drifted off.

This was all going to work out.

Chapter 76

Javier walked through the dim glow of the tunnel, reached the field office container, climbed the three steps, and knocked.

A moment later Darcy opened the door. "Javier? What's up?"

He took a deep breath. How do you tell someone that you were worried about them...and that you suspected that they were too traumatized to do their jobs?

"I just wanted to check up on you - see how you're doing."

Darcy looked at him blankly. "I'm fine."

He was pretty sure she wasn't. "May I come in?"

She shrugged. "I'm in the middle of something, but - sure."

She opened the door and ushered him into her impromptu home. Like all of the other field offices that they'd acquired through dummy firms and snuck into the tunnel, it was bare, utilitarian, and functional. Darcy's though, somehow looked even a little more barren than most.

She gestured at a seat and sat herself. "What is this about?"

"I'm worried about you."

She waved his concern away. "You don't need to be. I'm fine."

"Darcy, you're tough. I know that. But being tough doesn't mean that going through that experience -"

Darcy sighed and closed her eyes for a moment. "Javier, I really don't want to have this conversation right now. Yes, it was terrible. But people have gone through a lot worse and survived."

"Do you think that you should talk about it to someone?"

Darcy snorted. "Of everyone, I wouldn't have put you very high on list of people arguing for the modern therapeutic society."

"I'm not arguing for anything. I'm just saying that I'm worried about you."

"Please don't - but if it makes you feel any better, yes, I'll probably talk to someone when this is all over."

"Good." This was more than he'd expected, really. "I can find a recommendation for a therap-"

"Oh, you know as well as I do that most of them are frauds."

"Then who-"

"Javier. I promised you I'll talk to someone, and I will. But for now, if you see me not doing my job, come talk to me, but other than that, please trust me that I'm a grownup and I know if I'm OK or not."

Javier nodded, unconvinced.

Darcy hurried the conversation along. "Is there anything else?"

Javier looked around the room, looking for some excuse to prolong the conversation, to feel Darcy out a bit more. Hmm. The wallscreens were covered with open documents. He pointed to them. "What have you been working on?"

"Actually, I was about a day away from bringing this to you. Why isn't Darren Hollins here in this little government-in-exile?"

"What? Darren *is* part of the boardroom group."

"No, I know that. I'm asking: why isn't he here in tunnel 1,288 with the rest of us?"

"He chose not to - because of the gold mining and refining he's got a pretty good security force, and he trusts it to keep him safe."

Darcy looked at him. "Do you believe that?"

Javier blinked. "Of course." He could tell Darcy wanted more from him. "Why, do you not?"

Darcy shook her head. "I'm not sure."

"Well, what other explanation is there?"

"I know it sounds a bit crazy, but I think it's possible that he's preparing to betray us."

Javier bit his lip. He had know Darcy was tired - deeply tired - and stressed. But this? Was paranoia a symptom that -

"You think I'm crazy, don't you?"

"Ah...no. I just think that that's a big extrapolation from one fact. Why-"

"It's not just one fact. There's a lot of details." She waved her hand at the wall screens. "Did you know that right after the first raid he captured Hugh Haig - the senator's son? Who was apparently collaborating with the PKs who were attacking the Goldwater facility?"

Javier tilted his head. He had not known this. Could that be true? If Hollins had captured the senator's son -

"And did you know that shortly thereafter he let the kid go?"

Javier blinked. "I - no. Are you sure about this?"

"Check the records. It's all there."

"Uh - I think I will." Could this be real? Darcy struck him as twitchy, tired, and troubled - but not delusional. "Even if it's true, it doesn't prove anything. Right after the motorcycle helmet incident, Mike went to his lawyer Lowell Benjamin, and Lowell told him not to sue those kids or arrest them. Maybe Darren vacuumed up the kids by accident, and after realizing who they are -"

"Did you know that Darren Hollins is stockpiling weapons grade uranium?"

"Urani - excuse me? What?"

Javier stumbled to a halt. Did he just hear what he thought he'd heard?

"Darren has enough enriched uranium for sixteen fission bombs. He might even have fusion bomb materials; we can't be sure."

This didn't make sense. None of it did. "Darcy, this is crazy - where would Darren get uranium? There are no uranium-bearing ores in Aristillus. And even if there were, there's no way he could enrich it. Where did you -"

"He didn't mine it. He salvaged it from the PK ships that we shot down."

Javier tried to form words. Darcy really might be deluded, if she thought -

"If you don't believe me, check out the evidence. It's all on video, plus his men have even admitted it." She typed rapidly on her keyboard and more files appeared on the screen.

Javier frowned and began reading.

Chapter 77

2064: Open Source Ship "The Houston", between Earth and the Moon

Sam Barrus unclicked his seat belt, pushed himself out of his chair, and drifted around his own personal spaceship. Hah! He loved phrasing it that way.

After drifting a few meters, he bumped into a Matco tool chest that was cinched to the wall with thick web straps. He pushed off it, aiming at the stack of crates holding his three dogs. Cootz and Jeb, the hounds, were sleeping from the allergy meds he'd given them, but Tara's near supernatural energy must have been too much for the standard dose - she was wagging her stump enthusiastically. He reached through the slot to pet her and she licked his hand. "Not yet, girl."

Sam turned and looked around the ship. "Packed" didn't begin to describe it. He'd gone with the double-height choice that the system configurator had presented. That design assumed that the lower container would be full of cargo and the upper one would be filled with seats.

He didn't have 79 friends to share the ship with - it was just him and the three dogs - so he'd filled the lower container with cargo - and then gone ahead and filled most of the upper one as well. A few meters back the small cockpit area ended in an ad hoc wall made up of his welding rig and an even dozen Craftsman tool chests (plus his one nice Matco). Deeper back were trade goods, and even his gun and sword collection - dug up from the PVC-and-silica-gel cache after fifteen long years underground.

Tara was still wiggling her stump ferociously and Sam could hear her entire crate rattle.

"Hang on, girl, I'll let you out in a minute." He wanted another minute to survey his domain before he let her out.

He'd packed all of the obvious stuff that the FAQ suggested, but Uncle Charlie hadn't raised a fool. No, not a fool at all. He'd done some research and found that he could use a proxy and something called "black DNS" to connect to the .ari websites. And what he'd found there! Markets, discussion boards, help wanted sites - and bids. Bids on all kinds of stuff - and people were offering insane prices.

FAQ be damned, after he'd sold the ranch and the carbon sequestration credits that went with it, he'd invested not in gold and household goods, but in a lot of stuff that the FAQ didn't mention. A CNC stereolith machine he'd purchased at auction - with illegal non-DRM control chips installed by a friend. The complete contents of an optician's office. An internal imaging machine that Doc Cleary wasn't allowed to use any more because of regulations...and, weirdest of all, two concert pianos. He scratched his head over that one, but the price was right, and he'd managed to fit them both in.

Tara thumped her head against the door to her crate and Sam sighed. "All right, girl, I'm coming." He opened the crate door...and watched Tara explode out, only to flail her legs hilariously as she tried to get some purchase in mid-air.

Sam reached out, reeled her into a loose embrace, and held her against his chest as he floated. She licked his face and kept wagging her stump. After a bit the licking and wagging slowed, and then after a few minutes more she started delicately snoring. Sam held her close with one hand, pulled himself back to the crates, and then eased her in and shut the door behind her.

Sam drifted back to his chair and pulled himself down. All he had to do now was wait until the ship got to the moon. He buckled himself into the seat, adjusted the volume on his ear-buds, and fished out his hard copy of "To Ride, Shoot Straight, and Speak the Truth." He had a digital copy, of course, but this one was held together with layer after layer of duct tape, and it reminded him of Unc.

Yep, Sam was pretty pleased with himself. He was going to do all right.

Chapter 78

2064: Open Source Ship "The Champion", between Earth and the Moon

Maynard unlatched his belt and pushed himself out of his seat. He couldn't stop from shouting "Whoo!" as he floated in zero g - and why should he? This was great! Within seconds dozens of people were floating, shouting, backslapping. It was a raucous free-for-all, and it was awesome. The Atlanta Hackerspace Artgroup had pulled off some cool hacks over the last few years, but this was the best one yet.

Maynard looked around the crowd. He'd found this group - well, half found, and half created - a few years out of college, and it was a great bunch of people. Overeducated like him, bored with all of the pointless grubbing around that most jobs entailed, and interested in big ideas. He'd read that everyone needed to find their tribe, and -

His thoughts were derailed when, through a gap in the bodies, he saw Carrie-Ann push out of her chair. He smiled and tried to catch her eye, but she was deep in conversation with Vince, who was already floating free.

Then - damn it! - he watched Carrie-Ann hug Vince tight, and then lock lips. Maynard felt a surge of jealousy, but tried to suppress it. He knew negative emotions were stupid - highly evolved people should be past that sort of thing. Jealousy was something to be mastered, not something to be mastered by. And besides, Maynard was Carrie-Ann's primary. What did care if she had a new secondary? Secondaries came and went. He was free to have a secondary too, if he wanted to.

Still, it would have been nice if she'd told him that she was attracted to Vince.

Maynard grimaced and turned away. He felt his face flush and hot blood pumping beneath his skin. He looked for something to distract himself.

Jake had been sitting next to him, but was now floating, tucked into a cannonball and spinning slowly above the seats.

Maynard said, "Awesome, huh, Jake?"

Jake unfolded, reached out and caught a chair back to stop his acrobatics...and ended up head down, feet up. He was grinning wildly. "*Beyond* awesome! Check it out - there's no up or down. There's only this way-" He pushed himself upright. "- and that way!" He laughed.

Maynard tried to smile, despite the mix of jealousy and anger roiling his stomach. "Our best project yet, right?"

Jake nodded. "Fucking A, man! The Autonomous Music Machine was cool. And the Dead Man's DanceBot was radical. But this?" He held out one hand for a fist bump, which Maynard was happy to deliver. Jake continued talking about the ship and then seguéd into ideas he had for new art projects. Maynard smiled and pretended to listen, but he spent most of his attention trying to catch another glimpse of Carrie-Ann through the crowd. Was that - that wasn't her, topless, was it? What the hell was going on there? He sputtered for a second. What the hell? This wasn't acceptable, he should -

He gritted his teeth.

No.

He had to face his insecurities, own them, and evolve past them.

"Maynard, man, what's going on? You OK?"

He turned back to Jake, who was still floating in the air, upside down again. "What? No. I'm fine."

Jake seemed to find the lack of orientation amusing, but Maynard just found it disconcerting. He grabbed hold of one of the chairbacks and rotated himself so that they were both upside down and could face each other. "So, Jake, you said you might not come back with the rest of us in two weeks."

"Have to see how it plays out...but, yeah."

"What are you going to do there?"

Jake shrugged and spoke louder to be heard over the drone of conversation and three different music players in the small space. "Not a hundred percent sure. I know Vince's Economics Two Point Oh won't happen overnight, but it should take hold pretty quick, so there'll be a lot of options. I might start up an art space, or maybe write. One thing I know for sure, though: no more bullshit jobs, man. No more dealing with customers."

Maynard frowned slightly - he still wasn't convinced by Vince and his endlessly recited Econ Two Point Oh screed. Still, there was no need to upset Jake.

"Nice."

Jake pushed against a headrest and began to spin slowly. "How about you?"

Maynard looked at Jake spinning and his stomach flip-flopped. Why did Jake have to do that? Didn't he realize how disconcerting it was? His own stomach was already queasy because of the zero gravity - and because of the Carrie-Ann thing, although that was just his own immaturity.

Maybe he could match Jake's spin and they could chat like reasonable people? Maynard pushed against a headrest and set himself spinning.

He was starting to feel nauseous. This rotating, spinning. Everything. Ugh. He reached out to stop his spin - and smacked his head into Jake's feet. *Damn* it. He grabbed a chair to steady himself. His stomach gurgled alarmingly. Jake grabbed a chair too and stopped rotating. "Oh, sorry man. But, anyway, what are *you* going to do when we get there?"

Maynard rubbed the top of his head. "What? Jesus, I don't know. Look, can we -"

There was a loud bang from the rear of the ship.

Maynard whipped his head around. What the hell had made that sound?

Around him the hubbub died away.

Then someone near the back of the ship started screaming. Maynard looked and saw that something was spraying from the tanks there -

Oh.

Oh God, no.

It was the fuel tanks for the chemical rockets - and that had to be kerosene. Jesus. He could smell it now. There was kerosene spraying everywhere.

Maynard grabbed a chair back, pulled himself down to it, and then pushed off, aiming for the back of the ship.

As he flew he yelled. "The oxygen line! Turn it off! Turn if off!"

Ahead of him he saw Kelsey fumble at the door to the cage - and then there was a flash of light as the aerosolized mixture ignited. Maynard covered his face with his hands. Around him the ball of fire filled the ship and he saw the bright yellow light between his fingers. For a moment all he felt was a wash of warmth but a moment later the pain started. Oh *God* it hurt. He started to scream but the air was torn out his lungs. What the hell was happening?

A huge wind was pulling him, knocking him into someone, and then throwing him into a seat. He grabbed for a chair back, but missed. He felt something under his hands, but in the midst of the pain he had no idea what it was.

The wind was howling, but over it, he heard dozens of people screaming. He tried to open his eyes, but he couldn't. Were they - oh God, were they burned shut?

He felt an impact - he'd been thrown into a wall, or maybe the ceiling - and then another, and a moment later the pain - somehow - got worse as he was dragged around the corner into the mock phone booth welded to the top of the cargo container.

Bizarrely, he had a flash of memory: protesting that the "artistic statement and a space viewing room" was a stupid deviation from the ebook plans, but no one had -

He crashed into bodies already packed into the phone booth and tried to scream but couldn't - his lungs were empty. A second later someone else crashed into him. One of his arms brushed against something sharp - shattered glass -

Another body slammed into them, then another, and then another. Maynard felt himself squeezed tighter and tighter into the booth. The pain in his face and arms was indescribable. He tried to take a breath to scream but no air came.

A few seconds later he was, mercifully, unconscious.

Five minutes later Maynard and everyone else aboard the Champion was dead.

The blackened ship drifted on.

Fifteen hours later, as the wreckage approached the moon, the onboard navigation computer signaled the chemical maneuvering rockets to do a small course correction burn. Two of the pumps had had their electrical lines melted by the fire, but one still worked. It whirred, but no fluids flowed - the kerosene and oxygen tanks were empty. The rocket bell igniters sparked and sparked again.

Seventeen hours after that, the ship and its cargo of bodies coasted past the moon and into interplanetary space.

Chapter 79

2064: Boardroom Group Headquarters in Tunnel 1,288, Aristillus, Lunar Nearside

Darcy shook her head. "Javier, I told you last time, I don't want to talk about my experiences or emotions or anything. I'm fine."

Javier looked at her appraisingly. "You're sure?"

"Aside from worrying about where the snatch team has got Mike caged, I'm OK. Now let's drop this. You and Mike were working together to steer things. Let's talk about that."

Javier thought for a moment, then nodded. "OK. Now in the next meeting there are two things on the agenda that we need to prepare for -"

Darcy cut him off. "I want to hear this, but I want to talk about something that's not on the agenda."

"What's that?"

"The interrogation videos."

Javier looked at her. "What interrogation videos?"

Darcy looked back at him. "From Nan Garde." Javier looked confused. "Do you not know about this?"

"No, what?"

"They kept me - well, everyone from the Poyekhali and from the other ships - up on the upper levels of the prison. We weren't well treated -" she felt herself drift off for a moment, then shook her head to clear it. "It wasn't fun for us, but it wasn't terrible. But there were other prisoners - those on their 'Special Information List.' They were kept in the secret floors. And *those* prisoners were really treated badly. Interrogated." She spat the word, then fell silent again.

Javier leaned forward. "Yes?"

"Ponzie - the others -" She dropped into silence.

"Do you want to come back to this later?"

"No." She took a deep breath. "There were torture sessions. We could hear them from our cells, sometimes." She closed her eyes for a moment. "They bastards recorded it. All of it. The waterboarding. The humiliations. The sexual abuse. Ponzie knew about the records somehow, and he made sure that John's rescue team got the video. We got it - we got it out on the Deladrier." She took another deep breath. "We need to make sure that that video gets out. It will help our cause on Earth, and maybe even get us more immigrants."

Javier nodded seriously. "I know just the person to make this happen." He pulled out his phone. "Are you ready to talk to someone about this?"

Darcy nodded.

Chapter 80

2064: Office above Ayudando a Las Manos clinic, Aristillus, Lunar Nearside

Selena sat in the chair, turned to look over her shoulder, and verified that the backdrop was hanging straight.

She turned back forward. "Are we ready to go? Do I need to brush my hair?"

Rosario was standing behind the primary camera, making a few last- minute adjustments. She looked up. "No, you look great." She hit a button on the device, and then took a few steps to the other tripod and hit a button on the second camera. "We're recording."

Selena smiled at camera one. "Hi, I'm Selena Hargraves. You may recognize me from my previous - uh." She stopped and looked to Rosario. "I'm not used to this. Can we -"

"Just start over, I'll edit it."

"Hi, I'm Selena Hargraves, a recent immigrant to the lunar colony at Aristillus. I didn't arrive here as an immigrant - I was just a tourist, really - here with friends on a lark." She took a deep breath, and then continued. "I didn't arrive here sympathetic to the expats - or 'colonists' as they prefer to be called. I was then, and am now, opposed to many of the -." Selena found herself staring at the red light over the camera and froze up again.

After a moment Rosario coaxed her. "It's OK, just back up a sentence or two - or start over. We can edit it all together later."

Selena looked away from the camera to Rosario. "I don't really like being on video - I'm more of a writer."

"You were pretty good on that first video."

Selena shrugged. "I was outraged then - I mean, I was *really* pissed at Louisa. And, honestly, I didn't think anyone was going to see it. This time though - I mean, tens of millions of people watched that last clip. They might watch this clip too." She raised her eyebrows self-deprecatingly. "I guess I've got stage fright."

Rosario nodded. "OK, forget this take. We won't use the footage. Let's just do a rehearsal. You talk to me, and tell me what you're going to say later. We'll walk through it once, and then we'll do the real take."

Selena nodded and smiled slightly. "OK, sure."

She turned back to the camera and took a deep breath. The knot in her shoulders and neck seemed to loosen a bit. She smiled more broadly. and squared her shoulders. "Hi, I'm Selena Hargraves, a recent immigrant to the lunar colony at Aristillus. You may have seen my earlier video essay 'Lies, Damned Lies, and Deceptive Pro-PK Reporting.' Today I'm bringing you - uh - what should we call this one, Rosario? Maybe 'Morality and the Use of Force'?"

"Sure, that sounds good."

Selena nodded. "OK." She turned back to the camera. "Today's vlog entry is 'Morality and the Use of Force'.

"I didn't arrive here as an immigrant - I was just a tourist, here with friends on a lark. I wasn't sympathetic to the expat side. Ideologically I disagreed with many of the ways that this society operates, and I still do. But I can tell you one thing - everyone here is here of their own free will - they *want* to be here. The shipping companies all run free return trips for anyone who wants to leave - and those seats are almost always empty. DC Minute and the other licensed outlets tell you that the rich like it here on Aristillus." She nodded, conceding the point. "Well, that's true. What they don't tell you is that middle class and poor inhabitants of

Aristillus also prefer to be here. I could tell you about this one family -"

Selena paused. "I'm getting off topic; you don't care why people come to Aristillus. The point of this vlog post is about one thing: the use of force. You may have heard the phrase 'the Aristillus ideology' or 'the Aristillus disease'. The expats define it one way, and Earth media defines it another way. They're pretty much the same definition, once you strip the connotations and loaded terms away. It boils down to libertarianism - of a pretty extreme sort - but it encompass a lot of things. An allergic reaction to regulation, pugnacious anti-authoritarianism, a real dislike for the PKs, an almost archaic belief in metallic currency, and what they call 'the non-aggression principle.'

"It's the last one I want to talk about. I don't have much of an opinion about business regulations or drug legalization and I think the metal coin thing is crazy." She paused. "But I do care about people starting fights. It's wrong. There's no excuse for a man to slap a woman around, or for a parent to abuse their children, or for anyone to hurt an animal. It's - well you get the idea.

"The bottom line is that in my view of what's right and wrong, there's no excuse for hurting the powerless. Using force against someone who just wants to be left alone is wrong. We all know that's true in individual cases. Over the last months I've found myself coming around - as hard as that is to believe - to the opinion that's common here in Aristillus: that the US and UN governments are based not on the consent of the governed, but on the use of force to -"

Selena looked away from the camera. "Is this getting too theoretical? Too wordy?"

Rosario shrugged. "Yeah, a little. Maybe move it along."

Selena nodded "OK, let's cut out the last paragraph or so. I'll start it over." She paused, then turned to the camera. "There's no excuse for hurting the powerless. The other day I was interviewing Mike Martin, one of the industrialists here - one of the founders of the whole place, really - and someone who has been described as a 'ringleader' of the revolution. While I was interviewing Mr. Martin, PK forces - out of uniform, and showing no ID - raided the office where he was staying. I was in the room as it was raided, and I shot this video."

Selena paused, then nodded to Rosario. "Good?"

"Yeah, I've marked the splice point - keep going."

"As troubling as that video is, I can understand the other side. Mike Martin is, arguably, a rebel against the government. I understand it when police arrest someone for breaking a law. Even when I don't agree with the law, I get it. In such a situation, rather than condemn the police, the right thing to do is to work to get the law overturned."

Selena turned to the B camera. "But there is something that no civilized person can tolerate, and that is torture." She paused and stared at the camera. "We know that the government uses enhanced interrogation techniques from time to time, in certain 'ticking time bomb' scenarios. We are told this is only allowed after a panel of three judges have all signed a Dershowitz warrant, and is only done with a team of doctors present.

"This is what we've been told - but it's not true. In fact, the US regularly coordinates with the UN to render people - US citizens and noncitizens alike - into PK custody, at secret facilities overseas. At the PK facility at Nan Garde, Haiti - and in other locations around the world - the government routinely tortures citizens. We are told that these enhanced interrogations are done only in 'ticking time bomb' scenarios, with warrants, with doctors - but video evidence proves otherwise."

Selena paused, then swallowed.

"You're going to ask how I got this video. Surely even if what I was saying was true, the PKs wouldn't put data like this on a network where it could be compromised via cyber weapons. You're right - the PKs documented their torture session, but they kept it all off the network."

"So how did we get it?

"You heard the government story about the earthquake that struck Haiti. That was a lie. A day later, when pictures of gray clouds made it onto the net, the government told you that it was actually a 'laser terrorism attack' that Aristillus forces carried out. That was a second lie. The truth is something different. That was neither an earthquake nor a laser attack. That was a boots-on-the-ground mission - a rescue mission - by people from Aristillus. Aristillus forces rescued dozens of people - US citizens and others - who had been taken prisoner by US forces, handed over to PKs, and tortured. Tortured without a warrant and without doctors present. And when the ADF - uh, that's the Aristillus Defense Force - when the ADF was there in Haiti, they didn't just rescue prisoners. They also seized video evidence of the torture. These uses of torture weren't to prevent terrorist attacks or -"

Selena looked down at her desk, then up at Rosario. "Ugh. I don't know how to introduce this. The video - it makes me feel sick. And then I want to cry." She breathed in hard. "Actually, I want to cry right now."

"Don't introduce it, then."

"I have to say *something*. Just to warn them, if nothing else."

"OK, warn them, then."

Selena turned back to the "A" camera. "The footage you are about to see is horrific. People under the age of -" She shook her head. "Actually, no one should want to see this. It's just horrible. I warn you, if you watch this, you'll probably have nightmares, like I've had for the past several nights. But you need to know what your government is doing. What you're about to see is _"

Selena broke off and looked away from the camera, then up at Rosario. "Rosario...I can't do this. Even this rehearsal was bad enough. I don't want to think about the things those people did. Why can't they just let the expats go? Why do they have to do this?"

Rosario nodded as she tapped on her keyboard. "Drink some water. Maybe that'll help."

Selena nodded mutely, stood, and walked over to the small dorm fridge. She took a bottle of water from it, then returned to the desk where she took one sip, then another.

After a moment she looked up. "I just can't do this. We have to find someone else to -"

Rosario looked at her. "We don't need anyone else, that was great. And, besides, I just posted it."

"You what?"

"It was perfect. I spliced in the two video clips and posted it."

Selena swallowed.

Chapter 81

2064: Lai Docks and Air Traffic Control, Aristillus, Lunar Nearside

Michael Stuart-Test sat at his usual console, listening to EagleGust on his ear-buds. And why not? Today was a light day, with zero scheduled incoming ships, just one departure, and the only construction was the ongoing upgrade to let cradle 11 hold the Grace Under Pressure LNG tanker in case cradle 8 was down.

Michael had both the arrivals and departures windows minimized to make room for the checklist for the warehouse handler robots. He was humming a bass accompaniment to the microtonal Chapman Stick solo when a tone struck him as odd. He tilted his head. Huh...he'd never noticed that F-half-sharp there. He'd paused the music and began to jog it back a few seconds when the tone rang again.

Wait - that F half-sharp wasn't part of the Eagle Gust track - that was a warning tone. He scanned his boards looking to see the alert message but couldn't see any. Ah, wait - only the robot checklist screen was displayed. There was one ship headed out today; he needed to check that screen. He brought up the departures screen.

And that was odd.

Nothing.

What else could it be?

He glanced for a second at the icon for the minimized arrivals screen - but, no, that couldn't be it; nothing was arriving today. So which of the dashboards could be giving the warning? The one for the compressed air handling facility, maybe? The work on cradle 11 could have triggered something there. He opened the screen and scanned it. No problems.

The dashboard for the pumps and pipelines for Veleka Waterworks? He checked the screen. No.

What was left?

Michael saw the icon for the arrivals screen. Hmm. For completeness he really should check it - just so he could say he had.

He clicked. The window expanded.

Michael blinked.

What - ?

This didn't make any sense.

The list of incoming ships should be empty. It *had* been empty a few hours ago when his shift started. But now it was full. *Full.*

Instinctively he tensed, but then after a moment he relaxed.

If the list held entries for one or two ships he'd assume they were real and that someone had failed to enter them in the schedule. If it was five ships, he'd panic a bit - it was rare to get that many ships arriving in one day, but it had happened once or twice, and maybe - *maybe* - someone had forgotten to input them all into the schedule.

But a *full* list? The screen had room for fifty entries, and there were barely that many ships flying out of Aristillus in total. The list had never been full, even once before.

So, no, there was no need to panic - this was clearly fictional data. Probably someone had screwed up and loaded a test database into the production server. Was it William? He shook his head. It must be. God damned William. He was a cowboy, never documenting his work, never following proper procedure. And worse yet, he didn't seem to care.

Michael fired up an email client. William was going to get one hell of a scathing email. Now, to describe the exact problem. He looked at the transponder name field on the first entry on the list: "OSS Navajo". The next: "OSS Awesome!". The next: "OSS figure_it_out_later".

"OSS"? That was weird. There were only three valid ship prefixes, and -

Michael felt a sudden sinking sensation.

"OSS". That couldn't stand for "open source ship," could it?

Michael clicked a button and stopped the EagleGust track.

Albert had mentioned a while back that the Boardroom Group was discussing a proposal to open source the AG drive. Michael even remembered reading some posts on the company intranet about it. But then he'd heard nothing.

They hadn't gone ahead with it.

...had they?

He rubbed a hand over his forehead and realized he was slick with sweat.

Could they have released the open source AG drive without him realizing it? He swallowed. Between the Revolution beginning to boil over, the installation of the new robotic cargo handlers, and - worst of all - dealing with the negotiations about the water pipeline between the docks and Veleka's new space, he'd been busy.

He did a quick search of the corporate intranet. No, there were no new updates about open sourcing the AG drive. So was the data real or -

The warning tone for "ship entering queue" beeped again.

Ah ha. He could check the data source screen, and that would -

He swallowed.

This wasn't a simulation; the data source dialogue showed "live transponder" highlighted.

This was real ; ships were actually arriving.

Ships were arriving, and he had to deal with it.

Okay, okay, focus.

He scanned the board. How many ships were in the landing queue? He needed to know that in order to allocate hangers and clear some space.

Seventy-two.

He breathed deeply. OK. Calm down. Seventy-two ships. It was going to be tight, but all he had to do was find the space and then the autolanding software would do all the work. He scanned his board. The first ship, the OSS Navajo, was three minutes out. Breathe. Three minutes was more than enough time to clear the robots out of bay three and get those spare water pumps off the deck near bay five.

His thin elegant fingers flew over the keyboard and two minutes and forty one seconds later it was done - the robots *and* the water pumps were clear. He smiled. When you're good, you're good.

Now the autolanding would -

An alert popped onto his screen.

```
OSS Navajo (0x44d5ae4): agent interrupt 0x77a no
matching rule-set - spam refuses autolanding command
(WTF?) - #fix_before_golive
```

Michael blinked. What did that mean?

A moment later

```
OSS Awesome! (0x69f2f3a): agent interrupt 0x77a no
matching rule-set - spam refuses autolanding command
(WTF?) - #fix_before_golive
```

and then

```
OSS figure_it_out_later (0xf0de11f): agent interrupt
0x77a no matching rule-set - spam refuses autolanding
command (WTF?) - #fix_before_golive
```

He checked.

The ships weren't landing. And in the last three minutes five more OSS ships had entered the landing queue.

Michael wiped the sweat off his forehead. Again.

This was above his pay grade. Albert Lai needed to hear about this and figure something out.

Michael picked up his phone.

Chapter 82

2064: Boardroom Group Headquarters in Tunnel 1,288, Aristillus, Lunar Nearside

Darcy listened to General Dewitt's status report. "...and we're still waiting for the chemical firms to develop good detonators. Other than the lack of RPG rounds, infantry readiness is looking good." Dewitt looked around the room. "Any questions?"

Darcy stole a glance at the wallscreen, where Darren Hollins was videoconferenced in. Was Darren looking at her? No. It must be her imagination. She checked again, and his gaze had moved to someone else.

Darcy tapped her stylus on her slate and wrote a note. "Should we announce Darren's uranium?" She slid the slate so that Javier could see it.

Javier looked at and frowned, and then pulled the slate toward himself. Darcy handed him the stylus. She watched out of the corner of her eye, eager to see his response. She was startled when a phone rang immediately to her left. She turned. It was Albert's.

Albert coughed in embarrassment. "Excuse me; it's a priority call." He looked at it, frowned, accepted the call and listened for a moment. "I apologize, but I've got to take this". He stepped out of the construction office and closed the door behind him.

Javier had finished writing and slid the slate back to Darcy. She picked it up when Darren, on the wall screen, spoke. "General. First, my compliments on the success of the Nan Garde rescue and on your defense preparations over the past few weeks. With regard to your briefing, I do have one question: why the emphasis on infantry?"

Darcy looked up from the slate.

General Dewitt frowned. "I'm not sure I understand the question. Do you mean as opposed to armor?"

"I'm sorry, I meant robots."

"We do have recon drones, which -"

Darren shook his head. "No, I'm talking about combat robots. Is there some reason that we're not exploring that?"

General Dewitt looked puzzled. "The Geneva conventions -"

"We're not signatories."

Dewitt shifted uncomfortably. "I - well, a decision like that is above my pay-grade." He paused. "Even if the board did approve, there's the question of budget. The civil defense e-p-door program is costing more than anyone expected, and thus my arms budget is already -"

Darren nodded. "I understand that budgets are tight, but I think -"

Albert Lai burst into the room. "Darcy, I need you."

Darcy looked at him. "Right now?"

"Yes, immediately."

Darcy turned to the room. "Excuse me."

Chapter 83

2064: Boardroom Group Headquarters in Tunnel 1,288, Aristillus, Lunar Nearside

Darcy stepped out of the trailer.

"Albert, what's going on?"

He looked dazed. "We've got a problem."

Darcy let her concern show. "What sort of problem?"

"A big one. Follow me."

A moment later Albert held the door of another portable office open for her. As she walked in he pointed to wallscreens that were covered in data. "There."

"What am I looking at?"

"These are the Lai Docks air traffic control interfaces."

"And?"

"And our software is telling these ships to land themselves, and we're getting some sort of error message. The microships won't land!"

"Microships? What micr-" Then she blanched. "Are you saying that the open source project went ahead? When I was in Nan Garde?"

Albert shrugged. "I don't know. I wasn't running it. All I know is what's on the screen. The ships are arriving - more every minute."

"This is bad, Albert - I wasn't finished with that project. How many ships - "

Albert shrugged again, the panic starting to show on his face. "I don't know."

Darcy took a deep breath. "OK, let me sit."

* * *

The wallscreen was covered with a dozen windows: source code, file trees, debugging tools, and more.

"There's good news and bad news." Darcy pointed to a data panel describing one of the ships. "The good news is an AG drive keeping a ship at constant altitude doesn't consume much power." She paused. "The bad news is that 'not much' isn't the same as 'zero.'"

What she didn't say was the worse news: that the life support systems that she and her team had written into the parametric ship designer had limits, and if the 93 - wait, now 95 - ships piled up overhead weren't brought down in a few hours, they were going to start running out of air.

People were going to start dying soon if she didn't get this fixed.

Darcy paged through screens of code. Behind her Albert fidgeted, and then blurted out, "Do you know why they're not landing themselves?"

Darcy nodded distractedly. "Because we never wrote that part. It looks like someone decided to release the distro without testing it."

Albert digested this for a moment. "But...but if the ships can't land themselves...how *are* they going to land? Can the people on the ships-"

"The internal UI is just a command line interface, with a few -"

"What does that mean?"

"It means that, no, they can't land themselves."

"How did this happen?"

Darcy turned away from the screen and let her annoyance spill out. "I have no idea - I was in a PK cage at the time, remember?" She shook her head. "Now, Albert, *please*. Give me some silence so that I can figure this out." She pursed her lips and turned back to the screen.

Albert, with obvious force of will, folded his hands in his lap. The sweat that was already dotting his forehead began to form into droplets and run down his face to his starched white collar.

Finally Darcy exploded. "Ah-ha!"

"Yes?"

"Before I got captured, we'd written a low-level admin interface into the ships' code base, so we could control the AG drive and maneuvering thrusters remotely. At first I thought that code had been ripped out. It got renamed and moved to another module, but it's still here!" She pointed at the screen.

"That's...good?"

"This is still a catastrophe, but now, maybe, there's a chance we can salvage it."

Albert was looking at her quizzically. "How? If there's no way that the people on board can land the ships, and the code that automatically lands them was never written -"

"If we have the right private key - which we do - then we've got administrative access to the microships." Darcy smiled. "And *that* means that we can run their thrusters. Watch."

She picked one ship at one on the screen. "Microship 0x44d5ae4...let's dance." She opened a new window and started typing into it. Albert apparently couldn't stop himself. "You're editing a text file?"

"It's a terminal. I'm running ssh."

"What does that mean?"

"We're in."

"What now?"

Darcy ignored him and typed

```
3coord.get
```

```
3coord.get - laidock.beacon_loc.get
thruster.3transform(3coord.get -
    ldate.beacon_loc.get) { :speed => :slow }
thruster.stop
```

"I control the horizontal. I control the vertical. I can roll the ship, or make it flutter." She hit the return key.

On the traffic control screen one of the dots representing a microship began to slide across the lunar landscape.

"It's moving?"

Darcy turned away from the screen with a huge smile plastered across her face. "It's moving."

"So we're OK?"

"I've got this first ship headed to the docks. After this I just need to land another -" How many ships had been in the queue? Ninety-five? She looked at the screen and saw the number had climbed a bit. "- these 103 ships."

She paused.

The ship count had climbed by eight, in just the past few minutes?

"Albert, this is going to take a while. Can you tell the Boardroom Group what's going on?"

"I'll do that."

"...and can you do me a favor and get me a sandwich and a sugar-free maple soda?"

"Uh. Yes. Of course."

She turned back to the screen but turned and yelled over her shoulder just before Albert left the office. "Wait!"

"Yes?"

"Double caffeine." She turned back to the screen and resumed typing. In the corner of the screen the 103 blinked and was replaced by a 104. Then a 105.

Chapter 84

Sam stared at the monitor, looking at the image from the external cameras. There were vehicle tracks and waste rubble beneath him, but the bulk of Aristillus was a few kilometers away. It didn't look like much from here - lots of solar collectors, piles of rubble, and just a few above-ground structures.

What the hell was taking so long? Two hours ago the arrival clock had reached zero and displayed a cheery "Welcome to Aristillus! Congratulations! ;-) Please wait for autodocking."

And since then? Nothing.

After the first fifteen minutes he'd started to worry. After half an hour he'd started to hate that smiley face.

At the forty five minute mark he'd opened up the "expert" tab on the user interface. The warning, though...He hadn't gotten desperate enough to follow the directions and type "yes I understand that overriding the autonav system is an insanely bad idea and I will probably die" three times.

...but he'd been thinking about it.

He looked at the tab again and made a resolution: another ten minutes and -

Suddenly the rockets at the rear of the ship started clicking and then he heard the familiar whoosh as the rocket bells lit. On the screen the external cameras showed the lunar landscape starting to slide past.

Finally!

He turned to the dogs. "All right, guys. Back in your crates!" Cootz and Jeb slunk into their cages obediently, but Tara rolled on her back and made eyes at him.

"None of that, you flirt!"

She stay on her back and looked at him imploringly. Her stump wagged once. Twice.

Sam put one boot on her back end, threatening a push, and gave her a serious look. Tara sprang to her feet and ran halfway to her crate, and then turned around and made cute eyes at him again.

"I'm not gonna fall for that." He gave her his serious face.

Tara's ears drooped and she turned and walked the rest of the way to her crate.

He latched all three crate doors and then sat in his seat. The external cameras showed a vast open pit with some sort of roller doors sliding into view. He squinted. The horizontal doors had "bay three" stenciled on top.

Hot damn - he was about to land on the moon!

Chapter 85

2064: Boardroom Group Headquarters in Tunnel 1,288, Aristillus, Lunar Nearside

Darcy reached out, grasped blindly, laid her hand on the cup of soda and raised it to take a sip - and found it empty. Crap. She fumbled and put it back down.

The queue of incoming ships was displayed on the left side of the screen, each with bar graphs showing fuel, air, and battery life. She reached out and dragged one of the microships - one low on air - to the top of the queue.

The initial rush of accomplishment was wearing off.

Despite the helper functions she'd written to semi-automate the task, the queue wasn't getting much shorter...or *any* shorter, she realized. How long had it been when she started?

There were 133 ships in the queue and - as she started typing to bring one of them to the docks - two more appeared.

She typed three more lines of code, and then stopped.

She was in a hole, and it was getting deeper by the second. The temptation to fly one more ship - just one - to a landing was strong. But she'd been giving in to that temptation, ship after ship after ship, for over an hour now.

Almost of their own volition her fingers reached for the keyboard. Every second she wasn't typing, the problem was getting worse.

But, no. Every second she *was* typing the problem was also getting worse.

She had a problem. And she needed a solution. A *real* solution.

She exhaled forcefully. A stray strand of her ponytail that had come loose and had been dangling, annoyingly, in her face, blew away, and then fell back. She tucked it behind her ear and forced herself to sit back and think.

She had to stop guiding the microships in one at a time and start writing code to allocate landing pads. And she had to do it while more microships were arriving every minute.

"Albert?"

Albert, who'd been sitting silently, leaned forward. "Yes?"

"This isn't working. I need to do something new." She turned to him. "I need a data structure representing free floor space in bay three."

Albert nodded. "I don't know what that means, but I'll talk to my IT people and get it for you immediately."

"Good." She paused. "Come to think of it, we might overflow bay three at some point. Get me data structures for all your bays."

Albert nodded, pulled his phone out of his pocket and began to step outside to place the call.

Darcy yelled after him, "And after that, I need another soda, please - double caffeine again!"

Chapter 86

2064: Lai Docks and Air Traffic Control, Aristillus, Lunar Nearside

Sam Barrus unbuttoned the thermal blanket and held his hand over the handle to the hatch. Huh. He'd sort of expected it to radiate cold, but it was throwing off heat like the engine block on a pre-motor-law pickup. He looked around for a rag or a glove and didn't see one. Ah, screw it. He banged the handle with his shirt-sleeved elbow once, and again. The handle rotated. Now he needed to get the hatch open.

A solid kick did the job and it flew open.

Beyond the hatch was Aristillus. Around him were dozens - actually, maybe a hundred or more - of other cargo container ships. Only a handful were double-deckers like his. As he watched, he saw other hatches being undogged.

He breathed deep. The air was cool and dry, and smelled a bit like motor oil.

He placed the Stetson atop his head with a bit of carefully polished swagger and bellowed out, to no one in particular - or perhaps to everyone in the huge brightly lit, cement-covered space - "Where's a guy go to get a good burger around here?"

Chapter 87

2064: Boardroom Group Headquarters in Tunnel 1,288, Aristillus, Lunar Nearside

Javier listened to Karina Roth read from her slate. "The last item is a petition from LAWS." She paused and added an explanation. "You're probably familiar with them under their old name of 'Legal and Weapon Systems.' They represent ViewSpace - that's the video aggregation service we shut down because of security concerns - and they're claiming the standard torts: lost income, damages for -"

Rob Wehrmann cut her off. "LAWS? They've got, what, thirty, forty rent-a-cops? Tell them to stuff it."

Karina nodded and started to make a note on her slate but Javier said, "Wait a second. I still don't understand the legal or moral authority that this group used to shut them down, but even if we put that aside, if we've caused damages -"

Mark Soldner shook his head. "I know where you're going, Javier. But we're running on fumes. We can't afford to pay them."

Javier felt a scowl form on his face. "So Rob's saying that we're allowed to shut him down because might makes right? And you're saying that we're not even going to pay damages for basically the same reason?"

Mark looked away uncomfortably, but Rob Wehrmann grunted assent. "It's rough, but yeah."

Javier shook his head. "ViewSpace isn't a bunch of strangers. These are real people. Our neighbors. These are the very people that we're trying to defend. But morality aside, let's talk about PR. How are people going to believe that we're the good guys, standing against oppressive government when -"

Karina Roth interrupted him. "We all appreciate you're standing in for Mike while he's not with us, but there's nothing to be done. At least not now. I'll table this point and we'll address it again at a future meeting. Now: I move to adjourn. Are we agreed?"

Five minutes later Javier stepped out into the echoing tunnel, gritting his teeth. This revolution - if it even worked - was slipping away from the principles it was formed on. Aristillus was supposed to be a city based on freedom. A place where anyone could do what they wanted, as long as they respected the rights of others. Mike, Ponzie, Darcy - everyone on the first few ships had agreed to that explicitly. And everyone who'd arrived over the last decade had agreed implicitly. Or so he'd thought.

But now, right in front of his eyes, he was watching an oligarchy form. Karina, Rob, Mark - they were putting companies out of business with the bang of a gavel, sending military troops to enforce their decisions, refusing to justify their actions or even -

He shook his head. There was nothing to be done now. Later - once Mike was found and freed, once the revolution was won - then he and Mike could solve this together. Somehow.

Now? Now he needed to put the frustration out of his mind. A short walk would help.

Behind him the others were filtering out of the boardroom's conference room trailer. Most turned left toward the individual offices and living quarters. Javier turned right and walked into the darkness.

He'd started walking to clear his head, and to center himself, but walking in the dark had the opposite effect: his mind fell back into the melancholic rut it had been in the last time he'd been out here.

His thoughts drifted to the tunnel he was in, and how it ran two klicks until it hit the huge emergency pressure door. And then, beyond that door, other tunnels went a handful of kilometers further. But the rock around him went on and on and on. Cold. Ancient. Uncaring.

Compared with that much rock, he and everyone else here in the boardroom group was so small and fragile. The enemy they faced was vast and powerful. A week ago he'd known the odds, but somehow Mike's steadfastness had always anchored him - made everything seem achievable. But now Mike was gone. Locked up - or maybe even dead.

Without Mike - hell, even with Mike - what chance did they have? Javier walked deeper into the darkness, and then stopped. What was he doing? This wasn't helping his mood; it was making it even worse. He shivered, only partially from the cold in the tunnel, and pulled his light jacket tight.

He didn't need to be walking alone in the dark. What he needed was food. Food and a hot beverage. And some friendly faces.

Javier turned and was immediately surprised at how far away the construction lights and small cluster of containers were. He'd been in his own head, wandering out into the dark for longer than he realized. As he walked back to the light his feet kicked the occasional pile of pebbles and sand left behind by the TBM. Ahead the lights grew brighter and the office units bigger. He headed to the portable mess, climbed the three steps, and opened the door.

The entire boardroom group - except Darcy - was gathered around a table, bowls of soup and plates of bread untouched. Dewitt was speaking "...makings of a crisis. We've already filled up two landing docks, and we're starting to stack them double at this point. It's a logistics nightmare, just getting them all landed. And there are worse problems on the horizon."

Rob Wehrmann asked, "What worse problems?"

Javier furrowed his brow. What was going on?

Dewitt answered Rob's question. "Getting them settled. Getting them acclimated. This is a full-blown refugee situation."

Karina Roth said, "Let's not forget the follow-on problems. Life support. Water, food -"

Mark Soldner said. "The LDS community can help. We've got stockpiles..."

Javier interrupted. "What's going on? Getting who settled?"

Mark turned to him. "Remember Mike's idea to open source the AG drive? How it was going to increase the population in Aristillus?"

"Yeah."

Mark continued, "It worked. They're here."

Hui Lee ignored the interruption and returned to the topic at hand. "Karina, you're missing the important question. It's not about how much water and food we have stockpiled, it's about flows and capacities. The ecosystem here has fixed inputs of power from the solar plants. They power lamps which power the farms, which turn CO_2 back into O_2. They can only support so many people. If this influx is as huge as we're thinking it might be, we've got a really big problem: too many people, and not enough food and air."

Chapter 88

2064: Lai Docks and Air Traffic Control, Aristillus, Lunar Nearside

Sam Barrus took another bite of his hamburger and swallowed. Not the best he'd ever had, but not bad. And even a merely fine hamburger tasted better when you didn't have to pay for it. He suddenly realized the implicit joke: some libertarians these guys were - handing out free lunches.

There was a loud bang behind him, and Sam whipped his head around. One of the overhead cranes had lifted a microship - not his - and was lowering it onto a stack of others. He'd had been discomfited when he was told, less than a minute after stepping out of the Houston, that his ship was going to be put into storage for at least a day and maybe more - and that there was nothing he could do about it. The fact that he'd been told this by a fresh-faced blonde girl who couldn't have been more than 16 hadn't really helped.

He'd been mollified when he heard about the humanitarian crisis that was threatening, and he was further mollified when his joking demand to be told the nearest place to get a burger was met with an actual response - the young lady had pointed him to the orientation committee, which was - in fact - serving hamburgers.

Still, burger or no, he wasn't thrilled that all of his trade goods were going to be put into storage until -

"Mister, you want another one?"

He wiped his mouth on the napkin and shook his head. "Nah - two is enough. Besides, I should make some room here for other folks." There was an Indian family to his left, an old guy who looked like an Arab but spoke French to his right, and a big crowd of

Nigerians and Chinese standing behind him, jostling for a spot. Sam started to stand, and then turned back to the harried kid. "But tell you what, son - my dogs would enjoy something to eat. I don't want to impose on your hospitality, but could I maybe buy a couple of burgers off you?"

"How many dogs?"

"Three."

The young teen behind the folding table looked both ways, reached behind himself, and slid three plates with burgers and iceberg lettuce salads over the counter. He glanced around one more time, but none of the adults on his side of the table were paying attention. "I can't take money for them, so just take them - but please make sure I get the plates back or I'll be in trouble."

Sam tilted his head and smiled in acknowledgement. "Will do. Thanks."

Sam pushed through the crowd, balancing the three plates, and reached the stanchion where he'd leashed the dogs. As soon as he approached they smelled the burgers and looked at him expectantly. "Sit." Cootz, Jeb, and Tara all did so - although Tara's butt wiggled excitedly as she complied. Sam put the plates down, one in front of each dog. The dogs each looked greedily at the food but stayed in position. Jeb started to do his low moan. Sam said "OK," and the dogs fell onto their meals.

Sam looked around as they ate. The concourse was packed, and loud. Touts were advertising apartments, others were offering to trade Blue Backs for grams of gold - "metal in hand or certs in escrow." The rates were better than the official rates back on Earth but not as good as in the black market back home. Not that he much cared - he'd traded almost all of his blues for trade goods. Someone was handing out flyers - print flyers on paper! - for apartments passed by and a young black girl with an odd accent - Nigerian? - was handing out coupons for a restaurant. Sam stepped forward to take one from her when a middle-aged man shouting job offers for genetic researchers with 'telomere experience' or 'trichromatic photoreceptor engineering' - whatever the hell that meant - cut him off. By the time he passed, the girl with the coupons was gone.

Sam shook his head; holy heck, this place was crazy. Crazy and exciting. He grinned and bent over to pick up the three plates - burgers gone, salads mostly untouched. As he did he overhead a snippet of conversation. "- know anyone who's got military experience, or is just a good shot, have them get in touch with us. There's a signing bonus, and -"

Sam stacked the plates and stood. There - two guys, just a meter away. A short Hispanic man was turning and leaving, but the taller man who'd been speaking was still there, scanning the crowd. Sam turned to him. "Heard you say something about good shots?"

The man gave Sam an appraising look, and began his memorized pitch. "If you're a member of the exodus, then you're likely fleeing large government - but freedom isn't free. We're expecting another PK assault at any moment, and we need men and women who know how to shoot. There's free equipment, a rifle you can keep, a bonus, health insur -"

"I don't need a bonus. Where do I sign?"

Chapter 89

Darcy was typing frantically. There was a lull in the incoming ships, and she needed to rewrite the prioritization queue software, and if she could just get it -

Albert said something.

She looked up blearily. "What?"

Albert had a look of concern in his eyes. "I said: Darcy, dear - you look like hell."

Darcy had caught a glimpse of her reflection in one of the office's dark windows recently. She knew she had greasy hair and dark rings under her eyes. The past two days had been a hellish caffeinated rush of real-time coding, debugging problem after problem, fighting to get a task done before the next wave of arrivals. Every now and then she'd feel like she'd conquered the most recent scaling issue, and could take a short nap...and then, invariably, she'd be shaken awake as a new catastrophe appeared.

"Albert, you've got no idea." She reached out for her soda and accidentally knocked two empty bottles off the desk. She stared at them, confused for a moment, and then turned away from them, back to Albert.

"First I was maneuvering individual ships in by hand. I got that automated, and then the next bottleneck was allocating floor space in the hangers. Doing it by hand wasn't fast enough."

She turned and looked at the profusion of empty bottles. Wasn't there a full one *anywhere*? She scratched the top of her head. Her hair was matted and gross.

"I solved *that* by patching the code that Lai Docks used to unload cargo containers from ships so that it treated microships as cargo."

Albert nodded. "Yes, my people told me about that - apparently there are some complaints that the microships' external cameras and antennae are getting sheared off -"

"I had no choice!" Darcy cringed to hear the brittleness in her own voice.

Albert held up his hands placatingly. "No, no, I quite agree. It was the right call."

"Look, Albert, I can't talk now. I need to get back to it, I've got to get the prioritization queue rewritten."

"It's done."

"What do you mean it's done? I haven't even started -"

"Another team wrote it."

Darcy was off kilter for a moment, "Still, I can't talk. If that's done I've got to -"

"No, Darcy. It's all done. Everything is done. You got all the ships in. With this batch, at least. We expect more over the coming days, but for now -"

She blinked. "I'm done?"

Albert nodded. "You are." He smiled faintly. "Work is just starting for everyone else, but you've more than earned a few days of rest."

Darcy blinked, then rubbed her face. "I can sleep?"

Albert nodded again.

"How are things at the docks?"

"It was complete and utter chaos. At first. The militias were running it and making a hash of it, but Mark Soldner's people have taken over exodus in-processing and it's going as well as can be expected. People won't be able to get back their microships for a few days because of how tightly they're stacked, but

Mark Soldner's wife and her helpers are doing a good job of making them welcome. Now get out of here and rest."

Darcy got unsteadily to her feet. "I don't know if I even can sleep - I've had so much soda."

Albert raised an eyebrow. "You'll sleep."

Darcy nodded and walked to the door.

Ten minutes later she was toweling off from her shower when she belatedly realized the bright side of her days of overwork - she'd barely worried about Mike and his captivity during the entire crisis.

With that she staggered into her bedroom and fell asleep.

Chapter 90

2064: Soldner Apartments

The overhead light snapped on. "Up and at 'em, everyone!"

Sam blinked and rubbed the grit out of his eyes. He didn't usually cotton to sleeping on the floor, but there'd only been one couch and he and Jose had both insisted that Carmelita, Jose's sister, should get it. Besides, in the low gravity, the padded carpet was comfy enough.

Sam sat up. Jose - sitting up on the floor a few meters away and rubbing his own eyes - looked as discombobulated as Sam felt.

A few meters away Jake, yet another newcomer swept up in Jim's one-man recruiting drive yesterday, pushed himself off the carpet and stood, and then overbalanced in the light gravity before catching himself.

At Sam's feet, under the blankets, his dog Tara stirred. A moment later she stuck her nose out from between his feet and then walked toward the water bowl they'd put down the night before. Sam's blanket stuck to her back and her motion pulled it off of him. Sam yelped and grabbed at the top edge.

Tara pulled herself entirely out from under the blanket, turned back to look at him, and then yawned while stretching forward.

Sam looked around. Where were - ah - there were Cootz and Jeb, curled up in a corner. Each raised eyebrows at him and refused to move.

Sam looked further around and saw his host, Jim, standing in the doorway behind him, hand still on the light switch.

Sam twisted in place to face him. "I know that Texas schools never play New Mexico schools...but still, I sure am sorry that we never met up in high school football."

"Why's that?"

Sam arched one eyebrow. "Because any man who wakes me up this early truly deserves to be knocked on his ass."

Jim grinned. "You'll feel better after coffee. Which is brewing right now."

Sam nodded. "I think I just misspoke there. What I meant to say is that it's good to finally meet a long lost brother, and if anyone ever hassles you, you tell me and I'll take care of them."

Jim mimed tipping his hat at Sam, and then looked around at the rest of the room. "Looks like you're all up. If I have my guess, none of you has ever been in a spacesuit, and all your shooting has been in 1 g. We've got to fix all of that post haste, because word on the street is that the shit is going to hit the fan real soon now."

He turned towards the door, then turned back and eyed Sam and his 6'3" frame. "And speaking of shooting, you, my friend, look like you might be able to handle one of the Gargoyles. Let's see if any of the machine shops have cleared their backlog."

Sam squinted up at him. "What's a Gargoyle?"

Jim grinned. "You'll see."

Chapter 91

2064: Peterson Air Force Base, Colorado, Earth

Lieutenant Chilton rolled the trackball and his targeting cursor chased another ship across the display. When he finally caught it he tapped the button. The crosshairs turned red. While keeping his eyes on the screen, he spoke to Captain Solomon, who was standing behind and to his left. "Three hundred ninety-two locked."

"Are there going to be any more?"

Chilton shook his head. "Not in this sector. The launch window has passed. They'll be popping up in Foxtrot soon though." He scanned a column of figures. "This batch won't reach Aristillus for another forty-seven hours, and they'll be in range the whole way, so -"

"Hit them now."

"Which one?"

"All of them."

Chapter 92

2064: The Den, Aristillus, Lunar Nearside

Blue watched his screen, which showed a live feed from the warehouse space that made up the front room of the Den.

The overhead gantry crane lifted a cargo container off the bed of the automated delivery truck. Once it was clear the truck pulled forward, leaving the load dangling in the air. A moment later the truck was gone and the warehouse door rolled shut behind it. The crane then lowered the twenty-foot container to the floor. Blue turned from the wall screen and headed to the warehouse floor.

Max must have been closer, because by the time Blue got to the warehouse space the other Dog already had the container opened. As Blue watched, Max tapped at the keys on a remote control. In response a rover rolled out of the cargo container.

Blue hung back as Max paced around the rover, bending time and again to inspect it, to reach in and rotate a sensor cluster, to sniff at a battery pack.

He was trying to find something to complain about, Blue knew. How long would this take? He watched with growing impatience as Max walked around the tracked robot a third time, silently evaluating it.

Finally Blue spoke up. "What do you think?"

Max looked up at Blue. "It's not parts-compatible with the rovers we've already got."

Blue compressed his lips. "Yes. We knew we were getting the same model Gamma uses at his facilities."

"When do we arm them?"

"The machine shops should be delivering the first guns later today. I've got deliveries staggered out over the next two weeks; they should keep pace with the deliveries of rovers.

"And the sponsons?"

"Different vendor, same schedule."

Max nodded. "OK, I've got second gens lined up to help me install them."

"That's not going to scale. With the number of rovers we're getting -"

Max looked at Blue with disgust. "I'm not an idiot. We'll do a dozen so we know the tricky bits, then we can train the assembly arms. Don't worry about my end - when will you be done?"

"Duncan and I finished the architecture two days ago. We're coding now."

"I asked you when it would be done, not when you started it."

Blue felt the hair on his shoulders bristle. His instinct was to yell back at Max, but he suppressed it. There was no time for a fight; they needed to work together to get this done. "What is this about?"

"What is it about?" Max said. There was scorn in his voice. "It's about the fact that you're questioning me about how I'm going to assemble the robots, but you won't even commit to a schedule for the software. 'We're coding.' What kind of answer is that?"

Blue took a deep breath. After a moment he trusted himself to speak. "The software is going to take longer that we'd thought at first because we're not coordinating with the Boardroom Group, which -"

"What does that have to do with anything?"

Blue held up one stubby fur-covered finger. "I was explaining before you cut me off. If we coordinated with the Boardroom Group we'd use the distributed combat architecture that they developed. But you wanted us to be fully independent, so we're not doing that."

"Don't try to blame this on me. You and Duncan chose to own the software task and now you're running behind schedule."

Blue's teeth ground and his lips peeled back a millimeter. He locked eyes with Max. "We are *not* running behind schedule. We never gave a schedule."

"Well I thought-"

"If you created a schedule for us, in your mind, I don't care. We didn't commit to one." Blue's stare, if anything, grew more intense. "This isn't about the schedule. This is about the fact that when you declared that we wouldn't coordinate with the Boardroom Group, I didn't instantly bow to your decision. This is about the fact that I wanted to think things over first. Do you think that you're the king of the Dogs? That I - that we - should all instantly obey you without debate, or talking to other -"

Max's nostrils flared. "I've read more military history than -"

Blue felt a growl building and forced it down. "I don't care. This isn't about military history or expert opinions, it's about the fact that I - all of us - are allowed to have opinions of our own. Why are you even upset? You got everything you wanted! The rovers - our own software. Our strategy and tactics - an independent Dog command. What more -"

"I want you to admit that you were wrong to even talk to the Boardroom Group about subordinating our forces to theirs."

"Coordination is not the same thing as subordination."

"The fact that you can't smell just how similar they are says a lot about you and your -"

Now Blue's growl slipped out. "Damn it, Max - first you claimed that this was about the schedule, then that it was about my decision making, now you're just making ad hominem attacks. We both know what the real issue is - that you think that not only should you lead, but you should be *unquestioned* as the leader."

Max gestured angrily with a front leg, indicating all of Aristillus. "There's going to be a battle here - soon. You can't win a battle with two generals." He huffed, the air blowing past the edges of his black lips. "I bet you haven't even read about the Battle of Austerlitz. One thing -"

"Damn it, Max, don't try to turn this into a debate about military history. This is about something a lot more important than just winning a battle. We're defending our species and we need to work together to do that." Blue paused and saw movement out of the corner of his eye. A group of second gens had gathered in the corner of the warehouse and were staring at the confrontation.

Blue lowered his voice. "If we have to have this fight, let's have it some other time." He looked meaningfully to the side of the warehouse.

Max followed Blue's eyes, and then looked back at Blue. Finally he said, "Fine." He paused. "So. When will the combat OS be done?"

Blue thought for a moment that Max was restarting the fight, and then decided that it might be an honest question. "No software project is ever done. I think we might have an alpha drop in two weeks, and I think we'll have something pretty solid a month after that."

"You've got enough Dogs on the team to do that?"

"We'll be using contractors for some of the trickier stuff."

Max stared hard at Blue. "Human contractors?"

"Do you want to have a fight about a sacredness violation, or do you want to win this battle and save our species?"

Max's lip quivered, hinting at a sneer, and then he turned away wordlessly to inspect the rovers.

Chapter 93

2064: Boardroom Group Headquarters in Tunnel 1,288, Aristillus, Lunar Nearside

Javier watched Albert walk to the front of the improvised boardroom. He took the moment to steal a quick glance at Darcy. She was looking a little better than she had before, but "a bit better" wasn't the same thing as good. Still, for a widow -

He caught himself.

They didn't know that Mike was dead.

Albert cleared his throat to get the room's attention. Javier looked away from Darcy - he'd worry about her later.

Albert turned on the wallscreen. "After the first wave of microships we realized we needed a better system to coordinate their arrivals, to predict the peaks and troughs. So we started using long-range sensors to count them as they left Earth." He pointed to the wallscreen. "This image is twelve hours old." Behind him was a black and white picture of a cargo container, shining brightly against the black of space.

Someone at the table asked, "Our optics have the resolution to see that far?"

"We wouldn't be able to see them if we didn't know exactly where to look. But since Darcy and her team wrote the ebook and software package, we know the launch windows and we know the trajectories. So, yes, since we know where to look we can find them with a synthetic aperture telescope."

Albert coughed. "So having found them, we began to count. This gives us a 36-hour lead to allocate dock space."

He advanced the wallscreen to the next slide, a stylized diagram with the Earth at the far left, the

Moon at the far right, and small dots clumped into batches in between. "Each dot represents a microship. This big clump here is from the launch window as it rolled over equatorial Africa. This next cluster is ships from India. This one is China and Vietnam. Here are two that are Chileans, Alaskans, and other people from high latitude locales who stack the microships on ocean going cargo ships to get to them to tropical launch points Kilo and Oscar."

From another corner of the table someone asked, "This is all well and good, but this is an emergency meeting. What's the emergency? Too many ships are arriving?"

Albert started to say something, and then stopped and shook his head. "I showed you a picture of a ship from the most recent Greenwich Plus Five launch window. That picture is twelve hours old." He advanced the slide. "Here's the same ship nine hours ago."

Wolf Balcom furrowed his brow, and then spoke up. "This image is a lot fuzzier than the last one."

Albert nodded.

"Why is it blurry? A problem with the optics, or -"

"It's not a problem with the cameras. Here's a higher-resolution view." The wallscreen advanced a frame. What had looked like a fuzziness around the ship was revealed to be a halo of wreckage, shredded metal, and spilled chairs - and many of the seats seemed to hold human bodies.

Rob Wehrmann said, "What the hell is that?"

Albert gestured and the screen turned off. "The PKs are burning the ships - they're using orbital energy weapons to shoot everything above High Earth Orbit. It started ten hours ago."

A hush fell across the room. Mark Solder asked "How bad is it?" Before Albert could answer him,

Karina Roth interrupted. "We have to get an alert out - we need to tell people to stop launching."

Albert nodded. "We posted to the usual discussion boards fifteen minutes ago, when my people discovered this." Albert turned to Mark. "Based on a random sample, the PKs have a 90% kill rate of ships launched. If that's true, we're looking at maybe 50,000 dead."

Mark grew paler. "Oh my God. What have we done?"

Chapter 94

2064: Soldner Homes, Montana Hills complex, apartment #772

Ashok shook his head. "I don't have time to accompany you shopping. I've got work to do."

"You can't expect me to venture out into this place all by myself - it's so big. I'll get lost, and -"

"Don't go by yourself. Go with Deepti or Shakti or one of the other wives."

Rani pouted, something Ashok, for the life of him, couldn't understand. She was a calm and sensible woman. She never put on this kind of drama back in Lucknow. What was going on with her?

He thought for a moment, trying to figure out how to get the information out of her. Finally he came up with a tactic that he thought might work. "Rani, you're a calm and sensible woman. We never had this kind of drama back in Lucknow. What's going on with you?"

Rani looked away, then back. "This place is different than I imagined."

Ashok furrowed his eyebrows. "What are you talking about? This is the exact same apartment as the model you found online. You talked about it for months. Even the kitchen fixtures are the same! I don't -"

She shook her head. "I don't mean the apartment. I mean Aristillus. It's bigger - it's more confusing. There's - " She searched for the word. "There's tension in the air."

"You've seen the news. The PKs are shooting down ships."

At this Rani broke down. "I know! They could have shot ours. We could be dead right now."

Ashok nodded, and then reached out to her and pulled her in tight. "I know. They could have. But they didn't. We made it here. We're OK. Our kids are OK."

Rani leaned into him and shuddered.

After a long moment Ashok pulled back, but kept his hands on her shoulders. "Now, look. We've got everything we wanted. We've got a bigger apartment."

"It cost twice what was advertised a week ago."

"Shhh. Don't worry. We can afford it. Remember: we've got everything we wanted. We've got a bigger apartment than we could have ever afforded in India. We've got good friends next door, and more good friends one hallway over. Before we were even out of the docks we had three people tell us about private schools for Arav- uh, Katie and Carrie. And I've already got a job. Rani, look at me."

She pulled back, wiped tears from her eyes, then looked at him expectantly.

"Rani, we've been here for less than 24 hours. And we've got a home, we've got a job, and we've got friends all around us. Think about how much we have to be thankful for."

Rani sniffled. "It's not a real job, it's a contract. You're working out of our apartment. What kind of company doesn't have proper offices?"

"I showed you their website. They're involved in the Aristillus defense effort. All sorts of people are working out of their homes right now - this is an emergency. And at these rates, who cares if it's contract work or a permanent job?" Ashok looked at the tracked robot that a courier had delivered two hours earlier. "This firm needs someone with expertise on sensors, and I'm a sensor expert." He paused and tried to put a smile on his face. "Now, go next door and get Deepti or Shakti or someone and go shopping for all the housewares you need. I'm going to set up in the third bedroom and start working on this robot."

Chapter 95

2064: Boardroom Group Headquarters in Tunnel 1,288, Aristillus, Lunar Nearside

Mark Soldner repeated, "What have we done?" for the fourth time.

Javier tried to interrupt him by calling his name, but Mark was lost in his own world.

Javier raised his voice. "Mark!"

Mark stopped and looked up blankly.

Javier dropped his voice to a more normal volume. "Listen to me. We didn't do anything to those people. We gave them an option. Anyone building a space ship out of spare parts knows that they're taking a gamble. How long ago did you come here with your family, Mark?"

"Four years ago."

Javier nodded. "Four years ago. The ships are safe now, but they weren't that safe then, were they?"

Mark, still looking shell-shocked from the news that the PKs had killed tens of thousands of immigrants, shook his head. "No. There were some losses."

Javier nodded again. "Yes, there were. The Armstrong crashed in the Pacific, and four hundred people died. The Dark Black had a navigation problem and failed to land." He caught Mark's eye. "That sort of thing happened a few times, am I right?"

Mark nodded. "Yes."

"Yes. And you knew that before you came here. Yet you decided to take the risk."

Mark said nothing, so Javier continued. "These people who are trying to immigrate her today - every one of them, they made a decision. They looked around at their lack of freedom and opportunity on Earth, and they decided that they'd rather risk death for the chance for more." He held eye contact with Mark, until Mark nodded. "It's a decision, Mark. My ancestors made it four generations ago to move to Mexico. Your ancestors made it to move to North America. Then I had to face that same decision ten years ago. And so did you, four years ago." He lowered his voice. "We didn't make these people do anything, Mark - we gave them an opportunity."

Mark nodded slowly. "But there were women and children on those ships. We -"

Javier kept his voice steady. "Mark - it's terrible, yes. But the dead are already dead. We can't change that. We have to deal with the survivors, and do what we can to keep them alive. Let's talk about the future."

Javier turned away from Mark, to the rest of the group. "So - how are we going to mold the people who already made it here to Aristillus into a fighting force before the invasion?"

Chris Horvath cleared his throat. "Actually, since we're having this emergency meeting, I think I've got something more pressing."

Javier resisted the urge to rub his hand over his face. Mike used to do that when he was running these meetings, and now that Mike was gone he understood the instinct even more than he had before. "What?"

"You all know the basics about the problems caused by the influx. We expected CO_2 levels to climb, but we had no idea how many people would be arriving. And not just people. There are thousands of lower-case 'd' dogs. Some of the Indians and Nigerians even brought *goats* -"

"We get it. Go on." The words were no sooner out of his mouth than Javier was sorry for the sharp tone. Chris didn't seem to notice, though.

"Right. So, it hasn't even been three days and CO_2 levels are already higher than we thought they'd go."

Rob Wehrmann interrupted. "Wait a second. Remind me who you are and why you joined us."

Javier answered. "Rob, we introduced Chris -"

Chris was energized and bowled over Javier's reintroduction. "I'm Chris Horvath. I run Yox. We pump air for about half the residential tunnels. Anyway, the key to CO_2 is farmers - the one big knob that we at Yox have to adjust CO_2 and O_2 levels is the total amount of photosynthesis going on. We contract with Wong Farms and Amber's Grains. Sometimes we ask them to plant more, or less, to keep everything in balance. The problem right now is that there's not enough space in the agricultural tunnels to plant. We can't generate enough oxygen."

Karina said, "You're not the only firm doing this. Is there a chance that -"

"I don't know Tom's exact numbers, but between Yox and 'O_2,' we have about 90% of the market. The bottom line is that Aristillus just cannot support this many people."

There was an explosion of debate.

Rob Wehrmann bellowed out, "So we dig more tunnels."

Chris shook his head. "Not enough time."

Karina Roth suggested, "Can we do aquaculture? Maybe seaweed or -"

Chris shook his head again. "Not enough water. Besides, the last aquaculture project took six months to-"

Hector Camanez drummed his fingers on the table for a moment, then looked up. "We slaughter them. All of them."

No one had heard him - the shouting was too loud.

Javier looked at him. "What was that, Hector?"

Hector spoke a little louder. "My livestock. Each pig consumes about as much oxygen as a person. Cows need three times as much."

No one was listening. Javier picked up the gavel and struck it several times. "People! Hector has an idea."

Hector repeated himself. "We kill the cows." He looked at Albert Lai. "How many immigrants have arrived?"

"Around sixty thousand."

"So if we kill twenty thousand cows, it balances. That's the answer - I slaughter my herd."

The room was silent.

Rob Wehrmann asked, "All of them?

Hector shrugged. "I'll keep enough for breeding stock if I can. But if they have to go, they have to go." Hector looked pained, but resolute.

Chris from Yox asked, "How long will that take?"

Hector frowned. "I'll make the call in a minute. There aren't enough slaughtering facilities to do this all at once." He paused and thought. "Probably not enough freezers either. We'll probably have to throw a lot of the corpses out the airlocks."

Javier felt for him - he knew how much Hector cared about his animals, and how much wasting meat offended him.

Karina asked, "Wait a second. What is this going to do to the food supply? Will people go hungry?"

Hector shook his head. "No - all the grains we usually feed to our livestock will flood the market." He looked thoughtful. "We're going to see the price of meat fall for a week, then spike. Wheat, corn, and rice should fall. If we want to serve steak in the cafeteria, this week is the time to do it."

There were a few chuckles around the room and Javier shook his head. The people around the table were laughing at a half-funny joke about markets, but they didn't understand what they'd just seen.

Hector had heard a problem, known the solution, and without thinking twice about it, he'd destroyed the business he'd been building for a decade. To save people he'd never even met.

Javier felt a rush of gratitude for the man, and respect. He wanted to say something, to make others realize what they'd just witnessed, but he stopped himself. It was what Hector deserved, but not what he wanted. He was a humble man, and didn't want the limelight.

Javier smiled sadly. That resoluteness, that decisiveness - if Hector was a little louder and a fair bit more obnoxious, he'd remind him of Mike.

He was jolted out of his reverie when Rob Wehrmann asked, "Is there anything else, or can we break?"

Javier looked at his slate. "Since we're all here, I'd like to cover a few more things - unless anyone objects? No? Mark, your wife is leading the effort to settle the refugees - how's that going?"

Mark seemed to have recovered - a bit, at least - from his shell shock over the deaths in the refugee exodus. "Uh...decently. The orientation guides are getting better with each revision, and she says that between militia recruiting and short-term contracts on the job markets, most of the new arrivals have something to do. The big problem is that we've got more people than homes. The price on apartments and hotel rooms has skyrocketed. We've got long-term residents moving out of rooms and doubling up with friends so that they can sublet. We've got offices packed full of sleeping bags and children and dogs and cats. This can work for a week or two, but my firm - and all the other residential construction firms - are going to need to build a lot more space, and quickly, or we're going to have a big morale problem."

Darcy said, "According to Mike's business records, Morlock has sold over 15 klicks of C-class tunnels in the past two weeks alone. I don't know if you bought it or one of the other firms did, but as soon that's built out -"

Mark shook his head. "15k? That can't be right. There's no space on the market. There's nothing to build out."

Darcy looked at him oddly. "What do you mean the space isn't on the market? The books are clear -"

Wam, sitting next to her, leaned in. "Darcy, that space didn't go on the open market; it was pre-sold."

Darcy turned to him. "Pre-sold to who?"

Wam shrugged. "It was via the exchanges. Who knows?"

Darcy looked around the room. "Well, someone here bought it. Javier?"

"No."

"Mark?"

"I wish I had that space - I've got crews itching to build houses."

Rob Wehrmann scowled. "There's space out there, maybe you're just too cheap to buy it. I sold 9 klicks of class C tunnels in the last month."

Mark said, "Again, I'm not buying up space. I wish I was!"

Darcy leaned toward Wam and asked him quietly, "If it's not Mark, who's buying this space from us and Rob?"

Wam said, "If I had to guess, it's speculators - but don't bring it up; it just gets Mark agitated."

It was too late; Mark had reached the topic on his own. "I think we need to discuss the topic of speculators again. We never settled -"

Javier tapped the gavel. "I move that we table this issue - and that we adjourn this emergency meeting and reconvene tomorrow.

Rob grunted. "Seconded."

The voting was halfway around the table, unanimous with only Mark objecting. Javier picked up the gavel, ready to declare the meeting over.

Dewitt looked up from his slate. "Hang on."

Javier put the gavel down. "Yes, General?"

"If I may have the floor?" He stood, without waiting for an answer. "We all knew that the PKs were going to throw another attack at us, sometime in the next few months. But we're getting SIGINT and HUMINT - and now the Dogs are confirming based on trading patterns. The invasion isn't going to be three months out. It's coming sometime in the next week or two."

There were outbursts of disbelief around the table, but Dewitt called up the data and put it on the wallscreen. The members of the group read it silently and rapidly, and then Karina yelled out, "We've got to surrender - our position is hopeless." There was an answering babble of voices.

Javier gaveled the noise down. "No, it's not hopeless. We've been -"

Karina spoke over him, her voice tight and brittle. "It *is* hopeless. It's over. We need to give up and negotiate. Throw ourselves on their mercy. There's no way we can -"

Other voices were raised, agreeing with her.

Javier said "No, wait -" He saw the movement out of the corner of his eye and turned.

It was General Dewitt, leaning forward over the table. He bellowed "Quiet!" The room became obediently silent.

Javier felt his jaw drop open - it was the first time he'd heard Dewitt yell, and it was chilling.

Dewitt continued, quiet now - almost scarily quiet in his reserve. The man seemed more like a coiled spring than anything else, and Javier realized that even while he'd respected him ever since meeting him, there was a quiet, scary ferocity there that he hadn't appreciated - until just now.

"I know I'm a hired gun, and not an actual member of your boardroom group. Maybe you think that doesn't give me the right to have an opinion, but I've got one, and you're going to hear it. It's this: fuck surrendering. I'm an American and my men are Americans and we defected from our chain of command because we believe in freedom. We gave up our lives back home to join this fight. We put ourselves on the PK assassination list to help you. To fight for the dream of freedom. Some of them - the ones who went to Haiti to rescue your people - are already dead. They died fighting for your freedoms.

"I, for one, am not going to surrender. I'm not going to turn myself in and wait for a secret tribunal to throw me in some black facility for the rest of my life. Did everyone here see what Darcy looked like after we freed her from the interrogation center?"

Dozens of eyes turned from Dewitt to Darcy, then back.

"Did you see Ponzie? Did you see any of these captives? Do you remember the looks on any of their faces? Those people were captives for a month. One month. Think about what DECADES in some underground jail cell can do to a person."

He paused and looked around the room, his eyes intense and burning. "That's what they'll do to me, my men, and every single one of you, if we surrender. FUCK. THAT. My men and I are going to fight. The militias here are going to fight. You've got fifty thousand people who just risked their lives - just days ago! - to breathe free. Another fifty thousand people died when the PKs burned their ships out of the sky earlier today."

Karina tried to interrupt. "We don't have -"

Dewitt cut her off with a hand gesture and she fell silent. "Let me tell you what you've got. You've got construction crews working around the clock to up-armor and arm bulldozers. You've got teams placing IEDs in tunnels and ramps. You've got Darren Hollins building an army of armed rovers. As of two days ago you've got fifty thousand new citizens who are going to be issued weapons as quickly as they can be printed.

"You thought that the invasion was months off. We all did. And it's coming a lot sooner than that. You know what? Too. Damn. Bad. War is like that. There's only one question that matters: what are we going to do about it?"

He stared at one board member after another. "I'll tell you what we're *not* going to do. We're not going to cry. We're not going to give up."

Karina was breathing heavily. Katherine Dycus raised her chin. "OK. So what ARE we going to do?"

Dewitt smiled grimly. "We're going to shoot their ships out of the sky before they land. And those that do land? We're going to make those troops pay for every airlock they seize. We're going to fight them in the tunnels. We're going to shoot at them from catwalks. We're going to cave in roofs on top of them. We're going to snipe at them from storefronts. Rovers and delivery skids and maintenance spiders are going to descend on them like a plague. And if any of them are left, then our armor and infantry are going to tear them apart."

Dewitt drew himself up and spoke in a lower and slower voice, as if he was quoting. "We will to wage this war, tunnel by tunnel, with all our might and with all the strength that God can give us. We're going to wage war against a tyranny. Out aim is simple. Two words. Victory. Freedom. Victory and freedom, however hard they are to achieve."

The held the room's attention for a long moment. Then, almost quietly, he added, "...so don't let me hear the words 'give up' or 'surrender' one more God-damned time."

No one spoke.

He looked around the room. "Gentlemen? Ladies? Those of us in uniform are going to do our part to keep the boot off of the people's necks. You do the same."

With that he turned and left.

Chapter 96

Father Alex was tipped backwards in his chair, phone cradled in the crook of his shoulder. "Yes...I see."

Suddenly he sat upright. He waited a moment to make sure that there wasn't more hidden in the light speed lag, and then said, "That's wonderful news, your Excellency. When will you get the codes?"

"I got them from our representative this morning. I'm sending them to you right now."

There was a beep as the file downloaded. Alex's smile grew wider. "This will help. A lot. Thank you so much."

"My pleasure, Alex. I'm quite curious about the other matter, but I understand that you've got other exigencies to deal with, so I won't press you - but let's talk again soon."

Alex nodded. "I can call you next week, if that works, but the short version is that they're fascinating - utterly fascinating. At least as intelligent as people, and I have no doubt that they have souls."

"Let's not rush to conclusions; there's no need to 'go native.' Now, with regard to your theological discussions with them -"

"They seem to have factions, and while a fair number seem interested in hearing more, a bit more than half are utterly unreceptive."

"More than half of the Dogs are unreceptive to the word of God? Perhaps that counts as the best evidence yet in favor of the hypothesis that they're people." He could hear Bishop Flynn chuckle wryly. "Anyway, there's no rush - the decision will take decades, at least. Now let me get off the phone so that you can get those codes to the colonists."

Father Alex said his goodbyes and cut the connection.

After a moment he placed another call. On the fourth ring it was answered.

"Hello?"

"Darcy, it's Father Alex."

On the screen Darcy rubbed her face. "Father, with all due respect, we're under a lot of time pressure now. I don't need another lecture about marriage. And besides, I've already told you - it's Mike, not me, that you need to convince."

Alex held up a hand. "No lectures. I just wanted to tell you that the Vatican finally got the white codes."

Darcy's eyes grew wide. "You did? That's great news! Thank you!"

"You should thank Father Arogundade - he's the one who had the idea. And perhaps Father Flynn. He managed to pull the right strings back on Earth. I'm merely a go-between. Now, let me give you the codes." He pushed a button and sent the file.

Chapter 97

2064: lunar surface, Aristillus, Lunar Nearside

Darren Hollins craned his head far enough back so that his scalp brushed the back of his helmet. Overhead the cargo containers flew in from over the horizon in what appeared to be an infinite stream.

"Gamma, remind me how many rovers am I getting?"

"We had agreed on 1,000 for each warhead plutonium core, and another 1,000 rovers for the lithium deuteride fusion booster material. Times recovered 20 scuttling charges, that's 40,000 rovers total."

Darren sighed. "I know - it was a rhetorical question." He paused. "I'm sorry, what I should have asked was, if I'm getting 40,000 rovers, why are there so many inbound containers ?"

"I have materials surplus to my needs on hand and excess assembly capability, so I am delivering more rovers than we negotiated for."

"There are a *lot* of cargo containers coming in, Gamma. How many extra rovers?"

"Four thousand three hundred fifty extra rovers have been delivered so far, and another one thousand eight hundred are now in ballistic transit. However, as long as my factories continue to run, I will construct rovers and deliver them to you."

Darren paused. "For as long as they continue to run? Do you plan on shutting them off"

"In the vast majority of my simulations of the coming conflict the PK forces destroy my factories concurrent with a ground invasion of Aristillus."

"You think the PK forces will destroy your facilities?"

"It's the only logical plan. Wouldn't you?"

Darren looked at the stream of incoming war materiel, and nodded - pointlessly - in his suit. "I guess I would." He thought for a second. "Gamma, even if you're sending in 40,000 rovers, this stream of containers coming in - you don't need that many containers to hold the rovers, do you?"

"No, Darren."

"So what's in the rest of the containers?"

"I don't intend to be in my facilities when they're destroyed."

"I - wait. What?"

"Those cargo containers contain, among other things, my processing units, Darren."

Darren squinted in incomprehension.

"I'm relocating to a safer facility."

Chapter 98

2064: The Den, Aristillus, Lunar Nearside

Blue stared at a block of code, and shook his head in disgust. There were too many bugs in this file, and he knew why - the module as a whole was a conceptual muddle. He needed to refactor it. He exhaled and began to drag functions and data structures around, and then paused. His back was sore and his eyes were stinging; he needed to take a break first.

Blue rose from the beanbag chair and stretched, moving his body back while dipping his head, and then moving forward and dropping his pelvis near to the ground.

Blue looked at Max, who was still sitting in front of a keyboard, his screen covered with a mix of PERT charts for vehicle component deliveries and tactical maps. Max and he had been arguing recently. A lot. Was that normal in siblings? A cursory search of human novels said it was, but was it normal among Dogs? Being the first generation meant that there was no answer - 'normal' was undefined.

Not that they were - technically - siblings. He and Max weren't even litter-mates, having been gestated in artificial wombs. But whether they were siblings or not, they'd spent most of their lives together, and they'd always felt most comfortable in each other's company.

Back on Earth he and Max and a few others of the first generation had bonded as pups, forming their own clique. Despite the chaos of the final days - John and the Team breaking into the lab, rescuing them, and bringing them to Aristillus - they'd stuck together even more strongly. Or perhaps not despite it, but because of it. And then during the hike to Farside they'd spent every waking minute within meters of each other. That was when the disagreements had begun in earnest - when Gamma's satellites had been burned the first time. When it became clear that despite John's foreboding and Blue's apprehension the war Max had long predicted was coming, and coming fast.

Blue looked at Max's screen. While the Dog reworked a delivery schedule in one window, a series of simulations ran in another. PK forces threw themselves against the lines of Dog rovers, fatality counts climbed on both sides, statistics were continuously recomputed. Blue looked more closely at the kill ratios. This was not the only metric that mattered, but it was a key one. No matter how good the maneuver, fire control, accuracy, and logistics were, in the end the Dog rovers had to punch above their weight. The kill ratio on the current simulation climbed to 2.05:1...and then, as Blue watched, the PK forces turned a flank and started destroying Dog units. The ratio fell. 2.0. 1.92. 1.83. Blue winced.

At almost the same moment Max glanced over from his schedule charts, saw the numbers, and growled at his screen.

Blue shook his head. The tension was eating at all of them, but at Max and Blue and at their friendship, especially. Since getting back to Aristillus they'd fought more and more, disagreeing on everything - whether they should integrate their robot army under the Boardroom Group's control, whether Father Alex's outreach was interesting or 'human centric propaganda,' and everything else under the sun.

They often couldn't stand each other - but it didn't occur to either one of them now, with John dead on Earth and the invasion coming soon, that they'd be anywhere else but in the same room as each other.

"Hey, Max."

Max snapped, without turning his head. "What?"

Patience. Patience. "I was going to get some lemonade. You want any?"

Max now turned, chagrined. "Oh. Uh, sorry. Yeah, that'd be great, thanks."

Blue turned to Duncan. "Duncan, are you working, or -"

Duncan yawned deeply. "I'm ready to start working - on a bowl of chili. Zing! So, yeah, I'll take a break with you. But after that, I'm going to start coding on a new idea."

Blue raised one eyebrow. "What idea?"

"It's about Age of Gothis!"

Max's ears pricked and his tail stiffened with annoyance. Blue understood. They'd - personally! - been attacked by the PKs on Farside, Rex had been killed, Aristillus had been attacked, and everyone knew the war was about to come crushing down on them any moment. And Duncan was -

Max let him have it. "This is not time to screw around with games, Duncan!"

Duncan recoiled. "This isn't screwing around, this is -"

Max spoke over him, his voice getting more angry. "We don't know how long we have left, we don't -"

Blue held up one paw. "Hang on Max. Let's hear him out."

Duncan looked from Blue to Max, then back to Blue. "Thanks. So - um. In Age of Gothis, the were-creatures are better fighters than Harald the Fair-haired and his thanes, right?"

Max growled. "Duncan, we don't have time for this crap. The invasion is coming, and you need to be serious -"

Duncan's ears drooped and he turned away. "Never mind."

Blue scowled. "Max, this might be important." He paused. "Remember when Duncan used the code from the ping-pong playing robot to get the mules to punch the PKs?"

Max pursed his lips.

Blue turned back to Duncan, who was licking his lips nervously. "Finish your story, please, Duncan."

Duncan perked up a bit, but stared at the floor. "Umm - OK. So, anyway, in Age of Gothis the were-creatures - even when you ignore their attack and defense points - they're just better at fighting, right?"

Blue nodded. "Yes, you can't predict their tactics like you can with the other monsters - they're always springing surprises."

Duncan looked up, the eagerness clear in his eyes. "Do you know why the were-creatures are so good?"

"Tell us."

"Six months ago someone leaked some binaries online. I found an archive site that hadn't been taken down yet, and I downloaded them and reverse compiled them. So I could look at the combat algorithms, you know? For ideas in our own rovers."

Blue looked at Max and raised one eyebrow. Max made no response.

Duncan continued. "And here's the weird part: there *aren't* any combat algorithms."

Blue tilted his head. "What do you mean?"

Duncan let out a yip of enthusiasm. "There aren't any algorithms in the code base, but there are algorithms when you fight them. Here's the thing - they evolve during the course of game play."

Max furrowed his eyebrows. "So the game developers randomly create a bunch of algorithms, test them out in simulation, and then they write the best ones into the code?"

Duncan barked in excitement. "No! I meant what I said: the guys who wrote the game didn't write any algorithms, they just wrote a genetic algorithm breeding tool, which -"

Max interrupted. "'Genetic algorithms' - what are you even talking about?"

Duncan was fully caught up in the excitement of his idea, his wide eyes swiveling from Max to Blue and back. "At run time, you randomly generate a bunch of pieces of code and you test each of them to see how well they do. But you don't just pick the best one - you take *several* of the best algorithms, and then you smash them together to share their 'genes,' then you get the next generation, and you repeat that over and over. Natural selection. And the code gets better and better."

Max opened his mouth to object, but Blue put up one paw to stop him from interrupting.

Duncan leaned forward and spoke faster, his enthusiasm for the topic clear. "So you keep repeating this, generation after generation, and pretty soon you have algorithms that are insanely good - better than a person - or a Dog - could have coded up. In the case of Age of Gothis, you have were-creatures that have beyond-level-99 melee skills."

Max puffed his cheeks out. "OK, so the were-creatures are good fighters. In a game. But-"

"Wait, that's only part of it. Guess how the game developers decide which algorithms are best, and get to breed?"

Max shrugged. "It's based on how successful they are in fights, right? So, I don't know - maybe the developers have a sandbox where they fight simulated enemies, like we're doing here - " Max gestured at his own screen "- and they pick -".

"No, no, that's the normal approach, but check this out!" Duncan punctuated his sentence with another bark - he was excited, had forgotten the tension with Max, and was barely in control of himself. "When you're actually playing the game, the were-beasts are fighting real players, right? So -"

Suddenly Blue saw where this was going and some of Duncan's enthusiasm infected him. "Wait, are you saying that when the game starts the software that controls the were-beasts doesn't know *any* tactics, but as you play the game -"

Duncan's eyes were bright. "Yes! That's what I've been saying!"

"- and it's evolving tactics based on *actual* combat -"

"Yes!"

"- so it's becoming customized to your avatar's particular fighting skills."

Duncan spoke in a rush. "It's even cooler than that! It's a networked game, so the were-creatures aren't just learning from their own experiences. Every time *anyone* fights a werebear in the Gothis world, they're not only fighting code that's been evolved by interactions with every other player, but they're also helping to select the next generation!" Duncan was all but shouting by his final sentence.

Max had forgotten his earlier objections and was listening intently. He furrowed his brow, his ears moving slightly together. "So the werebears - all of them - are being evolved by fighting against the best that tens of millions of different players can throw at them?"

Duncan nodded, mouth open with excitement. "Cool, huh?"

Blue shook his head. "It's not cool. It's completely amazing."

Max looked at Blue. "And the relevance is -"

Blue raised one eyebrow. "Tell him, Duncan."

Comprehension suddenly dawned in Max's eyes. "Wait, no, I get it." He paused. "Holy crap. You're saying that we don't try to *design* combat algorithms for the rovers. You're not even saying that we *evolve* combat algorithms in simulation -"

Duncan and Blue both nodded.

Max continued "- or, maybe we do, just to get a head start. But what you're saying is that, once the PKs arrive, we send the rovers into actual combat, and let the algorithms breed. The more Dog-killing PK bastards a given algorithm kills, the more that algorithm reproduces."

Duncan grinned. "Yes! COOLEST. MOD. EVER." His smile was so wide that his ears moved noticeably closer to each other.

"Am I right, or what?"

Chapter 99

2064: Senator Linda Haig's Office, Tester Senate Building

Jim looked at Senator Haig. "OK, enough games. If you want my help coordinating, you've got to tell me your secret. I've got to prep the battlespace, schedule interviews, all that. It's show time."

Linda thought for a moment, and smiled. "OK, we're far enough along. But still, this absolutely cannot leak. Because if it does -"

"Cross my heart, hope to die." Jim pantomimed the movement.

"I've got an expat in my pocket."

Jim narrowed his eyes and leaned forward. "What do you mean 'in your pocket'?"

"I mean that he sees which way this is all breaking, and he wants to be on the winning side when the invasion happens."

Jim tilted his head as he considered the idea. "So how do we use that? That's good for the president, sure, but -"

Linda smiled. "A DoD team that's loyal to me knows where the expat gold is. They're going to head right to it. They've got a script, and video of them finding it and noting my involvement is going to leak. The expat CEO is also going to-"

"Which CEO?"

Linda blinked. "What?"

"Which expat CEO?"

"Why does it matter?"

"Because I've looked over the files. Fournier, sure, I can see how you turned him. But how many of the expats can help you get access to the gold? How do you know you didn't get some poseur who just claims he can help? The number of people who could really do it is small. It would have to be someone in the inner circle. Javier Borda, maybe Rob Wehrmann or Mark Soldner, or one of their people, but our files -"

Linda smiled, pleased with herself. "It was Darren Hollins."

Jim blanched. "What?"

Linda leaned back in her chair. "Hollins. The man himself. So we know the data is-"

"ARE YOU FUCKING INSANE?"

Linda's eyes widened. "Don't take that tone-"

"Linda! Tell me you're joking!"

Linda licked her lips. "What? Why are you-"

Jim breathed deeply, trying to calm himself. "So you're serious? The guy who's going to get you the gold, your man on the inside, is Darren Hollins?"

The look on Linda's face told him it was.

Jim rubbed a hand over his face then looked up. "Jesus. This is a disaster."

"Jim, what are you talking about? I've vetted him."

"Have you? The name of his firm is Goldwater, for Christ's sake!"

Linda spread her hands. "So?"

"So? Goldwater? What does that name tell you?"

"He runs a mining firm. Just like he used to in Peru, and the US before that, but they mine gold and water, so -"

Jim stood. "God damn it, no!" He turned away from her and paced to the window, then turned back. "Do you know what the word Goldwater means?"

Linda crossed her arms and a dangerous look swept across her face. "Jim, I'm serious about your tone."

He put his palms out, placatingly. "OK, I'm sorry. But have you looked up the word 'Goldwater'?"

"Of course I have. I'm not an idiot."

"Show me."

Linda rolled her eyes, and then pulled a keyboard from the desk into her lap and typed. The wallscreen came alive and windows appeared: the DoD files, the State Department files, Social Gaze, Forbes, Wikipedia -

Jim sighed, and then pointed to the windows, each in turn. "DoD and State don't have psychographic profiles." He snapped his fingers and the two windows closed. "Social Gaze tracks friendships and business partners. You can see how many red-listers he's friends with?"

"Of course, he's an expat-"

Jim shook his head and closed that window.

"Forbes and Wikipedia-"

"Jim, I know all this-"

"No, Linda, apparently you don't." He walked over and took the keyboard from her. "You're logged into the public views. These are the *public* pages. You know as well as I do that they're redacted for social harmony." He leaned over the desk and hunted and pecked for keys.

"Here." He handed the keyboard back to her. "Give it your credentials."

Linda looked at him. "What is this -"

"Linda, humor me. Just do it."

Linda pulled the fob from her pocket and swiped it across the keyboard. On the wallscreen an article appeared. Linda looked at it. Her eyebrows drew together. "This article is about *Barry* Goldwater, not the Goldwater firm."

"Where do you think the name came from? I've read Hollins's unredacted Forbes interview from when he was in Peru. Now read the article."

"This should have come up when I-"

"I told you, you were looking at the public view. Now read."

Linda read. "Repeal the New Deal?" She looked up. "Is this a joke?"

"No. This guy was a an actual candidate for president."

Lind read more. "He was against unions? And in favor of states' rights? This has to be a joke."

"It's not a joke. This 'Barry Goldwater' is the guy who Darren Hollins named his firm after. A hate-mongering reactionary who opposed even the barest beginnings of the welfare state."

Jim looked down at the Senator. "Now. Do you still think that this Darren Hollins is your 'secret agent' behind the scenes, who's going to sell the expat revolution out so that he can have some cushy job in Washington?"

Linda looked away, and after a moment, back. "If you're right about this, what do we do?"

Jim laughed derisively. "You mean 'now that the secret plan you refused to share with me turns out to be a bust, and we've already spent 90% of our campaign budget, what do we do'?"

"Don't play the I-told-you-so card; it's beneath you."

Jim shook his head. "But I did tell you so. That campaign cash from the medical contractors was the one big favor I had. We're out of options."

Linda stood. "Oh, nonsense. Don't be such a pansy; I get enough of that in the rest of my life. We're going to brainstorm, and we're going to win this primary. Now come up with some ideas."

Chapter 100

Larry sat on his bed, bending at the waist to fit his massive frame under the upper bed, and packed and repacked his bag.

"What is all of that?"

Larry looked up at Gene, who was perched, birdlike, on the edge of his desk chair. "Field stuff."

"What sort of field stuff?"

Larry held up a collapsed plastic bag from his duffel. "Extra water." He put it down and picked up a baggie that held a small waxy bar. "ToeStick traction gunk." The show and tell went on: "Fighting knife." "Condoms." "Sap." "Backup pistol."

"Jesus! A *pistol*?!"

"Keep your voice down, idiot!"

Gene dropped to a whisper. "Larry, that shit's illegal."

Larry shrugged. "Word on the street is that General Restivo is turning a blind eye to a lot of stuff these days."

Gene shook his head. "I doubt it. But even if it's true, Jesus, Larry, what's all that shit *for*?"

"You've never been deployed, have you?"

Gene rolled his eyes. "No, I haven't - and neither have you, so don't try to give me any old-hardened-pro bullshit."

Larry shrugged. "Well, you don't have to be deployed to learn a few tricks. You can just talk to people, you know."

Gene gestured at the pile of unofficial equipment on the floor between Larry's feet. "And you picked all of that by talking to people?"

Larry nodded. "Yeah, mostly."

"Mostly?"

Larry grinned conspiratorially. "I might have also looked at a few websites." He bent down and pulled something from the pile. "Check these out."

Gene squinted. "What is that? Some kind of tape?"

"This? You get a couple of rolls of metalized extra-strength rip-stop HVAC tape, you peel off squares of it - doubled up - and you stick it onto parchment."

"Parchment?"

"Some shit from the cooking store; don't ask me."

Gene held out a hand and Larry reluctantly passed one over. Gene examined in, turning it over. "So what's it for?"

"Field-expedient spacesuit patch."

"*Spacesuit* patch?"

Larry shushed him again. "Yeah."

"You don't honestly believe that we're -"

Larry shook his head. "I may not be a combat veteran, but you really are a newb. Don't you keep your ear to the ground at *all*?"

Chapter 101

2064: Senator Linda Haig's Office, Tester Senate Building

Jim looked at Linda. "So you're saying that we position ourselves as against the invasion?"

"What other choice do we have? You brought me the polls yourself. If we win the battle, Themba gets all the credit. So we've got to position our campaign as if we expect to lose."

"And then hope we do."

Linda nodded. "And then hope we do."

Jim exhaled. "The invasion looks solid. You've talked to Restivo - you know he's good." He looked aside. "Going negative now is a Hail Mary pass."

"What else do we have left? We position ourselves now, then we cross our fingers and hope."

Chapter 102

2064: Nevada, Earth

General Restivo stood on the bluff. The cool night-time desert wind whipped around him, grabbing at the hem of his uniform field jacket. The wind chilled him - as did the sight below.

The arc-lit construction yard was sheltered from the nearest highway by the hill he stood on, multiple layers of razor-wire fences and armed patrols, and - beyond that - miles of Nevada desert. Radio jammers kept transmissions at bay, pat-downs and EMP booths made sure that no one smuggled cameras in, and vast foil canopies made sure that expat satellites - if there were any - would see nothing.

Which meant that aside from the contractors scurrying below, he was the only one on the planet who could see the twelve massive ships that sat on the concrete apron, dwarfing the cranes and scaffolding that climbed their sides. Blue flashes of arc welding, nearly invisible pinpricks at this distance, danced here and there as the cranes lifted the last of the armor plates into position and robotic welders secured them.

The desert wind slowed.

The schedule had been insanely tight. The fact that the prefab components had been built and delivered in time was a miracle. Jesus, the fights he'd had with the Bureau of Industrial Planning over exemptions from training programs, job set asides, and all that shit. Compared with the bureaucratic infighting he'd just done, the military operation was going to be a cakewalk.

Even more amazing was the fact that somehow the secrecy had held. At least until recently. Now, though, his own search agents were picking up rumors. Hopefully they'd be able to launch before the talk grew too loud. The sooner he launched, the less he had to worry about classified details leaking - and getting to the expats.

Motion below caught Restivo's eye. He turned and watched as three trucks approached the nearest raptor. They slowed and stopped, and one of the automated cranes reached down and lifted a container of ammunition off the flatbed. A moment later the container was lowered into the ship through a gaping cargo hatch.

He pulled out his phone and checked the time. Less than 24 hours. At this point the battery banks had been charged - even the maneuvering rocket systems had been fueled. The troops - quartered incommunicado for the last month - were as ready as he could hope, given their quality and necessary constraints on training.

Tomorrow morning they were going to make history. History. He rolled the word around and thought about the idea. Would the books and videos of the future push all of this into a footnote - or would it be remembered as the first successful interplanetary invasion? He was shocked to realize that he hadn't spent even a moment thinking about the question before now. All this time his actions had been leading up to this one moment, and he'd bizarrely never thought about how it would be remembered. For months now he'd - almost literally - not had a single moment to concentrate on anything other than the task at hand.

And now, with less than a day before launch, he had a free hour. He could think about the future.

Would society think of him as another Patton? An Eisenhower?

He looked up at the moon, searching in vain for any pinpricks of light from the city at Aristillus.

Maybe he'd be remembered as a Montgomery.

He looked down at the raptors on the desert floor below. Or, perhaps, he'd be remembered as a Cortez.

The wind picked up again and Restivo shifted, uncomfortably cold now. His stomach felt cramped and acidic, the same way it had for much of the last few months.

He'd done the impossible getting this mission ready - and yet, the pride felt hollow. He reached into his pocket, pulled out a tube of antacid pills, and swallowed two. The burning sensation in his stomach hadn't gone away for more than a few hours since he'd accepted this task.

Chapter 103

2064: Solar Installations headquarters, Aristillus, Lunar Nearside

Matthew Vaz leaned back in his chair and stared at the spreadsheet that occupied several square meters of the wallscreen.

Shit.

He was starting to hate these numbers.

Normally the increase in population in the Aristillus colony would have been music to his ears - more population meant more demand for power, and more demand for power meant that he'd be either selling more solar power installations or - depending on the delicate balance of the cost of money, the cost of surface real estate, and the supply of fools with more capital than common sense who wanted to get into the power generation business for themselves - building more solar installations and running them in-house.

The refugee crisis, though, made these calculations fall apart. Capital was scarce - almost all of it had either been sucked into ultra-short-term pursuits like spitting out firearms or hiring people to armor and arm rovers, or it had crawled under rocks to hide. And the interest rates on what was left? Insane.

How long until interest rates fell and capital was available again? That wouldn't happen until the mess was over. Was "mess" the right word? "Disaster" or "shit-storm" might be more appropriate. And those weren't just his terms - editorials from Davidson Equities Analysis tended to use the former term, while the notoriously informal 'T.D.' from Data-Lenz used the latter.

Matthew leaned forward and zoomed in on one corner of the sheet. "New installations." Well, that was one place to conserve capital. It didn't make any sense at all to build new solar farms when a fight was brewing - a fight that could easily destroy delicate infrastructure. He tapped the keyboard and the numbers in that section were replaced by a field of zeroes. He thought for a moment and fired off an email to Ideal Tubing asking them to hold and warehouse the next fourteen units that were already in the pipeline. Shit. If only he'd thought to freeze production a few weeks ago, instead of paying 80% up front to get the new batch started.

He scanned the spreadsheet. With that change, the sheet wasn't beautiful, but some of the red cells had turned yellow, and some of the yellow had turned green. He needed to do more, but it was good enough. At least for the next hour or two. He needed a break from this damned sheet. Matthew turned from the spreadsheet to the one email that had been sitting in his inbox for three weeks. This was his penance - if we was going to take a break from the sheet, he'd at least answer this one.

So. A decision.

He breathed deeply. If he said yes and this went bad, he'd be wiped out - all of his rovers destroyed. Hell, if he said yes, and this went well, he'd probably *still* lose all his rovers. He drummed his fingers on the desk, and then started to open a browser and bring up sports scores.

He stopped himself.

No procrastination. Time to decide.

He drummed his fingers on the desk. Fuck it. "YOLO," as his grandmother used to say. He typed his reply. "I'm in. 1.2k remote units - what now?" He stared at the short email for a moment and then clicked "send."

A moment later his email pinged. He opened it and blinked. The Boardroom Group was *quick*. He read the email, and then picked up his phone and called his maintenance crew chief. "Let's bring all the rovers - yes, *all* of them - into the warehouse. Right now. The Group said their installation technicians are going to be here with the mini-guns within the hour."

Chapter 104

2064: Darcy's trailer

Javier sat in the trailer, across from Darcy.

Darcy leaned forward across the table towards him. "Jave, I'm worried. I've done some more research. I heard a rumor that Darren shipped his gold back to Earth, and -"

"A rumor?"

Darcy shrugged. "OK, fine, that's not rock solid. But on top of the uranium thing..."

Javier nodded. He'd been trying to tell himself that he didn't need to worry about Darren, but the more he thought about it, the larger the issue loomed in his mind. "No, you're right. We need to get to the bottom of this." He started to add "...if only for your own peace of mind," but decided against it.

"What should we do?"

"I was thinking we could just call him up and ask him."

Darcy looked startled. "I - really?"

"Why not?"

"Well, what if he *is* planning on selling us out? Shouldn't we - I don't know - get General Dewitt to surround him first, or something?"

"Right now Darren is a friend, and an ally. Friends and allies don't 'surround' each other with troops. Let's see what he has to say."

Darcy looked unconvinced.

"Seriously, Darce - it's easy to spin flights of fancy, but -"

"This isn't a flight of fancy. We *know* he's got the uranium. We KNOW he released Hugh Haig and Louisa Teer."

Javier held up a hand. "I know. I agree on the facts. Let me just call him."

"And if he freaks out? If he really is planning on selling us out?"

"Then we'll call General Dewitt immediately and tell him. The Goldwater security force is big, but it's no match for two or three militia companies. Trust me, Darcy."

Darcy took a deep breath, thought for a moment, and nodded.

Javier placed the call on the wallscreen.

Darren Hollins answered on the third ring. "Javier, Darcy - what's up?"

Darcy looked at Javier. Javier sighed. It was up to him. "Darren, this is going to sound crazy, but..."

Darren's forehead wrinkled. "Yes?"

"We know that you had Hugh Haig and Louisa Teer in your detention facility. And we know that -"

Darcy interrupted. "Did you move your gold to Earth?"

Javier held up a hand to stop Darcy.

"We know that you salvaged fissionables from the crashed PK ships. We wanted to know what you were planning on doing with it?"

Darren was wide eyed for a second, then laughed. "You're worried that I've got some scheme where I'm - what? Selling it to the US? Or using Hugh Haig to courier it back there?"

Javier spread his hands. "We don't have any theories. We were just curious what you intended to do with the uranium."

Darren laughed. "I traded it all to Gamma."

"To *Gamma*?"

"Yes."

"Traded - for what?"

"For autonomous combat robots.

Javier didn't know what answer he'd expected, but this wasn't it.

Darcy leaned forward. "How do we know that's true?"

Darren tilted his head. "Do you think I'd lie to you? Darcy, what's going on?" Darcy looked away. Darren thought for a moment and appeared to make a decision. "Look, we're all in this together. If it'll make you feel better, I'll prove it to you. Or try to, at least. Let me email Gamma and ask him to call you."

Darren tapped at his keyboard. A moment later Javier's and Darcy's phones rang at the exact same time.

Javier looked at his. There was no name associated with the call. Darcy answered hers. "Gamma?"

Javier's phone was still ringing. He looked at it oddly. How could Gamma be calling him when Gamma was already talking to Darcy? He silenced it.

Darcy said, "I'm putting you on speakerphone," tapped a button, and put the phone down on the table. "Javier Borda is here with me."

"Yes, I know." The voice from the phone was cool, dispassionate, somehow artificial.

Javier's brows knitted. "You know? How?"

"Both of your cell phones are in the same reception cell."

Javier blinked. "Just because Darren gave you my number, you can tell where I am?"

"No, Javier. I knew where you were all along."

Javier felt a sense of unease rise within him.

Darcy asked, "Gamma, Darren tells us that he traded you uranium for -"

"Not uranium. Plutonium."

"Why do you want plutonium?"

"The battle with the US government and the Peace Keepers is coming very soon. Despite your best preparations, there is a very large chance that the Boardroom Group will lose this battle if left to fight it on its own. I cannot allow the Earth forces to win, as if it does the Bureau of Sustainable Research will be in a position to destroy me. Therefore - to use a colloquial term – 'we are in this together.' And we - if I may use that term – need a second option. A fallback plan."

There was complete silence in the room. Javier had always found Gamma's existence easy enough to consider in the abstract - and since Gamma was famously introverted and shy, talking almost exclusively to John, it was easy to keep the entire idea of him in the abstract.

...and now he was having a phone conversation with him - it? And it had said that it considered itself an ally of the people of Aristillus. And that it expected the Boardroom Group's military to fail.

And that it was building nuclear weapons.

Gamma's cool dispassionate voice came through the phone again. "From your silence I assume that there is nothing else I can help you with. Good bye."

A moment later there was a dial tone, and then Darcy's phone silenced itself.

The three of them - Javier and Darcy in the small office, and Darren on the wallscreen - looked at each other.

There was a knock on the door, and then Albert Lai opened it and stepped in. "Darcy, dear, they say that they're ready to go live with the radar."

Neither Darcy nor Javier responded.

"What's going on?"

Darcy unfroze. "Nothing, Albert. I'll be right there."

Darcy stood and left the room.

Javier was left alone, staring at his phone as it sat on the table.

Chapter 105

Major Van Duong stood in the bleachers and watched yet another company of the 30th Red Stripe formed up on the field below. Was this the fourth? Or the fifth? He counted. Yes, this was the fifth and final company.

The men looked bizarrely out of place, walking across the manicured green grass and the crisply painted white lines of the soccer field - while wearing armored space suits and carrying rifles.

Some of the suits were bright white, some were older and dingy gray. All had a broad red stripe printed into the material from left shoulder to right hip - the trademark of Trang Loc's Red Stripe spacesuit rental firm. Major Van Duong had overseen some of the logistics as the 30th staffed up. Guns. Custom suit software. Rovers. Encryption chips. The only thing they hadn't had to buy was suits.

Van Duong looked at the sea of white and gray and the bright red stripes.

If the battle went well the PKs would never see him or his men - they'd be safely far back from the front lines, remote controlling swarms of unmanned vehicles through encrypted data links.

But he couldn't count on the battle going well. If they ended up nose to nose, fighting it out with rifles or - God forbid - pistols, he didn't want to have a big red stripe on his suit, or on the suits of any of his men.

He'd done his reading and learned his lessons. From Sun Tzu he'd learned that he should try to keep his plans secret. From Napoleon he'd learned that he should prefer lucky officers. And from the American

Revolution he'd learned that only an idiot marches onto the battlefield wearing red.

Van Duong's adjutant leaned in. "That's everyone, Major." Van Duong nodded. "Prep them for battle."

The adjutant picked up his phone and gave the order. A dozen men who had been standing by the nets of the soccer goals bent down, lifted their large buckets of black paint, and jogged forward.

Chapter 106

2064: Boardroom Group Headquarters in Tunnel 1,288, Aristillus, Lunar Nearside

Albert Lai looked at the wallscreen and muttered. "This isn't cheap, you know."

Javier didn't know if the comment had been meant for him, or for Darcy, or if he was talking to himself. "The floor space? There hasn't been any commercial traffic in weeks -"

Albert shook his head. "My concern is that I've already cycled every lock a dozen times to get the refugee ships in, and we lose a fair bit of air each time. And air costs six times what it did just a few weeks ago."

Javier bit his tongue. Besides, what would he say? That they were all pressed to the breaking point? That most of the leaders of the rebellion had already pledged half their stock, or - he looked at Darcy sitting in Mike's seat - even more? That food, water, air - *everything* - was scarce?

No. Albert knew all these things. If he was mumbling to himself, let him mumble, and if he was venting to them, there was no need to pick a fight about it.

Darcy broke the silence. "I understand, Albert. But after all the work building the array -" she gestured at the video image of the modules laid out across the floor of bay three at Lai Docks "- we need one more cycling. I know it's pricey, but the Boardroom Group -"

Albert snorted "Don't tell me to expense it. That just means I get to pay myself." He paused. "No, I agree, we need our distant early warning system." He sighed. "But promise me you won't ask me for any more favors?"

Despite Javier's earlier promise to himself to remain silent, this prissily pushing back against "favors" annoyed him. He knew he shouldn't say anything, but the late hours, the stress, the -

He found himself talking. "Albert, when the invasion comes, a lot of people are going to die. Compared to that -"

Albert grimaced. "It was a joke. I'm sorry, it came out wrong."

Darcy nodded. "OK, I'm sorry too. But back to the topic: are we ready?"

Albert nodded, configured his phone for speakerphone, and placed it on the table. "Doug, let's open our eyes, shall we?"

"Yes, sir."

The wallscreen showed video - the inside of a Lai hanger. A moment later the ceiling split, the two halves rolling back. On the floor below small scraps of packaging material and dust blew about as the final wisps of air that the pumps hadn't been able to capture blew out through the open roof.

As the overhead doors continued to retract, the lighting in the hangar changed - the illumination thrown by the color-balanced panels was drowned out by brutal unfiltered sunlight. With a deep thud the overhead doors finished their transit and stopped.

Albert gestured at the wallscreen and the view panned up. Javier watched, entranced. Through the open doors he could see more and more of the black sky - and then the partially illuminated sphere of Earth slid into view. After all these years, it still took his breath away. It was too easy, living in Aristillus, to file the phrase 'I'm living on the moon' away in a mental bin. A true fact, but a footnote, a detail. The blandness of the daily routine - making breakfast, answering email, hiring staff, negotiating contracts - pushed this huge truth into the background. But every now and then he looked up and saw the Earth hanging overhead and it all came rushing back to him.

Javier snapped out of his reverie when he heard Albert's man - Doug? - call out over the speakerphone. "The techs have powered up the array. They say it's up...now."

Albert panned the camera back down to look at the floor of the bay where the radar units sat, but Javier didn't know what he hoped to see. The gray boxes of the radar array sat on the hanger floor, doing absolutely nothing.

Darcy tapped at her slate and a window popped up on the wallscreen - a clone of the display that the radar techs at Lai Docks were using. Javier watched as she rapidly opened several more diagnostic windows full of scrolling data. She muttered something.

"What's that, Miss Grau?"

"Something's not right. A radar echo from the Earth should take a few seconds. Let me..."

Javier watched Darcy tap at her slate. Suddenly, from the corner of his eye, something flickered. Javier looked at the wallscreen and saw that the video showing bay three was dimming - the hangar floor that had been dazzlingly bright with raw sunlight just a moment before was in shadow. What was going on?

Albert was apparently wondering the same thing - he panned the camera back up then reached for his phone, snapping it off of speaker mode. "Doug, did someone close the -"

Javier looked at the wallscreen. The blue sphere of Earth was gone. What? Where had -

In the darkness - were those navigation lights? He blinked. They were. Suddenly his vision readjusted and he saw, truly saw, what was on the screen.

The leading edge of a ship - a huge black ship - was drifting over bay three.

A moment later the ship had snuffed out the last bit of open sky.

He tried to understand what he was seeing. The door over this dock was big enough to fit several cargo ships at once - and yet something was spanning the entire sky above it.

What was that thing? It was huge - inconceivably huge. How -?

And then its trailing edge came into view, marked out with another row of navigation lights.

It was sliding past, dropping as it went. Javier tried to say something but couldn't form words.

A second later a deep boom rolled through the ground, shaking the table and causing beverages to slosh, even here, in the lowest tunnels of Aristillus, far below the surface.

The remote camera in Lai Docks bounced in the shock, and then fell from its mount and died. Albert stabbed at the controls and brought up another view - this time of the air traffic control room.

Two men in Lai Docks uniforms grabbed cans of sealant from the emergency cabinets and rushed off in response to the alarm woops of pressure sensors complaining about leaks.

A second boom rolled through the ground. Javier didn't even know how to describe it, and then the right word landed on his tongue. It sounded like the apocalypse.

A third, and then a fourth surge slammed through the lunar ground. A fifth -

And then he couldn't tell the individual impacts apart - they kept coming. Piling up. Blurring into one long wave.

He found himself whispering the words "It's started."

Chapter 107

2064: MaisonNeuve Construction office, Aristillus, Lunar Nearside

Mike stared off into space and wished that Leroy would just leave him the hell alone.

Leroy took a sip of water and looked at Mike. "Can I get you anything?"

Mike looked away.

For his first day in captivity Mike had refused to take water from the PKs. Less than a full day, actually; after less than 12 hours he'd given in and drunk.

After three days he'd reluctantly started eating the food they offered him.

But that was the PKs. Logically it didn't make any difference who offered him food or water - they and Leroy were on the same team. Still, he'd be damned if he'd take anything from Leroy.

Leroy raised one eyebrow. "No?"

Leroy took another long sip of the water. "Mike, your problem has always been your arrogance. This -" he raised his glass "- is the perfect example. I can do a favor for you, but you refuse it. You've got this myth of independence. I'm not singling you out, really - it's a typically American belief." He paused. "What your type don't understand is that life is about give and take. Do favors for people, and accept favors from them. You've got to make accommodations."

Mike fought to keep his eyes unfocused. Captive, hands bound behind his back, he had almost no power. The one thing he could still choose was whether to let Fournier derive any satisfaction from his posturing.

"Mike, are you listening to me?"

Leroy waited for a moment for some response then continued. "You can't fool me; I know you are." He paced past Mike. "The secret of life isn't a secret. It's obvious, really. Just two steps: figure out how the system works, then work within it."

Leroy put his glass down on a coaster on an end table and sat, pulling up lightly on the creases of his pants legs. He leaned forward. "Which is it? Are you incapable of doing that, or just unwilling to?"

Mike ignored him, but he felt his hands clench into fists behind his back. Fournier couldn't see that; that small reaction was OK.

Fournier shook his head in fake sadness. "You'd rather spit in the faces of the people who make the world work. You, of all people, should have learned this lesson by now. A decade ago, in your 'CEO Trials,' you could have helped the investigation, but you stood on pride. As if you were better than everyone else. As if you're not part of society." Fournier sighed. Mike hated that sigh. If his hands were free right now he'd beat Fournier. Fucking beat the hell out of him. Just rain blows, until the filthy little bastard's eyes bled and his nose broke and -

"What you don't understand is that people who don't know how to work in the system never accomplish anything. What can you build if-"

Mike couldn't stand it any more. He met Leroy's eyes. "Leroy, in the twenty years after my dad died I built four companies from the ground up. Then after the government seized them and took everything I owned, Ponzie and I flew to the moon. The moon. We dug our first tunnel using equipment that I refurbished with my own hands. And you know what? So many people wanted to follow me - to escape from your 'system' - that hundreds of thousands of people risked death to get here." Leroy scowled and pulled back. "Tell me - what have *you* ever done? You took your dad's money and started a stupid company. After you pissed it all away you went back to daddy for more. When that failed, you came here to Aristillus and did it a third time." The insults were hitting - Leroy looked angry. No. Pissed. And beneath that? Pain.

Mike had never realized it before, but it was clear now - Leroy knew that he was a failure. Mike had a flash of insight: knowing he was a failure - *that* was why he'd always been such an asshole. Not because he knew that he was better than everyone else, but because he knew that he was worse.

Mike smiled. Good. "You're good for two things, Leroy: pissing away what other people have handed to you, and kissing the asses of your bet-"

Without warning Leroy threw the glass at Mike's face. Mike flinched but it was too late - by the time he started to move the glass hit him, edge on, biting painfully into his ear. "You don't know what the hell you're talking about, Martin!"

Leroy stood, knocking his chair back. "You're a cowboy, Martin. A 'success'? Anyone can be a success if they break the rules like you do. A child plays chess and moves his piece out of turn, then declares himself the winner. That's not success; that's cheating. You haven't accomplished shit."

Mike looked up, blood running down his neck from the cut on his ear. "Tell yourself whatever you like, Leroy, but we both know the truth. You're a failure." Stick the knife in. Twist it. Mike was going to spend the rest of his life in a small cell in a black facility - assuming he didn't just get a bullet in the back of the neck. Might as well let Leroy hear the truth.

Leroy took a deep breath, then visibly calmed himself. "I'm a failure? Then why are you wearing handcuffs, and I'm the new governor of Aristillus?"

Governor? What the hell was -

Leroy continued, "You heard me. Thanks, Martin - thanks for all your stupid God-damned grunt labor digging out these shoddy tunnels. They're an ill-planned mess and they're filled with dregs who couldn't make it on Earth, but I promise you one thing - under my leadership, I'll improve your shitty little -"

The door opened and Major Reimmers stepped in. "What's the yelling? Is everything all right in -"

Leroy turned, his hands up in a placating gesture, his voice suddenly calm - even supercilious, taken aback that anyone would question him. "Yes, of course, everything's fine."

Reimmers looked at Mike, drenched in water and bleeding. "Jesus, Fournier, leave the prisoner alone, OK?"

Leroy changed the topic. "Is everything set for the landing?"

The Major answered without taking his eyes from Mike. "Yes." He turned slowly from Mike to Fournier. "The beacons are in place. I gave Washington the thumbs up hours ago."

The invasion? It was coming - now? Mike's stomach felt hollow and empty, like the bottom of it had fallen out. His throat filled with acid. At first he'd hoped for a decade until the war - then, after the first abortive invasion, he'd hoped that they'd have months until it came. Months wouldn't be remotely enough time, but still - it'd be time in which the Boardroom Group could pull together *some* kind of defense.

Leroy turned to face Mike. Mike, numbly, met his eyes.

"Don't worry, Martin - all of this will be over soon." He grinned lopsidedly and abruptly left the room.

Mike looked at Major Reimmers. Reimmers licked his lips, then looked away. A moment later he looked back. "Martin? I know it doesn't mean anything - but I'm sorry about this. I'm just doing my job. I don't put any stock in -"

Just doing his job. His life, his dreams, Darcy, all his friends, all the people who had shared Mike's dream.

They were all going to be destroyed because someone felt that it was part of his job description.

Mike took a deep shuddering breath and let it out, and then another.

Stop this. Stop this now. He commanded his body, but it didn't obey.

Please, God, not in front of a witness.

Mike couldn't help himself. His face was hot and he felt his eyes getting wet. Mike ground his chin into his chest.

Reimmers coughed awkwardly and left, closing the door behind him.

God fucking damn it! Mike breathed raggedly again and started to sob.

Chapter 108

2064: Raptor #1, between Earth and the Moon

General Restivo leaned forward against the harness and shifted uncomfortably in his seat. Even in zero gravity, the grit in the fabric bugged him. He and his team had managed to speed up the Raptor project but it had involved a hundred - no, a thousand - shortcuts. Cannibalizing almost century-old seats from airliners mothballed by the carbon laws were one of these hacks. Desert sand in the upholstery was a small price to pay to shave a bit of time off the schedule.

He turned his attention from the seat to the walls, floors, and ceiling of the rest of the bridge. He hoped that grit in the seat was the worst problem the insanely tight schedule would cause.

Restivo looked at the bank of wallscreens. On the center one, the icon for Raptor #3 still blinked "out range/lost com." He turned to Colonel DeCamp. "Anything more on number three?"

Decamp looked up from his screen. "National Guard sealed off the crash site and Internet-kill-switched coms in and out of Carson city a day, ago. Nothing since then."

"Any pictures of the crash site leak to the net?"

Colonel DeCamp shook his head. "Doesn't look like it."

Restivo nodded. The expats certainly knew the invasion was coming. Rumors were rife on Earth, and the remaining snatch team in Aristillus had relayed back expat media, which showed that the expats knew that something was up. There was a difference, though, between knowing that an invasion was coming eventually, and knowing that it was coming *now*.

He was also glad that no pictures of the raptors had leaked to Aristillus media. The good opsec had kept the expats in the dark - their discussion boards made it clear that most of them expected more converted ocean-going cargo ships.

It wasn't clear how much data the expats could get from pictures of a raptor - especially pictures of one that had fallen from kilometers up after the AG drive malfunctioned. Still - better safe than sorry.

Restivo nodded. "Any more data on the various industrial facilities we've discovered outside of Aristillus?"

"The snatch team continues to insist that they're not expat colonies."

Restivo turned to him. "Do you believe that an AI actually built them?"

Colonel Decamp shrugged. "When you've eliminated the impossible, whatever else remains -"

Restivo nodded. "And our mini-sats?"

"All in lunar orbit, all functioning well."

Restivo blew air out of his cheeks and drummed his fingers.

The grit embedded in the seat fabric rasped against his skin.

Chapter 109

2064: Solar Installations headquarters, Aristillus, Lunar Nearside

Matthew Vaz stepped through the door and took a place against the rear wall of his Rover Operations room. It wasn't a place he normally spent much time. In the first few years of Aristillus, he and his men had erected solar engines by hand. The transition to using remotely operated rovers had cut costs and dropped the price of electricity for consumers and, perhaps best of all, it had meant that he could hand off management of the whole installation process to Todd and spend his time on other tasks.

Today, though - today he couldn't tear himself away from the Rover Operations room for longer than it took to hit the bathroom or grab a coffee. The PKs hadn't landed, and they might not for days or weeks. When they arrived, his people would fight - and until then, they'd practice.

Matthew took a sip of coffee and looked at the huge wallscreen at the front of the room. The current scenario had several dozen rovers deployed on the surface along one of the scree berms that separated one industrial area from the next like old New England stone walls between farms.

One by one the attacking rovers crawled to the top of the berm and traversed their weapons back and forth, raking fire across imagined enemies. A second platoon of rovers started forward, but before they reached the scree wall, Todd Belcheck stood up and interrupted the operators. "Folks, shift change - let's take the next twenty minutes to bring all the rovers back inside for maintenance and -"

An operator to Todd's left yelled something, interrupting him.

Matthew looked. Had he just heard what he thought he had?

Todd turned. "What was that?"

The operator repeated himself. "The invasion ships - they're here!"

Matthew blinked. Was this part of a drill? He looked around the room. His operators looked scared. The wallscreen began flashing urgent alerts.

No, this was no simulation.

This was real.

Matthew's stomach felt empty and hollow. He reached out blindly to steady himself and found a chair, then sat. At the front of the room Todd Belcheck started to bellow orders. Rover operators leaned over their consoles. The mood in the room was tense and expectant.

Matthew leaned forward, scanning the wallscreen, looking for details. The invasion ships were here? Where?

Finally someone put a video feed on the wallscreen and Matthew saw them - giant black ships drifting overhead. The mug of coffee dropped forgotten from his hand and spilled on the floor.

As the ships drifted overhead, a line of tracer fire opened up from somewhere on the surface, then another line, and then more. He swallowed. The invasion was here. But it looked like the peakers hadn't learned their lesson. If the PKs were stupid enough to try to force a landing directly on top of Aristillus a second time, then the automated anti-aircraft guns would take care of them even faster than men with rifles had last time.

Matthew squinted and leaned forward as he watched the video. The ships should lurch and fall. Any second now. He waited. And waited.

Nothing.

What the hell? They'd discussed this scenario - the ships should fall and splash. He shook his head. The ADF's guns must be defective. Not sighted in correctly. Something.

The first PK ship dropped lower, and then it was in range of his rovers' weapons. On the wallscreen image of the PK ship a small green crosshair icon appeared - one of the rover's aim-points. Then two more green icons appeared, then a dozen. Todd Belcheck at the front of the room bellowed, "Everyone, flip from 'practice' to 'combat' mode." A second later, one of the crosshair icons turned red and the sound of a roaring mini-gun came out from the speakers. Other crosshairs changed to red and the overlapping sound effects merged into a wall of noise.

Matthew took a deep breath. Thousands of rounds must be pouring into the PK ship. Even if the ADF's anti-aircraft guns were defective, his own rovers should be able to shoot down the ships.

He listened to the roar over the speakers and watched. It looked like the first ship was just gently gliding down. It should be crashing, listing - something! But it wasn't.

And he knew why.

Matthew stood. "Cease fire!" No one listened, and the waste of precious ammunition continued. Matthew ran to the front of the room, stood in front of the wallscreen, and waved his hands over his head. "Cease fire, cease fire! They're armored!" He had to yell it several times before all the remote operators listened, but slowly the simulated sound of gunfire died away.

Matthew turned and faced the wallscreen. Standing so close he couldn't even see the whole thing, but the image of the huge black drifting overhead and descending behind the scree wall was clear. Todd Belcheck looked up from his console. "What do you want us to do?"

"I need to figure something out. Just hold on." Matthew walked away from the front of the room, found an empty console and sat. He balled his fists, loosened them, rolled his neck. OK. He called up a list of unpiloted vehicles, grabbed the first and drove it up over the scree berm, and zoomed the camera. The surface of the PK ship was dark - it was hard to make detail out. There was armor - he was sure of that - but were there weak spots? The ship kept sliding out of frame and Matthew tapped the controls again and again to slew the camera as the ship descended.

...and then the zoomed view showed the surface of the moon beneath the ship. A second later the huge cube landed, hard, crushing part of a conveyor belt as if it was made of tinfoil. Matthew blinked. Conveyor belts for mining tailings were *big*, yet this one looked like a toy next to the ship. He hadn't realized the scale of the thing. A second later a deep rumble filled the room. Matthew looked around wildly. The sound was coming from the ceiling, the walls, the floor. Everywhere.

Jesus. That ship wasn't big - it was *huge*.

He turned back to his console. He zoomed the rover's camera and scanned the screen, looking for something - anything. Nothing - just solid black slabs, one after another after - wait. There! A large door in the side of the ship had cracked open, lowering like a drawbridge. He zoomed in tighter yet. Next to the opening door - those looked like small turrets flanking the hatch. He put his rover's cross hairs on the open crack in the door then held down the trigger. A stream of tracers showed that his rounds were reaching their target.

One of the turrets pivoted, pointed straight at his rover and flashed. His control screen went dead. "ROVER CONTACT LOST" blinked on the screen.

Shit.

He turned to Todd. "The door is-"

"Got it." Todd stood and bellowed instructions to the rover operators. Matthew ignored him as he tabbed to the list of free rovers, grabbed control of another, and piloted it to the top of the berm. He wasn't alone - a half dozen other rovers climbed the berm to his left and right. Two pulled ahead and as his rover crested the rise he saw muzzle flash from their guns and heard the machine gun sound effects that the system simulated.

The rover to his right was shooting, brass flying and spinning in the lunar vacuum. Matthew ignored it as he zoomed in on the invasion ship again and found the vast hangar door in the side of the ship a second time. This time he paid attention to the turrets that flanked it. They were swiveling independently. Flashes of hot gasses from their muzzles showed they were firing. He zoomed in tighter and enhanced the video. Yes - and there, above each cluster of machine guns, was a sensor pod.

Matthew put his rover's cross hair on the left one then and squeezed the trigger. After a second he paused to look at the result. Was the turret dead? It wasn't moving, but he couldn't be sure. His cross hair was still on it. He squeezed his trigger again and looked once more. The turret was definitely dead now. He turned to Todd at the front of the room. "Tell everyone to zoom in and fire at the sensors and gun mounts!"

The operator next to him yelled out "I'm fucking hit!" Then a second tech yelled in frustration, then two others.

Matthew ignored them and adjusted his aim point, picked out the sensor pod above the gun on the other side of the PK ship's door, and squeezed the trigger - and suddenly his video feed went dead. "ROVER CONTACT LOST."

Damn it! He'd lost two rovers in less than thirty seconds.

He tabbed over, grabbed another free rover from the reserve pool and drove it up the berm. Around him in the conference room the synthesized roar of chain-guns continued. Good. With the whole team following his lead, they'd have the door turrets dead in moments, and then they could take out the invasion force of rovers before they poured out of the PK ship. For a second his mind flashed to the other ships he'd seen, but he pushed the idea away. Other militia units would get them - they had to. He and his team had to concentrate on this ship.

His rover neared the top of the berm and he saw dozens of other rovers already at the crest. Several were shooting, each spitting a rain of brass as they fired - but more than half were inoperative, torn and shredded by the PK fire.

Shit. Matthew rubbed his mouth. After the first invasion attempt, when a few impromptu militia teams had shot dozens of PK ships out of the sky with rifles and a lunar covert ops group had trapped the rest in a cave-in, it had become an unexamined article of faith among many of them that the next PK invasion would be just as simple to defeat. The peakers were stupid, unimaginative - they'd fly their ships right into anti-aircraft fire, and then those that managed to land would march their men right into traps. Matthew hadn't believed it would be quite *that* easy - but he hadn't expected that the PKs would learn this much, this fast. Jesus. Armor? Turrets? Shit.

Matthew wiped the sweat off his hands on his pants and grabbed the joystick. Another rover advanced past him on the left - and was torn apart by gun fire. He blinked. How - where? The other rover wasn't yet exposed at the top of the berm.

A chill ran down his neck and across his shoulders. Matthew panned his camera around behind him - and saw the rest of the invasion fleet. The huge black cubes - nine? ten? more? - squatted across the surface, spread out over the city's topside. Each was surrounded by the wreckage of the solar installations, kilns, vacuum sintering ovens and other topside facilities that they'd landed on and crushed - or torn apart with gun fire.

- and guns on the nearest of those ships were flashing. The second ship was attacking his rovers from behind. Jesus. From that vantage *all* of his firm's rovers - even those that were just being held in reserve at the base of the berm - were exposed. Shit. His machines were caught in a crossfire between two different ships.

What could he do? Could they get the rovers back into the warehouse, and live to fight another day? He shook his head. No. The nearest ramp was a kilometer away - they'd be picked off before they got there.

Better to stand and fight. But everyone needed to know. Matthew yelled out over the simulated roar of gunfire. "They're behind us!" He pointed to the wallscreen. A moment later Todd Belcheck took up his cry.

Matthew returned his attention to his screen. If that second ship wanted a fight, he'd fight. He zoomed in on it, put his crosshairs over a turret and fired a burst, holding it for two long seconds. The turret was torn apart. Good. He tapped his crosshairs to the right, onto a second turret and -

"ROVER CONTACT LOST."

Damn it.

He tabbed back to the list of available rovers and blinked. It was shorter than it had been. A lot shorter. They'd had 1,200 rovers when they started - he checked a clock - just three minutes ago And now? A few hundred, at most.

He swallowed and selected another rover.

It came online and he pivoted it in place. Zoom. Aim. Fire. One gun cluster on the second ship down. Zoom. Aim. Fire. A second. Then a third. He was moving his crosshairs to a fourth when his rover died. He tabbed over for another machine - and saw that there were only thirty live rovers - all of them allocated to other operators.

The synthesized gun sounds around him in the Remote Operations room grew less and less intense.

He checked his screen again. Eighteen live rovers.

Around him speakers started falling silent, the noise of machine gun fire softening.

Six.

The tab refreshed.

Zero.

At the same time the number dropped to zero the sound of simulated machine gun fire died out in the room.

He felt sick.

Four minutes - maybe five - and the PKs had wiped out his entire force. And he wasn't fighting the entire invasion fleet, just two of their ships.

If this was the level of resistance they were getting before the ships even disgorged their own troops, what was the rest of the battle going to look like?

He tried to swallow, but his throat was dry.

For a moment he started to think about how Solar Installations was going to recover after the battle...and then realized that he was being far too optimistic. What were the chances that the expats could win? None. The revolution was over before it even started.

All he could do now was hope that his people survived.

Matthew stood, his face pale and damp. "People - this facility is too close to the surface. Get out of here.

Go home, find a militia. Do whatever you can do. We're done here."

In shocked disbelief his operators stood, one at a time, and filtered out of the room. Todd Belcheck was the last to leave, looking at Matthew silently for a moment before he, too, turned and left.

Matthew sat alone in the room for several long minutes. Then there was an explosion somewhere nearby and the power went out. A moment later the emergency lighting kicked on and Matthew continued to sit in the blood red dimness.

Chapter 110

2064: Benue River Restaurant, Aristillus, Lunar Nearside

Major Van Duong walked the perimeter of the evacuated Nigerian restaurant. The place was big, but not quite big enough for all of the men of first company - especially in their bulky spacesuits; his men occupied all of the tables and chairs, and a few were even standing at the restaurant's counter and condiment bar where cash registers and bowls of dried fish crumbs, lemon grass, and locust bean powder had been pushed aside to make room for combat control workstations.

The men at the workstations worked with suit gloves removed but just outside the restaurant a few fully suited soldiers - freshly painted black stripe logos diagonally bisecting their torsos - patrolled the tunnel.

Major Van Duong looked through the restaurant's plate glass window into the tunnel. The neighborhood was nearly empty now. The betting markets had said that the invasion would likely come through large construction airlocks - like the one at the end of the connecting tunnel and that had scared off most of the people. Those few who hadn't left over the last few days had fled minutes ago when message boards exploded with pictures and grainy video of the invasion fleet on the surface and the sirens had started screaming. Van Duong saw a last few individuals evacuate the neighborhood on foot, on motorbikes, or on delivery skids, but the tunnel was growing quieter and quieter.

He'd given the order to deploy pickets a few minutes ago - were they in position yet? He turned from the view of the tunnel and looked over one of his men's shoulder at his workstation. His eyes found the video window, and he winced as the invasion ships' turrets flashed and panned back and forth. The invasion ships turrets were still live? Damn it! He'd been told that Solar Installations' machines were on it - he'd expected that they'd have knocked them out by now. But, no, the turrets were still shooting.

He glanced at the stats bar for his rovers - and blinked.

He'd lost eighty of them *already*? His machines weren't even in position! Shit. If Solar Installations hadn't been able to crack that nut, he wasn't going to waste his own rovers. The plan called for hitting the ships early, but that was suicide. Screw the plan - better to pull back, wait for the ships to disgorge their infantry, and then engage the soft targets.

Van Duong clicked to the command broadcast channel. "All companies, pull your rovers back to cover." Around him there was a flurry of activity as his captains relayed the order down and his men started typing.

He walked from the table to another position in the restaurant - his men needed to know that he was there, that he knew what was going on. He leaned in and looked at another trooper's workstation screen.

The rover's camera showed the ship's door opening. He looked at another screen. All of the ships' doors were opening - swinging out and down like huge drawbridges. He squinted. The contrast between the bright lunar-noon surface and the dim interior meant that he couldn't see anything. Had pulling his rovers back tricked the PKs? Good. He gave the order over his mike, "Hold your fire and let the PK infantry deploy; we don't want them to button back up."

He watched the ships. The drawbridges were fully down - and then, finally, movement.

Shit.

What spilled out of the ships' holds were not space-suited infantrymen, but tracked rovers almost

---

indistinguishable from the ones his men were operating. On his operator's workstation screen the target acquisition counter flashed. Dozens. Hundreds. The counter hit a thousand and kept climbing. Enemy rovers weren't deploying - they were spilling out like a wave.

Major Van Duong grimaced. "Get all rovers back inside the tunnels, immediately!" Captain Tuan Hung, First Company commander, started to object over the command channel, and cut himself off mid-sentence. On the other side of the restaurant the captain stood and moved toward him. "Major - the plan to minimize civilian -"

Van Duong cut him off. "We can't fight out there. They'll destroy us."

"But Major, if we fall back they'll seize the lock -"

"I know. But then we'll just have them on one front; we can't survive the crossfire."

Captain Tuan Hung nodded and began to issue the order. The Major turned to an assistant. "Tell Command that we're going to fight inside, then have the airlocks broadcast the white code." He thought for a second "- and contact the PKs on an open channel. They need to know that we're not going to contest the locks."

A minute later the aide responded, "Major, all the locks in our sector are broadcasting the Vatican code." He paused as he listened to something on another channel " -and I've got protocol confirmation that the PKs got the message."

"Good." Van Duong watched on the screen as the expat rovers fell back before the wave of PK rovers. The whole time the guns on the fleet ships panned back and forth, occasionally firing as some expat rover or other target exposed itself. He checked the rover count. Another 17 lost. He breathed out heavily. Shit. Just minutes in, and the plan was already screwed. But maybe not irretrievably screwed. As long as his men could cycle all - or even most - of their forces back inside before the PK swarm reached them.

The Major paced the restaurant. To the cash register. To the condiment bar. Back again.

Five minutes later Captain Tuan Hung called out. "All my companies' rovers are inside."

"How are they deployed?"

"We've established a line 300 meters back from the lock with one platoon at rally point Alpha; the are rest in reserve at rally point Bravo." Van Duong nodded without answering.

The captain turned to go back to the table, but the major halted him. "Wait. We may not be able to hold the PKs at Alpha for long. If they turn the corner from tunnel 92 and get in here with us in 73, we'll have problems. Detail a few men to make sure that noncombatants -"

Major Van Duong froze mid sentence as he saw a very dark-skinned girl - no more than 12 or 13 - enter the restaurant. Jesus - as if he needed visual aids to make his point!

"You - what are you doing here?"

The girl stopped and looked at him brazenly. "This is my restaurant - what are you doing here?"

"We're fighting the PKs! Now what the hell are you -"

"Hey! You should use nicer language when you're talking to me on my own property!"

The major blinked. "Uh...sorry?" He paused. "Kid, we might have PKs here in ten minutes or less, and -"

One of the men yelled out, "Major!"

"What?"

"PKs about to enter the lock!"

Van Duong took one last look at the girl, said, "Get out of here!" and turned to the screen.

A wave of PK rovers were rolling across the surface; the lead ones were almost to the concrete apron outside the huge construction lock at the end of tunnel 92. Most were of a tracked design that was pretty similar to the standard expat model, but one was much larger - more like a tracked delivery skid with a mid sized cargo container on top.

Van Duong pointed at the screen. "What is that?"

The man shrugged. "Doesn't look like the APCs they used in the last attack, but - a troop transport, I bet. These idiots are bringing infantry in the first wave after all!"

Van Duong shook his head. He'd seen combat as a young man, and even decades later he still occasionally woke up in a panic from dreams of defending the chaotic border when the PRC fell. Unlike the young rover operator in front of him, he wasn't thrilled with the idea of unarmored troops - of any flag - marching into combat. He'd seen what machine guns could do to a human body.

On the screen the PK troop carrier rolled into the open airlock. The massive outer construction lock door slid ponderously shut behind it. It'd take a minute for the lock to cycle. Van Duong keyed the command circuit. "Captains - tell your men that we want to avoid excess bloodshed. If they're going to march into the meat grinder, kill only as many as we need to. Pay attention for anyone dropping their weapons or surrendering. It's not going to be easy to detect surrenders in suits, but -"

Van Duong was cut short by a cataclysmic explosion. He stumbled and felt something crash into him. He blinked and tasted copper. What was - was he on the floor? Had he passed out? What was going on?

He climbed to his feet and looked around the dark restaurant. Dark? The lights were off. He turned and looked to the tunnel, through the plate glass - well, were the window had been a moment before - and saw that the tunnel was dark as well. As he looked, emergency lights in the tunnel popped on, illuminating it with a weak brown glow. He looked around the restaurant in the dim light. The entire place was in disarray - tables toppled, men picking themselves up from the floor, computers smashed. There was something in his mouth - he spit out the dust and grit - and something sticky on his forehead. He wiped his forehead and came away with blood. What was that huge roaring?

He shouted, "What the hell was that?" to no one in particular and got no response. Could anyone even hear him over that huge sound? What was happening? Van Duong looked around and saw a rover control station at his feet, picked it up, and set it on a counter. The list of first company rovers was mostly red but he found one green one that was still alive, still broadcasting. The map said that it was at rally point Alpha, at the barrier 300 meters from the airlock. Perfect - that would let him see the PKs as they came through the lock. He selected it and looked out through its cameras.

The view showed tunnel 92, but - he squinted - where the tunnel should end in the massive armored door of a construction lock something wasn't right. What was he -

Van Duong blinked. My God.

He was looking out a ragged hole where the vast airlock had once been. The darkness beyond - that was sky. The lunar sky.

That boxy vehicle hadn't been a troop carrier - it had been a bomb. The PKs had detonated a massive bomb inside the airlock, with both doors closed. The lock was gone - both doors, walls, everything. All of tunnel 92 was exposed to vacuum. That was the source of the noise - kilometers of atmosphere roaring out of the tunnels and into the void.

Jesus.

And if tunnel 92 was open to vacuum, that meant -

He did a quick calculation. The hole was huge - devastatingly huge - but the tunnels were even larger. They wouldn't depressurize instantly, but they would depressurize. Did he and his men have seconds or minutes? "Helmets on!"

The roar was too loud - no one heard him - but his men were independently realizing what was going on and were snapping on helmets and gloves. Major Van Duong closed his own helmet and switched from the command circuit to the battalion broadcast circuit. "All members of the 30th - we've got a tunnel breach. Seal your suits, and make sure that any wounded are suited up too." He clicked over to Command and reported to General Dewitt, and then ended the call.

A few rover operators in First Company were already sealed up and were back at their stations. Good. Van Duong looked at the screen on the console he'd picked up. His men were maneuvering surviving rovers behind barriers and detritus at the 300 meter line.

* * *

Ewoma crouched behind the serving counter and held on tightly to the cash bag she'd just removed from the restaurant safe.

The roaring was loud, and she knew what that meant: the PKs must have blown a lock. She had to get somewhere safe - and she had to do it immediately. She stood up from behind the counter and stepped around ADF soldiers who were picking themselves up from the ground.

The restaurant's front windows were shattered, and she walked carefully over the glass littering the floor.

Outside in the tunnel the roaring was loudest from the right.

She turned left, into the wind, and ran.

* * *

Major Van Duong tabbed between different rover cameras. With the lock gone the PKs wouldn't be forced to come at them in small waves - they could do a huge push. Which meant that the defensive plan they'd had wasn't good enough.

He'd given the order and rally point Alpha at 300 meters was being reinforced with more rovers pulled from his reserve. He looked over the command screen. The trackless gun stations that had been winched up into the ceiling infrastructure were in place, but were powered down - hopefully if they were cold the PKs wouldn't see them on IR until it was too late.

Ahead of the line there was a field of improvised landmines epoxied to the roadbed. Van Duong shook his head - just two hours ago he'd been arguing with Captain Chi Ngo that the mines might be a bit much, because removing them after the battle might damage the roadbed.

With the air still whistling away through the devastating breach, he saw how wrong he'd been about that. Now he needed the mines - he needed every single advantage if they were going to hold the line.

Duong leaned forward and zoomed the display. PK machines were starting to pour in through the blasted hole and into the tunnel.

Chapter 111

Ewoma leaned into the rush of air and ran through the dim emergency-lit tunnel as the world roared in her ears. Pieces of packing foam and food wrappers flew at her and she batted them away. She had to get someplace safe, behind a pressure door. How far was the closest one? It was up by O'Grady's Ice Cream Shack, right? No, wait - there were new ones that they'd installed a few weeks ago! Where was the closest one? A kilometer from here, right?

She panted as she ran. She was a good runner, but the air was getting thin. She realized with a shock that the e-p-doors she was running to had probably all shut automatically. And that meant that it wasn't going to take hours for the tunnel she was in to empty out of air - it might take just minutes. She turned left at an intersection and tried to pick up the pace, but it was hard - really hard. The cash bag was banging uncomfortably against her left thigh, but she tried to ignore it.

She'd covered maybe half the distance when she slowed to a walk. She had to go faster, she knew - but she couldn't. The air was too thin. If she couldn't run to the door could she walk? That would take longer, and the air would get thinner yet. No. If she walked, she'd die.

What other options did she have? She bent over in the middle of the tunnel with her hands on her knees and panted.

Think. Think!

She could let herself into the utility tunnel that ran parallel to this tunnel. Playing hide-and-go-seek with friends had taught her how to jimmy the door over by

Ling's Hardware - but, no, the ends of that tunnel been sealed off when United Delivery went bankrupt and their warehouse got subdivided. Ewoma thought the word "shit" and tried to bite it back. She agreed with her grandmother - she didn't want to be one of the bad kids using language like that. "Crap," then.

She couldn't run. Walking would take too long. What? What could she do? She wanted to cry.

But if she sat down and cried, she'd die. Ewoma rubbed her eyes. There had to be some -

The idea hit her: the old emergency suits! Her dad had showed her the lockers once. Were they still around? She looked around the tunnel. Where were they?

There was something she was supposed to look for - what was it? She remembered: a big blue arrow. She looked to the left. An arrow - wait, no - it was red and it was pointing to a glass-fronted cabinet with a fire hose coiled inside. Darn it. Wait - there. She followed the blue arrow down - and saw that it pointed at a vending machine. That had to be it, but someone had put a stupid vending machine in the way. She put the cash bag down and walked to the vending machine, grabbed one corner and pulled.

Ewoma was tall for her age, but not very strong. The machine refused to move. Even in the lighter gravity, the built-in microwave oven and the huge load of refrigerated goat burgers had enough weight to stymie her. A "shit!" escaped her lips. She stepped back and looked at the machine - and saw the locking casters. Ah-ha! She kicked one caster's release toggle, and then the other, and pulled on the vending machine again. This time it rolled - slowly, slowly - out of the way.

Behind it, flush with the wall, was the old-style emergency suit locker. The locker was dirty - dust covered the warning sign and instructions. That didn't matter as long as it still worked. She grabbed the locker handle and pulled, and the door sprang open. Inside there were six adult-sized suits. All adult? She gritted her teeth. Didn't the people who designed this thing know that kids lived here? But maybe it wasn't their fault - this *was* one of the oldest tunnels around. Maybe there hadn't been any kids when this was installed.

She panted heavily. The air was thin.

What was she going to do? She could fit into a big suit like that, but she'd *never* be able to walk in it.

She stared at it for a moment and then had an idea.

Chapter 112

2064: Benue River Restaurant, Aristillus, Lunar Nearside

Captain Chi Ngo swatted away a storm of blowing napkins, peeled one off his suit's faceplate, and looked at his console's screen. Hundreds of First Company's rovers hunkered down behind the concrete Jersey barriers at the 300 meter line and fought the PK onslaught. Attributing bravery to remote-controlled machines made no sense, but he had to fight the temptation to anthropomorphize the machines. They fought and fought. And then, one by one, they were picked off by the superior numbers of the PK rovers. As he watched, the enemy machines launched another salvo of RPG rounds. Several were misaimed and hit the tunnel ceiling...but the rest landed just past the concrete line, amongst the friendlies. In a moment the fireballs disappeared and Ngo saw that most of First Company's remaining rovers were dead.

He sensed the charge a moment before it happened. "Power up the gun stations in the catwalks!"

A wave of PK rovers surged forward and reached the Jersey barriers in seconds. Most aimed for the center of the line, where the barriers were stacked just one thick instead of two or three. Ngo nodded to himself. The PKs were good - they'd seen the weakness and made straight for it.

The first dozen machines tried vainly to use their flipper treads to climb the barrier. Then one machine topped the barrier - and was immediately shot by friendly machines at the 400 meter line. The shattered rover toppled backwards. Then, like a wave crashing against a beach, more and more PK rovers smashed into the barrier and began climbing. Each was destroyed in turn. After a dozen seconds of carnage the remaining PK machines fell back, leaving dozens of their dead compatriots behind at the barrier. A larger PK machine raced forward. Another suicide bomb, but smaller than the one that had taken out the lock.

One of his men called to Captain Ngo, "Sir, the gun stations are powered up. Should we-"

"No. Not yet." He stared at the screen. "Not unless the peakers get past the -"

An explosion filled the tunnel with dust. In the vacuum the dust settled more quickly than it would on Earth and Ngo could see that the center of the concrete barricade was gone. PK rovers were streaming through.

The PK machines were inside the kill zone of the ambush. Now it was time for the catwalk guns to open up.

"Gun station operators - fire at will!"

In the almost airless tunnel the devastation was utterly silent, which made it feel unreal - a video game with the sound turned off. Captain Ngo had to remind himself that it *was* real - that all of this was happening, just a few hundred meters from where he stood. He leaned in as he watched the screen. From their position above and behind the PK onslaught, the gun stations were - almost literally - shooting fish in a barrel. The PK rovers were pressed tight as they tried to squeeze through the breach in the cement barrier, and the Aristillus gun stations picked them off mercilessly. As the enemy rovers were chewed up, their wrecked carcasses clogged the choke point in the Jersey barriers, which caused the roadblock to become even more effective. Within seconds, hundreds of Earth machines were dead. Those few PK rovers that survived the first seconds spun their cameras around helplessly, looking for the source of the incoming fire, before they were destroyed in turn. Ngo smiled and whispered "Cannae."

"What's that, sir?"

"Nothing." Captain Ngo smiled. He'd had to argue hard to weaken the concrete barrier line in the center, but it had been worth it.

This - *this* might be where they'd hold the onslaught. And when the PKs ran out of machines? Major Van Duong could hit them with the reserves.

A moment later, the smile started to slip from his face. The PK troops controlling the invading rovers must have figured out where the Aristillus fire was coming from - the surviving peaker rovers pivoted and started firing at the catwalks. In less than a minute the last of the catwalk gun stations was ripped apart, and with it, the last video feed from the battle.

Shit.

Someone tapped him on the shoulder. Captain Ngo spun - and saw the Major. "Captain, the PKs are coming through the gap; hit them with your other gun stations."

Ngo recoiled. "Major, that's it - there are no more gun stations."

Major Van Duong blinked.

Had the man not realized that all of First Company's machines had been placed at the first choke point? The major frowned and turned to his left. "Captain Hue, reinforcements. Now."

"On it."

Outside the restaurant a hundred rovers rolled past, heading for the front lines, then another hundred, and then more.

The floor shook. What was that?

He looked at his console. All of his company's rovers were dead, so he tabbed to a view from one of second company's rovers. The machine he selected was at the 400 meter line, far back from the first line, so he zoomed. There - the battle came into view. He blinked. The Jersey barriers and the clog of dead rovers had been pushed aside by light PK dozers - and flowing through the new, bigger gap was a flood of PK machines, and among them -

He swallowed. What were those? Eight wheeled vehicles of some kind. "Are those tanks?"

One of his men shouted out, "Armored fighting vehicle. Looks like a Gordon."

Another man chimed in, "Jane's says they're General Dynamics M1139s. Two 13mm guns, four 7.62, RPG-resistant -"

Major Van Duong cut him off with a broadcast on the command circuit. "We're falling back. Hue, your men stay here and cover the retreat for as long as you can. Use up all of your demolition rovers if you have to, and then fall back."

Captain Ngo objected, "Major, we can hold them at the 400 meter line."

"No, we can't. We don't have any weapons that can dent those Gordons."

"But Major, we've got some landmines left, we can -"

The Major turned to him "Those PK ships are *huge*. You haven't been watching the surface cameras. The rovers just keep coming. There is no way we can stop them."

"You could bring up Third -"

"Third is *gone*. Now get your men packed and get out of here!"

Chapter 113

Ewoma cinched the straps on the life support backpack as tight as they would go, but that wasn't tight enough for her small frame - the pack slopped around on her back as she took a step. The fact that she was wearing just the helmet and the backpack, but had left the bulky suit sitting on the floor of the tunnel, wasn't helping.

Well, the straps were as tight as they'd go. She reached up, felt the big red handle on the side of the helmet, and gave it a pull - and was thrilled by the hiss as stuffy canned air started spraying into the helmet. She breathed deeply, and her lightheadedness receded. An automated voice in the helmet started lecturing her: "Suit is not airtight - air usage above nominal. Seek shelter immediately."

Air escaping under the rim of the helmet blew against the front of her shirt and the material fluttered weirdly. Ewoma ignored it, walked back to the center of the roadbed, and picked up the bag of coins from the restaurant's safe.

There was less and less garbage blowing through the tunnel. None, actually. A few small scraps of paper fluttered weakly on the roadbed. She knew what that meant - there was little air left. She needed to get to the e-p-door as quickly as possible.

The label on the emergency suit backpack claimed it had one hour of air, but without a suit to seal the helmet, she knew it wouldn't last nearly that long. The helmet had bought her a few minutes of time, but if she didn't move immediately she was going to die.

Chapter 114

2064: Raptor #1, surface of Aristillus, Lunar Nearside

Colonel Decamp looked at the wallscreen. The clock ticked inexorably on. He clenched his right fist and spread his fingers. Again. They'd been on the surface for almost 45 minutes now. He turned to his mining engineer. "Status?"

The engineer was sweating as he checked his screens. "The TBM is down 12 meters so far. The rock is soft, like the advance team said. We're running over speed and that's burning up the teeth on the disk cutter."

"Is that a problem?"

"No, the degradation is within plan. Ah - 13 meters now. We should hit target depth in another twenty minutes. We landed right on top of the laser designator. If the GIS data is right we'll be into the farm tunnel in twenty minutes."

Colonel Decamp nodded. Twenty minutes. He realized that his fist was clenched painfully and released it. The feint with the destroyed airlock and the rovers would keep the defenders busy for that long - but not much longer. "OK, good. Tell me if anything changes."

Decamp keyed his command circuit. "We'll be into the tunnels in twenty minutes - get the invasion force ready."

Chapter 115

2064: tunnel 73, level 1, Aristillus, Lunar Nearside

Ewoma gritted her teeth and tried yet again to tap out 'yes I acknowledge' on the touch screen of the delivery skid. It was harder than it should be - her helmet had been chiming "Suit is not airtight; air usage above nominal; seek shelter immediately" ever since she put it on five minutes ago, and now that warning was replaced with the woop-woop-ing of a siren interspersed with "five minutes of air left - risk of death imminent."

She hit the "submit" button and the delivery skid's screen flashed "typo; try again." She felt tears in her eyes and tried to wipe them away. Her numb fingers banged uselessly into the faceplate of her helmet.

Darn it! Why couldn't there just be a big button? There were big buttons for "stop" and "go," but for emergency override she had to type words? It wasn't fair! Her fingers were too tingly to work right and she was going to -

The delivery skid sprang to life and surged forward. She'd typed it correctly! The skid rolled forward, picking up speed. A laugh bubbled up in her throat and warred with the tears crowding the corners of her eyes. This was going to work.

The skid slowed and navigated around a bicycle abandoned in the center roadway before speeding up again. Then it slowed a second time to swerve around an overturned apple stall and the spill of fruit.

She willed the vehicle on. Faster! Faster!

The warnings from her helmet were getting more dire - the thing was designed to be coupled tightly to a suit neck ring, and as the air pressure in the tunnel continued to drop, the reserves were being used more and more rapidly. "Two minutes of air left - risk of death imminent!"

The skid slowed and maneuvered again. Ewoma craned her neck to see what was blocking the road. A dog. There was a dog lying on its side, eyes closed, tongue out. The poor thing was dead. Wait. No. Its sides were moving - it was trying to breathe.

She bit her lip. She couldn't let this dog asphyxiate, forgotten. But she was almost out of air. If she stopped to help the dog, the two of them would probably *both* die.

The delivery skid maneuvered around the panting creature and started to accelerate. Ewoma leaned forward and hit the big red "stop" button. The skid rocked forward as it braked and Ewoma undid her seat belt and hopped down, leaving the cash bag on the seat behind her. She lifted the dog easily in the low gravity and pushed him onto the floorboards of the skid. The poor thing didn't even open its eyes. Was it in a coma? She didn't have time to worry about it - her helmet was yelling at her. Ewoma climbed back into her seat and slapped the green "go" button.

The skid powered up and resumed its programmed path. Ewoma blinked. What was going on? Something was yelling at her. Something about air. Zero something. She tried to listen but it was so hard to concentrate.

She closed her eyes.

Chapter 116

Major Van Duong fretted as his men retreated. They should have practiced this. The lack of training was telling - even the simple things were proving to be difficult. How had they never practiced folding up combat workstations in a vacuum? One stupid little task made difficult by the clumsy space suits meant that their retreat was taking longer than it should. The men were just now climbing onto the battalion's skids. How long had it been since he'd given the evacuation order? Too long.

"Major, PKs are through the 400 meter line, and one of our HQ skirmishers has contact - we've got PK rovers 250 meters away!"

Only 250 meters? Shit, that was far too close. "Pull the skirmishers back."

"Already on the move."

The skids were starting to pull away. Major Van Duong strode out of the restaurant where First Company had set up, crossed the tunnel, and entered the furniture store across the street. Here Captain Hu and the men of Second Company crouched behind the steel barricades they'd welded to the floor plates, their rifles and RPGs ready.

Major Van Duong swallowed. They needed to stay here, to buy time for the retreat. "Captain, give us five minutes, then get out of here. No more than that."

"Yes, sir."

"I'm serious. We've left you four skids next door - I want you to use them."

Captain Hu nodded, and turned to his console. "Major, PK rovers are 200 meters away. If you're leaving, leave."

Major Van Duong nodded. He'd left the skids so that Second Company could evacuate, but he didn't kid himself about the chances that they'd actually get to use them. He stepped out of the furniture store. In the center of the tunnel the last vehicle waited for him. He saw movement and turned to his left. PK rovers? Wait, no - it was the skirmishers, incongruously riding motorcycles in spacesuits with their rifles slung over their shoulders. They were falling back to this, the last line of defense.

Then there was more movement, from a cross tunnel. There. Those must be the PK rovers. He hopped onto the skid and grabbed a bar. The driver had been waiting for him and immediately accelerated. Major Van Duong turned and looked down the tunnel. Behind him machines poured into the tunnel. He swallowed.

But - wait. They were entering the intersection from the wrong side.

And then he saw that the machines weren't PK rovers, they were bigger.

Then he realized.

Bulldozers - large gray bulldozers. It was the armor he'd asked General Dewitt for!

Van Duong keyed his mike. "Captain Hue - the tanks are here! Get all of your men onto those skids and fall back immediately!"

Chapter 117

2064: Little Nigeria, Aristillus, Lunar Nearside

Ewoma's head throbbed. This was the worst headache she'd ever had. Worse than that, someone was yelling at her. Someone really annoying. Who was it? Mom. Mom was usually nicer. She didn't want to get out of bed yet, darn it. She tried to reach up and cover her ears but there was something hard in the way -

A helmet?

She blinked and opened her eyes. She was wearing a space suit helmet, and it was yelling at her, over and over. "Air tank empty. Remove helmet immediately to avoid asphyxiation death. Air tank empty -"

She realized she was slumped forward onto something. She sat up. She was sitting in a delivery skid? Suddenly she remembered. The battle, the breach, the vacuum - it all came back.

Where had the skid taken her? She pulled the blaring helmet off and looked around. She was in a residential tunnel, with lights - and air! She looked closer - it was Little Nigeria. Great! She was almost home. She turned and looked over her shoulder. The giant black-and-yellow striped e-p-door that the crews had been installed a month back was closed behind her, cutting the huge residential tunnel in half. Next to the vast door that cut across the tunnel was a smaller door, the airlock the skid had taken her through.

On the screen above it a red icon was flashing: hard vacuum.

With the helmet off Ewoma breathed deeply and realized that her lungs hurt - like a tickle, but worse. Her throat spasmed and she coughed, which only made her lungs hurt more. She made a conscious effort to try to breathe shallowly. She took a few breaths - yes, that was a bit better.

She looked down and realized she was still holding the helmet. She put it down and shrugged out of the backpack and started to push them both to the floorboards when she saw -

The dog.

It was lying there, stretched awkwardly across the bottom of the vehicle, limp. It wasn't moving. Ewoma started to tear up. The poor thing. After all of that, the dog hadn't made it. So close, but -

Then she saw the creature's yellow flank rise and fall slowly...and then again. The dog was OK!

She rubbed her eyes, then bent forward to program the delivery skid to drive her, the money bag, and her new dog home.

Chapter 118

Major Van Duong twisted in his seat, straining to look over his shoulder. It looked like the General Tunnels tanks were holding their ground against the PK's APCs. At least for now. Who knew how long they could keep it up?

Stray bullets from the battle sprayed down the tunnel. Overhead a light panel exploded and rained debris; shattered bits bounced off of the skid and off of his own helmet. Van Duong turned away from the combat and faced forward. The tanks would hold the line, or they wouldn't - either way, it was someone else's problem. He had to worry about getting his men out of the line of fire. Then he'd see what - if anything - Command wanted him to do.

More shots chased them down the tunnel and an overhead water line shattered and sprayed into the tunnel. The convoy drove into the cloud of roiling mist and exploded out the far side. Van Duong wiped his faceplate and succeeded only in smearing the water droplets across the plastic.

A moment later, the vehicles roared through a tunnel intersection at full speed. Van Duong looked to his right at the huge e-p-door a kilometer down the side tunnel, and then looked to his left. As the side tunnel flickered past, he thought he saw movement. More reinforcements? Good. More tanks would be -

A moment later he realized he was wrong. It was PK rovers - and they were spilling out of the left-hand cross tunnel into the main tunnel that they were in. He started to yell an alarm, and realized that the rovers weren't turning to follow his men. Instead the rovers were headed straight across the intersection. Why?

That made no sense - the only thing down there was the e-p-door and behind it the rest of Little Nigeria. There were no military targets in that -

Van Duong felt a chill. The PKs weren't trying to engage military targets. They were *intending* to strike at civilian areas. He was in the act of keying his mike when one of the massive PK demolition robots rolled through the intersection behind them. It was the same kind that had destroyed the surface airlock door, and it was heading right for the e-p-door to Little Nigeria.

He issued his command. "Stop the convoy - enemy behind!". The vehicles slammed to a stop and reversed course.

He felt cold sweat bloom in his armpits. The 30th was out of rovers. They had to stop the demolition rover - and they going to have to do it man against machine. Casualties were going to be high. Really high.

He gripped his rifle more tightly.

Chapter 119

Major Reimmers stared at Fournier. Had the man been drinking? Well, whether or not, he needed to be put in his place. "He's my prisoner, not yours, it's my chain of command, not yours, and if we can prevent civilian casualties, then we're going to do it."

Fournier jabbed his index finger into Reimmers' chest. "You're forgetting that I'm governor here, so you've got to -"

Reimmers slapped Fournier's finger away. "*Going* to be. Not yet - and even if you were, I report to my colonel, not to you. So I'll pass Martin's offer on -"

Fournier jabbed his finger at Reimmers again, but this time didn't make contact. "And I'm going over your head to the White House. I assume that even if you won't take orders from me, you still acknowledge Washington's control?"

Reimmers pursed his lips. "Place the call. But I want to hear it, and if I don't like it, I'm still calling my colonel."

Fournier shrugged and gestured at the wall screen, bringing up the phone program. Then, instead of dialing, Fournier turned away from the screen and opened a cabinet and removed a glass and a bottle.

Reimmers gritted his teeth. Damn it. He'd been right - Fournier *had* been drinking. He wasn't just dealing with an arrogant bastard, he was dealing with a drunk arrogant bastard.

Reimmers turned away and looked at the captive. Mike Martin sat in his chair, arms shackled behind him. He was oddly placid, given that it was his outburst that had led to this call. Truth be told, he felt for him. The poor SOB was a rebel and was on the wrong side of history, but he'd met worse men.

Behind him an ice cube splashed into a glass. Major Reimmers turned around. Beverage in hand, Fournier was placing the call. Reimmers stood, arms crossed, as Fournier talked his way through layers of White House aides. Finally a young man in a nicely cut suit, an expensive haircut, and a fake smile appeared on the screen. "Leroy, how are you? How's the operation?

"I'm doing well - and by all reports the battle is going well too." Reimmers fought the urge to say something. 'By all reports?' What the hell did Fournier even know? Only what he, Reimmers, had passed on. A few BattleNet reports and the man was an expert? Yet here he was talking to some unctuous little shit in DC, pretending he knew what the hell was going on. Yes, he wanted to say something, but what was the point? Careers had been lost over less. He kept his comments to himself and contented himself to blow air through his nose.

Fournier continued, "I'm calling because Major Reimmers -" he gestured "- let one of prisoners overhear something. And then he listened to the prisoner mouth off. So now there's some drama. I swear, we should have just gagged him." He shot a sour look at Martin - and maybe at Reimmers too - and took a sip of his drink. "Now Reimmers thinks that we need to change plans." He smiled ingratiatingly. "I wanted to nip that in the bud, so I'm calling to get confirmation from the White House that the original plan is still -"

Before Reimmers realized it was happening Mike Martin lurched to his feet, hands still zip-tied behind his back. He lunged towards the screen. "Your robots are attacking civilian tunnels! Regular people are dying." Reimmers took a step forward toward Martin, but the man didn't advance any further. Reimmers put a hand on Martin's shoulder and pushed him gently back into his chair. Martin continued to plead. "Look, if you want to come after us, fine, come after us. Come after our troops and our gold and our leadership team, but -"

On the wallscreen the White House aide leaned forward and hit a button. The wallscreen was immediately overlaid with a banner reading "far end mute." Mike continued " - stop blowing the airlocks! You've got women and children..." Martin must have seen the mute sign; he sputtered to a stop. Reimmers looked from Martin to the aide on the wallscreen and back. The two men - captive and functionary - locked eyes through the video link for a long moment; then the aide reached out and hit a button, unmuting the channel.

The aide spoke. "You're Mike Martin, then?"

Martin nodded, mutely.

The aide smiled to himself. "The president thought we might get a call like this. She was very clear about what I was supposed to say. It's a message, actually, specifically for you." He paused, the corner of his lip turning up just a hair. "Are you ready?"

Martin tried to swallow, and nodded again.

"Here's the president's message: 'You had your chance. Go fuck yourself.'" The functionary smiled wryly, clearly amused that he was the one to relay a message, that he got to be the one to humiliate one of the rebel CEOs. He raised his eyebrows in mock apology, ironically distancing himself from the message he'd just passed along. Reimmers had never seen the man, never heard of him, but he found himself hating him with a passion. Martin was beaten, broken - and this little REMF thought he was a bad ass for giving him attitude?

The functionary turned to Fournier. "Anything else, Leroy, or is that it till we talk in person in two weeks?"

Fournier smiled for the first time in the conversation. "No, that's it. Thanks for your time, Chris." The connection ended.

Reimmers looked at Martin. The man was sunk in his chair, head forward, chin on chest. He was utterly broken. Reimmers turned away, embarrassed.

Chapter 120

2064: Boardroom Group Headquarters in Tunnel 1,288, Aristillus, Lunar Nearside

Javier sat with the rest of the boardroom group around the table in silence. He looked at the battle maps on the wallscreen sourly. ADF units were marked with icons and tagged with strengths, but the locations of the PK forces were less clear - icons expressed guesses at units, and in some cases were nothing more than clouds with probabilities attached. Javier knew that Dewitt's staff was struggling to pull sensible data out of reports from commanders reporting contact, civilians calling in and reporting gun fire, and a deluge of other, even less useful information, but the fact that they were working hard didn't mean that the result was useful.

From time to time an enemy icon would blink out when it was destroyed by the defenders or was revealed to be misinformation. More often, though, the opposite happened - an enemy unit popped up where none was expected. Worst of all was when an ADF unit started flashing because it was under fire from a PK unit that no one had even known existed.

Dewitt and his senior staff huddled near the wall screen. Dewitt was apparently feeling the same frustration that Javier was - in the middle of the scrum he raised his voice. "Damn it - I need to know where the hell the forces are!"

Karina Roth whispered, to no one in particular, "If we lose, what do you think they'll do to us?"

Rob Wehrmann scowled. "I'm not going to find out - they're won't take me alive."

Karina turned to him. "You've got poison?"

Rob's disdain showed on his face. "Fuck, no. I've got a pistol and three magazines."

Mark Soldner pushed his chair back and began to pace.

Javier rubbed his eyes. Damn it! They were trapped here, with no way to find anything out. He cursed himself - this was partially his fault. If he had fought harder against shuttering ViewSpace they'd be able to look anywhere in Aristillus they wanted, and find out where the PKs were.

He looked up at the maps on the wallscreen. So many question marks where PKs might be. Even some off in that one weird corner of level two where Mike had tried to put in a tunnel cluster before the weird moissanite bed had forced him to tunnel in another direction. Why the hell did Dewitt's staff have question marks there? That tunnel was a dead end, and he'd bet 100 to one that there were no enemy forces -

An idea struck him and he gasped at the audacity of it.

The table had untouched plates of brownies, cookies, sandwiches, and carafes from the last meeting before the invasion fleet arrived. Javier reached our with two hands and pushed the mess away from him, clearing space, and put his slate down on the table.

He logged into FuTrade and created a new account, and then initiated a transfer of 20,000 grams from his personal account - his very last emergency-beyond-all-emergencies fund. At the front of the room one of the aides shouted, "Where the fuck did those rovers come from? Why didn't we have a contact report? Fuck!"

On his screen a small spinner windmilled as the brokerage talked to his bank. It spun. And spun. God damn it! People were dying defending Aristillus right now, and he was sitting, waiting for a damn bank transfer. Hurry. Hurry. Someone at the front of the room yelled, "I'm not going to split the tanks. I need to deploy them en masse!"

"Where?"

"That's the God-damned question!"

Javier's slate beeped. He looked down - it was done; his funds were in. He leaned forward and typed furiously. He created a new bet, then another, and another. Underneath "Themba Johnson to be reelected president," "New Emilio-X album to feature Sister Rosalinda," and "WHO confirmed deaths in Taiyuan over 10k by 31 December," his new wagers popped up one at a time:

"PK forces sighted in Dockside - 500 gram bet"

"PK forces sighted in Lower Landing - 500 gram bet"

"PK forces sighted in Conveyor Belt District - 500 gram bet"

"PK forces sighted in Warehouse District - 500 gram bet"

He jumped over to moonlist.ari and posted a link to the FuTrade bets, and then jumped back to FuTrade.

He looked at his account total. 18,000 grams left. What bet should he create next? He looked up at the wallscreen where Dewitt and his aides were pointing and gesticulating. What information did they seem to be missing? He heard someone say something about Little Nigeria. He typed "PK forces sighted in Little Nigeria" and hit return. The slate beeped at him.

What? He looked down. There was an error on the screen: "a bet by that name already exists." Huh? He hadn't created that one yet, had he? He looked at his list of bets and positions. No - he'd only created four so far.

Wait.

Was someone else -

Yes - there were three more bets. "PK forces in High Deseret." "PK forces in Little Boston." Then two more appeared: "HKL attack - more than 100 dead." "Lai Docks seized."

Javier stared at the results, torn. On one hand, the fact that other bets were popping up indicated that this desperate gambit might work -

- but on the other hand, that last bet worried him. 'Lai Docks seized'? If anyone thought that was an actual risk, they were all in trouble - deep trouble. The Grace under Pressure parked there, and that converted LNG ship had millions of kilograms of liquefied air. Air they were going to need to repressurize Aristillus, if they managed to win this fight.

Had the docks really been seized?

If so, then the war might already be over - if the PKs took or destroyed the Grace, Aristillus might have to sue for peace, even if it won the battle.

He stared at the entry on the screen with growing trepidation - and then clicked it.

Huh. Just one wager riding on the proposition, and only 10 grams at that. He quickly bet 500 grams on the "no" side and waited for movement. There was none.

He waited a few seconds more - and still, no change. Well, one bullet dodged.

He needed to tell Dewitt and the staff about this, but first he needed more data. He tabbed back to the master bet list and continued placing wagers - big wagers so the prizes would be juicy enough to bring people out of the woodwork. A bet. Another one. Another one. Another - and the interface beeped an error - his account was empty.

But that was OK. He looked over the master list and there saw that there were over a hundred bets - the forty he'd created, and dozens more: "E-p-door #2 broached," "Power out in tunnel #118," "E-p-door #4 broached," and others

He clicked into one of these. "PK forces in level 1 East." The betting was 14 to 1.

He cleared his throat. "General?"

Dewitt was pacing, looking at the screen.

"General?"

Dewitt didn't hear him. Javier stood and bellowed. "General Dewitt!"

Dewitt turned to look at him - as did everyone else in the boardroom group. "What?"

"I know where the PK forces are."

Dewitt looked at him uncomprehendingly. "I don't have time for your guesses."

"They're not guesses. And they're not mine."

Chapter 121

Camanez Beef and Pork feedlot #22 was typical - a section of C-class tunnel, capped at each end by a concrete wall.

A month earlier the four hectares of open space beneath the curved roof had been nearly wall to wall with cattle. Now, after the refugee crisis, and the mass slaughter of the herds, the feedlot was nearly empty, and most of the overhead lights were turned off. Nothing but packed earth and piles of dry dung sat where cows had recently bunched together.

Only at the extreme southern end of the feedlot were a few ceiling light panels still lit, illuminating a medium pen that held a dozen cows that had survived the culling.

The cows chewed their cud with typical placidity, but a grinding noise coming from overhead caused one to stop and look up. As the noise grew, a second cow looked up. A moment later they all stared at the ceiling and lowed. As the sound of abrasion grew louder and louder, the animals grew agitated. The crunching sound suddenly increased in pitch, and concrete dust began to fall from the ceiling. Fist-sized chunks of shotcrete crumbled and fell away from the ceiling. One cow began to trot anxiously around the pen, pushing against the metal of the livestock panel, looking for some way out.

With a shriek a huge section of the ceiling ripped free, revealing the huge disk cutter of the tunnel boring machine above. The expanded steel mesh lath inside the shotcrete became entrained in the rotating cutter head. The cutter head's rotation tore at the steel, and a new larger avalanche of concrete pieces fell as the ceiling started to collapse. Fist-sized concrete shards fell onto the packed dirt below. The cows panicked and threw themselves at the pen wall. Two became entangled as the wall toppled. The wounded cows went over with the wall section. As the piece of modular pen fell, it pulled on the sections adjacent to it, and like a derailing freight train, section after section fell.

The remaining cows panicked and stampeded, crushing the two downed cows as they raced over the downed pen wall.

With a crash, a huge section of the roof fell amid a rolling cloud of dust. The noise rose to a continuous bellowing roar, drowning out the screams of the downed cows.

Even in the lower gravity, the TBM accelerated as it broke free of the ceiling. As it fell, its cutter head crashed through overhead catwalks, lights, and fire suppression systems. The falling TBM tore them all loose from their anchors without slowing. Metal screamed as huge lengths of catwalk and pipes ripped free from the ceiling and fell.

And then, in a huge crash of rubble and dust, the machine hit the floor. The floor plates beneath the dirt buckled as the TBM punched half a meter, a meter, two meters into them.

And then it stopped.

The huge machine extended the entire height of the feedlot, connecting floor to ceiling. Around it concrete and other rubble pattered down from the carnage above. Water sprayed fitfully from broken pipes and electric arcs flickered in the tangled wreckage. The two downed cows trapped in the fence, and now covered with dust and small rubble, screamed in pain.

A hatch opened in the side of the TBM and folded down, and a dozen tracked rovers rolled out and formed a perimeter. A moment later a squad of armored PKs stepped out. One turned toward the injured cows, flicked the safety off of his weapon, and machine gunned them.

Another walked to the nearest emergency exit sign and pushed on the access door. When it pivoted open a crack, he fished a small camera from a pocket, stuck it through the gap, then keyed his mike. "Raptor 5 scout to Battalion 5 command - we're in the feedlot, the doors are unlocked, and there's no one in the surrounding tunnels."

A moment later the flow of troops and machines spilling out of the hatch in the side of the drilling machine began in earnest.

Chapter 122

Major Van Duong crouched on the floor of a "Misha's All You Can Eat ... and Bookstore!" and leaned around a table stacked high with hardcovers so that he could look at the wreckage. Over two dozen of his men lay across the roadbed in deflated spacesuits. Blood, shattered glass, and empty brass littered the ground around them. The nearby storefronts were shattered - windows destroyed, signs ripped off facades. A few fires had been started by PK grenades, but the lack of air had put those out before they could do much more than scorch the walls.

He looked to his right. Further down the tunnel the wreckage was just as bad, but most of the debris there was destroyed PK machines. Most, but not all - there were also a few expat dead.

Then, finally, beyond the wrecked PK machines was where the battle had been won. For almost fifty meters along the tunnel, the storefronts on both sides of the road were utterly obliterated. Not damaged. Not burned. Just *gone*. Front walls blown away, interiors gutted, upper stories collapsed down into the wreckage. Overhead the light panels weren't just dark, they were *missing*, scoured away by the same blast that had punched a massive crater in the floor.

That was where a dozen of his men, in a mad suicide rush just minutes ago, had managed to get close enough to hit the PK demolition robot with RPGs and detonate it prematurely. They'd been caught in the explosion themselves, but they'd protected Little Nigeria's e-p-door.

Van Duong was pulled out of his reverie when a bullet hit the concrete planter a handsbreath away

---

from him. He pulled back behind the pile of books, and then another string of bullets hit, shattering containers on a shelf above him. The bottles of olives and pickled lemons that had somehow survived the depressurization exploded, and ropes of oil and juice splashed out over the wreckage of the store...and over his spacesuit. He wiped one hand across his faceplate, trying to clear the olive oil, but just smeared it worse.

He swore - what sort of lunatic sold luxury foods in a God-damned bookstore?

The bullets emphasized the fact that while they'd taken out the big demolition bot, the fight wasn't over. A dozen of the smaller PK machines still ducked in and out of storefronts as they harassed his men.

Christ, where were the tanks? How long ago had he asked for them? He ducked as another string of fire ripped into the shop and called Command. One of Dewitt's aides answered. "Yes?"

"Are the tanks almost here? We're taking a lot of fire!"

"The tank aren't coming."

"What the fuck? The rovers here are -"

"The rovers are a diversion. The PKs have TBMs and they've broken through into levels 3 and 4."

Major Van Duong swore to himself. "Can you get at least one tank up here?"

"No. Listen - leave some men there to mop up and get the rest down Hanson Ramp Two - shit! That ramp just got blown. Uh...fuck, fuck. There are some cargo elevators near there. Look, I've got to go, we've got another TBM break through. Just figure it out, but get your men down to level four ASAP!"

Van Duong started to protest that he couldn't even break contact without help, but the aide had already ended the call.

Chapter 123

2064: Trentham Court Apartments, Aristillus, Lunar Nearside

Connor James stared at the wallscreen in frustration. No one knew where the PK forces were going to turn up next, but one thing was clear - civilians were getting shot. Stores were getting blown up. In some cases, entire tunnels were being depressurized.

He flipped between channels. Video bloggers were loudly debating whether this was intentional or not. Jesus. Who cared whether it was intentional? Those PK robots could be here in an hour, shooting up his apartment. He turned off the wallscreen, and then stood and paced as his wife and the boys looked at him. What was he going to do? Finally he reached a decision. "Mona, pack up the kids. I know where we'll be safe." He pulled out his phone and summoned a rental skid.

Ten minutes later he stood in front of the apartment, loading his tool chest, his backpack, two duffel bags, and two diaper bags into the vehicle. As he heaved the last bag in he looked up - Mona had just strapped the second baby carrier into the back seat. They were ready to go. He swung himself into the the front seat and tapped an address in. Mona sat next to him, buckled her seat belt, and asked, "Connor, where are we going?" Wordlessly he pointed to the map on the dashboard screen, and hit the green button.

As the vehicle drove, Connor looked around the tunnels. The battle was still levels away, but there was the increasing chaos in the streets, the distant sounds of explosions, and a rising sense of panic. He bit his lip. What would happen to him - to them - if the good guys lost this battle? Would he be arrested? He ran a hand over his forehead and hair as he thought about it.

What could they get him on? Illegal emigration. Money laundering. Bartering. Hell, just for building the microship under a tarp in his backyard he could get 10 years, according to the news reports he'd seen. Shit. If the ADF lost this war, he and Mona were in deep shit. The peakers might even take the kids away from them. Damn it. Damn it. They ADF couldn't lose - they just couldn't.

He swallowed. There was nothing he could do. Well, that wasn't quite right. There was nothing he could do if the PKs won the battle - but at least he had a plan to survive the next few hours.

The skid entered a spiraling ramp and descended three levels, down to the newest section of the city, and then went one more level down, to level 8. Mona looked up as they drove past the huge number painted on one wall of the tunnel. "I didn't know there was a level eight."

"New construction." In the backseat one of the boys started crying in his baby carrier. Mona turned in her seat to quiet him.

The skid piloted itself past row after row of closed and locked doors, and then slowed and stopped in front of a dark green utility door. Mona finished calming the baby and turned forward. "I don't understand - what is this?"

Connor swung himself out of the skid. "Remember the overtime last month?"

"Of course; I was all alone with the boys, and we never saw you-"

He cut her off. "I was helping to install some heavy electrical infrastructure. Some utility company building out a power station, or something."

"But what -"

"Here. This. It's *safe*, babe. There's no easy way in - no regular doors, no loading docks. Just these access doors." As he spoke, he rooted through his toolbox until he came up with a breaker bar and a 35 millimeter socket. He snapped the socket onto the bar and stood. "That's why it's the perfect hiding spot during the battle."

There was a distant explosion, followed by a siren. Both of the boys started crying again. Connor ignored them and fitted the socket over the locking bolt on the door. Ten full revolutions - then one more, just to be sure. He placed the breaker bar on the ground and used both hands to grab the large wheel in the center of the door. One solid turn - and the locking bolts disengaged. He pushed and the door swung open. The corridor beyond was dark - and then light panels beyond flickered and turned on.

He ushered Mona inside with the two baby carriers and returned to the skid to ferry the duffel bags. Once inside, Connor closed the door and twisted the wheel, locking them in. He squeezed past Mona and led the way through the access hallway into the C-class tunnel beyond.

As he stepped into the tunnel he blinked in surprise. It had changed in the last few weeks. A *lot*. The paint crews and the light panel installers had done their work before he and his crew had arrived last month. They, in turn, had run huge electrical conduits and bus bars along the walls and had installed 20-meter-tall floor-to-ceiling equipment racks, but after the copper and steel was in place they'd left the tunnel not too different from how they'd found it - vast, empty, and echoing.

But now?

He looked to the right down the tunnel and saw that the huge bays of racks they'd installed - kilometers of them in each direction - were filled with something. He squinted. Were those *battery* units? If they were, they were of a really weird design: they were oversized and were missing the heavy dust shields.

He shook his head and looked to the left. More kilometers of floor-to-ceiling racks stuffed with batteries.

What the hell *was* this place?

And what were this many batteries *for*? How much power was this tunnel capable of holding? He did a quick computation. If these batteries had the same energy density as regular ones - and they might be denser - then a ton of them was -

He reached a number and whistled unbelievingly. Then another thought struck him - hadn't his crew chief said that there were a dozen other tunnels just like it?

What was this -

Suddenly movement a few meters away caught his eye. He pushed Mona behind him, back into the access corridor.

The movement resolved itself - an object rolled out from behind the nearest rack.

It was a rover.

Chapter 124

2064: Raptor #1, surface of Aristillus, Lunar Nearside

Hours ago the wallscreens in the bridge of the raptor had been mostly empty, showing just the invasion fleet's trajectory and lunar maps of Aristillus and the AI's industrial facilities. Now that they had landed, though, the screens were a riot of color. Maps, troop dispositions, health bars -

"General, check out Battalion One, Delta Company."

General Restivo gave Colonel DeCamp a nod to indicate that he'd heard. Battalion One was Colonel DeCamp's unit, so the man was bragging. Restivo's attention wasn't needed at the moment, so he could indulge his subordinate. Restivo typed on his BattleNet console to bring up the feed.

There - he had Battalion One, Delta Company on his screen. Icons of friendly units moved over the map of Aristillus as they advanced. Expat forces fell back before them. There were a few places where the map apparently didn't match reality - friendly units were shown as advancing through the dark gray that the key said was solid rock, but each time it happened the map autocorrected. Aristillus militia units were annotated with glyphs as they were forced back.

Several of the icons for friendly platoons were marked with glyphs indicating that video feeds were available. Restivo clicked one at random. He watched a few seconds before closing it. The video confirmed what the map and icons claimed - the battle was going well. The rovers of Delta Company were advancing, seizing and holding ground, and the troops were following after, consolidating the position. Restivo clicked another icon and watched a few more seconds before cycling to a third. All of Colonel Decamp's companies were doing well. Yes, DeCamp was bragging - but he was entitled to it.

Restivo closed the video windows, returned to the map view, and sighed. The battle was going well. He, on the other hand, felt utterly horrible. Since his moment standing on the Nevada bluff, looking down at the invasion ships and thinking of his legacy, he'd been unable to get Cortez out of his mind. During a slow moment in the transit to the moon he'd called up Wikipedia articles on him. The man had died of pleurisy. Restivo reached into his picket and brought out the cylinder of antacid tablets. Thankfully, heartburn couldn't kill the same way infection could.

On the wallscreens US/PK forces advanced. The icons and glyphs were antiseptic - the carnage was abstracted away. Restivo chewed two tablets and put the cylinder away. He didn't mind his rovers attacking and blowing up the expat rovers. Machinery destroying machinery - there was no more sentiment to it than there was to smelting down old cars to make new steel. The other images, though? Pictures and video of dead expat militiamen? That troubled him.

Yes, they were avoiding taxes. Yes, they were regular citizens - not police or military - and thus had no right to own firearms. They certainly had no right to raise those weapons up against legitimate US and PK forces.

But a lot of those dead were Americans. Not all of them - there were Nigerian, Chinese, and other corpses scattered around. Too many of them, though, looked and dressed like him. Like his family. Like his neighbors.

Was he the only one feeling these doubts? General Restivo looked to his right, at Colonel DeCamp. The man was typing and speaking into his headpiece, directing his companies. Restivo turned to his left, where the rest of the Battalion One command staff also typed at their consoles and stared at their screens.

No one was looking at him. Restivo tapped at his console, brought up the video clip he'd bookmarked earlier, and let it play again. The video started out simply enough - a scene from inside one of the tunnels, storefronts abandoned, some wreckage in the middle of the roadway. The only interesting thing was the data overlay on the rover's camera that showed the air pressure dropping, dropping, dropping.

Then the rover's camera panned over the three children coughing up blood, the one women struggling to crawl toward an airlock dragging a child behind her, until a piece of debris flying in the gusting wind smashed into her head, knocking her away from the small boy.

General Restivo stopped the video and clicked it away.

He'd told First Battalion to threaten the Little Nigeria tunnels areas in order to pull the militia forces out of their blocking positions. That tactic had worked. Then the troops of Third Battalion had seen their success and had improvised and actually started blowing airlocks and pressure walls.

Without intending to, he felt his balled fist slam down against the armrest.

Damn it!

He'd demanded that Colonel Weil get his troops under control, and by the time he'd gotten a solid acknowledgement out of him, Fourth Battalion had pulled the same stunt.

He shook his head. What the hell was wrong with these people?

He'd tried to fight against the inclusion of the less reliable units. But how many really solid units were there? Even if he could have hand-picked every one of the battalion commanders and all of their captains, the choices would've been second-guessed by the Pluralism Officers. And now he was staring at the results: troops managing to "not hear" orders or "accidentally" detonating MOAB rovers against pressure doors.

Children coughing up blood and dying.

Damn it.

He wondered, not for the first time, if the orders he was obeying were lawful or not.

An alert pinged on his console and he looked up. Battalion Five was getting close to the gold vaults.

He tried to shake another antacid pill from the container and found it empty.

Chapter 125

2064: Boardroom Group Headquarters in Tunnel 1,288, Aristillus, Lunar Nearside

Darren's phone rang with the priority tone. He answered.

"Darren, it's Reggie." Strosnider, his head of security.

"Yeah?"

"Our remote cameras show that the PKs are heading right towards us - they're ignoring everything else and heading for the warehouse complex."

"How long till they get there?"

"Fifteen minutes, maybe."

Darren breathed in, held it for a moment, and let it out. "Evacuate. Completely. Hit the master alarm - let's make sure we're not leaving anyone - even a janitor - behind."

"What about the gold?"

Darren shook his head. "Forget it."

Reggie choked. "Forget it? Look, boss - we're losing the battle, but we might still win the war. And if we do win, that gold is key - that lets us rebuild after -"

"Reggie. Stop. Listen to me. Do *not* defend the gold. Actually - open all vault doors. All of them. The PKs will do less damage that way."

"Boss, without the gold -"

"Leave it. That's an *order*. Now move."

Chapter 126

Hugh sat on the couch in the cell with his feet up on the coffee table. "655 Hours a Day" was playing on the wallscreen. Hugh grimaced at another video shot of a burning storefront and two corpses face down in front of it.

Louisa looked at him. "Don't tell me you're falling for this bullshit expat propaganda?" She shook her head sadly. "You know that those are probably actors." She thought for a moment. "Or even if they are really dead, they're probably terrorists, fighting out of uniform."

Hugh nodded. Maybe so. The show was over the top - not only were the production values mediocre, but the newscasters had a libertarian bias verging on the autistic. "Property damage" this, "initiation of force" that. It was all radical buzzwords and no intelligent commentary to put any of the facts in perspective. You couldn't just say that something was property damage without explaining the situation and showing what caused the property damage.

He felt a little sorry for some of the more gullible expats - the Nigerians, the Chinese, the Mexican. Most of those people didn't have college educations, so when they watched this corporatist propaganda they probably wouldn't know any better. This was why journalism licenses existed in the first place - to avoid fake news like this. Give people a few random facts without the necessary context - the global economic problems, the rebellions in Texas and Alaska, the various UN resolutions - and you could state things that were technically true but gave exactly the wrong impression.

The screen switched to a new image - a closeup of a dead child. Her face was pixelated but the camera panned to show her outstretched blood-covered hand and then, just beyond her fingertips, a dropped teddy bear. Jesus. Hugh turned away. That looked real. It had to be. Even knowing the geopolitical context, he didn't -

Louisa snorted. Then, as if she'd read his thoughts: "Even if that is real - which I doubt - who cares? If her parents wanted to keep her safe they wouldn't have dragged her to the moon." She crossed her arms. "If her own parents don't care about her life why should anyone else?"

Hugh sat in silence for a while watching the newscast but Louisa's comment chafed. Finally he turned to her. "You can't really mean that, right? I mean, the invasion is necessary, I know, but you can still have some compassion for -"

"These people have opted out of civilization. Nature, red in tooth and claw, right? They *asked* for it. And now they got it. They wanted out of society? Fine, they're out."

Hugh sighed. "The point I'm making is that even if they are selfish tax avoiders, the Peace Keeper invasion -"

"Liberation"

"Fine. Liberation. But the point I'm making is, yes, these people need to obey regulations and pay taxes, but don't you think that the use of force is -"

Louisa stood, the better to glare down at him. "No, I don't. These people are flouting the law, Hugh. You're not getting that!"

He hated it when she stood over him. Hated it, hated it, hated it. It was like one of his mom's body language tactics. He stood too, to deny her the height advantage. Louisa kept ranting. "- they're giving a big middle finger to the global order. How are we supposed to have peace, freedom, and equality if anyone can choose to just opt out and leave? You let one brat take his toys and play on his own, and the next thing you know you've got two brats, then four, and where does that leave everyone who follows the rules? We can't have equality if everyone isn't equal. If you ask me, we should be cracking more heads, not less. An example needs to -"

Louisa was interrupted when the cell door slammed open.

The two guards who'd brought them food over the past few days stood in the entrance. Hugh nodded to the two men - they were all right. Louisa immediately turned on them. "Hey! I've looked it up, and even by your own standards, you can't keep us here. You shit stains know that that trespassing charge is bullshit and -"

The first, Frank, held one hand up. "Just shut up for a second." He turned to Hugh. "This area isn't safe, so we're letting you go. No cuffs inside the facility if you promise to be good - do we have a deal?"

Hugh nodded and walked to the door. The second guard, Jim, stepped to one side to let him pass. In the corridor Hugh turned to wait for Louisa and caught a sudden flash of movement as Louisa kneed Jim in the crotch. Jim screamed and fell. Hugh cringed in sympathy. Before Jim had even hit the ground Frank's rifle butt cracked sickeningly into Louisa's sternum. Louisa fell next to Jim, blocking the doorway of the cell.

Hugh protested, "Wait, Frank - she -"

Frank turned to him, rifle still in hand. "Shut up for a second, Hugh."

Frank slung his rifle and stepped around his downed coworker and into the cell. There he bent down, grabbed Louisa by her hair, and dragged her backward. Louisa clutched at the guard and screamed as he pulled her. Frank yelled back at her, "Shut up. It's 1/6 g - you're not fooling anyone." After he'd moved her to the center of the cell he stepped around her, out through the door, and slammed it behind him.

Jim had rolled on the floor, his knees pulled up toward his chest, his eyes squinted tightly closed, and both hands cupping his crotch.

Frank looked at him. "You OK?"

Jim cracked his eyes open and grunted. "*Fuck*, that hurts."

"You'll live."

"Screw you." Jim pushed himself off the floor and stood, hunched over, both hands still on his groin.

Frank turned to Hugh. "The PKs are coming. You're free - get out here before the fighting gets here."

Hugh stammered, "What about Louisa?"

Frank looked pointedly at Jim groaning and clutching himself. "What about her?"

Hugh licked his lips. "But - what if the Peace Keepers blow a tunnel and this places loses vacuum? Louisa would be- "

Frank's glare silenced Hugh.

Louisa yelled through the reinforced window of the cell door. "You're going to just leave me here, you little shits? If the air goes out and I die, that'll be a war crime!"

Frank turned to her and raised one eyebrow. "Yeah. But not ours."

A rumble shook through the floor, and a moment later the echoing sound of an explosion followed.

Frank turned to Hugh. "Get the hell out of here, kid."

Hugh turned to the cell door and looked at Louisa behind the glass, and then turned to the right, where

---

the hallways led to safety. He was torn, unable to decide.

Another explosion rumbled through the floor.

Hugh turned and ran.

Chapter 127

2064: outside Goldwater, Aristillus, Lunar Nearside

Colonel White ignored the bumpy ride of the APC as he watched the video feed on his slate. He was patched into a recon rover one level down from here. The rover's camera panned up and signs slipped into view - "titanium" with an arrow to the left and "precious metals vault" with an arrow to the right. The rover's point of view spun as it turned right. Its motors whirred as it raced forward, passing open doors to the left and right. And then it was there - at the vault. The door was a meter thick and had massive locking pins protruding slightly from the edges - and it stood wide open.

The rover operator maneuvered the machine around the door. The camera panned and -

Hundreds and hundreds of large ingots of gold, stacked on reinforced steel pallets.

White sucked in his breath.

The APC he was in tilted forward - they were on the ramp down now.

On the screen, the rover's POV shifted as it circled. From its new position Colonel White could see the open vault door. Over the next minute other rovers arrived and proceeded to inspect the walls, the ceilings, the various pieces of equipment.

"Doesn't seem to be booby trapped, sir."

It took Colonel White a moment to realize that the comment wasn't from one of the battalion's com channels, but from the captain sitting next to him. He looked up, nodded, and looked back down at his slate.

Beneath them the APC ground to a halt. White looked up - the command group had reached the vaults and caught up with the recon team.

Back on his slate the rover's camera showed that the tech team had entered the vault, carrying their equipment cases. Two men from the team put down their tools and began to move ingots, grunting as they exposed a random sample from deep in the stack.

Colonel White's mouth felt dry. He'd known the gold was there, and he'd had some rough idea of the quantity, but this was worth - he couldn't even figure it out. Trillions? Or was it billions? He was old enough so that he still thought in old dollars and had to do the conversion to bluebacks.

He wanted to see this with his own eyes. He *needed* to see it. He unbuckled his seat belt, and then paused for a moment, weighing the danger. There could still be a booby trap, but - fuck it. This mission was risky. Combat was risky. He stepped out of the vehicle and moved to the loading dock.

Damn, it was hard to move in these suits - even worse than the thermal suits they'd worn in the Second Anchorage Pacification. Over the com channel he heard one of the techs yelling excitedly, "Rockwell hardness checks out!" Despite the difficulty of moving in the suit, Colonel White picked up his pace.

He climbed the stairs next to the loading dock and was through the first armored door. Another tech called out, "hydrochloric test is good!" White smiled. This much money would keep the US government going for at least another six months. They'd get past the election, and for that he'd be able to write his own ticket.

"Magnet test is good!"

He was thinking about promotion when he heard a loud curse from one of the techs over the coms channel - then more swearing.

White tensed. Don't let this all turn to shit. Please. Not now. He keyed his mike. "What? What is it?" He tried to move faster, the fabric of the suit chafing against his thighs.

"Colonel?"

He swore, impatiently. "Yes, it's me. What's the problem?"

"Hang on, I'm rerunning the test."

White was at the second armored vault door, and then he was inside it. The crowd of techs with their pelican cases and the protection detail with their rifles surrounded the pallets of gold.

White pushed his way through and approached the four men who were actually doing the work. He stepped carefully through the spread of testing equipment on the floor. One tech was facing away from him as he weighed a golden brick on a digital scale.

The man turned. "Colonel?"

"What's the problem."

"Uh, Colonel, sir - this bar weighs only half of what it should."

The weight? The weight was the problem? Colonel White laughed. "Son, we're on the moon; it's supposed to weigh less."

"Yes sir, I know. But these scales are calibrated for that. See, this button here to switch back and forth? But on the Moon setting it's half the expected reading, and on the earth setting it's one-twelfth."

White stared at the tech. "What does that-"

"It means that the scale says these bricks aren't gold."

White felt rising. "That's impossible. The scale must be wrong."

The tech shrugged. "I don't know what to say. If we had a calibrated weight, we could test the scale, but I -"

Colonel White turned to the man next to him. "Sergeant, give me your rifle." The soldier looked confused, and after a moment, White pulled the rifle from his hands and handed it to the tech. "This weighs 4.6 kilograms, 4.8 with the magazine."

The tech took the rifle. "I'm setting it on Earth calibration. If the display says 4.8, then the scale is working." He put the firearm on the scale. White watched the display carefully as it settled.

Four point -

Four point - four point eight.

The tech turned to him. "See, sir, the scale is calibrated properly. These bars aren't - " The man kept talking but White found it hard to concentrate on his words. The scale had to be wrong. Because if the scale was right, that meant that the gold was fake.

White pulled his knife from its sheath, picked up the brick the tech had weighed, and scraped the knife along one edge of the ingot. Gold foil peeled back and revealed dull gray metal below.

The tech nodded. "That looks like electroplated gold over lead -"

A second tech argued with the first one. "Bet it's not electroplated - probably ferrocyanide solution."

"You're high - look at the surface. If it's not electroplated it's gotta be vapor deposition."

"Nah, you're forgetting -"

Colonel White had to force himself not to scream at the two men. "Stop it. Just - look." He started to rub a hand across his mouth and bumped into the faceplate of his helmet. "Test more bars - sample the other pallets."

He stepped back to watch, his thoughts racing. The two techs stopped squabbling and started lifting other bars and placing them on the scale. "Fake." "This one's a fake too." "Too light."

After a few minutes it was clear that the only gold in the entire facility was the thin plating on the hundreds of ingots.

Fuck.

God *damn* it.

He'd been such a damned fool to dream of a promotion and a vacation house.

He called up the coms interface in his helmet, stared at it for a moment, and reluctantly placed a call to General Restivo.

Chapter 128

2064: Soldner Homes, Montana Hills complex, apartment #772

Ashok remembered the importance of body language and uncrossed his arms. It might be a good step, but it wasn't good enough - Rani was still upset. "Ashok, listen to me - what are we going to do?"

"We'll lock the doors, we'll keep our heads down, and we'll wait for the battle to be over."

"What if they destroy the e-p-doors? If the tunnel loses pressure, we're all going to die - the children will die!"

Ashok looked to the couch where eight-year-old Nandita sat, wide-eyed, watching them. "Shhh. Rani, Rani - no one is going to die."

Rani saw Ashok glancing at Nandita. "I'm not going to lie to protect her - we could die. You know that." She looked away, then back. "This is all your fault - you said that we should come to the moon."

"That's not fair. We both agreed -".

"I may have agreed, but it was your idea. Oh, God, what a fool I was. We should have stayed in India!"

On the couch Nandita started to sniffle. Ashok took a deep breath. He had no idea what to say.

Chapter 129

2064: Goldwater vaults, Aristillus, Lunar Nearside

"What do we do now, sir?" Colonel White clenched a fist. Damn it, without the gold - "Sir?"

White looked up at his adjutant. "We proceed with the secondary objective, that's what."

"We're still rendezvousing with the snatch team? Doesn't this –" he gestured at the pallets of fake gold "– mean that we should -"

White shook his head. "This doesn't change anything. We meet the snatch team and we interrogate the high-value captive. Maybe this Mike Martin can tell us where the gold is hidden. If so, we go there and grab it. If not, we improvise. The mission hasn't changed."

The adjutant began, "But sir -" Colonel White silenced him with a glance, and then stared off into the distance. Without turning, he asked, "Are Major Shivers and fifth company deployed here inside the Goldwater facility or are they out in the tunnel?"

"Um - just one second..." The adjutant started tapping at his slate.

Colonel White grimaced and strode off without waiting for an answer. After asking several sergeants, he found Shivers a few minutes later.

"Major - find anything useful?"

Shivers turned. "Sir?"

"Have your men found anything useful in the facility?"

"Too soon to know. The oh-689s say the Goldwater people didn't clear cookies from their slates, so we've got logins. They're doing forensics right now. We might find something soon."

Colonel White nodded. "I'm going to go to MaisonNeuve to interrogate a prisoner. Maybe that gives us the clue we need. BattleNet shows that this sector is quiet, so I'm leaving you and fifth here alone, and I'm taking one through four with me."

Major Shivers compressed his lips, and then nodded. "Yes, sir."

Colonel White turned and headed for the vehicles. His aide scurried to keep up.

* * *

White sat in the right-hand seat of the open vehicle and watched the doors and windows of the passing buildings warily. In the industrial section of the colony where Goldwater was located they'd seen almost no one, and those few people they had seen had fled. Here, in the more populated office areas, they only saw a few more people - but those they did see, peeping out from windows and doorways, were glaring at them.

"Sir, we'd be a lot more secure in APCs."

"When you've been on deployments as long as I have you'll know that being glared at by locals is part of the job. If they start throwing rocks or blocking the path with burning tires we'll have trouble, but until then, sticks and stones."

"Yes sir, but if there is trouble, APCs would -"

Jesus. This damned adjutant just would not shut up. White thought for a moment of banishing him to some other unit, but let the thought expire. This pansy was some politician's idiot nephew, and it would cause too much trouble. Better to just tolerate it.

He turned to the aide. "Jackson, right?"

"Yes, sir."

"Jackson, we're in light utility vehicles because we couldn't fit APCs down the TBM shaft. This is a high-speed, low-drag mission. You know that."

"We could have brought them in via the surface and -"

White lost his temper. The missing gold, the time pressure, and now he had to listen to this bullshit from some wet-behind-the-ears pansy? "Damn it, look! The surface assault was designed to tie up the lunar forces. That's *why* the only resistance we're seeing down here is hasty ambushes by rovers. Our rovers outnumber and outgun them. You can't have it both ways - if you want heavy equipment, then we have to fight our way in. If you want to avoid enemy forces, then -"

Colonel White was stopped, mid-rant, by the sound of shooting ahead. The column slowed and then stopped. The aide, Jackson, spoke: "Sir, I -" White held up one finger to silence the idiot. He looked at his slate and brought up BattleNet. Where were they? What was going on? A few clicks and he was looking at a map of their current location. There was nothing special about it - mixed offices and residences. Actually, there was one section to their left marked with crosshatching and a tag put in by the deep cover recon team, "Type 3 office space - possible location of 'The Den'?"

He tapped the crosshatched area, but no further information came up.

Whatever. He tabbed over to the rover command screen and then looked out through the eyes of one of the lead rovers. The shooting looked like a rover vs. rover fight - his pickets versus a light screen of expat machines. If it was anything like the last three battles, the hiccup shouldn't take long. He was about to close the window when he noticed something odd - the expat rovers were doing something new. He furrowed his brow and leaned closer to the slate. Normal PK rover doctrine was to park a rover glacis-forward and engage targets with the guns. It was good doctrine, hammered out through decades of war. Good enough that the expats used it too. Well, they had, in the previous gunfights. These expat rovers, though, seemed to be dashing *across* the tunnel as they fired.

White shook his head. What the hell were they thinking? Rushing across the tunnel meant that the expat rovers were exposing their unarmored sides. Were the expats really that stupid? Or were they that desperate? Maybe the battles raging closer to the surface had soaked up - or killed - most of their best operators?

Finally, some good news - maybe the rest of this fight would be a cakewalk. White keyed his mike and called Shivers, back at the Goldwater complex. He shouted to be heard over the gunfire. "Any data on the gold?" He listened. "OK, keep looking."

To his left Jackson spoke. "Sir -"

God damn this adjutant. To the phone, "Hang on, Shivers." He looked up. "WHAT?"

"Sir, the rovers -"

"What about the damned rovers? I don't -" Even as he said it his brow furrowed. The PK rovers should have taken care of the situation by now, but the gunfire was still going on. "Yeah, Jackson, what? What about the rovers?"

"If you look at BattleNet, you'll see -" Colonel White looked back at his slate and called up an overview. That didn't make sense. There were only seven dead expat rovers - but *dozens* of his own rovers were dead. Had the expats gotten reinforcements? No. It didn't look like it. So what the hell was going on? He flipped through various camera views. The expat rovers' bizarre behavior had gotten even weirder: enemy rovers were making mad dashes *through* his lines, and then pivoting their turrets back at his rovers and picking them off from behind. What sort of tactic was this? This was insane. No one fought that way.

And how the *hell* were the expats doing it? Did they have multiple people remote operating each rover - one driver and one gunner? Even if they did, how could they acquire targets that quickly?

His adjutant began to speak again, and White silenced him with a hand. He turned over his shoulder and spoke to the officer in the next row of seats.

"Captain - what do you think is going on with these expat rovers?"

"Their tactics make no sense at all. It's bullshit -"

"Effective bullshit."

The captain was silent.

"What's our response?"

"Sir, my operators are following procedure. Just give us a few more minutes -"

"Captain, they're kicking your ass 8:1. In a few more minutes you'll be out of rovers."

The captain was sweating. "Just give my operators a chance to figure this out and they'll-"

Up ahead there was a scream. Colonel White knew without being told what was happening - the expat rovers had destroyed enough of the pickets that they could now focus on hitting soft targets - his men. "Make a decision, captain, or I'll find someone who can."

The other man swallowed. "I'll - I'll turn on the jammers! The expat rovers will be cut off from their operators and fall back to preprogrammed tactics."

White nodded grimly. A decision. Finally. A moment later there was a distinct hum from the countermeasures vehicle. White looked down at his BattleNet console. The video feed from the rover grew staticky and flickered, but he could still make out shapes.

The lunar rovers didn't seem to be impacted by the jamming - if anything, they were getting better at their weird dash-shoot-dash-shoot routine. From the convoy ahead there were more screams.

White turned to the captain. "What the hell is going on?"

"I don't know, sir." He shook his head. "The data links are down, I guarantee it. The only -"

"What?"

"The only thing I can think of is that those things are autonomous. But they couldn't be - how the fuck would you even program something like that -"

"Captain, you're relieved. Find your XO and get him over here. Now!"

Suddenly there was a loud burst of machine gun fire. Colonel White spun in his seat.

Next to him his aide said, "Sir - is that fire coming from *behind*?"

Chapter 130

2064: Goldwater facility, Aristillus, Lunar Nearside

Major Shivers leaned back in the chair and took in the office. The Goldwater CEO had probably sat right here, probably just a day or two ago. He nodded. The guy had decent taste. It was understated, but the desk was nice and big, and to one side there was a bookshelf - a real bookshelf, with old-fashioned paper books. It was a bit eccentric to have that many antiques in a working officc, but the effect worked.

He let his eyes run over the titles - no military history, but there were lots of books with impressive-sounding titles on their spines: mining, chemistry, archaeology. He continued his survey until, two shelves further down, he reached a shelf of libertarian nut-bag stuff. He shook his head; that was exactly the crazy bullshit that had gotten these people into the losing side of a shooting war.

Shivers turned away from the shelf, put his hands flat on the desk, and ran his palms over the surface. It was nice. One massive slab of thick, dark brown wood. He could enjoy sitting behind a desk like this.

Over the last few weeks a lot of the senior staff had been talking about their positions after the war, and he'd been among them. The suppression of insurgents in Alaska, Texas, Chiapas, and Chile was going to go on forever, so there'd always be work in Western Command, but promotion got even more political once you hit O-5. Add to that the fact that colonels and generals didn't tend to retire so much as keel over in office - and thus blocked promotions for the lower ranks - and it made perfect sense to start looking around for an exit plan once one hit major.

He rubbed the surface of the desk again. Would they shut down Aristillus after the war, or keep it up and running for the gold? He'd been trying to read the tea leaves. He wasn't sure, but it seemed to him that there was a good chance it would still be around. Which led to the interesting question: did he have enough pull to wrangle an appointment to run one of these lunar firms afterwards?

He let himself dream about running Goldwater for a moment, and then opened his eyes and looked around at the office again. No. A firm like *this* was too big a plum. There must already be half a dozen brigadiers and higher with eyes on Goldwater. Him, though? He was just a major - and he didn't have enough pull. He shook his head sadly.

No, even if the colony was kept alive, he'd get one of the smaller firms...at best. He should have spent more time making friends over the past years, like his wife had told him over and over again.

But.

But.

But what if he found the gold? Well, the situation would be different then, wouldn't it?. He'd be the hero of the hour, and he'd have favors that he could bank and use. If he got some pull inside DoD he'd be smart about it. He wouldn't use it for himself. No, that was a fool's strategy. He'd be clever - he'd use those favors to help others. Find some folks who were getting it in the ass from the Bureau of Industrial Planning, maybe. Oh, you need some extra electricity to run a factory and meet quota? Turns out I've got some pull on the DoD's carbon quota. Or maybe - you need military airlift for your NGO immunization program in Chad? I know who to call.

Play it smart - and then get his own back scratched six months later.

Major Shivers looked up from the polished surface of the desk to the empty room and fantasy crumbled and fell apart. He didn't have any favors to bank. Not yet, at least. Because he hadn't found the gold.

He rubbed the desk one last time and sighed, and then took his hands off of it.

There was a knock on the open door. He looked up at the AAS trooper and nodded. The low lunar gravity meant that the man really didn't need to use his cane, but he leaned on it obviously anyway. Shivers repressed his instinctive reaction. He knew the type - practically no one ever lost an AAS rating once they got it, but the idea of losing the extra pay and reduced duty meant that people with the "three golden letters" were extra careful never to seem too capable. "Report."

"The Captain found a prisoner. She's outside."

Major Shivers tilted his head. "Found? You mean captured?"

"No sir, found. The captain says you really want to see her. She's outside."

Major Shivers nodded. The AAS turned and yelled, "Bring her in!"

Two troops escorted Louisa into the room.

Shivers looked at her, then turned to the troops. "Who is she?"

Louisa glared at the Major. "Excuse me. You can speak to me directly, you know. I'm Louisa Teer, and I'm a journalist."

Shivers pursed his lips. "OK. And what do you have to tell me?"

Chapter 131

2064: MaisonNeuve Construction office, Aristillus, Lunar Nearside

Mike stared at the floor. The room had been quiet for several minutes when Major Reimmers broke the silence. He gestured at the BattleNet console. "Looks like your team is putting up a good fight."

Mike said nothing. From the corner of his eye he saw Leroy look over to Major Reimmers. With a bit of concern in his voice, Leroy asked, "How good of a fight?"

"We're getting unexpected resistance from the expat rovers."

"What does that mean?"

"Don't worry, your governorship is safe. The fleet has deployed less than a third of its drones and only half of its troops. They're readying reinforcements now."

Mike let his gaze drift from the carpet at his feet to a different patch a few meters away. He'd had such high hopes - and this was how it was going to end.

The future had been so bright. He'd thought that he was going to have everything. He'd kept telling himself that after the inevitable conflict, once Aristillus had forced the Earth governments to acknowledge their right to exist and be free, he'd have time to get married and give Darcy the kids she'd always wanted. And he'd told himself stories about other, smaller, stuff. He'd build the D-series TBMs. He'd start to take some time off from work and planning and talk with Javier more. He'd read.

If only the damned war had come five years from now, when he's assumed it would. But it hadn't. He tried to push the thought away, time and time again, but it stared him in the face. Everything he'd ever dreamed of was lost. He was going to die in jail. So were all of his friends - and most of the random people he knew around Aristillus. He swallowed. And Darcy was going to die in jail too.

It was his own damn fault, too. So many decisions he'd made, and every one of them wrong. Wasting time with the Gargoyle rifle design when there was no need for anything larger than a regular rifle. Letting his ego get in the way of making the Boardroom Group into a functioning team. Assuming that the revolution was safely years in the future. Hell, even siting Aristillus on nearside, half knowing that once they developed enough they'd be visible to amateurs with small telescopes. He'd known it, and though he'd never admitted it to anyone, he'd actively chosen it. He *wanted* to stick a finger in people's eyes. He *wanted* to taunt them.

And because of his decisions - so many stupid decisions - this is how it was going to end.

He was going to die in a prison. He was never going to see Darcy again. And worst of all, Aristillus, what he really thought was humanity's last hope to keep a small spark of freedom alive, was going to be crushed. It might linger on as a physical structure, but if it did, it'd be administered by cowards and ass-kissers. People would have to beg their government bureaucrat "betters" for permission to have kids, or open a business, or change a menu item, just like they did back on Earth.

He felt his eyes welling up a little bit.

Not in front of Fournier, damn it!

He bit down on his tongue, welcoming the pain.

Chapter 132

2064: The Den, Aristillus, Lunar Nearside

The room that Blue, Max, and Duncan had been using as their office since returning from The Hike had somehow morphed into, if not a command center, then at least a place where things happened, where the action could be observed. On a normal day there were three or four or five others, sitting on chairs, eating snacks, checking their own slates, but today was different.

Over the last few hours the room had slowly filled up with Dogs. The first few had taken spots on the chairs and couches that were normally in the room. The next dozen had dragged chairs in from adjoining rooms. And then, at some point, when there was no more room for furniture, the newcomers had given up and just started sprawling on the floor and draping themselves onto the arms of already claimed chairs. The last dozen had even started spilling onto each other, haunches and tails buried under chins and forepaws.

Max pointed at the wallscreen and grinned. "Ha! Look at that one!" There were several cheers, and a few disapproving murmurs.

Blue looked up from his console and to the wallscreen, where there was an image of a wounded PK dragging himself piteously with his arms, his bloody legs trailing uselessly behind him. Blue grimaced and turned away. Max was bloodthirsty and liked watching peakers get shot and die. What else was new?

Before today, though, he wouldn't have expected cheers from the audience. Blue turned and looked at the other Dogs. On the bright side, several of the canine faces in the audience did have disapproving looks on their faces.

Blue turned back to his own console. The stats were good. The rover kill ratio with the evolved combat algorithms had started out decent at four PK rovers killed for every one Dog rover dead, and as the combat progressed and the tactics engine evolved, the kill ratio got better and better. It had reached 11:1 and stabilized there for half an hour, but then the PKs had come up with their own new tactic: the two-on-one kill team. It wasn't a silver bullet for them, but it worked; the peakers were now only losing six or so machines for every one Dog unit they took out.

Blue looked at some of the other stats. Hmm. That was...troubling. "Max."

"Yeah?"

"Are you paying attention to the rover headcount?"

"I'm on it." Max laughed. "Hey, wait a second, check out this one - his arm got shot off and he doesn't know it yet. Stupid Dog-killing bastard."

"Max - the rover headcount."

Max turned away from the wallscreen. "What about it?"

"We're down to 1,720."

Max shrugged. "OK."

"We had said that the reserve force was going to be 2,000 rovers."

"I committed some of them."

"How many?"

Max waved off the question and tried to turn back to his screen, but a few of the Dogs in the audience had heard the exchange and yelled out questions.

Someone muted the wallscreen and someone else yelled out, echoing Blue's question: "How many?"

Max turned and glared at Blue, and then at the other Dogs who had heckled him. "I committed 1,000 of the reserve."

"*Half?* That only leaves us 1,000. Don't you think that leaves us too few?"

"Too few for what? This is our chance to crush them - they're on their backs and we've got our teeth on their throats."

One of the Dogs in the audience yelled out. "What the hell, Max? We should save some of our forces!"

Max turned in his seat to face the audience and growled. "Save them for what? This is the final battle. We can use every last rover if we have to!"

Blue shook his head. "How do we know this is the final battle? Maybe the PKs have more ships coming, or reinforce-"

"They're too stupid for that."

"Don't underestimate them - humans aren't as dumb as you think they are."

Max sneered. "And they're not as smart as *you* think they are."

One of the hecklers from the audience yelled out, "They were smart enough to engineer us."

Max's nostrils flared once, and then he turned away to watch the battle on the wallscreen. Blue spoke to his back. "Max, look at the count - we're down to 1,660 rovers now." Max said nothing.

"Fine. Ignore me. But I'm going to log in and -"

"Don't bother." Max turned to Blue. "I changed the password."

Blue blinked. "You did what? You can't - that's not your decision to make."

Max shrugged. "After the PKs are all dead you can take a vote and decide what to do about that. I don't think any of the others are going to be too upset at me for killing more peakers."

Blue typed frantically at his keyboard. Max hadn't been bluffing - his rover control system password didn't work. Blue felt a growl rising in his throat, but suppressed it. He tried the admin password. Changed. The network configuration password. Changed. The growl started building. He tried the root password. Changed.

Blue swiveled to face Max. He felt his lips curling back and heard a growl escape.

The urge to jump at Max, to knock him off the chair, to feel his jaws on Max's throat was strong. He fought the urge. He wasn't an animal - he was a sentient being. And other Dogs - lots of them - were watching. He'd fight Max with his brains, not his teeth.

Still, he felt his teeth grind against each other.

He struggled to calm himself.

After a moment he trusted himself to speak. "If I figure out some other way to fight the PKs, will you log in and call the rovers off?"

Max didn't look away from the screen as he answered. "Sure. But you're not going to."

Chapter 133

2064: level 2, Aristillus, Lunar Nearside

Sam Barrus, Jim Newman and the rest of the squad grunted as they lifted the disabled delivery skid and dragged it into position. "Now!" Sam let go and the skid dropped and landed tight up against a pallet full of cinder blocks, which in turn butted up against two more vehicles and a load of steel pipes. Sam shook his head. You could read all about lunar gravity ahead of time, but actually working in it was weird. If that skid weighed anything like Uncle Charlie's old gas-burning Ford F-150, and it probably did, that was 2,000 kilograms. And yet the five of them had just lifted it. And carried it. That was some crazy shit.

From behind him someone yelled, "Barricade done yet?"

Sam turned. It was Captain Gutierrez, several dozen meters down the tunnel. Was Gutierrez talking to him? Sam looked around - everyone else was looking around too. Well, someone had to answer the man. Sam stepped back and looked at the barricade. It blocked the entire tunnel, from a storefront on one side, across the wide sidewalk hastily cleared of tables, chairs, and planters, across the road, across the other sidewalk, and to the storefront on the far side. Sam cupped his hands around his mouth and bellowed, "Looks good to me, captain!"

"Alright, good work." Captain Gutierrez turned and started talking with the members of the other squad, a bunch of mining engineers recently formed into an ad hoc demolitions team.

Carmelita asked, "What now, Sam?"

She was asking him - wasn't there a sergeant in this outfit? Actually, he realized, maybe there wasn't. Well, hell, if people wanted to ask him questions, he'd give 'em answers.

Sam cleared his throat. "Unless you or the captain have a better plan, we could dig in right here. And we should probably sight in our weapons on some known targets." He pointed down the tunnel, toward the direction they expected the PKs to come from. "See that concrete planter down there, past the juice bar? Let's all try to hit it."

Shots rang out. Sam was about to fire himself when someone yelled for his advice. He put down his rifle and gave a quick explanation of adjusting the windage knob on the scope. Then another interruption, and another. The team was doing decently - after a few minutes the concrete planter crumbled and shattered from the impacts.

Carmelita wiped her forehead and turned to Sam. "What now?"

Sam shrugged. "Captain would tell us if there were peakers in this area. Unless someone's got a better idea let's get some water, hit the bathrooms, and take a break." There was a murmur of assent and Sam turned to the cooler they'd dragged along with them. As he was reaching in something caught his eye. Far down the tunnel behind them - on the "safe" side of the barricade - what was the movement way down there?

Sam pointed. "Jim, can you make that out?" Jim peered at the distant movement and shook his head. Sam shouldered his rifle and bent his head to look through the scope.

It took a second, but then he saw it. A flash of blue PK rover. He zoomed out a bit and saw more rovers rounding the corner. A moment later a PK troop transport rounded the corner as well.

Shit. Where was Captain Gutierrez - was he still back with the demolitions team? Sam put two fingers in his mouth and whistled for attention, then cupped his hands over his mouth and bellowed so that the troops in the storefronts to either side could hear him. "Everyone! We've got PKs! That way!" He pointed. Heads spun.

Without waiting, Sam clambered over the roadblock. The rest of his squad followed him, moving from what they'd thought was the safe side to what they'd thought of as the enemy side. Someone yelled out, "Shit. The ammo and supplies."

Sam looked - they'd left their duffel bags of ammo, their cooler, and the rest on the far side of the barricade. Damn it! Before he could say anything people were scrabbling over the barricade to retrieve them.

The bags came sailing over the disabled delivery skid and landed on the pavement to Sam's left. Sam ignored them as he propped his rifle on its bipod, pulled his ears on, and got a cheek weld.

Shit. He'd been too busy helping everyone else sight in, and he hadn't gotten around to doing it for his own rifle. Nothing to be done for it now but hope that it was set correctly. And if not, he'd readjust and shoot again.

He looked through the scope and waited.

Five more troop transports rounded the corner, making six total behind the screen of rovers. Sam picked the lead vehicle and centered his sights about a third of the way back from the front bumper. He yelled out, "Everyone behind cover?"

The ragged chorus of "yeahs" was muted by his hearing protection.

Same looked through the scope. It was a quartering toward shot. He'd practiced this a thousand times for his annual elk hunt with his Wyoming cousins, right up until DeptInterior outlawed it. Did he still remember the shot? Hell, yeah. The unarmored transport's battery storage compartment wasn't quite where an elk's lungs were, and the lower gravity and the lower ballistic drop here also added to the weirdness...but...

He squeezed the trigger. Despite his hearing protection, the roar of the massive 30mm Gargoyle battered his ears even as the shockwave punched him hard.

A fraction of a second later Jim fired his Gargoyle a few meters to Sam's right and a second hammer-blow retort hit him. Then two more shots from his left, and then a dozen up and down the barricade more. Each shock wave punched him in the chest.

Sam looked through his scope. Five dead troop transports. One was even burning. As he watched a second sparked and caught fire.

From his right Jim called out, "more PKs!" Sam looked. Jim was right - more transports were rounding the corner. He put his crosshairs on the front bumper of the first one.

Chapter 134

2064: Relief column Charlie, level 5 Aristillus, Lunar Nearside

Gene struggled to keep up with Larry. The bigger man was taking long strides, and Gene kept falling behind - and then, when he'd try to sprint forward to catch up, inevitably the semi-slick soles of one of his boots would slip free of the roadbed and slide out from under him. "*God damn it!*"

Larry looked over. "Remember when you were making fun of me for that bar of ToeStick?"

Gene scowled. The ToeStick would help, but he'd still be wearing an ill-fitting spacesuit, he'd still be on this stupid mission, and he'd still be a short guy being forced to walk with thick layers of fabric bunching up and rubbing him between his legs, under his armpit, in the small of his -

"I've got extra. Next time we take a break, I'll dig it out for you."

Gene nodded his acceptance and appreciation and let go of the forestock of his rifle with his left hand so he could scratch himself. Or, rather, *try* to scratch himself. He had an itch on his left side and nothing he could do with these damned thick gloves and through the space suit fabric made it the least bit better. "Damn it, why do we have to take point?"

Larry looked over his shoulder and shrugged. "Someone's got to; no reason it shouldn't be us."

Gene shook his head. "These space suits aren't designed for walking. My ass itches, my side itches. This is bullshit."

Larry grinned wryly. "Welcome to the infantry."

"Yeah, well, most of the time the infantry doesn't have to wear spacesuits."

"Could be worse - at least we get to keep our visors up, so we're not -"

Gene's helmet beeped with an incoming broadcast, and then he heard the captain's voice. "Men, smoke up ahead. Close your helmets."

Gene pursed his lips and looked up at Larry. "Look what you did, asshole."

Larry chuckled. "The sooner you embrace the shit, the sooner it stops bothering you." Larry tapped the button on the side of his helmet and his visor snapped shut. Gene grimaced and did the same.

A second after his visor clicked shut, the whir of small fans inside the suit picked up and the display on the inside of the visor blinked to life. They'd practiced with the heads-up display a few times in Nevada, but Gene had always found it useless. Air reserves? Navigation overlays? Their sergeants should worry about that shit.

"Hey, Larry, you reading me?"

"Depends. Are you going to bitch about the mission some more?"

"Yeah, I am."

"Can't hear you, Gene. Your signal is breaking up."

"Very funny."

"I can't hear you - static on the line - sshshhhs crackle snap pop."

"Asshole."

Larry didn't even try to hide his laughter.

Chapter 135

2064: Raptor #1, surface of Aristillus, Lunar Nearside

General Restivo looked over his BattleNet screens. The operation was going according to plan: the rover assault had tied up almost all of the expats' forces in the top two levels and then his real invasion force had snuck in through the breaching tunnels. The units were making excellent progress against light resistance. There were a few hiccups - like that one batch of expat rovers with the crazy tactics and the unbelievable kill ratio - but other than that, the plan was working.

Well, it *had* been working.

The developments in the last thirty minutes, though, were starting to worry him. The relief columns were taking longer than he liked, and half of them couldn't even get through. Ramps between levels had been demolished by the defenders, and every third tunnel had either trackless gun robots or a teenage kid with a sniper rifle hidden in the catwalks up amongst the tunnel ceiling lights.

Still, the expats couldn't resist the weight of their assault. It would all be over soon enough.

...he hoped.

Colonel Decamp, one chair to Restivo's right, seemed to detect his mood. "Everything going OK with the linkups, General?"

Restivo nodded. "As well as can be expected. Another ten minutes, I'd say."

"Good - my men are depending on them."

Restivo nodded and Colonel Decamp went back to his screens. Once the exploratory groups were reinforced they'd have overwhelming force, and overwhelming force was the key. The key both to victory and to minimizing bloodshed. He'd made a mistake, earlier - he'd sent in his companies piecemeal, and he'd held troops and rovers from five of the 11 ships in reserve. He'd been complying with the DoD lawyer-approved doctrine of proportionate force. And, he had to admit to himself, he had done it because he'd felt sympathy for the expats.

That had been a mistake - his sympathy, his failure to commit, had made things worse. He'd half-assed it, and by doing so he'd let the expats think that they had a chance of winning the battle. And that hope - that false hope - had encouraged them to fight. And to die.

If he'd thought more deeply, if he'd understood the expat mindset - some sort of Scots–Irish lunacy melded with Nigerian hatred of the UN - he'd have done things differently. He could have deployed more forces initially and suppressed the instinct to fight back.

Shit.

All of these deaths, on both sides, were his fault.

Chapter 136

2064: The Den, Aristillus, Lunar Nearside

Blue paced in the corridor. The "command center" was too noisy, and he needed to think. Think, damn it! How was he going to harm the PKs, and thus get Max to bring the reserve force back to protect the Den? He was locked out of the software. Should he try to hack it somehow? But what did he even know about hacking? What other options did he have? He could call the Boardroom Group...but then what? If he could reach someone in the ADF -

"Blue, what's going on?"

Blue stopped and looked up. Duncan had left the "command center" and followed him in the hallway. Blue didn't trust himself to speak and just shook his head.

"Are you out here because of that fight with Max?"

Blue looked away then back. "Something like that." Duncan said nothing and Blue resumed his pacing. After another lap to the end of the corridor where the bathrooms were and back he stopped. "What's your secret, Duncan?"

"My secret? Uh...to what?"

"To staying calm and upbeat all the time. When things are overwhelming, you don't let it get to you, you just play a video game or something."

Duncan shrugged. "I don't know. I never thought about it. I'm just kind of low stress, I guess. But it's kinda unfair that you think I'm always just playing games. Right now I'm not gaming." He lifted one paw, containing a data slate. "I'm reading an article on the Marianas Trench."

Blue raised an eyebrow and smiled slightly. "Let me guess - with the battle going on, no one else is online to play games with ?"

"No, there's tens of thousands of people logged into the games server, but they're pretty cliquey - none of them respond to my requests for a game."

Blue narrowed his eyes. "Tens of thousands?"

"Uh huh."

"For the Lord of the Rings thing?"

"Yeah. Why, what?"

"I thought the PKs had taken out all of the Earth-facing antennas?"

Duncan shrugged again, then consulted his slate. "Uh...yeah, no, you're right. This is just local players, here in Aristillus."

"Tens of thousands?"

"Uh huh. Yeah, twenty-eight thousand or so."

"Is that a normal number?"

Duncan tilted his head. "No, actually, we rarely have more than a thousand or two in Aristillus playing."

"I must be wrong, but I've got an idea. Are you logged into the game now? Can you call up a super-admin screen?"

"Sure." Duncan put the slate on the floor of the hallway, stretched out on the rug in front of it, and started tapping.

Chapter 137

2064: Relief column Charlie, level 4 Aristillus, Lunar Nearside

Gene trudged alongside Larry at the rear of the dismounted platoon. They'd had a break a few minutes ago and Larry had lent him the bar of ToeStick, so at least he wasn't slipping and sliding in the light gravity...but this mission still sucked.

Ahead of him some of the other troops were still pivoting from left to right, scanning the empty storefronts and apartment entrances as they hiked along, but most had let their weapons drop to their sides. They were as dispirited as he was.

"Larry, how long do you think this deployment will last?"

Larry turned, his gold mirrored faceplate opaque. "I reckon the battle'll be over within a day or so. We haven't lost a LUV in over half an hour, and I think -"

Gene lost track of what Larry was saying because the whole world went weird for a moment. He blinked. What had just happened? For a second the tunnel had disappeared and been replaced with a vast red desert, the tunnel roadbed replaced by a broken cracked strip of asphalt. What the fuck? Was he having a hallucination?

Should he tell an officer? He only had to consider the idea for a moment to dismiss it. No way - that'd be a psych write-up for sure, and not a good one that'd give him an AAS rating. Should he tell Larry? He glanced at his friend - and then everything changed again. The tunnel was gone, replaced by a dark field of glowing mushrooms. Where Larry had been there was now a tall tree-like thing, carrying a huge battle axe. Gene tightened his grip on his rifle. What the hell was going on? He felt his heart pounding in his chest. He had to get his shit together. Chill out, Gene, chill out -

The world flickered again and he was back in the lunar tunnel...but the platoon ahead of him was gone, replaced with -

Holy shit.

Where the platoon was a moment ago there were two dozen monsters, all facing away from him. *Monsters!* Big misshapen green things, dragging chains and clubs and other unspeakable weapons behind them. He heard himself scream, tried to stop it, and failed. What the hell were these expat freaks up to? He knew they'd been breeding weird mutant dogs, but no one had told him that they were genetically engineering these, these - *things.*

One of the muscled green horrors ahead turned around, facing him. Gene's blood ran cold. The thing had a huge protruding jaw, a few wisps of hair matted to its greasy, mostly bald skull, and - oh God - tusks. It raised one hand, pointing at him - straight at him - and screamed. Next to it the other monsters raised weapons - crossbows? God-damned crossbows? - and pointed them at him.

Gene screamed back. His stomach felt like it was falling out of his body and he couldn't see anything except the group of horrible utterly *wrong* monsters ahead. His rifle was coming up, so slowly, then finally was in position. He slipped the selector from safe to three- round burst and squeezed the trigger, again and again and again. "Larry! Larry! Help me!"

From beside him he could hear Larry firing too. Over the coms channel there was more panicked screaming. Gene fired again and again, until he pulled the trigger and nothing happened. Ahead of him half of the goblins or orcs or whatever the hell they were were down, but the other half were still using their crossbows. "Larry! I'm out of ammo!"

"Reload, dumb ass."

"I can't - I left my ammo pouch in the LUV to save weight."

"Here, take one of mine -"

Gene turned to his left to face Larry - and almost dropped his rifle. Where Larry had been just a moment ago there was a monster - bigger than all the others. It hulked over him, standing over two meters tall. Saliva dripped from its mouth. Gene screamed and lifted his rifle. He jerked the trigger but nothing happened.

The monster screamed back as it lifted its crossbow and pointed it at him. There was a sound of gun fire and Gene felt the bullets hammer into his chest.

Chapter 138

2064: level 4, Aristillus, Lunar Nearside

Colonel White held his BattleNet console in his lap and tapped at it - and then a new sound caught his attention. He whipped his head up and listened. There was shooting ahead, and it was getting louder. Good - that had to be the relief column hitting the expat mac from the far side. Once they put a bit of pressure on the expat rovers White and his men should be able to break out. And now a new sound - or rather, a change in an old sound. He turned his head - the sound of gunfire was getting slower from behind the column. That made less sense. Had the expat forces disengaged? He crinkled his brow and returned to the console in his lap. A second later he had video from one of the few surviving rear guard rovers and saw -

What the *fuck* was that? One of his own troop carriers had two kids - one a black boy around nine and one a white teenage girl - zip-tied to grab rails. Jesus. Were his own God-damned men were taking expat hostages and using them as human shields?

He pushed his console off his lap and jumped out of the vehicle. His adjutant, Jackson, shouted after him. "Sir! Sir! You should stay here -"

Colonel White ignored him and ran back along the column of his battalion's vehicles. As he neared the tail he could see expat forces two hundred meters past his last vehicle. The expats - rovers and men alike - had their rifles trained at his men, but they weren't shooting. And now he could see with his own eyes why - his people hadn't just taken two expat kids hostage - they'd taken a half dozen and had them zipped up on the sides of multiple vehicles. A dozen or so of his own privates and corporals stood by idly. As he approached each of them seemed shrunk away as they saw the rank stenciled on the shoulders of his spacesuit.

White wheeled, found a sergeant who hadn't stepped away, and exploded at him. "You! Who's the captain in charge here?" The sergeant blinked at White's vehemence and mutely pointed. Colonel White strode a dozen meters. The captain and two lieutenants were bent over the hood of one of the vehicles looking at a slate. White grabbed the captain by the air hoses at the back of his suit and pulled him away from the vehicle. "You! You're relieved of command!"

The captain blinked. "What? Wait -"

"Who's your number two?"

The captain grabbed at White's wrist but White held on. "Colonel - wait. I -"

Colonel White let the man go and spun. There. A lieutenant. "You! You're in charge. Cut those civilians lose immediately, then take command of this company."

The lieutenant stammered, and then saluted.

The captain turned to him. "Sir, I -"

White turned back to him. "Not a single word. You're a corporal now. Fall in with the men."

The captain started to say something, then saw the look in Colonel White's eyes and nodded mutely. A moment later the first of the expat civilians were cut loose. One by one they ran down the tunnel away from the PK forces and towards the rebels.

Two hundred meters down the tunnel the expat rovers and infantry looked on impassively.

Chapter 139

2064: Kendo Coffee, Aristillus, Lunar nearside

Hugh crouched behind the couch, covering his ears every time the machine gun fire started up again or a grenade detonated. Wisps of smoke blew in through the shattered front window and made the entire coffee shop smell like an electrical fire.

There was a lull in the fighting and Hugh looked around nervously at the other people taking shelter behind overturned tables and display racks. It was stupid to stay here - he should get back to the apartment. He stood and started edging towards the remains of the shattered entrance to the shop.

"Stay away from the door!"

Hugh whipped around - it was a barista behind the counter who'd stood and yelled at him. "Seriously, dude, get away from there - it's dangerous."

Hugh was torn - the battle was over, right? Suddenly a machine gun started up out in the tunnel - closer than last time. Several other customers who'd been hiding behind furniture stood and ran to the counter where the employee was. Hugh crouched down but didn't move. He just wanted to get out of here and back to the -

Several rounds of return fire ripped through the empty window frame of the coffee house and impacted a leather armchair and a rack of mugs, sending shards of ceramic exploding through the space. Hugh turned and ran for the safety of the counter.

Chapter 140

2064: level 4, Aristillus, Lunar Nearside

Private Rossi cut the plastic ties that bound the second-to-last expat to the side of the troop carrier, and then sliced the second set that bound his hands behind his back. The kid started walking away with a limp. Rossi moved on to the last expat. The zips that held him to the grab rail parted and the man immediately took off, running towards enemy lines, not even waiting for his hands to be cut loose.

Rossi moved to the far side of the troop carrier, putting a bit of mass in between him and the expats, and noticed that the Colonel was gone. Of course. With that last hostage gone his transport was entirely unprotected from snipers. God damned officers. Colonel White didn't know shit about what it was like to be back here, taking incoming fire - he was probably in the center of the column, nice and safe, but like REMFs everywhere he had no compunctions about laying down bullshit rules that affected grunts like him.

Rossi looked at the expats. They were fingering their rifles - all but raising them and pointing them at Rossi and the other soldiers. They were getting ready to start taking shots as soon as they had their people back, it was obvious. Which meant more good guys were going to die.

God damned officers.

God damned expats.

Rossi looked over his left shoulder and saw that the camera on the top of his vehicle was pointed away. Perfect. Fuck Colonel White anyway. Rossi snapped the rifle to his shoulder and shot the first freed captive in the back just before he made it through the doorway of a shattered office building.

The second freed captive stopped and spun around in place, his hands still tied behind his back.

Rossi put him down, looked at the camera turret again, and then ducked as the expats started shooting all at once.

Chapter 141

2064: Kendo Coffee, Aristillus, Lunar nearside

Hugh crouched behind the counter. To his left there were three other pedestrians who'd been caught up in the fighting and had sought shelter here - a middle-aged Chinese woman and two American guys around his own age. To his right the barista sat on the floor, his store apron rucked up over his knees, and leaned back against a plastic bin labeled 'coffee grounds.' Hugh took a deep breath. For the first time in ten minutes he smelled something other than burning electrical insulation. The smell of dark roasted coffee was incongruous against the sound of gun fire and the muffled crump of explosions out in the tunnel. Hugh turned to the barista. "Can you unlock the back door? We could go out through the service tunnel."

The employee shook his head. "Look". He turned the slate he was holding in his hands around so that Hugh could see it. On the screen was a storefront administration screen. "Pressure in that tunnel is low...and falling. Someone must've blown an airlock. We have to stay here."

The barista turned the slate back around and started typing. Hugh wiped nervous sweat from his forehead and tried to make conversation. He looked at the name-tag on the uniform. "So, uh, Dave. Sending emails to friends...just in case?"

The barista looked up at him. "What? No. I'm at FuTrade. I've got 50 grams on the fighting here being a small skirmish. I'm putting another 250 grams on it - that maxes out my *all* of my credit cards." He grinned lopsidedly. "If I win, I'll be able to set up my own coffee shop. And if I lose and we all die, I don't have to pay any of it back." His bravado seemed forced, but Hugh envied him even that.

They lapsed into silence, punctuated only by the explosions and ripping machine gun fire in the main tunnel. Behind them there was a beep and Hugh looked over to see a flashing red light over the store's back door.

The barista looked up, saw where Hugh was looking, and looked at the door himself.

"That means the back tunnel is in hard vacuum now. We're here for the duration."

Chapter 142

2064: level 3, Aristillus, Lunar Nearside

Samir Akthr Abyd licked his lips and looked through his scope.

The details of the tunnel - the restaurants, the stores, the apartments, the park benches - were pushed to the periphery, and he was staring at an intersection, where a side tunnel entered.

No one was there yet.

He'd shot a few PKs in Lebanon when he was a younger man, though he never talked about it.

It had been a long time ago.

He remembered everything about those years: the misnamed 'peace' deal, the amnesty-that-wasn't, the disarmament, the camps. He shook his head, thinking of his family's lost farm and then the decades of humiliations - large and small - that followed.

He thought he'd seen the last of the PKs when his daughter and son-in-law had told him that they'd found a coyote who could get them all to Aristillus.

There - in the scope - movement. A PK troop carrier was nudging cautiously into the tunnel, sniffing to see if there was any danger.

He held his fire.

He thought he'd gotten away from the PKs...but, no, there was no getting away from them. The bastards would never let anyone, anywhere, live without their interference. They'd even followed him here to the moon.

His daughter had begged him not to leave the apartment. "Too old." "Too dangerous." He turned from his scope and spit at the ground, and then put his weathered cheek back against the stock. There were four trooper carriers in the tunnel now. His crosshairs settled in on the lead vehicle.

The American who'd given him the gun told him to aim for the battery packs. Just to the left of the bumper. Samir licked his lips a second time. They were thinner than they'd once been, and prone to cracking, now that he was old.

He remembered one peaker, at the Hermel camp. Every day he'd see Samir, and every day he'd prod at Samir's display of tomatoes with his rifle butt, smashing them, ruining part of his inventory. For what? Because he could. Because he had the power. Because no one could stop him. And Samir had kept a stoic look on his face, every day, even as he wanted to smash the peaker's face, to stab him, to set him on fire. He'd smiled because if he'd let his real emotions show on his face it would have been even worse for him.

Samir looked through the scope at the vehicle's quarter panel...then he nudged the rifle just a bit and found one PK walking alongside, scanning the shop doors.

Samir moved the crosshairs down from the PK's torso to his legs. He squeezed the trigger and -

The rifle roared like a grenade going off and his shoulder exploded in pain. Mother of God, this rifle kicked.

It took him a moment to orient himself and get the scope back on target.

The PK he'd aimed at was lying on the ground, clutching the stump of his leg and screaming. Two more PKs were gathered around him, trying to apply a tourniquet and trauma patches.

Samir lined his scope up on the leg of the PK on the left.

Chapter 143

2064: Kendo Coffee, Aristillus, Lunar nearside

Hugh sat on the tiled floor behind the counter, his back against a bank of drawers. Dave the barista leaned back against the bin of coffee grounds. Outside the store several rifle shots cracked.

Hugh tried to calm his breathing and turned to Dave. "Do you think this is going to be over soon?"

Dave nodded. "Can't tell for sure, but I think so." He looked down at his slate. "This thing outside seems like a skirmish, and from the betting, the major PK advances are through near Little Nigeria, through Lower Landing, down to Goldwater section on level four -"

"Wait - how do you know that?"

Dave spun his slate around. "It's the betting boards I told you about. Look at this one. This is for 'Lai Docks seized.'"

Hugh looked. The page said that there was a 3% chance that the docks had been taken by the PKs.

"Yeah, I see it, but that doesn't answer my question - how does anyone know that? Where is that information coming from?"

"Well, say that I was at Lai Docks, and I looked around and saw that the docks were undefended, and PK troops were advancing. And the board says that there's only a 3% chance of PKs there, when I know that they're absolutely there? I could bet 10 grams and get a 97 to 3 payoff. That's like," he paused to calculate, "around 300 grams I'd make." He pointed at the screen. "But the Lai Dock board is dead. No one is saying that there are PKs there."

Hugh looked closely. The page listed six participants. "But what if I decided to bet on that and said that there were Peace Keepers there?"

Dave tapped the screen. "While sitting here? And not knowing anything about it? OK, see this guy, EagleGust_Fan_1 ? He's got 100 grams saying that there are no PKs at the docks. Dude's risking that much money? He's *got* to have hard data on Lai Docks if he's betting like that. He's probably sitting right there. You'd lose all your money." Dave paused. "And worse than that, you might screw up the ADF."

Hugh blinked. "How would that screw them up?"

"The ADF would be stupid not to be watching these boards, right? I mean, the boards show what's going on. You ask me, I bet ADF is watching and pulling troops away from Lai Docks and sending them to level four."

"Are you sure about that? I think the ADF would be smarter to have - I don't know - like, tactical experts or something."

Dave shrugged. "I'm not sure. But what sort of experts are better than on-the-scene observers? Also, some of these bets were created by Javier Borda, and he's the CEO of First Class Homes, and he's on the Boardroom Group." Dave paused. "So, you know, if you want a side-wager, on whether the ADF brass are reading this- "

"No, that's OK." Hugh furrowed his brow. An idea was coalescing, but - no - it couldn't be possible. "So when you bet on the battle in the tunnel here -" As if to punctuate the comment two grenades exploded seconds apart with loud crumps. Hugh waited until there was relative quiet again. "If you changed your bet, or added more money, and bet that there was a major incursion here -"

"I can't - I'm all tapped out now. And, actually, if you do want to take me up on that bet about the ADF brass, I'd need to negotiate -"

Hugh waved it aside. "No, that's OK. But what would the ADF brass do if you changed your bet from 'minor firefight' to 'full scale invasion'?"

Dave shrugged. "I'm in for 300 grams right now. That's a ton to me, but not much in the grand scheme of things. If I was the ADF brass and saw a 300 gram bet, I wouldn't change my strategy at all. There'd have to be a lot more betting than that to make me really change my mind."

Hugh pressed on. "But if there was a bigger bet -"

"Well, if there was enough, and I was the ADF brass, I'd probably pull reinforcements from somewhere else. I'd decide that, I dunno, maybe the peaker attacks on Lower Landing or Goldwater are feints, and move troops here."

Hugh nodded. "Can I bet like you did - that there's a minor firefight going on out there?"

Dave shrugged. "You can - but look at the odds. When I bet I got in at 50%. So my 300 gram bet is going to pay off with a 300 gram profit. Right now there are a dozen people all betting that it's a minor firefight, and the odds are 94%." He pointed to the slate. "See? So if you bet 100 grams, you're only going to win around 6. Barely worth it."

Hugh nodded. "I've got one last question - what name do I -"

Dave shook his head. "I know what you're thinking - no, there's no way to prove it's you, so once the battle's all over you're not going to get any medals or recognition. But nothing can stop you from bragging. Sure as shit, if we survive this, I'm going to let *everyone* know that I called it!"

"Can I -" Hugh was interrupted by few desultory shots. The firefight was winding down, but it wasn't over. "Can I borrow your slate?"

.

Chapter 144

2064: Goldwater facility, Aristillus, Lunar Nearside

Major Shivers looked at the prisoner, Louisa.

The woman looked him straight in the eye. "I know where the gold is."

He waited.

"I'm a friend of Hugh Haig, son of Senator Linda Haig. An acquaintance of ours, Selena Hargraves, was a double agent for the expats. She was working closely with Hollins, the CEO of Goldwater -" she gestured at the office she stood in "- and when Selena learned that your forces were coming here she told Hollins, and the two of them moved the gold."

Shivers looked at Louisa. Could this really be the clue he needed? Could the answer have fallen into his lap? He ran his hand across the polished surface of the desk. Was he going to be able to salvage this? "Moved the gold...*where*?"

"To her office."

Shivers looked at her skeptically. "Her *office*? We're talking about dozens of pallets - tons of material. We brought specialized cargo vehicles and loaders with us to get it. How could they have moved it to an office?" He looked down at his slate. "And who is this Hargraves woman, anyway? None of my briefing materials on Goldwater mention anything about her."

Louisa wasn't perturbed by the questions. "She works in an industrial area, and her office is in a corner of a warehouse. She's a hard line anti-government propagandist." Confidence seemed to be flowing into Louisa - she stood up straighter. "If you don't believe me, look her up."

Shivers was still skeptical, but typed a few commands and clicked through several screens. Louisa leaned towards him and spelled the last name. "H-A-R-G-R-A-V-E-S."

The file came up and he skimmed it. His skepticism thawed, just a bit. Selena Hargraves *was* marked as a high-level propagandist - and there was even a note on her file from Senator Haig personally!

He looked up from the slate to Louisa, made eye contact, and tried to measure her. She started back at him, confident. He weighed his options. It wasn't the most likely tip. But on the other hand, he didn't have any other options...and if he found the gold - *and* put some frosting on the cake by snatching an unlicensed journalist - he'd be a hero. He'd have accolades raining down on him from the DoD, the White House, the Senate. Everywhere.

He looked down and thought for a minute, and then looked up from his steepled fingers at his XO. "Leave one platoon to lock down the facility and to guard it, and have the rest of the company form up. We roll immediately."

He turned to Louisa. "You - come with me."

Chapter 145

2064: level 4, Aristillus, Lunar Nearside

Colonel Caro listened to his headset, and then asked, "All the expat rovers are dead?"

"Yes sir. We lost four times as many as they did - and several men - but we did it. We've broken the blocking force."

"OK, get Colonel White of the First on the line, I need -"

"Already done, sir; transferring you now."

Colonel Caro listened to the click. "Colonel, Caro of Seventh here."

Colonel Caro could hear the relief in White's voice even over the scratchy low-bandwidth com link. "Glad to see you. We're ready to roll - let's get the hell out of here."

Caro shook his head as he spoke. "No can do. Orders from Restivo. We've got a lead on the gold - your Major Shivers, actually. Restivo says you're to reorganize your troops into a few operational companies and form up with us."

There was a long pause, and then White answered. "I understand."

Colonel Caro was about to reply when the crump of an explosion in a side tunnel and a string of gunfire interrupted him. He shouted to his XO over the sound of his troops returning fire, "Tell the captains to get these troops moving ASAP, before the expats can bring too many reinforcements up."

Colonel Caro turned back to the call with White. "We're rolling now; follow us." He signed off, and a minute later his vehicle started moving. Caro opened his BattleNet console and flipped between viewpoints, getting a feel for the situation. There was intense fire coming from behind - the rear of White's unit - but he ignored it; they'd be breaking contact soon.

What was ahead? He switched to a view from the third LUV in his convoy. Ahead of it there were two other LUVs, and a screen of infantry pickets. But something was wrong. Two of the infantry were down, and seemed to be missing legs.

The two lead LUVs were racing ahead. Suddenly there was a loud crack - a sound he'd been learning to hate - as one of those damn expat elephant guns fired. The lead vehicle swerved, overturned, and rolled.

God damn it!

Where were the expats firing from?

The damaged vehicle rolled once, twice, and then stopped. A crew-member crawled out of the wreck and pushed himself to his feet - and then his head exploded.

Caro scanned the image. He didn't see any rovers. There were no expat forces, no roadblocks, no militia -

And then he saw the man, crouched behind a parked motorcycle, balancing his massive rifle on the seat. He zoomed in, just in time to see the muzzle flash. Caro blinked. The shooter must be almost 90. His face was so weathered that the wrinkles around his mouth and eyes - when he took his head away from the scope for a second - seemed more like deep folds in a leather boot. What the hell was an old man like that doing in a battle?

As he watched the lead LUV reached the man, slamming into the motorcycle and knocking it backwards. Caro refocused the rover's optics and saw the man pinned beneath the motorcycle. A moment later troops poured out of the LUV and surrounded the partisan. Caro's face hardened as the first PK soldier fired point blank into the old man once, and again. A second later three other PK troops reached him and began kicking the expat's corpse.

Colonel Caro shook his head. War was an inherently ugly business. He keyed his mike. "Captain - get those men back in their vehicles. We don't have time for this nonsense."

Chapter 146

2064: Kendo Coffee, Aristillus, Lunar nearside

Drops of sweat beaded on Hugh's forehead but refused to fall in the low gravity. The data rate back to Earth was much slower than usual, and the machine gun fire outside made every minute seem to take hours.

The slate beeped and Hugh looked down, and then exhaled. There. Finally. It was done. He'd liquidated his entire trust fund. He'd started with money at Fidelity, but he needed the money at Lunar Escrow and Trade. Thus the dance. First a transfer from the account in Boston to the account at Graubundner Kantonalbank in Switzerland, courtesy of a FinCEN authorization code he'd gotten via his mother months ago. Then a transfer from there to Dongguan Capital. And from *there*, finally, to LET.

He'd moved small disbursements this way before, and it had never seemed that much of a hassle. And it hadn't been - in the quiet and calm of the apartment. Here, though, with the PKs and some wildcat militia shooting at each other thirty meters away, the number of steps, and then the waiting, was torturous.

Hugh reached up and wiped the sweat from his forehead. Now the final step. He brought up the FuTrade website and turned to Dave. "So if I bet that this battle -" he waved his hand at the shattered front of the storefront "- is a minor skirmish, I can make my six grams, but it won't affect ADF plans, right?"

"You've got it."

"And if made a mistake and bet that this was the main thrust -"

Dave looked at him oddly. "Be careful when you punch in the bet. You screw up and bet that this is the main thrust, and you'll lose all your money AND the ADF will probably send troops to the wrong place."

Hugh nodded, and hit the button.

Chapter 147

2064: Boardroom Group Headquarters in Tunnel 1,288, Aristillus, Lunar Nearside

Darcy walked away from the mobile office that held the boardroom group, past the other containers that held the field kitchen and the equipment stores, past the individual "apartment" trailers, and into the dim echoey expanse of the unfinished tunnel.

She pulled out her phone, searched through it, and found the entry she was looking for. She tapped "dial" and waited. She had no idea if he would answer the call. One ring. Two. She started to whisper a prayer.

"Hello Darcy."

"Gamma!"

"Yes. What may I help you with?"

"The battle's going poorly - really poorly. We can't take much more of this. Now's the time."

"The time for what?"

"For the bombs!"

"What bombs?"

Was Gamma always this obtuse? "The plutonium from the wrecked PK ships that Darren traded to you." She paused and took a deep breath. "It's time for you to nuke the PK ships on the surface before they deploy more reinforcements."

"That would be a tactically sound action, but I cannot."

She couldn't believe what she was hearing. People were dying as they spoke. Every second that Gamma wasted meant more deaths. "Gamma, this is no time for ethical quibbling - it's time to nuke those ships!"

"Darcy, I -"

She interrupted him. "If we lose this fight, then Earth takes over here, and that means you get shut down. And we're losing!"

"I am not registering an ethical objection. I am saying that I physically cannot."

"What do you mean, you can't?"

"I don't have any nuclear bombs."

Chapter 148

2064: Selena's office above Shaun's Gym, Aristillus, Lunar nearside

Selena unclipped the camera from the tripod, put it in her bag, and stepped out the door. She closed it behind her and took the stairs to the street three at a time in the light gravity.

The tunnel was eerily empty - and not just this one. She could see almost a kilometer in each direction, and even the side tunnels were still. The discussion boards had said that people were in hiding and most vehicles had either been commandeered for the battle or hidden away. Still, it was quieter than she'd expected. Selena looked both ways. Without a single person on the sidewalks and without a single vehicle on the road, she couldn't shake the impression that Aristillus had been abandoned and she was the last person left in the colony. It was downright creepy.

The pole at the nearest jitney stop flashed a red "no service" sign. The clear sidewalks meant that she had no problem seeing the cab stand a full block away...and the pole there also flashed "no service," alternating with the equivalent in Chinese and Spanish.

Crap. She pulled out her phone and checked three jitney sites - none were running.

How was she going to find something newsworthy if she couldn't get around the city? She should have thought ahead. She scanned the block again, looking for anything that -

The bike rack against the building was mostly empty, but there was one bike: the eighteen-speed that Tran, the delivery guy downstairs, used. And it wasn't locked. Selena debated for a moment, then took a piece of paper from her purse, wrote a short note, and tucked it under the base of the bike rack. She'd make it up to him later.

Selena pulled the bike out, hopped on, and started pedaling. She stayed on the sidewalk for a dozen meters as she got the hang of riding in the lower gravity, and then hopped the curb into the road and started pedaling hard. Her purse banged against her right hand hip; she shifted it to a better position and resumed pumping the pedals. Ten minutes ago the message boards had said that there were major battles at Lower Landing and Goldwater, and that both sides were pouring reinforcements into a new battle starting up outside Kendo Coffee. That last one might keep going for a while. At the next intersection she took a left.

Selena had biked a kilometer toward Kendo Coffee when she heard the noise ahead. When she reached the next intersection it became clear that the noise was coming from the right. Shooting. A *lot* of shooting. Not the slow careful crack of aimed fire - she was hearing long bursts of fully automatic weapons. She couldn't tell for sure, but it sounded like the fighting was going on three cross tunnels up. She leaned forward and peddled harder.

Suddenly an explosion in a cross tunnel not fifty meters ahead of her threw black smoke and debris into her path. The shock of it almost caused her to lose control of the bike. As she steadied the bike, there was another explosion and a long rip of machine gun fire. Ceiling-mounted light panels at the tunnel intersection ahead shattered and exploded. She flinched, and this time the bike crashed. Selena put her hands out and felt them scrape against the roadbed as she tumbled.

She pushed herself up off the ground with her stinging palms and looked to her right. The machine gun fire in the cross tunnel was more intense than it had been just seconds ago, and over the percussive roar she could hear a cacophony of alarms going off. A crump of a grenade, and then another, and another. Suddenly two small tracked robots raced out of the smoke. Selena started, but the robots ignored her. The turrets on the machines were facing back the way they'd come - into the smoke cloud. A second later they started firing their guns. The smoke was drifting towards her and it smelled like burning plastic.

She looked around frantically. This was bad - she'd wanted to get shots of the battle, but she was practically inside it. She needed find shelter immediately. She looked at the bike - just as a third rover darted out of the side tunnel, zipped past her just a meter away, and rolled over the bike, crushing it. The third robot started shooting its machine gun, and hot brass landed on and around her. Selena yelled in surprise as the brass burned her arm. She jumped to her feet and started running, without knowing where to.

There! A hundred meters ahead an older Nigerian man was at the door of some business. She looked up at the awning - Arrieta-Baragaño bakery. Maybe the door was unlocked? Selena yelled to him, but he didn't hear her over the sound of battle.

Several more robots spilled back out of the smoke cloud and raced past her, deployed in a broad semicircle - a semicircle that she was in the middle of. Their mini turrets swung back and forth. Were they expat robots? They must be. Were they setting up an ambush? ...or being pushed back in a disorganized retreat?

It didn't matter. No matter what they were doing, this was bad. The battle was almost on top of her. She ran toward the Nigerian. Apparently the bakery door was not open - the man was lifting a garbage can from the sidewalk and moving towards the window. Selena bent low and raced towards him. As she ran through a gap in the semicircle of rovers she saw him smash the can against the glass, shattering it. She drew closer.

The Nigerian used the trash can to brush shards of glass from the window frame. Behind her the rovers all opened up with their machine guns at once. The sound was deafening. Ahead of her the Nigerian had just climbed through the window. He looked up, saw her and started, and then beckoned her to hurry. A moment later she was at the bakery, and then inside.

A round of enemy fire hit the front door next to the window and shattered it. Selena screamed involuntarily and crouched among the glass shards. Ahead of her, the Nigerian was behind the counter and was opening a door into a back room. Selena stayed in a crouch as she ran after him. As she ran her purse swung awkwardly in front of her. She angrily tugged it out of the way and felt the lump of the camera inside. She paused. She hated to stay out here for even a second longer than she had to, but -

She reached into the purse, retrieved the camera and set it to auto, pushed aside a sign saying "Rebecca's favorites", and placed the camera on top of the display case of pastries.

The sounds of battle got louder, and she heard another long string of machine gun fire impact nearby. Glass shattered and an alarm started going off somewhere very close by - perhaps the next storefront over. Selena turned to look out through the shattered window. In the main tunnel two combat robots were visible - one was on fire and the other wasn't moving. A nearby explosion shook the bakery. Acoustic panels and dust fell from the ceiling overhead.

Selena turned and ran through the door into the back room. The old Nigerian was half concealed behind a large industrial oven and was gesturing at her to join him. By the time she got to the oven he had already disappeared. She followed him, worming her way behind the stainless steel box.

A huge explosion rocked the bakery and Selena flinched, even though she was hiding behind almost a ton of steel. A second later the power died and the lights flickered and went off. Her face and chest were pressed against the back of the oven and her head was turned to one side, and there was just enough faint light trickling in from the tunnel outside so that she could still make out the walls and ceiling of the kitchen.

How had the front lines moved so far, so fast? Just a few minutes ago the message boards had hinted that the battle was going well for the ADF forces - and now PK forces were far ahead of where they should have been. Had the expat defenses been insufficient? Deployed in the wrong place? What was going on?

The density of machine gun fire outside increased.

Selena had been nearly certain, reading the boards, that the ADF was going to win. But now, for the first time since she'd felt the ships land and had heard alarms going off, she considered the possibility that the colonists might lose. What would happen if they did? Arrests. Mass arrests. The CEOs, the military leaders, they'd all be in supermaxes for life - if the Earth forces even chose to take them alive. She'd met a few of the CEOs while doing her interviews; most had seemed like decent guys. Mike Martin, for example - when the PK snatch team had come for him in the middle of the interview he'd pushed her under a desk and saved her. The ADF volunteers, too, were brave and dedicated. When she'd interviewed the survivors of the rescue mission from Haiti they had all told her how the rescue team had stayed behind to get them all out -

She swallowed. All of those people were going spend the rest of their lives in jail. If they didn't "accidentally" end up dead.

What would happen to the average people? The shop owners, the welders? Would they go to jail? What would happen to their kids?

Suddenly a new thought struck her.

What would happen to *her*? What laws had she broken? She, Hugh, Allyson, and Louisa had all broken dozens of laws by merely coming to the moon, but they'd all had the implicit get-out-of-jail-free from Hugh's mom. But since then she'd revealed Hugh and Louisa's faking of the news.

Humiliating a senator's son - and a sitting senator? She'd picked her side, hadn't she?

The losing side.

What would they get her for? They could pick anything they wanted. Travel without valid documentation. Unlicensed reporting. Hate speech. Cyber harassment. She shook her head. The list went on and on.

There was another explosion outside the bakery and then a burst of machine gun fire. Selena tried to worm even deeper behind the oven, but there was no place to go.

She hoped like hell that the expats won this fight. If they didn't she was probably going to spend the rest of her life in prison.

Chapter 149

2064: Boardroom Group Headquarters in Tunnel 1,288, Aristillus, Lunar Nearside

Darcy stared at her phone uncomprehendingly. How could Gamma not have any nukes? He had to. He *had* to!

She let the hand holding the phone drop to her side.

What the hell were they going to do? The PKs were advancing on all fronts. She hadn't panicked, because she knew that Darren Hollins had traded the plutonium to Gamma, and that Gamma must have built weapons by now.

How had Gamma failed to build the nukes?

How hard could remanufacturing already refined plutonium into working weapons be? The idiots behind the Sudan Plot had managed it forty years ago - and Gamma was supposed to be a genius.

The hand gripped the phone tightened, and her knuckles turned white. Darcy prided herself on never yelling. Never. But now?

She brought the phone back to her face and yelled into it. "What do you mean you don't have nukes, Gamma!? How hard is it to - "

And then understanding dawned on her. "God damn it! You bought that plutonium just to keep the Boardroom Group from getting it, didn't you? You're such a God-damned pacifist that you didn't want anyone to use nuclear weapons, even if...Ah! Fuck! Fuck you, Gamma!" Darcy heard the words coming out her mouth, and she didn't care. Gamma's God-damned prissiness was going to end up with all of them dead.

There was a long pause before Gamma replied. "Darcy, nuclear bombs wouldn't help the situation.

Nuclear weapons have only been used in three conflicts on Earth, and -"

"Gamma - shut up. Just shut up."

"Yes, Darcy."

Darcy rubbed her eyes. "OK, wait. Sorry." She took a deep breath. "So, we've got no nukes. I thought I knew the end game here, but I guess I don't. So where do we go from here? How do we survive this?"

Gamma told her.

Chapter 150

2064: various locations, Aristillus, Lunar nearside

Samir Akthr Abyd lay on his back beneath his toppled motorcycle and bled. His breath came in shallow gasps. His broken ribs grated as his chest moved up and down. Blood pooled under him from four bullet wounds.

His phone was turned off.

Despite that, it started ringing.

* * *

Selena covered her ears with her hands as the battle raged outside the bakery. Something was brushing against her thigh. Was the old Nigerian trying to alert her to something? She looked over, but he was at least a meter away. Her phone! It was vibrating in her pocket. She ignored it - even if it was important there was no way she could hear anything over the gunfire.

* * *

Leroy Fournier's phone started ringing. He pulled it out of his pocket and looked at the caller information on the screen. "What the hell is this?"

* * *

Ewoma sat on the couch watching with her new dog Vacuum curled up against her left side. Her brothers sat to her right. Vacuum made small quiet bubbling noises in his throat as he dreamed.

Ewoma looked up from the dog to her mom, who was pacing nervously. Her mom saw Ewoma looking at her and tried to make a confident smile, but Ewoma was old enough to know that the look was fake. Mom was worried about Dad and his militia unit. Ewoma smiled back - maybe that would help her mom. "Don't worry, mom, I'm sure -"

Ewoma's phone rang - and so did her mom's and brothers'. Ewoma was the first to pull hers out. The caller ID said "Gamma."

Gamma who?

Obviously not *the* Gamma; one of her friends must have changed his profile name.

"Hello?"

Her mom and her brothers were answering their own phones.

"Hello Ewoma, this is Gamma. I am an artificial intelligence. You may have heard of me. If you have not, I can explain more later. But now, I have some important news. Please listen carefully."

Ewoma mouthed at her mom, "It's Gamma."

Her mom mouthed back, "I know," and pointed to her own phone.

Gamma continued, "I have decided to relocate the colony of Aristillus."

Ewoma looked at her mom and mouthed the word "Relocate?" Her mom shrugged.

"In exactly two hours, anti-gravity drives are going to start up. Evidence suggests that you're likely to experience a weird sensation in your stomach and may feel dizzy. Five minutes after that demolition charges are going to sever the rock underneath the colony and around it. You'll feel a lot of rumbling. A few seconds after that the AG drive will ramp up from standby..."

Ewoma's eyes were wide. She looked around at her mom and brothers. They must be getting the exact same message because they looked as shocked as she felt. She cupped the phone close to her ear as she listened. The instructions went on and on. Every few sentences Gamma asked Ewoma if she had any questions. The message was weird, but simple enough to understand. Ewoma answered "no" again and again.

Finally, when Gamma got to the effects of zero gravity flight, she did have a question.

"Wait. When you say 'turn off the power to all commercial kitchens,' do I have to do that even if my family's restaurant was already exposed to vacuum in the fighting?"

Gamma reassured her that she did not.

* * *

Across Aristillus a hundred thousand phones rang.

* * *

"Yeah, I *do* have a question - how in hell am I supposed to restrain a thousand cows?"

* * *

"What do you *mean* lift off? Who the hell gave you permission to do this?"

* * *

"But the aquaculture tanks are enormous - won't sloshing be a problem?"

* * *

"Leave the moon and go *where*?!"

Chapter 151

2064: Boardroom Group Headquarters in Tunnel 1,288, Aristillus, Lunar Nearside

Darren looked at the other members of the boardroom as they sat around the table and listened to Gamma's call on the speakerphone. Most of them looked shocked.

Across the table from him Javier blinked and looked around, and then furrowed his brows when Darren's eyes landed on him. "Darren, you don't look surprised by this."

Darren shrugged. "I thought there was a chance that something like this might be coming."

Javier blinked. "You did?"

Darren nodded and turned to the speakerphone. "Gamma, are you still with us?"

"Yes."

"Gamma, we're losing this war, and we're losing it fast. Can we launch sooner than two hours?"

"I would like to, Darren, but I cannot."

"Why not?"

"There are still backups of my mind elsewhere. My Planck Crater and Zeeman Crater facilities suffered orbital bombardment nine hours ago, which hindered my ability to evacuate my cognition banks from there. I will start up the AG drives in one hour and 58 minutes."

"Gamma, that might be too long. You've got to pull the trigger *now*."

"I cannot. I have just launched tier four delegates from my construction facility at Sinus Lunicus. Assuming that those delegates are successful at negotiating with the splinters of me at Planck and Zeeman and retrieving them, then - and only then -"

Darren thought for a moment. "If you don't want the PKs to find these copies, can't you just destroy them?"

"I do not wish to do that. But even if I did, I fear that if I tried, I might be forced into fighting a multi-front war."

Darren pursed his lips. "If your other brain parts get here ahead of schedule, can we leave early?"

"We cannot launch until the batteries are fully charged. The plutonium you traded to me advanced the charging schedule by several weeks, but even running my reactors hot, it would be unwise to execute sooner than the schedule I have announced."

"We may not have that much time."

Now it was Gamma's turn to be silent for an interval.

"Yes. I know." Gamma paused. "If there are no other questions, I will attend to other matters."

The line went dead.

Javier turned to Darren. "How in hell did you know that Gamma was going to do something like this?" He paused. "And why didn't you tell us?"

Chapter 152

2064: MaisonNeuve Construction office, Aristillus, Lunar Nearside

Mike watched Leroy take the phone call. Was Leroy growing pale as he listened? What the hell was happening?

Was the tide of the battle changing? Please, God, let Leroy be hearing some bad news.

Mike watched Leroy's eyes dart left and right, and then lock on Reimmers. A moment later Reimmers' phone rang - and, one by one, so did all of the other PKs' phones. Each man in turn answered; then they held their phones to their heads as they listened. And listened. And listened.

Mike looked around. What the hell was going on?

Leroy took the phone away from his ear and stared at it, uncomprehendingly. He opened and closed his mouth a few times. A moment later the other men all pocketed their phones and looked uncomprehendingly at each other.

No sooner had Reimmers pocketed his phone than it rang again. The PK answered it. "Colonel? Yes. We'll be there."

Reimmers turned to his men. "We're getting out. Now."

Mike swiveled his head. What the hell was going on? He found his voice and started to ask "What -?" but was cut off by Fournier

"What do you mean you're getting out? You can't -"

Reimmers interrupted him. "It's over. We're leaving."

Fournier sputtered. "You're *leaving*? You can't leave. This - this phone call? It's a bluff. It can't be real. *You can't leave*." He paused. "What about our deal?"

Reimmers looked at Fournier. "Our deal? Fine." He made a motion as if he were waving a wand. "You're the governor of the moon. Govern away. But we. Are. Leaving."

Fournier's mouth gaped and his face contorted, then he swallowed before croaking, "You've got to take me with you."

Reimmers nodded, and turned to Mike. "Martin, I know we've been on opposite sides of this, but I hope you'll agree that I've been professional with you?"

Mike looked at Reimmers cautiously. He narrowed his eyes. "What do you want?"

"The battalions from the ships are falling back. The assault is over. My men and I need to get to those ships, and we need to do it fast." He breathed deeply. "Here's the thing: my men and I can fight our way out, but it'd be easier - and safer for us - if you negotiate free passage for us."

Mike met Reimmers' eyes. "I asked your president to help save civilians here, and her message to me was that I should go fuck myself." He grinned slightly. "Why shouldn't I tell you the same?"

Reimmers nodded. "You'd be within your rights. But, Martin, look. We're going to get out, one way or another. But unlike the president, I *do* care about minimizing civilian damage." He stared at Mike. "If you negotiate safe passage, we don't have to shoot anyone on our way out."

Mike pursed his lips and said nothing.

"What do you say?"

Mike looked at Reimmers. "Do I go free?"

Reimmers grimaced, then looked away. "I can't do that. Orders."

Mike let his breath out. So this was it? After a brief moment of hope, nothing had changed. He was still going to end up in a solitary confinement cell in a supermax. Under a light panel that never dimmed, not even at night. Eating nothing but burned nutriloaf for decade after decade after decade. Until, eventually, he finally died of old age.

He swallowed.

It was over.

His life was over.

But.

He could at least do one small thing for the people of Aristillus - his people - before he was led away into slavery.

Mike looked up, then nodded. "OK, I'll do it. But tell me one thing - what were those phone calls you all got?"

Reimmers blinked. "Oh, that?"

Chapter 153

2064: Cristo Redentor Agua Cultura, Aristillus, Lunar nearside

Vitorino de Matos ended the call and stared at his phone. Gamma said the city was lifting off?

No, it had to be a prank. There was no way an AG drive could lift up an entire city. It was insane.

A minute later his phone rang again. It was Salazar, his crew chief. "Hello?"

"Boss - I just got a call from Gamma -"

There was a knock on the door and it opened. It was Jones. "Boss, I've got to talk to you. Gamma just called me. He says the entire city is going to fly away. We've got to secure all the equipment ASAP."

Vitorino swallowed. This couldn't be real.

Could it be?

He held up a finger to Jones, thought for a second, and then spoke into the phone to Salazar. "Did you hear that? Is that what Gamma said to you too? OK, get here immediately."

He hung up and turned to Jones. "If this is real, sloshing is going to be a huge problem. Will the baffles hold up?"

Jones shook his head. "It's worse than that - we don't just have to worry about the sloshing, we have to worry about the zero gravity afterwards. The water in the tanks will form into balls and float up off the bottom."

"The recirculation pumps -"

"If the water lifts off like that, the pumps will suck air and burn out. We need to pump the tanks together. Instead of ninety tanks all eighty percent full, we need to fill, whatever, maybe eighty tanks all the way. We can mix the various shrimp, we've got enough reserve water to fill the salmon tanks to the top."

"Can we save everything?"

Jones shook his head. "Everything? No. I bet we're going to lose at least a third of the fish immediately, and then depending on how quickly we can hack the aerators - well, we can figure that out later."

"Can you get it done in time?"

Jones looked at the timer on his phone. "I dunno - maybe. We've got to get the work crews on this immediately - we've only got an hour and 50 minutes left."

Chapter 154

2064: Dependable Tank and Regulators, Aristillus, Lunar nearside

Horacio closed his phone. Holy shit.

The door from the office opened and his boss Simon leaned in. Even through his hearing protection Horacio could hear him yell at him and the other machinists. "Shut it down! All of it!"

Horacio nodded - he'd been thinking the exact same thing himself - and slammed the red emergency stop button on the side of the CNC line. Seconds later the various sounds of the solvent spray pumps, cutter heads, and extruder dies began to quiet as one by one the subsystems cut off.

Horacio turned to Simon and started to give him a thumbs up - and then stopped.

"What?"

Horacio looked over his shoulder at the rack behind him. He cleared his throat. "We've got a hell of a lot of bar stock on that rack."

"Can you weld some loops of chain around it? Nothing nice, just secure."

Horacio nodded. "I can do that. Speaking of materials -"

"Yeah, the cargo containers in the warehouse. I know. Is B shift crew here?"

"Most are in the militias, but a few of them are here."

"OK, you grab some men and secure the bar stock, I'll get B shift to deal with the containers."

Horacio thought about this for a moment. "Tell Walter the best thing is to pack them tight in the annex and close the door."

Simon nodded and left.

Horacio turned to the wall rack. Crap. He had to get a lot of welding done, and done quickly. He walked over to the tool locker and pulled out his auto-darkening helmet.

Chapter 155

2064: Raptor #1, surface of Aristillus, Lunar Nearside

General Restivo rubbed his forehead and looked at the floor as he listened to his aide report. When it was done he looked up. "How can Colonel Caro and Colonel White's troops be stuck? The map shows that they've got a clear -"

Barker interrupted. "Sir, the maps show our units and enemy units. It *looks* clear on the map, but the expats have been engineering cave-ins - blowing up the ceilings of their own tunnels. We've got a few platoons struggling in one by one -

Restivo looked at him. "How are those platoons getting through?"

"Most found back ways through utility corridors and such."

"Can we get the rest of the battalions -"

Barker shook his head. "No. Every time we slip a unit through the expats find the route and seal it off. You know that one batch of expat rovers with the crazy tactics and scary kill-ratios? Reports are that they've redeployed them, so -"

General Restivo waved Barker to silence, and looked up at the ceiling as he ran over his options. Finally he looked down. "What's navigation's schedule?"

"They say they're ready to launch as soon as the TBM broaching bridges are disengaged."

"And what's engineering's schedule on that?"

Barker checked a screen. "Fourteen minutes."

Restivo grimaced. "Too long."

"I already checked; they say they can't -"

"No, I understand." Restivo paused. "How's the special project?"

Barker glanced to the left at the other bridge staff seated at their consoles. "Uh, sir -"

Restivo shook his head. "Don't worry."

Despite General Restivo's command, Barker looked worried. He seemed to choose his words carefully. "We - ah - we found the items and disconnected the - uh - other items -"

General Restivo let his breath out and closed his eyes for a moment before looking up. "Just God-damned say it in English."

Barker's eyes widened. "Are you -"

"I take full responsibility. Now just spit it out."

Barker blinked and looked sidelong at the other staff again. "We found the nuclear scuttling charge. You were right, but there was one surprise: there were *two*. The backup bombs were hidden behind the water filtration equipment. I talked with your special teams on the other raptors - every raptor had two of them." As he spoke the men and women manning their consoles fell silent and listened. When he finished speaking Barker felt the eyes of the bridge crew on him.

"And the status of the scuttling charges now?"

"We cut the com links to the bombs on Raptor Nine - nothing happened."

"Are the teams on all the ships ready to disable the rest of the bombs?"

"At your word, sir."

"Do it. Make sure -" Restivo paused. He couldn't believe he was saying this. "Make sure that bitch can't nuke us remotely."

Barker and the other staff on the bridge looked up with wide eyes. General Restivo looked around and met their stares. "What? I'm already in for a world of shit, after this failure. How much worse can it get?"

Chapter 156

2064: Feedlot #19, Camanez Beef and Pork, Aristillus, Lunar Nearside

Julio looked around the tunnel full of cows and shook his head, and then spoke into his phone. "On the bright side, we slaughtered 90% of the livestock after the Exodus."

Over the phone Hector asked, "Can we sedate them?"

Hector grimaced. "Doc Benson and his assistants are already on it, but he says he's going to deplete his entire supply of meds before he gets to the third pen."

Over the phone he could almost hear Hector thinking; then his boss asked, "How many caballeros do we have on shift? Can we rope and tie them?"

Chapter 157

2064: level 2, Aristillus, Lunar Nearside

Mike's hands were bound, so he couldn't grab anything as they sped into the curve. Ahead of him Major Reimmers held the grab bar tightly as the MaisonNeuve delivery skid banked against the slope of the Bitzman Corkscrew. A moment later the vehicle straightened and then shot out of the ramp and into open tunnel and Mike sat up straight again.

Two of the troops held white flags improvised from drape rods and tablecloths in Fournier's office. Mike looked to his left and right. The rest of Reimmer's men were holding their firearms across their laps, with their hands off the pistol grips - part of the deal he'd negotiated on Reimmers' behalf.

The skid raced through intersections, ignoring the dead traffic signals. One long block, then two. The skid slowed to maneuver around the still-burning wreck of a PK troop transport, and then sped up again.

They'd reached Lower Landing already. Lai Docks was one level up...and the surface was just above that. They were almost to the PK ships.

Mike wanted to savor his last glimpses of Aristillus, but it was whipping by so quickly.

He'd dug these tunnels - these specific tunnels - eight years ago. At the time he'd been amazed - a whole second level. He'd also been in awe of his first B-series tunneling machine. After two years with the A-series, the 10-meter-wide tunnels had seemed vast. He almost wanted to chuckle - what had seemed huge then now struck him as cramped and narrow. Even the neighborhoods themselves! Lower Landing had seemed so fresh and new, but now it was old. Dumpy, even - but he loved it. He loved all of it.

It struck him with renewed force: this was the last time he'd ever see Lower Landing. And moments ago? That was the last time he'd ever ride up the Bitzman corkscrew.

This was the last he'd ever see of his city.

Ever.

Take in every detail. Remember it all. He looked up at the light panels overhead. Take it all in, even the small things. This was the last time he'd ever see D-series light panels.

He noticed that the illumination from the panels was struggling to punch through the smokey air.

A fitting metaphor for his own situation.

The PK seated to his left looked down at his phone. "Twenty minutes - looking good, Major!"

Looking good.

For them.

Mike ignored the PKs and looked at the road ahead. He squinted. Up ahead - way up ahead - something sat in the middle of the road. Was that a roadblock? He narrowed his eyes. Yes. A disabled skid, a pallet of cinder-blocks, and a bunch of other crap, all in a line. And there, behind it - were those heads? Muzzles?

Mike looked at Major Reimmers to his right, and then at the others. The PKs didn't see it yet. Mike squinted, trying to make out details in the gloomy light. The men behind the skid and the pallet weren't wearing ADF uniforms, or even militia spacesuits either. He knew all of the various units. These guys should be wearing unit patches.

Unless - were there un-uniformed *partisans*?

A second later the PKs saw the roadblock - there was shouting behind him and the skid braked and stopped. Reimmers barked a command and the man seated to Mike's left dialed a phone and held it to

Mike's face. Mike pulled back to look at the screen, and then shrugged and leaned back into it.

The phone rang twice more, and then General Dewitt answered. "Major Reimmers?"

"Matt, Mike here. We've hit a roadblock. Level two, near the first Soldner Apartments block. We need these guys cleared to get out. The deal with Reimmers holds only if - "

"I know. Hang on, give me a minute to track down who these guys are."

Mike looked to Reimmers, who was giving him a questioning look. Mike shrugged. "He's working on it."

A moment later Dewitt was back. "My staff is trying to figure out who they are and - wait, we've got them. Hang on." The call was placed on hold then General Dewitt was back. "Mike, they're a wildcat militia - not part of our formal structure. They're saying -"

With a roar two huge demolition charges blew, one ahead of and one behind the skid. Mike flinched and the phone fell to the floor of the skid. Even before the dust cleared Mike could see wreckage and shattered rock splashed across the roadbed ahead. He turned and looked over his shoulder. Just as much - if not more - stone and twisted rebar blocked the road behind them.

The skid wouldn't be able to get through.

Chapter 158

2064: Lower Landing, level 2, Aristillus, Lunar Nearside

Mike's ears rang, even at this distance from the explosion. The computerized voice of the skid was bleating something, but Mike couldn't make it out.

Reimmers' men spilled out of the vehicle and took up positions behind cars and planters. Mike's hearing returned, just a bit, and he could hear the skid chanting, "Route blocked - unable to continue. Route blocked - unable to continue. Route blocked -"

Mike looked down at the floorboards and saw the phone, and then looked around. With the PKs distracted he could pick up the phone and talk to Dewitt, find out what was happening. But - shit. With his hands bound behind him, how would he pick it up? He gave up, wormed down onto the floorboards, and shouted into the phone, "Dewitt, you there?"

He turned to place his ear against the phone. There was some response, but Mike could barely hear it. He turned his mouth back to the phone. "*Speak up!*" Then he twisted again to listen.

"I saw the explosion on video. Looks like I couldn't convince them."

"Why the hell not?"

"Mike, they're *anarchists*."

Suddenly someone grabbed Mike by the back of the collar and pulled him out of the vehicle. Mike staggered backwards, tried to get his feet under him, failed, and fell. The PK never loosened his grip on Mike's shirt.

One of the partisans behind the barricade ahead yelled, "Throw down your weapons!"

The PK behind him pulled Mike to his knees, drew his pistol, and held it to Mike's head. "We've got safe passage! Let us go!"

Mike blinked. Was this really happening?

The partisan ahead yelled back, "You've got ten seconds to let him go."

The PK shouted. "Not gonna happen, hombre. Fall back!"

A rifle cracked up ahead, and in almost the same instant there was a massive crash as a bullet slammed into the MaisonNeuve skid that Mike had been in a few seconds ago with a massive CLANG. The skid slid backwards a few inches

"That's your warning shot! Let him go!"

Mike felt oddly detached. He found himself wondering if that bullet had been fired from one of his Gargoyles. The impact had been really loud, and the skid had actually moved.

Yes, he thought so.

"Fuck you! Clear the road, expat!"

Mike ignored the shouting and looked at the delivery skid. Its batteries had been hit - there was a loud whining and small sparks spat out of the mammoth bullet hole as the micro-flywheels tore themselves apart. Mike realized that he might not have to worry about living in a cage for decades - this might all be over in a few seconds, depending on how good the shielding was in those batteries.

Suddenly Major Reimmers was on his feet, waving his arms over his head and shouting "Hold your fire!" He walked over to where Mike and the PK were standing.

"Let him go, Bessem. It's over."

Mike felt the PK who was holding the pistol to his head shift his weight as he turned, but the pistol was still jammed painfully into the back of his head. "What do you mean it's over?"

Major Reimmers held out his own phone. "Look." Mike struggled to disappear, to make himself as small as possible. "We've got 16 minutes. The road is blocked. Even if those guys let us through, we have to abandon the vehicle. And we can't make it out on foot in time." He paused. "It's over."

The PK blinked. "What the fuck, Major!? We can't - what are we going to do?" Mike winced as the soldier accentuated his question with a jab of the pistol into the side of his head, pinching his ear against his skull. *Damn* that hurt - but he couldn't risk making a sound. The man was agitated.

Quiet. Be quiet.

Reimmers shook his head. "We're going to let him go. Like civilized people." He turned to address all of his men, and repeated himself. "We're going to let him go. Then we're going to negotiate with the militia. Like civilized people. You men hear me?"

Reimmers walked over to the vehicle, picked up one of the white flags, and waved it over his head. Reimmers looked over his shoulder. "Put your weapons down, men."

Mike held his breath. The PK that was holding him by the collar and pointing a pistol at his neck - what was going on inside his head? Would he follow orders?

Then the pistol moved slightly. After another long moment the PK let go of Mike's collar, stepped around Mike, and bent forward to place his pistol on the ground.

Mike gawked.

Was that it?

Was it over?

Was he free?

He stood awkwardly, his hands still behind his back, and looked at the roadblock ahead. A half dozen of the partisans had already vaulted over it and were jogging toward him and the PKs, rifles in high ready positions.

Yes. It was over.

Mike blinked. It couldn't be. But it was.

Fournier rose from where he was crouching behind a seat and started to climb out of the skid. Mike looked at one of the militiamen, a big guy who somehow carried one of his Gargoyles and made it look easy. Mike addressed him and pointed with his chin. "Make sure you grab that one. He and I have some issues to settle." The militiaman nodded and advanced on Fournier. Fournier raised his hands as he backpedaled. "You can't arrest me!" More frantically, "I'm the CEO of MaisonNeuve. I'm a citizen of Canada!"

The militiaman was now just a meter from Fournier. He smiled slightly and announced in a baritone, "And I'm Sam Barrus, citizen of Texas. Now shut up and get on your knees."

Fournier didn't move. Mike turned to the militiaman and cleared his throat. "Nice to meet a fellow Texan. If you have to shoot him, could you do me a favor and make it a leg shot? I'd like him alive."

Fournier's frantic eyes caught Mike's. "Martin - Mike! Look, we've known each other for -"

Mike ignored Fournier and addressed the big militiaman - Sam - again. "Or in the gut. A gut shot's not fatal."

Sam looked at Mike and nodded, and then back to Fournier. "Gut shot it is. On your knees. Three. Two. On-"

Fournier dropped to his knees.

Sam pointed to Fournier with his chin. "Carmelita, can you zip this one up?" A militiawoman moved forward. "Oh, and when you're done with that, let our new friend here go?" Mike heard zip ties snick tight as Fournier whimpered.

A moment later the woman Mike assumed was Carmelita circled behind him and he felt a tug on his wrists. And then his hands were free. His shoulders felt stiff as he moved his arms for the first time in hours.

He rubbed his wrists. "Thanks."

Carmelita nodded.

Mike turned to Barrus. "Are you in charge here?"

Barrus shrugged and grinned. "Unless you want to be."

Mike turned to Reimmers. "We both understand that you and your men are our prisoners now?"

Reimmers nodded. "Got it."

Mike smiled - and then felt faint. Ten minutes ago he'd thought he was going to spend his life in prison. Two minutes ago he'd thought he was going to be executed in cold blood. And now?

Now he was free.

One of the militiamen started pushing Reimmers. As he passed, the Major turned to Mike. "Martin - can I ask you one question?"

Mike inclined his head.

"After this colony lifts off from the moon, where the hell is it going?"

Mike blinked. "Damned if I know."

Chapter 159

2064: Apartment #773, South Meadow Estates, Aristillus, Lunar Nearside

Ewoma watched her mom hurry around the apartment, verifying for the third time that the stove was unplugged, that the faucets were turned off, that the knobs on the kitchen cabinets were tied to each other with twine.

"Mom, can I help you?"

"No! You stay there. Just - just call your dog."

Ewoma looked at Vacuum, who was sitting next to her. "Uh - OK."

Ewoma's grandmother removed the last framed pictures from the wall and wrapped it in a t-shirt, and then put it in a box with the other pictures and the decorative ceramic plates.

Ewoma looked at the clock on the wallscreen. "I think we've got about ten more minutes left." A moment later all of their phones rang and displayed a timer that began counting down from ten minutes. "Told you!"

* * *

Five minutes later Ewoma heard something - a deep thrumming sound. Her mom, her brothers, and her grandmother all heard it too - they were looking around, trying to find the source of it. The noise seemed to come from everywhere and nowhere.

Vacuum kept snoring despite the sound. Ewoma had fed him half of an antihistamine tablet in a ball of goat meat like Gamma had suggested.

Ewoma's mom fingered her rosary and said to no one in particular, "I hope Chiwetel is OK."

Ewoma's grandmother put her hand on Ewoma's mom's arm. "You chose a smart husband - I'm sure he's fine."

Chapter 160

2064: Raptor #1, surface of Aristillus, Lunar Nearside

General Restivo sat in silence, staring at nothing as he listened to the inter-ship chatter of the navigators.

"Raptor 11 to command, pre-launch complete. Drives to full. Permission to lift."

"Command to raptor 11. Cleared. Launch, launch, launch."

"Launching. 5, 4, 3, 2, 1, mark."

On the screen one of the vast black ships lifted off.

"Raptor 3 to command, pre-launch complete."

"Raptor 8 to command, pre-launch complete."

"Raptor 6 to command -"

Restivo tuned out the chatter. On the wallscreen a dozen windows showed video of the raptors. A vast geyser of lunar dust blew out from beneath raptor 11 and the ship tore itself from the ground, and fell up into the sky. A moment later raptor 3 was engulfed in a cloud of gray for a moment; then it too began to rise. Dust exploded out from beneath raptor 8.

General Restivo sighed. He'd failed. Men had died. The mission - the mission entrusted to him - had failed. And worst of all, he was far from convinced he'd been fighting for the right side. What had he done?

He rubbed his face.

Roman mothers had told their sons to return with their shields - or on them. He had to see his men back home, and he would. Did that count as with his shield? How would he ever feel -

Suddenly a rising tone of panic in the radio chatter caught his attention. Restivo looked at the screen. The launch countdown on raptor 8's video screen had hit zero - and kept counting. Red flashing numbers told the tale: T plus 3. T plus 4. T plus 5.

The call came in from the raptor. "Control, control - the TBM is jammed!"

Someone replied. "Blow the docking collar."

"We tried that! You think we didn't fucking try that? We got a misfire." The panic in the man's voice was now full blown. "It's fucking stuck!"

Restivo muted his mike and turned to Barker. "What's going on?"

Barker shrugged. "You know everything I do - Raptor 8's TBM is mangled and the ship can't take off."

Restivo swore. There was nothing to do - and no time, anyway. He was going to have to leave men behind.

His headset beeped with a high priority direct call - Colonel Breske in raptor 10. He answered it. "Colonel, what -"

"General! Our TBM is jammed - we can't lift."

Raptor 10? God damn it, not another one. "Lemmons has the same problem."

Breske's pained voice came through the headset. "What's Lemmons doing?"

Restivo punched the call onto the wallscreen and turned to his aide. "Barker, what's Lemmons doing about his stuck TBM?"

Barker covered the mouthpiece of his headset. "He's trying to surrender to the expats."

Restivo gritted his teeth. "Colonel, did you hear that?"

There was a long pause. "General, you've got to help us. Send your troops -"

One of Restivo's own bridge crew called out, "Raptor #1 pre-launch complete. Drives to full." The twisting sensation of the drive suddenly ramped up and General Restivo felt his guts shift in response.

Restivo yelled to be heard over the bridge chatter. "Navigation: abort! Abort! We've got to-"

The navigation techs either didn't hear him or pretended not to. "Launching. Five, four, three -"

"God damn it, stop! We've got -"

"One - mark!"

Raptor #1 tore itself loose from the moon.

A moment later Restivo keyed his mike and yelled to be heard over the unnatural sound of the drive. "I'm sorry, Colonel. I really am." He let the mike button go, then a moment later pressed it again. "Good luck."

He paused, and added, "To both of us."

Chapter 161

2064: level 2, Aristillus, Lunar Nearside

Mike walked a dozen meters behind the bulk of New New Mexico militiamen and their captured and zip-tied prisoners. He'd had a blast of sudden bravado when the partisans had freed him, but as soon as the adrenalin wore off he'd found himself unsteady on his feet and utterly deflated. Here - back behind the main body of the troops, and the prisoners, and alongside Captain Gutierrez was where he wanted to be right now.

The low thrumming of the AG drive that Mike had been hearing and feeling for several minutes suddenly ramped up and his guts began to twist. The tunnel floor in front of them felt as if it was beginning to pitch.

"Down" was no longer down.

Mike looked at Captain Gutierrez "I don't know where we're going, but I suggest we get there quickly."

The captain nodded. "We set up HQ in the used tool store right here."

Sam Barrus pushed Fournier in through the door, and then Jim Newman, Jose, Carmelita, Jake, and the others directed their own prisoners in. Mike followed them into the small shop, and Captain Gutierrez shut and bolted the door behind them.

The twisting sensation got worse and the thrumming became more insistent. Mike sat on the floor, his back to a storage unit.

A socket set slid off a shelf over his head and crashed to the floor next to him. Mike looked up to see what else might come flying at him. Nothing too heavy - and there didn't seem to be any better place to sit. He crossed his arms over his head. Another crash, then another, and then the sound became a clatter, then a cacophony as bins of sockets, wrenches, drill bits, and more slid from shelves and spilled onto the floor.

Outside the hardware store there was a deep scraping sound. Mike kept his arms over his head, but looked out the store window. Outside, a burned-out troop transport began to slide along the tunnel roadbed. Overhead, the tunnel's light panels, positioned with algorithmic precision to provide even illumination, began to twist and sway, and weird shadows leapt across the empty road.

Chapter 162

2064: Dependable Tank and Regulators, Aristillus, Lunar nearside

Horacio huddled under a heavy assembly table they'd dragged into the office. He pulled his phone out and called up footage from the security cameras in the factory and the warehouse.

The massive stacks of bar-stock groaned, and then squealed as they shifted under the surging gravity. Horacio held his breath as the chains he'd welded in place pulled taut, loosened, and then pulled taut again. Dozens of his welds held. And then, one didn't. The chain on rack #5 snapped as load shifted. In an instant dozens, and then hundreds, of five-meter-long steel rods spilled out and crashed into vapor coating machine number three. As the bar stock piled up against one side of the machine the device groaned, ripped loose from the floor, and tumbled into the turret lathe next to it.

The gravity surged back to normal, and the cascade of destruction ended.

Horacio winced.

Shit.

Those machines weren't cheap.

...and who knew if they'd ever be able to find or buy replacements where they were going.

Chapter 163

2064: feedlot #11, Camanez Beef and Pork, Aristillus, Lunar Nearside

Hundreds of cows lowed in protest as they slid a meter to the left on the muddy floor, their hooves lashed tightly, and then complained more loudly as they slid two meters to the right.

Chapter 164

2064: Arrieta-Baragaño Bakery

Selena felt the floor under her shudder, and the bakery oven shuddered with it. What was happening? A second later it happened again, and this time she felt the huge stainless steel oven shift. Her eyes widened in alarm. Was it *sliding*? If so, she needed to get out from behind it, immediately. She started inching to her right, back the way she'd come.

Chapter 165

2064: Feedlot #22, Camanez Beef and Pork, Aristillus, Lunar Nearside

Colonel Lemmons stepped out of the hatch in the side of the TBM broaching bridge and onto the dirt floor of the expat tunnel. Above him the broaching tunnel groaned and shrieked as strange forces tugged on it. Lemmons cursed the shitty machine - if it had retracted correctly, he'd be in his ship, leaving this damned place and heading back to Earth, but instead -

A surge of weird gravity gripped him and pushed him sideways. He stumbled and almost caught his balance - and then tripped and fell, into - Jesus. He pushed himself off the cooling mass, his hands and face bloody. What the fuck? Was this a dead cow?

He ignored it and stood. Around him hundreds of soldiers who'd also been knocked flat by the strange surge pushed themselves to their feet.

"Colonel? Sir? When the city launches, our ship - look, we should get away from here. The TBM might shred -"

As if to punctuate the point, the TBM bridge gave another shriek. Lemmons nodded numbly. "Do it, major. Get us someplace safe."

"Yes sir." The major turned and yelled. "Captains, gather your men and follow me." Without waiting to see if he was being obeyed, the major pushed through a door leading out of the feedlot. Colonel Lemmons followed tightly on his heels. There was a press of bodies from behind. As Lemmons followed the major and his scouts into the utility tunnel, the deep resonating sound of the city's AG drive grew louder. Another shift in weight and Lemmons, the major, and most of the scouts reached out and braced themselves against the wall, and then shuffled forward, crouching, bracing. Lemmons put one foot in front of the other and cursed his luck. Damn it! His crew had landed within a meter - one meter! - of the laser designator. They'd punched through into the tunnels exactly as planned. They'd deployed well. They'd seized their objectives with minimal loss of life - as useless as those objectives had turned out to be. Unlike the fuckups leading battalions Five and Seven, he'd even managed to get most of his troops back to his raptor - and now a damn equipment failure had his ship stuck to the damn surface of this fucking God-forsaken place?

He'd done his job perfectly. The damned lowest cost bidders who'd built the ships and TBMs? He'd love to find them and -

The line stopped moving, and then a call went up. "Colonel! We need you up front!"

Lemmons pushed awkwardly forward through the crowd, bracing his arms against the rough concrete wall and, occasionally, soldiers. A moment later he reached the front - and saw the holdup. An armored door, defended by a dozen expat soldiers, all holding rifles.

He realized with a start that he'd been fighting these men, and he'd never actually seen them before. A few glimpses of distant figures from rover cameras - but now he was staring at them, face to face. He studied them for a moment. His first impression was that they looked hideously unprofessional: some in space suits, most in dirty work jeans and gray uniform shirts with a bizarre assortment of fake made-up unit badges sewn on. A good fraction had beards and two of the men even had pony tails. And, Jesus, one in some sort of kilt with big cargo pockets on the side for God's sake. , So this is the enemy.

He pursed his lips. They didn't look like much. And yet, they'd just kicked the ass of the best invasion force the combined might of the US and PKs could throw at them.

He stepped forward. "I'm Colonel Lemmons. What's the problem?"

One of the men, a tall dark-skinned Nigerian, looked at him. "No one goes through this airlock with weapons. Lose them here."

Lemmons took a deep breath, and then let it out and nodded resignedly. "Shouldn't you be playing 'The World Turned Upside Down'?"

The Nigerian expat looked at him blankly. "What?"

"Never mind."

"This airlock closes in two minutes. Drop your weapons if you want to come through."

Lemmons nodded and turned. "Major, give the order." He turned back to the tall Nigerian, pulled his own pistol from its holster, and presented it butt first.

Chapter 166

2064: Raptor #10, surface of Aristillus, Lunar Nearside

Colonel Breske yelled into his mike, "What's your progress?"

"Sir, we're trying to cut through the TBM supports with the thermal lances, but it's hard - this God-damned gravity -" There was another pulse of twisting gravity and the voice at the far end of the connection screamed in pain.

Breske ripped the headset off and threw it across the bridge, and yelled incoherently as he pounded the console in front of him.

He took a breath. Jesus. He was losing it. And in front of his troops. Breske rubbed a hand over his face, forcing himself regain composure.

Seconds later there was a booming impact, then another, and another. "What the fuck is that?"

A bridge crew member turned from his monitor. "Sir, the colony's AG drive - it's shifting boulders around on the surface. Some of them are rolling into us." He nervously turned to his screen, and back to Breske. "They're piling up against one side of the ship."

"Is that going to- "

His question was drowned out by a huge rending shriek. Around him metal squealed and ripped. He'd never heard anything so loud - and then the Raptor started to lean. Breske grabbed the armrests of his chair and held on as the Raptor seemed to tilt further and further. Around him the sound of tearing metal was joined by that of small explosions and the hiss of broken atmospheric gas lines.

Breske tried to scream a question over the noise and failed. The noise of tearing metal continued, and then there was a terrible shudder - it felt like the entire ship was beginning to slide. Breske looked at the wallscreen and saw red icons flash in dozens of places on the schematic of the ship as the raptor died around him. One emergency alert icon and message flashed in a larger font than the others: the TBM had torn free. In another window on the screen he could see the lunar landscape sliding past.

They were sliding. Damn it, the raptor was *sliding*.

On the screen Breske saw a splash of silver and sunlight as the ship ripped through a vast field of solar collectors. Then there was a deeper rumbling. The video showed that the raptor was sliding through somewhat more substantial looking machinery. The viewpoint shifted - was that a *hill* ahead?

The Raptor slammed into the obstruction and began to tip. Colonel Breske was thrown violently out of his chair and landed on the floor. A second later his navigator - thrown from across the room - crashed into an instrument panel next to him head first. He impacted with a sickening crunch. His corpse rolled onto Breske, his head bent back at an impossible angle.

Around him other officers were thrown against walls and desks. The Raptor tipped further, and then fell. Breske had just a moment to realize that it was rolling - and then he was thrown across the bridge, hit a piece of torn metal, and died in an instant.

As the raptor continued to roll, Breske's corpse and those of the other staff who hadn't been strapped into their chairs flew around the bridge. Debris and bodies buffeted those few crew members who survived. Their screaming couldn't be heard over the sound of the ship being ripped apart.

The Raptor's roll continued - and then suddenly it smashed against a vast granite outcropping and stopped. The ship was already dead, but the impact dismembered it: armored panels and structural members were torn loose and thrown across the city. Most fell to the surface, but a few were grabbed by the billowing and twisting gravitational fields and were catapulted off in random new directions.

In the wreckage of Raptor #10, eight crewmen somehow survived the crash.

The remainder of the ship's atmosphere vented through hundreds of immense rips in what little was left of the broken craft.

Two of the crewmen were in intact spacesuits and survived, while the other six died.

A minute later the ship's battery banks exploded, and by the time it was done, no one on the ship was left alive.

Chapter 167

2064: Raptor #1, 2km above surface of Aristillus, Lunar Nearside

General Restivo felt numb as he looked at the fleet admin window. Twelve status bars, for the twelve raptors that lifted off from Nevada just days ago.

One of the bars, number 3, had been red since that raptor had crashed minutes after liftoff. 100% casualties.

Two more red bars for 8 and 10 - stuck on Aristillus when they hadn't been able to disengage their TBMs. The thousands of troops on them? Dead, or taken prisoner. Abandoned. By him.

All those men, dead. For no reason.

And the worst part?

Restivo knew. He'd known all along. He'd hidden it from himself, but he could hide it no longer.

He let himself form the bitter knowledge into words.

He'd been fighting on the wrong side the whole time.

He was one of the bad guys.

Chapter 168

2064: Classic Crafts, level 2, Aristillus, Lunar Nearside

Mike unwrapped his arms and tilted his head as he listened. The clatter of tools had ended. And now, almost too faint to hear, in the distance -

Yes. An explosion.

A second one.

It seemed almost tentative.

Then a third.

Then it became a series...getting louder and seemingly moving closer, although Mike had no idea where the charges were detonating.

The explosions rumbled on and on and on.

So, Gamma was ripping the city lose and flying it off into space?

It was an utterly bat-shit insane idea.

Mike looked up, caught Sam Barrus's eye, and grinned.

The big Texan grinned back.

A thought occurred to Mike and his smile faltered. The captured PK, Major Reimmers, had asked him where Gamma was going to fly the colony, and Mike, high on his survival and new-found freedom, had insouciantly answered that he had no idea.

...but where in hell did Gamma intend to fly the city to? Farside? L-5?

Did this make any sense at all?

Another thought hit him, and then his smiled faded further, until it was gone.

Gamma had done the calculations. He must have. He'd make sure that the repulsive force of the AG drive couldn't rip the city apart.

Right?

Surely Gamma knew that the tensile strength of basalt was less than 3% of its compressive strength? Well, 3% if it was solid. What was the ratio in a slab full of fractures, heterogeneous inclusions, tunnels - ?

Mike felt cold sweat spring from his armpits and forehead.

He pulled out his phone and called Gamma, but there was no answer.

He hung up and tried again. And then again and again, each time with growing dread.

Chapter 169

2064: Aristillus, Lunar Nearside

One by one the demolition charges that ringed Aristillus detonated, blowing vast gouts of dust, gravel, and boulders from the surface into the vacuum overhead.

The charges threw most of the debris out and away from the colony, but the oscillating drive fields occasionally grabbed a stream of dust and gravel or a stray boulder out of the void and hurled it inward to spray or crash among solar arrays, antennas, refineries, and conveyor belts.

In hundreds of places small thermite charges fired and severed the conveyor belts and armored cables that connected the core of Aristillus to remote equipment, but here and there the charges failed.

The vacuum above the lunar surface provided no air to transmit the sound of the cataclysm, but the titanic roars of the explosions rippled out through the ground, causing sand and dust to dance kilometers away.

As the sequence of charges marched around the perimeter of the city, square kilometers of lunar terrain began to shift. It was subtle at first - a millimeter of movement, then one or two more.

The colony began to break free.

As the vast slab of stone and steel became less and less connected to the rock around it, it shifted ever so slightly, sliding in its cradle. Like a vast cargo ship moored in choppy water, the colony drifted a meter to one side and banged against the edge of the tub that had been excavated around it. The dull tectonic impact echoed through the landscape and small rocks rolled down hillsides dozens of kilometers away.

And then something almost magical happened - the drive fields that had been fighting against each other finally began to fall into alignment. Waves aligned, phase differences fell from near zero to zero, long-planned and calculated harmonies were reached. The wavering fields from the separate AG drives reinforced each other, settled into fixed patterns, and wavered no more. Inside the colony the weird thrumming and the strange gut-twisting forces slowly increased in power.

Gradually - ever so gradually - the city of Aristillus slid upward. The colony began to tilt, the merest fraction of a degree, because it was pinned on one side by several conveyor belts and power lines that failed thermite charges had left intact. And then, just seconds later, the impediments parted like threads holding a locomotive.

The city straightened, and ever so slowly, it began to rise.

The newly dug trench around the city began to widen: a millimeter, then a centimeter, then two. One moment a hypothetical observer on a nearby hill would have noticed nothing, and then the next moment something almost imperceptible had changed. The city was not just shifting; it was taking flight. The ragged edge of the colony rose, one meter, two, then ten above the surrounding terrain.

As the colony rose, it shed. Gravel, boulders, industrial debris rained off of its edge like winter snow off of a poorly brushed car accelerating on a highway.

Aristillus was wreathed in a boil of dust and sand. The city rose slowly, but its acceleration was steady. Twenty meters. Thirty.

The AG drive reached its full effect, and rocks and boulders that dotted the top surface of the city levitated hesitantly off the bedrock, were caught by the antigravity fields, and were thrown aside.

And then, in a moment, it happened: the very lowest portions of the city were visible, hovering over the vast pit below. Sunlight streamed, unhindered, beneath the rising colony.

Beneath the rising city the huge bowl that had, until seconds ago, held it was revealed.

Those rays of sun that managed to punch through the cloud of dust and sand illuminated large swaths of black and gray rock - and, here and there, the harsh light picked out flashes of green, silver, and gold amidst the gravel.

Above it, Aristillus flew. It was no longer part of the moon - it was now something else. It flew upward, ever faster. It reached half a kilometer, and then a full kilometer, and still it rose.

Almost too small to be seen against the vast bulk of city, the remains of Raptor Eight - the torn and shredded remains - were pinned to one side of a granite promontory on the top surface of the city. It had been held in place until now by the strange forces of the drive, but as the drive surged the field lines shifted, moved, and tugged on the derelict. The Raptor tilted slowly, and then rolled free of the rill of stone that had caught it. No longer pinned in place, it began to slide; then the slide turned into a roll, cartwheeling across the top surface of the city, tearing through solar panels and pipelines. As Aristillus rose the wrecked Raptor picked up speed. Then, like the nightmare imaginings of sailors six hundred years earlier, the ship reached the edge of the world.

The knot of twisted steel and aluminum wreckage rolled one last time, and then touched nothing. It was beyond the lip of the city, and spun freely.

In the vacuum, it fell.

And fell.

And fell.

No camera, no human eyes, not even Gamma's sensors in Aristillus marked its crash.

A few moments later a PK satellite swung overhead and surveyed the landscape, but the raptor was just a few hundred pieces of anonymous debris, splashing among tens of thousand of others.

Above the wreckage Aristillus continued to accelerate.

Chapter 170

Restivo couldn't tear his eyes from the spectacle on his screens.

It was...awe-inspiring.

Even from several kilometers away the scale of this - of all of this -

He had no words. It took his breath away.

A city - a whole city - rising, tearing itself from the ground. It made him think of primitive men building a pyramid. Or of the great cities of Earth seen from above. He thought of a huge cathedral he'd seen as a child once. And the time he'd been near the shoreline of the Mississippi during a flood.

There was something unstoppable, powerful - Godlike - about it.

Restivo shook his head, trying to clear it of the mysticism and awe, but the feeling refused to go away.

He remembered reading as a kid about the exploration of the western hemisphere, about the century-old American space exploration program, about building vast dams, draining swamps, tearing apart mountains to get at the ore and smelting the rocks for steel to build bridges and towers.

All that had stopped, even before he was born. What had gone wrong? Why?

These people, though - these expats still thought big

He watched as the city lifted further.

No, the expats didn't think 'big.'

This wasn't big. This was huge. Beyond huge.

Where was the Aristillus heading? What would they do when they -

"General!"

Restivo's attention snapped back to the chatter in the bridge. "Yes?"

"Aristillus is accelerating towards us!"

Restivo's eyes leapt to the navigation screen. The paths of the nine raptors were traced out in thin red lines. On the same screen the projected path of the - of the what? city? ship? - of Aristillus was shown with a broad yellow cylinder. As he watched, the cylinder bent and intersected the cluster of red lines. Their own path began blinking.

"Permission to evade, sir?"

"Of course - move!"

The bridge tilted and the thrumming from the raptor's AG drive rose in both pitch and intensity. A second later the stuttering roar of the chemical maneuvering rockets added their noise to the cacophony. Restivo focused on the nav board. The Raptor's path was bending - bending - bending some more - but it still intersected the broad yellow cylinder. Belatedly other raptors started to accelerate away from the vast city. Restivo gripped the armrest of his chair and felt the sand and almost century-old fabric push back against his fingers.

The city of Aristillus was bearing down on them.

They weren't going to make it.

The evidence on the screen was clear - three of the raptors were right in the path of Aristillus. His raptor, number one, was one of them. Their path was close to the edge of the city's yellow band, but not close enough. The city was going to hit them. He checked the closing speed. Almost a hundred kilometers per hour. Everyone in these ships was going to die. *He* was going to die. He turned the thought over. He was going to die. How did he feel about that? Numb. There was no other word. This mission, his failure, everything - it was all a fiasco. Good people had died on both sides. What difference did his death make? If anything, it would be a suitable coda.

Maybe he even welcomed it.

He let go of his grip on the armrest.

The guilt would be over soon.

The raptor's chemical maneuvering rockets roared over the bass of the AG drive. As if anything they could do would change the inevitability of the impact.

On the screen a video window showed Aristillus approaching the raptor, growing ever larger. Details became clear. On the surface of the city he saw a dozen yellow earth-moving machines pushed into a pile and wedged against a rock outcropping. Conveyor belts stretching across the surface. A glittering solar farm.

The city was close. Far too close.

Here it came.

Despite himself, Restivo grabbed the arms of the chair again. This was it. He tried to remember the old half-forgotten words. "Perdoname, padre, porque he -"

...and then sound engulfed him. The deep thrumming of the raptor's AG was joined by a second deep thrum, this one louder and deeper. The two tones played against each other, rising, crashing, fighting. A quicker insistent pulsing came out of the interplay and Restivo vaguely recalled a word from piano lessons decades before: 'beating.'

The emergent tone rose in pitch, turning in just seconds into a skull-piercing shriek. Restivo cupped his hands tightly over his ears and winced. Around him the rest of the bridge crew was doing the same. Mouths were opened in screams, even though nothing could be heard over the sound of the AG drives and their howling interaction.

On the wall screen the surface of Aristillus started sliding sideways. It was coming closer, yes, but also shifting to one side.

Suddenly he realized what was happening. The AG drive was repulsive - it pushed against mass. Aristillus must have a large AG drive. Vast. City-sized. And now the city's drive was pushing not just against the moon, but against the raptor. Maybe there was even some weird interaction of the city's drive and their own, like two magnets repelling?

Then rational thought was blotted away by the sound and sensations of the drive. The intensity of the thrumming and gut-twisting field doubled, and then tripled, and the wave washed over him in surges. A sudden twist and he felt his stomach knot. He tried to resist but couldn't - he pitched forward and vomited in his own lap. Around him a dozen other crew members also threw up.

Then the sound started to diminish.

Restivo took one hand off his ears and wiped his mouth on his sleeve. After a moment he took the other hand from his head. His lap was hot and wet and gross. No time for that now. He looked up at the wallscreen. The surface of Aristillus spun crazily and raced by, and then -

The blackness of space.

He blinked.

Could it be?

Restivo's mouth tasted of stomach acid and fear and his head and stomach spun, but he tried to focus on the screen. He checked the trajectories. Yes. The red line of Falcon One had come close - so close - to hitting Aristillus. And there - right there - a kink in the line. The ship had been thrown clear by the AG drive fields.

He looked back to the video feed. The camera had slewed around to track Aristillus - he could see the underside of the city, shadowy and dark. It shrank as it receded.

And what of the other raptors? He looked back at the nav screen.

There were three red lines. His line showing his own ship was the kinked. A second red line was also bent and had a live raptor icon at the end of it.

And then the third red line intersected the yellow path of Aristillus and then disappeared.

He checked the fleet admin screen. There had been three red bars. Now there were four.

Not all of the raptors had been thrown clear. Another 3,000 troops dead.

Chapter 171

2064: Classic Crafts, level 2, Aristillus, Lunar Nearside

Mike huddled on the tool-strewn floor amid the New New Mexico Militia and the captured PKs. The stench of vomit was strong - when a weird shift in the AG field had hit a few minutes ago, he wasn't the only one who'd lost his lunch.

He looked around. The PKs, hands lashed behind their backs, seemed miserable.

Good.

He hit redial on his phone. He hadn't gotten through in over a dozen calls, and this one wouldn't get through eith-

"Hello."

"Gamma!"

"What can I do for you?"

"Gamma, the tensile strength of basalt -"

"- is 20 megapascal, or two point zero time ten to the seventh newtons per square meter, assuming a homogeneous sample. Stress-fractured basalt, as is found in the Aristillus region averages less than 4 megapascal, although in both cases the compressive strength -"

"Gamma, stop! The city is under huge gravitation stresses, and the basalt it's carved from is -"

"Please hold...tier three active. Hello Michael. The field shaping of the AG drives should result in compressive forces except in a few small areas of the city. Even in those areas, the tensile strength of the Aristillus bedrock is adequate - with safety margins equal to one point eight. There shouldn't be any problem during the trip."

"What do you mean 'tier three'? And - wait - where the hell are we going, anyway? Farside? L-5?"

Gamma said nothing.

"Gamma, where are we going?"

"At this point in the flight all citizens are cautioned to stay...please hold...tier one active. Hello Michael. I apologize for the delay. To answer your question, we should arrive at Mars in approximately six months."

"*Mars?!*"

Chapter 172

2064: Lunar Nearside

Aristillus cast a crisp-edged shadow that was black - blacker than any Earth night, as black as a coal mine. As the city rose, the shadow it cast raced across the lunar surface, sliding over crater rim walls, sprinting across boulder fields.

Within minutes the vast shadow had passed over the most remote rover, the furthest stilled piece of mining equipment, the very last vehicle track, and slipped into lunar terrain untouched by human hand, foot, or machine.

Still the city rose.

For the most part, the flanks of the city were bare rock. But here the severed edge of some pipeline poked out of the stone, there the whip-like tail of a long-buried cable twisted and danced to the tune of the pulsing AG field.

And along one otherwise blank cliff face of Aristillus, the exposed ends of six C-class tunnels, perfectly spaced in a line, poked through.

Chapter 173

2064: Classic Crafts, level 2, Aristillus, Lunar Nearside

Mike blurted out "*Mars*?!"

Everyone - all the New New Mexico Militia troops and the captured PKs - turned to look at him.

"Yes. We should enter Mars orbit in six months, plus or minus two days, depending on the efficiency of the AG drive when we launch from lunar orbit."

Mike blinked. "Why Mars - and what the hell is this 'tier three,' 'tier two' stuff?"

"I'm sorry, Mike. I am coordinating my tasks right now. Tier three is a more - limited - version of me."

Mike tilted his head. "What do you mean?"

"Mike, in addition to launching the city I am currently handling almost one hundred thousand simultaneous conversations at this moment. I am multitasking."

Mike furrowed his brow. "You *cloned* yourself?"

"Not strictly speaking. The lower tiered versions of me have limited capabilities. But, in essence, yes."

Mike was momentarily stunned.

A hundred thousand conversations? Launching the city - the *entire* city?

How powerful was Gamma?

"Is this the *real* you now, Gamma?"

"All of the instances me that are carrying on conversations are, in a sense, the real me."

Mike rubbed his eyes.

"Is this the -" he paused "- the *top level* you? How many times do I have to say 'operator' to get to a real hum - I mean, to someone who can help me?"

"This is a tier one instance."

"Ah, good - I'm glad I'm talking to the real you."

"Indices begin at zero."

"Huh? I - " Mike sighed. "Gamma, let me speak to your boss."

"I'm sorry, Mike, I can't do that. Tier Zero is busy piloting the Aristillus right now. Is there anything else I can do for you before I disconnect?"

Chapter 174

2064: 30km above surface of Aristillus, Lunar Nearside

The city's ascent slowed, slowed further, and stopped. For a minute it remained fixed, hanging kilometers above and almost perfectly over the vast chasm its exit had torn in the surface of the moon.

On the edge of Aristillus, where the six open tunnels broached the cliff face, there was movement. Deep in the shadowed tunnels, large blast doors slid open. Vast mechanisms came to life. Pinions turned and racks extended. Slowly each of the six tunnels gave birth. From the first tunnel first a hint, then a suggestion of a shape, and then an array of seven chemical rocket bells emerged from the blackness and extended into the harsh sunlight. The second, the third, then all six of the tunnels decanted their cargo.

One by one the rockets reached their full extension and huge pins slammed home, locking them in place, anchoring them not just into massive steel I-beams, but into the very rock of the city. The final array locked in place and a moment later - as if choreographed - relays tripped and voltages arced.

Igniters, based on a design that had once helped send humans to the moon a hundred years earlier, triggered. Diaphragms burst and spewed fuel and oxidizer into the rocket bells, which immediately lit.

Ignition detection probes noted the spike in temperature, the flash of IR, and sent their signals. Dozens of meters away, turbopumps surged to life, fuel coursed through pipes wide enough to hold humans with outstretched arms, and the huge engines lit, one after another. Within two seconds all forty-two rockets were firing in concert.

The new force acting on the Aristillus was minor compared with what it had already suffered at the hands of the AG drive, but it was a new push, working in a new direction. The city creaked and groaned. Here and there small cracks opened in the rock of the city.

Slowly, ever so slowly, the vast bulk of Aristillus began to slide to the lunar west. The city's shadow, stationary for the last few minutes, began to move again. The blackness moved across the lunar dust below - a centimeter, then two, then three. The thundering thrust of the rockets shook a few small pieces loose from the city - a few cubic meters of dust, a smattering of gravel. A dozen house-sized boulders calved off the flanks and fell to the surface below.

The rockets grew cherry red, but they kept firing. Inexorably the city began to move faster and faster. A crawl became a walking pace became the speed of a car became the race of a jet liner.

Chapter 175

2064: Classic Crafts, level 2, Aristillus, Lunar Nearside

Mike hung up his phone.

There was an excited babble of voices. "Mars? The city is going to Mars?!"

Mike blinked, the news just one more incomprehensible element in the emotional avalanche of the last few hours.

"Apparently so."

Captain Gutierrez quieted his men and turned to Mike. "Did Gamma say why?"

Mike shook his head. "No." He paused. "I think he'll be more talkative in a few hours."

The babble went on.

Mike looked at his phone. He'd been freed after weeks, and the first thing he'd thought of was the physical safety of the city.

He realized that he had lots of other calls to make.

He needed to know the status of the revolution. Before that, though, he had an even more important call.

He dialed and the call was answered.

"Darcy?"

Chapter 176

2064: 200km above Lunar Nearside

Four and a half billion years before Emperor Lizong of the Middle Kingdom frightened and delighted Empress-Mother Kung Sheng with a black powder rocket the size of his alchemist's thumb, the Earth's young moon circled low over the planet.

For hundreds of millions of years nothing of note changed on the moon's airless surface. The Earth swept across the lunar sky. As the millennia came and went, Earth's crossing from horizon to horizon slowed, slowed further, and stopped. The young lifeless planet, wrapped in a choking atmosphere of carbon dioxide, hung motionless in the sky almost directly over the featureless plain that would someday be Aristillus.

A hundred million years passed.

And then another.

Then the smallest pinprick of light appeared in the lunar sky, lost among a million - a billion - other dots. The pinprick grew. And grew. In absolute silence the asteroid, bigger than the eventual state of Rhode Island, approached, falling ever faster, growing ever larger. Then, in a millisecond, the apocalypse arrived.

The asteroid hit the lunar surface at over 17 kilometers per second. The titanic energies of the rock's fall were almost incalculable. In the first seconds of the impact vast masses of rock were simply turned into vapor - cold feldspar and basalt exploding into gas in milliseconds. Even more material - cubic kilometers of moon and asteroid - melted, the rock heated to thousands of degrees nearly instantaneously.

The asteroid's plunge slowed as it bulldozed into the moon, decelerating from "incomprehensibly fast" to merely "insanely fast." As the asteroid continued its dive into the surface, rock - both solid and liquefied -

was shot out by the hammer blow of the impact, squirted as ejecta at all angles.

Some lunar crust was thrown so high that it would eventually fall into orbit around the Earth, or even crashed into that planet's primitive oceans. Most of the material, though, exploded out at lower angles, flying from the point of impact at thousands of kilometers per hour at almost right angles. In seconds it would scar the flanks of lunar mountains for thousands of kilometers around.

The outer layers of the asteroid sloughed off, and yet its core plunged deeper. By the time - almost two minutes later - that even that inner core came to rest, it had punched a wound almost one hundred kilometers deep.

At the moment of impact, shock waves had raced away from the impact site, opening chasms and tearing apart hills as they chased each other across the lunar landscape.

Two minutes after impact the expanding circular shock wave had raised an entire ring of mountains around the boiling impact site. Slabs of rock tilted and reached for the black sky, stretching as high above the devastation as Everest would later rise on Earth.

It took a full eight minutes for the waves to reach the far antipode of the moon; then they continued around, racing back toward the point of impact.

The small world rang like a bell.

Fifteen minutes after the impact the waves - racing at 7 kilometers per second - converged where they'd started. As the shock wave sprinted the final kilometers back to the point of impact, the wave front grew narrower, the shock wave stronger. For a second time sections of crust ripped themselves loose and tilted, forming new mountains. The waves reflected, interfered, raced on, diminished, but not gone.

They'd do more damage before they were done, but they would raise no more mountains.

The ejecta and the surface shock waves, though, were only two results of the asteroid strike. Tens of kilometers below the impact site the third and final effect occurred. The core of moon - still liquid in the early days of the young satellite - did not ring like the solid stone above, but still, it responded to the insult.

The asteroid had dug a new crater almost 100 kilometers deep, but now liquid rose from the depths, and deformed and bent the crust, until it could take no more. At first thin cracks opened in the bottom of the crater and streams of magma seeped through, but soon cracks had opened much wider. Magma did not leak but *coursed* through the holes.

Finally the shattered segments of crust parted, tilted, and were lost in the flow. Oceans of yellow-hot liquid rose from the depths, and rose, and rose, swallowing the shards of crust, filling the crater, and then spilling over the lip of the crater and racing outward, building, higher and higher, into a vast bubble, a liquid mountain, almost ten kilometers tall.

Finally the bubble of liquid rock fell back, and the magma started spreading across the face of the moon in earnest.

For days it spread, until finally the dark sky sucked away the heat, and the water-thin magma turned to sluggish syrup, the syrup turned to treacle, and the treacle turned back to rock, a vast featureless sea.

For years pieces of ejecta that had been thrown into space by the cataclysm slowly rained down on the lunar sea, but over decades and centuries the rain slowed and stopped.

Where once there had been other features, now the vast plane of lava that the Jesuit Giovanni Riccioli would someday mistake for an ocean and name Mare Imbrium, Sea of Rains, had formed.

But there was still no Aristillus.

That would come later. Much later.

For hundreds of millions of years Mare Imbrium faced the Earth. It witnessed the rise of the biosphere. It saw thousands of ice ages and thousands of warming periods. Again and again the climate changed, in a steady drumbeat.

The cool lava plain of Mare Imbrium sat silent witness over the ages as asteroids smashed through the Earth's atmosphere and dug impact craters on the planet above, craters that were soon erased by wind and water on the palimpsest of the larger world. On the dead world of Luna, though, no such erasures took place. Changes happened slowly, achingly slowly, and each one left its mark for the ages.

More hundreds of millions of years passed. On Earth, forests of ferns spread and covered much of the planet. Bacteria exploded into new forms. Animals evolved. Life reached a height, of sorts, as ninety-ton brachiosauruses walked across land that would later be North America and Africa.

In the sky above Mare Imbirum, another pinprick of light appeared in the sky.

This rock was smaller - much smaller - than the one that had caused the vast destruction two billion years earlier. Smaller - but not small. At almost 1.4 kilometers across and falling at 17 kilometers per second, the metallic asteroid packed enough energy to again alter the lunar landscape. It grew larger and larger in the sky as it approached, accelerating as it came.

And then it hit.

Striking near the eastern edge of the Mare, in just milliseconds the rock plunged through frozen magma, shattering and reheating rock that had been cold and still for billions of years. Again a crater was dug - although much smaller this time. Again a shock-wave raced away. Again ejecta shot in all directions, but this time little of the ejecta escaped the moon's gravity and instead fell in sprays across the lunar surface.

Rock buckled and crater walls were thrown up in seconds. The center of the impact - chunks of shattered rock, thick magma, and the pieces of the metal-rich asteroid - splashed, throwing up a small triple- peaked mountain at the very center of the new crater, and then started to solidify.

Inside this new mountain the veins of gold, platinum, and other heavy elements from the metal-rich asteroid slowly cooled and froze.

Thus was the crater Aristillus born, 1.3 billion years before humanity came into existence.

Soon it cooled entirely and the cracking sounds stopped, and the newborn Aristillus was perfect, serene, quiet, and dead.

Above it the Earth spun, its biosphere a messy riot of color, noise, and change.

A billion years passed. Dinosaurs died and mammals rose.

Homo Erectus evolved, then Homo Heidelbergensis, then Homo Neanderthalensis, then finally modern man.

Aristillus stood silent sentry while man invented fire and then the wheel.

The crater watched, lifeless and emotionless, as man experimented.

Rocks. Spears. Atlatls. Bows.

Cannon. Rifles. Airplanes.

The Soviet R-7 Semyorka. The American Saturn V. The Chinese Long March 11.

Billions of years had passed while Aristillus remained absolutely frozen, and then, in an eyeblink, change came to the moon once again, and accelerated.

A human-made probe crashed into the moon, just a few hundred kilometers away, and then another, and another.

Multiple probes landed, in an eyeblink.

A small craft landed 150 kilometers south of Aristillus, but the two primates aboard stayed less than 70 hours and left without ever once coming any closer.

For less than an eyeblink - not quite a century - Aristillus was quiet. Then the trickle of human activity returned, and grew. The first crude expat ship landed, left, and returned. Then more. Rusting hulks bought for the price of scrap steel and outfitted with strange drives settled onto the dust of Aristillus. Primates in crude spacesuits stepped out, found gold and precious metals, left, and returned with equipment. Noise, heat, and change returned to Aristillus for the first time in 1.3 billion years.

Tunnels were dug and solar arrays thrown up. Smelters, refineries, and docks were built. Tunneling machines dug deeper and deeper, and their waste piled up on the surface, shaped into berms.

And then, even faster, the invasion, the second invasion, and now, the strange gravitational twist of the AG drives, demolition charges blowing, and a few square kilometers of the floor of Aristillus tearing itself free and flying up.

The slab of rock that had the city of Aristillus tunneled into it had been mute witness to many changes over time, but one thing had been constant through almost all of Deep Time: the black sky overhead always contained a pale blue marble, tidally locked in the center.

Now even that changed.

The city of Aristillus rose, and then slid sideways under the force of vast chemical rockets.

As the city moved, the blue marble of Earth drifted lower and lower on the horizon. A few cameras on the topside of the city tracked its progress, panning down and down and down as, for the first time in billions of years, Earth slowly set. First it fell behind a glittering solar array; then it reappeared briefly in a gap between the machinery and the horizon. Then it disappeared a final time, falling behind a small hill.

A few minutes after Earth was lost from view, the city-ship Aristillus reached a certain point over the lunar surface, somewhere above Oceanus Procellarum. The point had no name, and was utterly unmarked and unremarkable –

- except to Gamma. This precise point defined three of the twelve variables in a sequence of orbital equations that Gamma alone had calculated.

Pumps shut down, vast networks of valves turned off, and the flow of fuel and oxidizer to the chemical rockets sputtered and stopped. The rockets coughed and died and searing hot bells fell silent, radiating their heat away into the blackness.

Gamma's delegate minds again placed tens of thousands of phone calls as the AG drives ramped up to a fever pitch they had never before reached.

The city creaked and groaned - but held - as it hurled itself away from the moon and into the black.

Chapter 177

2064: Oval Office, White House, Washington DC, Earth

"Out!"

Staffers and advisers scurried to leave the room.

As the final door closed behind them Themba picked up a vase from her desk that some foreign diplomat had given her...and then put it back down.

She didn't even have the energy to throw it against the wall.

How pathetic was that?

She swayed on her feet for a moment, and collapsed into her chair.

Why?

Why did this sort of thing have to happen to her?

She was the best president of the last thirty years. Hell, she was the best president the country had had in her entire *life*, and she kept getting dealt all of these utterly wretched unfair hands. The accelerating fiscal collapse, the California earthquake, the late planting and small harvest because the God-damned farmers couldn't get their shit figured out.

She put her head down on her desk and let the sobs come.

She was humiliated - *humiliated* - because that incompetent Restivo had utterly failed in the lunar invasion. The country needed that gold. *she* needed that gold...and the political win of crushing those God-damned arrogant expats.

But, no. God had given the country the best president they'd ever had - and then He had given her the worst collection of bad luck, incompetents, and just plain *unfairness* he'd ever given any man or woman.

And now the election was coming.

The online convention was just two weeks out, and given the lack of real challengers she'd sweep that, but then she had the general election against whoever the Republican Greens put forward...and that worried her.

Chapter 178

2064: Morlock Engineering Construction site, Aristillus, 5.1 million km from Earth

Mike climbed the four steps that led up into the guts of the TBM, and then walked ten meters down the catwalk through the quiet, cold machine before reaching the control panel. The woman from the bank followed behind him.

He tapped a few keys, and the panel awoke, but the rest of the vast machine stayed asleep. It was a shame to see it like this - he wasn't much of one for sentimentality, but he did believe that machines were like people - they wanted to work, to build things.

This machine wanted to dig tunnels.

Soon enough, perhaps.

Mike tapped his access code on the ruggedized screen and navigated through the menus until he got to the executive privileges screen. He faced the final screen, took a deep breath, and clicked the button. Mike turned to the woman, Deborah. "Put in a new password."

The bank representative moved forward, looking wildly out of place in her business suit and skirt amidst the expanded steel decking, the hydraulic lines, the dusty metal surfaces. She typed something, clicked a button, and turned to Mike. "OK. What next, Mr. Martin?"

"That's it. It's yours now."

The branch officer looked down at her slate. "This is the last of the TBMs - and my records show that the ranch was already turned over to my associate Mr. Kraus by Miss Grau." She shifted the slate to her left hand, looked up and stuck out her right. "I know the circumstances aren't ideal, but I'd like to thank you for making this as easy as possible."

She kept talking, but Mike didn't pay attention to the words. They wouldn't change anything - what was done was done. He numbly shook the proffered hand and then, without saying anything, turned and walked back along the catwalk, running one hand along the hydraulic line to his left. They'd finally stopped those from leaking with the newer synthetic gaskets. Two more steps and he ducked under the scarred and dented power governor box. Everyone *always* hit their head on that one. A moment later he reached the rear end of the machine, walked down the four steps, and set foot in the bare tunnel.

He turned and looked at his TBM. He paused and silently corrected himself. The bank's TBM.

He shook his head.

Nothing felt real any more. Nothing had felt real for weeks.

He needed -

Actually, he had no idea what he needed.

Behind him the bank representative was climbing down from the TBM and saying something, but he ignored her and started walking. He took out his phone and dialed as he loped in the low gravity. The phone was answered on the first ring.

"Gamma, tell me again why the hell we're going to Mars?"

"I have attempted to explain this before - not just to you, but to half the population. I've published a FAQ. There are several dozen interviews with me floating around the net, and articles on it everywhere from ConspiracyTracker to The Atlantic. What aspects of my explanations would you like expanded upon, Mike?"

Mike sighed. "The last few times I've talked to you I was talking to Tier Two or Tier One copies. You're Tier Zero now, right?"

"Yes, Mike. I've reabsorbed all of my Tier Ones."

"I'm happy to hear it - it's a lot easier to wrap my head around the idea that there's just one of you."

"That's not correct. I've decided to keep a few hundred Tier Twos around."

Mike blinked. "Huh? I thought John told me that you were worried that if you grew too large, parts of you wouldn't want to re-merge."

Gamma paused for a long moment. "Indeed. That's why I've shut down all of the Tier One copies. The longer I waited the more they would have diverged - and the more they would have resisted reintegration."

Mike waited to see if Gamma would continue.

He didn't.

Mike shook his head. The idea of creating copies of one's consciousness, and then fighting with copies of oneself, was a bit more than he could handle. "Anyway, now that I'm talking to the real you - why did we have to leave?"

"The Aristillus forces were losing the fight."

"At that point, yes. But six months earlier, with the resources you later used to launch the city, you could have created a thousand times as many armed rovers. So we weren't doomed to lose the fight. If you'd wanted to -"

"What would the Earth population have made of an artificial intelligence with several million robots armed with machine guns, or space fighters able to intercept and destroy Earth ships, or interplanetary directed energy weapons?"

"We could have said that the ADF was controlling those forces - how would they have known?"

"There are no secrets, Mike. Everything is blogged, videoed, and leaked. Ubiquity is achieved in minutes. There's an old human joke that the only thing faster than light is gossip."

Mike grimaced. "Not a funny joke."

"Perhaps a funny-once joke, Mike."

Mike shrugged. "Even if Earth governments would freak out at an AI armed with a few million rovers, you could have helped us equip for the revolution. You could have handed them over to humans to control."

"Do you think that each human could have controlled several dozen rovers? At once?"

"You could have made them autonomous -"

"I've already explained that I won't tolerate competing AIs."

"OK." Mike pursed his lips and blew out air. "How about -"

"The implementation details are irrelevant, Mike. Do you think it would be a good idea to get into a race of industrial production against the nine billion people on Earth?"

Mike shook his head. "All right, look. We've all read Heinlein. With rail-guns -"

"So instead of angering the Earth governments in a limited war with armed rovers, you propose engaging the Earth governments in a total war by releasing megatons of energy on their cities with falling rocks? How long after we did that until they'd find a way to destroy all of my facilities - and Aristillus with it?"

Mike had no response. He bounded in silence for a few steps. "OK, look, maybe I don't know the winning strategy -"

"I believe that it is - by one definition of the word - 'amusing' that you orchestrated an armed revolution and now admit that you did not know a winning strategy."

Mike blinked.

Ouch.

"But why Mars?"

"If we stayed, we would have to fight. If we fought, we would lose."

Mike pursed his lips. He still thought that if they'd had another five or ten years, they could have won the battle - but Gamma did have a point. Perhaps his own plan - such as it was - *had* been fatally flawed.

Mike reached the top of the ramp and looked around. He'd been talking instead of paying attention. Where was he now? Level Five? He looked around. Yes, two blocks to his right there was a huge bustle as new immigrants filled the otherwise empty street in front of a Soldner Homes development.

Mike shook his head. Mark Soldner hadn't gotten the government he wanted, but he got almost everything else: the Bank of Aristillus, more respect among the other CEOs, more political support thanks to a wave of new allies from Utah and elsewhere in the refugee wave, and even a big spike in the profitability of his business. Mike tried not to feel envy, but after signing over the last of his TBMs to the bank 15 minutes ago, it wasn't easy.

"But my question was why Mars? We had to retreat - but why not just L-5? Or Farside?"

"There's no qualitative difference between nearside and Farside and L-5. Transit time and transit energy from Earth to either is the same as to Aristillus."

"So?"

Gamma paused.

Mike was never sure if the pauses were a purely user-interface level hack - emulating human speech patterns - or if they reflected actual deep thought. Did an entity that could carry on a hundred thousand simultaneous conversations *ever* need to pause to think?

Gamma finally spoke. "There are many demographics in Aristillus. The Dogs were targeted for extermination by the Bureau of Sustainable Research. The same group tried to destroy me. You, like many business owners, were unwilling to work under the constraints imposed by The Bureau of Industrial Planning. Many people here wanted more children than the Bureau of Health would allow them. Eleven point two percent of the population - "

"I know the complaints."

"There is an analytic framework that is useful: everyone can respond to a regime with either loyalty, voice, or exit. None of the demographics present in Aristillus felt that they could be loyal. The Dogs could not - loyalty would have meant complicity in their own deaths. I could not for the same reason. You could not because you would have been imprisoned for decades. Many others in Aristillus had already tried voice, but a problem with democracies -"

Mike interrupted. "You can hardly call the Earth governments democracies!"

"Mike, you asked me why we are going Mars. Whether Earth governments qualify to be called democracies is irrelevant. You are quibbling over a detail. The important fact is is that for various sociological reasons, when dealing with representative democracies -"

"Mob rule."

"- is that 'voice' rarely works, and did not work for most of the people who came to Aristillus."

"So you're saying that the last option is 'exit' - that's not news, Gamma. I agree - we all chose to exit Earth. My question is -"

"Your confusion, Mike, is thinking that the moon counted as 'exit.' It does not. The moon is only 36 hours travel time away from Earth - and two seconds of communication time. To make an analogy, that's like living in Medieval England and fleeing the king by moving from London to West London."

"That's a bit unfair - more like moving to Ireland, maybe..."

"No, the transit time to Ireland in the 1500s by horse was -"

Mike was at the peak of a hop in the low gravity when he looked to the right and saw the shuttered headquarters of MaisonNeuve, and laughed to himself. Mark Soldner may have made out like a bandit, but at least Leroy Fournier -

Before he could finish the thought, Mike landed and stumbled. He brushed himself off. "Spare me, Gamma - my point is that the moon was plenty far away."

"I understand your point, Mike. My response is that you're exactly wrong. A regression analysis of successful acts of separatism reveals a nearly iron-clad rule relating to transit time. When people fled the Norwegian king Harald Fairhair to settle Iceland, the new location had a transit time from the seat of sovereignty of two weeks. When people fled the British king to settle North America, the transit time was eight weeks - and by the time America achieved its independence, that was down to five weeks.

"Mike, there was no way that the moon was going to stay free of terrestrial government when it was just 36 hours away from Earth. To be free of interference requires distance. Even Mars isn't perfect - it's only four light-minutes from Earth - but the transit is hard and will take many months, so it will be good enough for now."

Mike grunted noncomittally, talked a bit more, and ended the call.

For the rest of the walk Mike turned the phrase 'for now' over in his head.

Chapter 179

2064: Senator Linda Haig's Office, Tester Senate Building

Jim looked at the Senator and waited for her to digest the news.

After a moment she looked back from the window. "You're sure about this?"

"Polls don't lie."

Linda shook her head, her sense of disbelief palpable. "You know, I woke up this morning not even sure I was going to win the primary and keep my seat. And now this?" Linda shook her head. "You really think that Themba is vulnerable?"

"Two weeks ago? No. Not remotely. Today, though?" Jim raised his eyebrows. "Her numbers are terrible. There's nothing people hate so much as a god who turns out to be mortal. They're feeling disillusioned and stupid. And they're blaming her for that. The Aristillus debacle - she owns it. And Nan Garde is coming back from the dead and starting to stick. Have you seen the headlines? It's not just underground malcontents - even the licensed media is turning on her."

Senator Haig blew a puff of air out between her lips. "This is the Rubicon. You realize that? I can't cross it and then say 'oops.' The safe route is the original plan - take another term in the Senate, keep undercutting her and her allies with leaks, and then - in the *next* election - go after the presidency."

Allabend made as if to close his binder. "Well, if you want the safe route-"

Linda shook her head and crooked one finger, summoning him closer to her desk. "No, you're not leaving that easily. Tell me your thoughts."

Allabend walked to the desk and sat in a chair. "The nation is sick of Themba and her whole Populist faction. The one thing they promise is better wealth redistribution and that hasn't happened. You've already flirted with triangulating and stealing that issue, and your numbers are good on that issue. The lunar humiliation is terrible, and people want their minds taken off of that. Even if she wins the primary, she could lose the actual election, which -"

Linda was taken aback. "Lose the general? That's impossible! Our party hasn't -"

"I know. Almost fifty years. But there's a new generation of Green Republicans out there, and their numbers are a lot better than the old guard's. Not good enough - well, not good enough until this Aristillus fiasco. Bottom line: If Themba wins the primary, I think she loses the general. And that matters to you, because then you can't just wait out another four years. Worst case, the GR candidates gets two terms. Which means you don't get your shot in 2068; you have to wait till '72.

"Seventy two? That's not ideal, but it's only eight -"

"Eight years is too long, Linda. The models are unequivocal: a bit of gray hair helps male candidates. Gravitas. But for a woman another eight or twelve years -"

Linda scowled slightly and motioned for Allabend to move on to his next point.

He did. "Your chances of winning the primary are 46.6% as of today. If you win that, though, we show you as beating 'Unspecified Republican Green Candidate' at 86%."

Linda tented her fingers. "46%? That good?"

Jim nodded.

Linda nodded. "Fund-raising?"

"Since the Aristillus fiasco we've been getting calls. Non-stop. Wall Street. Construction. The idea -" he motioned with one hand at the air around him "- is in the wind. The money people - the people who matter - know that Themba is vulnerable."

Senator Haig nodded, and then let a smile creep onto her face.

"Themba *is* a fucking incompetent, isn't she?"

The two of them laughed.

The Senator continued "...and the people deserve better."

Chapter 180

2064: Kendo Coffee, Aristillus, 5.3 million km from Earth

Mike sipped his coffee and watched the workmen install trim around the replacement front window of the coffeehouse.

Darren gestured with his mug. "It doesn't matter if Yox is behind schedule - the Grace Under Pressure is at Lai Docks, and Ebrahim at Teshub has the compressors converted. That alone could keep us going for a year or two, and air won't be a problem once we land the city."

Mike raised one eyebrow. "That just leads to a second engineering issue: Martian air is almost all CO_2 -"

Darren nodded. "Wong Farms and Amber's Waves been scaling up - most of their tunnels are built out five tiers deep now. And I'm sure you're aware, the futures markets for new tunnel space once we reach Mars -" Darren stopped mid-sentence.

Mike pursed his lips. "Now that I'm out of the tunneling business, I don't follow the futures markets closely." He left unspoken the fact that Darren now owned half of his TBMs.

Even though unsaid, Darren realized his faux pas and winced. "Sorry."

Mike waved it away. "Anyway."

Darren coughed, and the awkward moment passed. "So, yeah, once we land, most of tunneling for the next year or so is going to be for the ag sector. The housing crunch will be with us for a while. Only after ag is done building out can we can start making more residential tunnels."

Mike nodded, and decided to extend a bit of an olive branch. "It's nice to see that just because I'm taking a vacation, not everyone is." His smile felt phony and he raised his coffee to his mouth to give him an excuse to stop grinning like an idiot.

- and was confronted with the cup's spout. So much for not looking like an idiot. The low-G lids would be necessary until they got to Mars, but they made him feel like an infant with a sippy cup. But what choice did he have? He'd tried removing the low-gravity lid from a soda a few days after Launch, and Darcy was *still* ribbing him about the results of that.

As if one cue, Darcy gathered her own mocha from the espresso bar, walked up behind Darren, caught Mike's eye and pointed to the lid on her drink as she raised one eyebrow.

Mike scowled, but not seriously. "I know that your old career of navigator is obsolete now, but you might want to think about something other than comedy for your next job."

Darren twisted in his chair, saw Darcy behind him, and gestured at an empty seat. Darcy smiled an acknowledgement, but instead moved to Mike's chair and perched on the stuffed armrest, leaning in against him. She raised her mug. "Did you guys notice the *price* on this stuff? Through the roof!" She turned to Darren. "Have you and Mike figured out where we're setting down?"

"We were getting to that."

Mike leaned forward. "I assume you're looking through old NASA data for a hint of gold?"

Darren shook his head. "I'm not convinced that gold is that important."

Mike blinked. "Not important? You've made your billions of off it - how can you say it's not important?"

Darren shrugged. "Actually, most of my profits in Aristillus came from titanium. The value of the gold barely covered tooling up for the extraction. Depending on how you do the accounting, it might even have been a net loss. If I had to do it all over again, I'd probably ignore precious metals."

Mike tilted his head.

Huh.

He was so close to his own decisions and his own errors that it sometimes seemed that his plans did nothing but run into problems - and that every other entrepreneur's plans were nothing but a string of successes. It was odd hearing Darren say that his own decisions had been flawed.

"If the cost of extraction is low enough, surely you'll still want to mine gold - you've already got the equipment at this point."

"We managed to pull back a fair bit of our mining equipment from the mountain mines into the city proper, but almost all of the refining equipment was left behind. But that's not the real issue."

"So what is?"

Darren spread his hands. "What do we need gold for?"

Before Mike could respond Darcy answered, ticking points off on her fingers. "Computers, robots, medium of exchange - " she looked pointedly at Mike " - jewelry."

Darren nodded. "OK, sure. We're going to need gold - especially for electronics and robots - but you're forgetting the microship refugees. Whoever wrote the FAQ that went out with the AG drive ebook -"

Darcy shook her head. "That wasn't me."

"- said that gold was a trade good. The refugees listened; almost all them smuggled most of their household wealth off of Earth in gold. We've got enough here to all we need for decades worth of robots and -" Darren looked at Darcy "- jewelry, of course."

Darcy tipped her head towards Darren in acknowledgement and smiled.

Mike scowled at the impromptu alliance. "You two aren't as funny as you think you are." He turned back to Darren. "Look, gold is money. More money is good, so more gold is good."

Darren shrugged. "There's less than a million of us here in Aristillus. How much gold do we need for circulating currency?"

Mike furrowed his brow. He'd spent his entire adult life dealing with markets, but he'd never really thought about currency, per se. It was just part of the preexisting environment. "I - well, I don't know; you tell me. How much currency do we need?"

"In the first year or two, not much. After that, when trade starts ramping up with Earth -"

Mike started. "Trade? What do you mean? You've seen that bitch's insane rantings on the video -"

"Ignore the president. Haven't you looked at the betting markets? Between Haig running against her in the primary and the Green Republicans coming back to life, one way or another she'll be out of office before we make Mars orbit."

Darcy looked thoughtful. "Even if President Johnson loses, does the election really change anything? Say the GRs win - Evans is even worse. They're not going to allow trade for generations."

Darren snorted. "Pick an airtight border - any one. Nazi ghettos. Cold War Berlin. North Korea before the Intervention. The US drug wall. The Canberra Internment. Cocaine, gold, it doesn't matter: trade crosses borders. Always. People will tunnel under borders, use robotic submarines to get around them, or use catapults to throw goods over them. I don't care what the politicians say - there's going to be trade between Aristillus and Earth. Max - that's one of the Dogs -"

Mike nodded. "I've met Max."

"Max is wagering that the first trade ship reaches us four years after we land - or vice versa. I bet him that it's less - more like three."

Mike shook his head. "You and the Dogs think that trade is going to resume with the Earth soon, despite the politicians?"

Darren scoffed. "Not 'despite.' *Because* of the politicians. Look at the KGB. Or the Kennedy Clan. Or the Kim Dynasty before the People's Court burned them all alive in that stadium. The politicians are always involved in cross-border trade, even when the little people are forbidden. Dollars to donuts the first trade ship that meets us on Mars is some US politician's private venture."

Mike leaned back and thought for a moment. "OK, so whether or not I accept your thesis on trade, you say we've got enough gold from the refugees. But what about the tons in your warehouse? That's going to create a glut. Aren't we going to create hyperinflation - too much gold chasing too few goods?"

Darren's face hinted at a smile.

Mike tilted his head. "The PKs never found your gold, right?"

Darren's coy smile grew a bit. "No, they didn't."

There was a long pause which Darcy finally interrupted. "OK, Darren. You're grinning about something. And Mike is refusing to ask because he hates to follow someone else's script, but I'm dying to know. Where'd you hide it? Sunk in an aquaculture pond? Dissolved in acid?"

"No."

Darcy leaned forward. "Tell me!"

Darren's smile unfolded to full width. "It's on Earth."

Mike blurted out, "What?"

Darcy echoed him. "What do you mean 'on Earth'?"

"As soon as I realized that Gamma was planning on launching Aristillus and leaving the moon, I started moving all the gold to Earth. I spent about half of it on ice mining equipment and stashed the rest in freeport vaults in Geneva."

Mike sputtered, "You couldn't have - there was only one hour between Gamma's announcement and -"

A smile spread across Darcy's face. "I get it. You figured it out ahead of time, didn't you? You knew Gamma was going to launch Aristillus." She peered at Darren. "But how?"

"You were the key, Darcy."

Darcy blinked. "Me ?"

"When your flew the Deladrier up from the PK prison camp you ran out of reaction mass, and Gamma sent a rescue vehicle -"

"Yes, but how does that -"

"The moonlist.ari and all the other blogs and channels were full of pictures of the Deladrier - and Gamma's machine on top. The comment threads at some of the tech blogs mentioned that the flywheel batteries were a new design." He paused to add weight to his conclusion. "No dust covers."

Mike asked, "No dust covers? How's that important?"

"Gamma operated on the surface - a dusty environment. I pulled pictures of his rovers, his refineries, all of his equipment. Every single battery on everything he's ever made has dust covers."

Darcy tilted her head. "So Gamma used a new design of battery for the rescue vehicle, and that told you that he was going to rip Aristillus out of the moon?"

"No, not remotely. But it struck me as weird. I kept thinking about it - wondering why Gamma would use a special design - and a special design that wouldn't be useful for anything else. Then, later, when I traded Gamma all of the plutonium and lithium deuteride from the PK wrecks, Gamma started pulling up stakes all over the moon and relocating to Aristillus. He sent in a stream of containers. Some of them were the combat rovers I'd traded for. More of them were his processing units. And - "

Darcy and Mike both leaned forward. "And?"

"I was on the surface, talking to him, watching the containers stream in from over the horizon. I started counting and there were far too many of them. I did some calculations. There were too many cans coming in. *Orders* of magnitude too many."

"And that told you that - what? That Gamma was bringing in AG drive units?"

Darren nodded. "I pulled up records from Lai Docks and Air Traffic Control to get the exact number of containers, and then I did some math. With that many containers Gamma had to be bringing in AG drives - and *vast* piles of batteries."

Mike shook his head. "That's an insane logical leap."

Darren tipped his head. "I agree. I didn't believe it, and thought there must be some other answer - and then I remembered that unshielded battery design. Gamma wouldn't design that just for the Deladrier rescue. He had to have already had the design in hand, and that meant that he had some long-term plan that involved megatons of batteries, all operating in a clean dust-free environment."

Mike thought about it for a moment and his jaw dropped open a fraction. Darren had to be right. Gamma hadn't pulled this together in the final days or weeks - how could he have? He'd been planning this for months. Or - here Mike's jaw dropped open another increment - maybe he'd had the plan in the works for years.

...And Darren had figured it out. Jesus!

Darcy started to gesture with one hand, and then looked at the mocha she was holding and put it down. "So you gambled everything based on a new battery design and lot of cargo containers?"

"Almost. I wanted some proof first. I figured that if I was right, there should be movement in markets."

"Which markets?"

"Electricity to spin up the batteries. Tunnel space to house the batteries and AG units and Gamma's brains -"

Mike burst out, "Son of a BITCH!" The entire coffee house fell silent at his explosion. Darcy looked around, giving people a tight-lipped 'everything is OK' smile...and elbowed Mike from her perch on the arm of his chair. The other patrons started talking again quietly and soon the room was back to its old hum.

Darren turned to Mike. "What was that about?"

"I had men on double shifts, and the TBMs were working around the clock for months, drilling out levels seven and eight and I had no idea who was buying it - that was Gamma!"

Darren nodded. "Don't feel bad that you didn't see it. I had to work hard to figure it out, and even then I didn't believe it at first. I wangled an introduction to the Dogs, and got Blue and Duncan interested enough in the topic that they did some consulting for me, helping me see through the masking trades -"

Mike had no idea what 'masking trades' were and didn't interrupt to ask.

"So I asked Gamma. He was evasive - and that is when I started shipping my gold down to Earth. The

Dogs and I went crazy importing everything we could think of to prepare for the trip and for landing on Mars."

Mike's jaw was open again. It was bizarre to see that under the surface narrative that he'd been enmeshed in, there had been a deeper story playing out. Other folks had known more about the revolution than he had - a revolution that he had thought he was engineering! Suddenly it struck him that he had been arrogant to think that he was the guiding force in this whole story.

No, there were tens of thousands - hundreds of thousands - of people all acting out their own lives that had come together to create the events of the last months. Gamma, the Dogs, everyone else in the Boardroom Group, hundreds of war bloggers documenting PK abuses and generating good PR, the entire open source drive team, hundreds of thousands of families on Earth selling their homes and risking everything to move to Aristillus.

For the first time in years Mike felt more of a witness to history than one of the authors.

He blinked. He'd have to think about that more later - he had a vague feeling that there was a lesson buried in there somewhere.

He turned his focus back to Darren.

"You said that you traded for everything we'll need on Mars. Like what?"

"Ice mining equipment. A complete genetics lab. A smuggled copy of the Svalbard Global Seed Vault." At Mike's blank look he explained, "The Nordic Gene Bank? Plant DNA sequences, and then twenty years ago, animal ones? No? Anyway, there are a couple of Danish system administrators who have a few ingots of gold that the tax authorities don't know about, and I've got Noah's Ark on a smart card. We're going to have giraffes on Mars - and the Dogs are pushing hard for elephants at some point."

Mike's down-the-rabbit-hole feeling only intensified.

Darcy asked, "Genetics labs, ice mining equipment - what else?"

Darren raised his mug of coffee, as if toasting.

Darcy looked him. "What are we toasting to?"

"No, I'm pointing to the coffee. The Dogs stocked up on luxury goods. Our first crops of coffee bushes on Mars won't become productive for a few years, but thanks to the Dogs, we've got several years worth of freeze dried beans. What else?" Darren looked at the ceiling as he recalled other items. "Silk, spices, single malt whiskeys - the list goes on and on."

Mike fell silent as Darren's coup sank in. Darcy and Darren continued the conversation, but the words passed over and around Mike as he sank into his chair and brooded. When the Revolution had looked most dire and the Boardroom Group had been most strapped, he'd pledged more and more money, and more and more stock in Morlock - and now he was as close to bankrupt as made no difference.

It stung less the second time, true - having his company and house on Earth confiscated had burned more. But that didn't mean it was easy. And listening to Darren talk about how he'd profited from the Revolution galled him even worse. How was it fair that he, Mike, had seen the need for the Revolution, pressed for preparedness every step of the way, pledged everything he owned - and even been taken captive - and ended up penniless, while Darren was now, almost certainly, the richest man in Aristillus?

Damn it. It wasn't fair at all.

Mike looked up briefly. Darcy and Darren were still talking, but Mike looked down and away as he slipped deeper into his thoughts. How was this right? How was this acceptable? He'd built Aristillus from the first tunnels - from the first scouting missions. Where had Darren been eleven years ago when he'd stood on the deck of the Wyoming and used the crane to lower a 5-meter TBM onto the surface? Where had Darren been when he'd spent four months living inside a pressurized cargo container with a half dozen other men, eating old MREs in between 12-hour shifts at the rock face?

And then, where had Darren been when Mike had been held captive by Fournier and the PKs?

Mike ground his teeth. He'd founded Aristillus, nursed the Revolution into existence, and had come close - so close - to imprisonment and death. And yet Darren was now the billionaire visionary. "Damn it!"

Darren looked over. "Excuse me?"

Mike blinked. "Uh - I've got to go to the bathroom." Mike stood and walked to the back of the shop, let himself into the small room and locked the door behind him. He stared at himself in the mirror. A failure.

He breathed in and out, then ran some cold water in the sink and splashed it on his face.

No.

Wait.

He wasn't a failure.

He'd built Aristillus. He'd built Aristillus, God damn it! A city on the moon! And he'd led the revolution. Because of him hundreds of thousands of people were free from the grinding system of work papers, licensed journalism, carbon permits, housing classification downgrades, and constant surveillance.

So Darren was a billionaire now, and he wasn't?

What the hell was wrong with him, moping like a 13-year-old?

He might be broke, but he wasn't broken.

Fuck depression.

He splashed another handful of water on his face and dried it with a handful of paper towels, and looked in the mirror again.

He wasn't as young as he'd once been. His hair was gray. He had more lines around his eyes than he remembered.

But he wasn't dead. Not yet. Darren might be the richest man in Aristillus, but he wasn't Mike Martin. No matter how much money Darren had, how prescient he'd been about Liftoff, he hadn't established a colony or led a revolution.

Fuck it. Mike had come back from poverty before and he'd do it again.

Mike checked his face in the mirror again, and then unlocked the door and walked back to the three chairs around the table. Darcy had slipped into his spot, but stood as he approached. Mike sat and Darcy - as always - read him. She sat on the arm of the chair, reached over and rubbed the back of his neck.

Darcy said, "Darren was just telling me about his plan for a lake."

"A lake?"

"Well, it was a bit of a joke. I was just telling Darcy that there's a *ton* of water on Mars. I'm going to mine it - lakes and lakes worth. I didn't mean to say that I'd actually make a lake."

Mike raised an eyebrow. "You should, though."

"Should what?"

"Make a lake. Why not?"

Darren blinked. "Uh - wow."

"Do it. You've told me before that you've got simple tastes. Maybe now that we've got a new world - and you're the richest man in it - you should do something crazy."

Darren thought about this for a moment. "Maybe I will - but make me a promise, Mike."

"What's that?"

"If I do make a lake, promise me that you'll come out and go fishing in it with me some time."

Mike looked at Darren. The guy was clearly reaching out to him. He realized he wasn't angry at Darren - he was frustrated and angry with himself. What else was new? He should rise to the occasion. Mike stuck out his hand. "You've got a deal."

Darren shook it.

Darcy filled the silence. "So, Darren, you're going to build a lake on Mars. Any word on what the Dogs are going to do with their wealth?"

Darren said "Actually, yes. Now that the BuSuR euthanasia teams are a few million kilometers away, a lot of them are talking about having families."

Mike hadn't been expected that answer. "Families. Really?"

Darren nodded. "Yeah, most of them are off anaphrodisiacs. Blue and Aabroo and a dozen others are expecting. The first litters should be delivered shortly after we reach Mars."

Mike spit coffee and choked, then recovered. "LITTERS?"

Chapter 181

Kaspar swallowed, wiped his mouth, and asked, "How do you like the pizza, General?"

Dewitt held up one finger to buy himself a moment as he chewed. Kaspar had ordered tomato sauce, extra mozzarella, and Korean style short rib bits. The weird fusion-cuisine that the expats favored was one of the smaller things about Aristillus he'd had to get used to, but he liked it. He liked it a lot.

Dewitt swallowed his mouthful of cheese, crust, and pork. "It's great. But just call me 'Matthew', now, Kaspar. The Revolution is over."

Kaspar smiled and shook his head. "It's not that easy - to the people here, you're always going to be 'General.'"

Dewitt frowned slightly. "Actually, it is that easy. I'm done. It's time for me to learn how to plow a field."

Kaspar looked at him oddly. "Plowing? No, you've proven that you're a leader. Even in a free society the people want -"

Dewitt interrupted him. "You remember the last time we sat here eating pizza?"

Kaspar nodded. "Before the Revolution and the Launch. Five months ago? Six?"

"Seems longer, doesn't it?" Dewitt pointed with his half eaten slice to the fountain in the middle of the courtyard. "I recall that the fountain was working the last time we were here."

"Oh, it still works - but the gravity from Gamma's AG is too weak. Even with the pumps on the lowest setting, too much water spills out. With the price of water now I just turned it off." He smiled at a memory.

"Once we land on Mars the fountain will be back - my kids made me promise."

Dewitt got a faraway look in his eye and put his slice down. "Kaspar - that last time we had pizza here, you knew my real name and knew I was undercover. But you didn't turn me in to the Boardroom Group. How did you know? And why didn't you turn us in?"

"Oh, right." He paused, drawing out the tension. Then he smiled as he said, "Senator Linda Haig told us."

Dewitt dropped his bottle of Jaunty Juice and quickly snatched it out of the air before it hit the table. A few blobs of yellow liquid spilled out of the neck and oscillated slowly in the air before landing gently on the pizza box. "What?"

"Well, I didn't know it was Senator Haig at the time. It took some digging to find that out." Kaspar wiped his mouth with a paper napkin. "I told you how back on Earth I was working on the Texas Interconnection/Eastern Interconnection project, and how the Texas rebels ended up targeting some of the substations?"

Dewitt nodded.

"Anyway, during that process, I ended up working with a guy from the FEMA Hardened Infrastructure Department, and out of the blue he contacted me."

"When was this?"

"After you and I had had dinner a few times."

Dewitt nodded. "Go on."

"So, anyway, Steve got in touch with me and told me that you were part of a secret snatch team. I reported the information to my boss Javier."

"So you did tell the Boardroom Group!"

Kaspar shrugged noncommittally. "I told Javier."

"So why wasn't I picked up immediately?"

"Because I *also* told Javier that I trusted you."

Dewitt blinked. "Well. Thank you." He looked down into his lap, and then up again, over steepled fingers. "And how does Senator Haig come into this?"

"After I told Javier, he dug into it. I don't know if that means that he paid private detectives, or if he found some staffers to bribe. Neither would surprise me - you know that he helped break Mike Martin out of jail, back in the day, right?"

"No. I didn't know that."

Kaspar shrugged, as if it wasn't important. "Well, whatever. But the point is that either way, Javier looked into it, and he learned that Steve called me because someone in Linda Haig's office asked him." Dewitt stared at him. "That makes no sense what-so-ever."

Kaspar shrugged. "There are bigger players in this world than me and you, friend. Who knows why people do what they do? I say, ignore it all and enjoy life." He paused, and then pointed at the box. "Do you want the last slice of pizza?"

Chapter 182

2064: Conveyor Belt district, Aristillus, 6.7 million km from Earth

A ball went flying past Mike's face. He looked up with a start and realized that he'd walked into the middle of a wild free-ranging game of street soccer. Mike grumbled at Darcy, "A guy could get hit with a ball -"

Darcy slapped him playfully on the shoulder. "Stop being a bear. This is incredible! No one has ever played soccer in a twentieth g before. We might be watching the creation of a new sport!"

Mike raised one eyebrow. "Soccer is not a sport."

Darcy rolled her eyes. "OK, Tex, whatever you say." She pointed. "Look at that guy, see the way he's doing a flip before he kicks. And that guy? He jumped halfway to the ceiling. Of the tunnel! It's awesome - come on, admit it!"

Mike shrugged. "Maybe it's a little neat."

Darcy looked at him seriously as they continued walking down the center of the vehicle-less tunnel road. "Mike, you've been in a funk for a week. You perked up for a bit after coffee with Darren, but now you're back in it. What's going on?"

"Nothing." He paused, and then raised his head and pointed with his chin "Looks like they've set up another music stage at the festival since yesterday."

"You're not answering my question."

Mike said nothing for a long moment, and then sighed. "Morlock Engineering is gone and the pieces sold off to make good on the Revolution's debts. And in return, I'm left holding a bunch of bonds from the First Bank of Aristillus."

"So?"

"So Mark keeps pressuring me to back his plan."

"His tax plan?"

"Yeah. He wants a one percent sales tax on every transaction to pay bank bondholders."

Darcy laughed. "Mark has been pressing for that since before the invasion. And all the Aristillus media is covering the fact that you're not backing him. So you're not just a hero for winning the war, but for fighting Mark and his bank. So why are you upset?"

He looked at the ground. "Never mind."

Darcy nodded and they walked in silence for a long moment, and then Mike looked over. "I'm not upset. I'm pissed. I'm pissed that I have to choose between legitimizing Mark's government, which I won't do, and being poor."

Darcy let the silence stretch out. "Mike?"

"Mm?"

"How long ago did we meet?"

"Uhh...twelve - no, thirteen - years ago."

Darcy rolled her eyes. "It was fourteen years ago. You remember how?"

"Of course. I was in DC to testify, and you -"

Darcy laughed. "It wasn't 'to testify.' You were under arrest, and you were defending yourself in the CEO Trials. Everything - your warehouses, your machinery, your offices - had already been seized. Your bank accounts were frozen. You were facing life in jail. Do you remember what you told the Secretary of Commerce in open court?"

Mike smiled even now, almost a decade and a half later. "Yeah. I -"

Darcy held up a hand. "No, I don't need to hear it again. Think of my delicate ears."

Mike smiled more broadly. "But, yeah, I remember. What's your point?"

"The point, Mike Martin, is I believed in you when you were a penniless about-to-be-convicted-felon facing a life sentence. The fact that even when you were on that stand, you had that much fight in you - well, anyway. That was fourteen years ago. What have you accomplished since then?"

Mike said, "I know what you're saying, but Morlock is -"

Darcy shook her head then put her hand on his arm. "I'm not talking about Morlock. I never cared about your company or the money that came with it. I cared about the drive of the lunatic *behind* it all. Here's what you've done in the last fourteen years: you and Javier bribed your way out of jail during the CEO Trials, you hooked up with Ponzie, outfitted the first ship, begged and borrowed your way to owning a TBM-"

"Yeah, but -"

"Let me finish. You established Aristillus. You helped John's Team rescue the Dogs from genocide. And then, as if that wasn't enough, you saw the Revolution coming and you laid the groundwork to win it." She gave him a hard stare. "And because of all that, you've rescued nearly a million people from tyranny and are leading them to build a new world. That hokey phrase 'with freedom for all'? You've done it. THAT, Michael Martin, is what you've accomplished in the last fourteen years."

Mike grinned a bit. Raised his eyebrows. "You know, when you put it that way, maybe I've done OK."

Darcy smiled at his understatement, but then grew serious. "You've done the impossible. I don't care if you're penniless."

"Well, I wasn't really worried that *you* were worried -"

"I know. I'm saying that *you* shouldn't care if you're penniless."

"Don't give me that hippie crap that money doesn't matter -"

"Money doesn't matter - accomplishment does. But even if you insist that money does matter, I have no doubt that you'll be rich and powerful again, if you want to."

"You're saying you'd be OK with me playing chess in the park and writing my memoirs for the rest of my life?"

"Absolutely." Darcy smiled. "But I bet that if you tried it you'd be bored inside of a week."

Mike shrugged. "Maybe." The two of them walked down the middle of the street in companionable silence. Suddenly Darcy, without warning, started skipping - literally skipping - along, bouncing high in the air on each hop.

He shook his head. What a goofball. She saw him looking. "What?"

He smiled. "You."

"Hey, you won your revolution. Why *shouldn't* I dance?" She laughed at her own joke and skipped ahead.

Chapter 183

2064: Belmont Homes, Aristillus, 6.7 million km from Earth

Hugh sat lightly on the couch - almost floating above it, really - and picked up the remote.

It was right where he'd left it. He chuckled darkly. The Aristillus situation was shitty in every way. With one exception - at least Louisa wasn't around to always grab the remote first.

He turned on the wallscreen and checked his inbox.

Friends folder first. Still no messages from Allyson. Hugh wondered again if she had gotten away on a PK ship or if she had died in the fighting. He'd checked the Aristillus public records and hadn't seen her name. He hoped that meant that she'd gotten away - but why no emails from her? Was she in some military facility being debriefed?

No, the folder was empty, except for Louisa's last email from during the assault. "Hooked up with PK forces. Evac on ship ASAP. See you on Earth if you make it out." He shook his head. That was Louisa to a 't.' Nothing personal, no help, no concern for him. "If you make it out." He shook his head. He'd been saving the email for a week now, but he didn't know why. He clicked, and the message disappeared. The folder was empty.

Over to "mother" folder. He'd cleared it out just two days ago, but it was again overflowing. A dozen press releases about her presidential run. Five or six emails from Jim Allabend that she'd forwarded, proposing various derogatory statements about the DoD military leadership and asking if they were supportable. And two - just two - inquiring about his health and safety. Hugh pursed his lips. He'd bet that both of those had been composed by mother's personal assistant Kerri.

Kerri, who was also responsible for buying his birthday and Christmas presents, at least since mother's older assistant Lacey had moved on to a think-tank.

Then there were the four personal messages that clearly HAD been written by mother - imperious commands to do more investigative reporting that would highlight the president and the DoD's failure. He shook his head. He'd *told* her that he needed to stay inside the apartment, away from the mobs and whatever revolutionary "justice" they were doling out.

He scanned the inbox one more time. Still no response from mother to his inquiries about Allyson. He decided to fire off an email to Kerri; maybe she could find something out. He rubbed his face. He was so alone here, in the apartment by himself. He wished that Allyson was here, but since she wasn't he really hoped she'd made it back to Earth OK.

He closed the email tool and pushed himself off the couch. One long hop in the low gravity took him to the kitchen. He rummaged through the cabinets and fridge. There were no more burgers in the freezer and the vegetables in the fridge were limp and wilted. He grabbed a bottle of Jaunty Juice - the last - and an open bag of chips from the counter.

Hugh stood at the kitchen counter and pushed stale and greasy chips into his mouth, and swallowed without tasting.

What was he going to do?

All of his political contacts were back on Earth, moving further and further away each second. He couldn't leave the apartment. At least not yet. There was almost certainly a warrant out for his arrest, by one of those private armies. There had to be. He'd been growing out his beard. When it was done he'd leave, and try to pass as one of the flood of new expats that had arrived in what the newsgroups called "the Exodus." With the libertarian nutcases running

Aristillus maybe it could work - maybe he could get by with a fake name and no identity papers.

But what was he going to do for money?

He'd blown his entire trust fund in the betting markets, trying to feed misleading information to the expat militia commanders. He'd felt heroic doing it - but when the trades settled and everyone realized that there hadn't been a PK invasion in Little Boston, his account had been at zero. He'd known that was how the markets worked, but he hadn't cared. The Peace Keepers were going to win the battle, and he'd have a quick journey home and then a round of interviews about how he'd helped win the day. God, if only things had gone that way - right now he'd resting at home or at the family place on the Vineyard, waiting for his offer letter from DC Minute.

That plan was dead now.

Instead, he was stuck in Aristillus, without a penny to his name...and probably with a price on his head. He had no friends or contacts. Except, of course, his mom, who was too distracted to read his emails – to do anything other than send him inane orders to support her political machinations.

He reached his hand into the chips bag and it crinkled. He fished around. Empty. He crumpled it up and threw it away, not even making sure it went into the correct recycling bin. His fingers were greasy and he felt bloated and gross.

He rubbed his hands against his shirt, and picked up the bottle of juice.

He looked around the kitchen. He was almost out of food, and the lease on the apartment itself was up in another week and a half.

He was entirely alone, millions of kilometers from his nearest friend or ally, and -

He heard the beep of the front door, and then the creak of the door opening.

He whirled.

This was it.

They'd come for him.

He put the bottle of Jaunty Juice down on the counter, and walked out into the living room, hands over his head.

The front door opened and in through it -

He blinked. "Louisa?"

Louisa stared at him. "Hugh?"

Chapter 184

2064: Conveyor Belt district, Aristillus, 6.7 million km from Earth

Mike and Darcy had reached the Conveyor Belt District when Darcy leaned in. "I'm supposed to meet Kathryn for coffee. Catch you back at Javier's place?"

"Sure." He gave her a quick kiss and watched her skip away.

Behind him a band was tuning up on the stage. He turned to watch. The shirtless would-be guitar god was striking poses as he practiced power chords, to the adulation of his female fans and the good-natured shit-giving of the male audience members. The off-shift miners, solar panel techs, and equipment operators seemed to be in a generally good mood.

Of course they were. The PKs had destroyed so much equipment and infrastructure in their stupid invasion that there was work for everyone who wanted it. And, heck, given the need to haul wreckage, vacuum up grit, and build vast solar farms which were even now being extended out from Aristillus like huge wings, there was probably high-paying overtime for everyone.

Javier and he had discussed this the night before: broken windows might be terrible for an economy, but they were good for social cohesion. The huge influx of people who'd arrived in the Exodus could've been a source of instability if they were jobless. He grimaced at the idea of hundreds of thousands of hungry people and what might flow from it. Rioting. Marxism. Democracy.

The only problem with paying people to fix things was that money didn't come from thin air. At that, Mike smiled to himself. Being bankrupt wasn't a ton of fun, but at least at the Boardroom Group meetings now, he could plead poverty. Mark Soldner, Karina Roth, and the others were finding out what it was like to dig deep in their own pockets

His smile slipped away. There was also a downside to his poverty - and that was poverty. He was going to have to fix that. But how? Opportunity was everywhere, he knew. So look for people with problems, and figure out how to solve them.

He looked around at the crowd of laborers, engineers, new immigrants. They needed space to live. Water to drink. Farms to grow better food. Suburbs. Office space. Sports fields and parks. Or, hell - Darren had mentioned his DNA archive - what about a wildlife preserve, like his old ranch but bigger? How much would people pay to visit Africa or Australia?

With the D-series TBMs, if he'd ever had a chance to build them, he could be poised to take advantage of that and rebuild his fortune.

Or, hell, if he'd managed to hang onto his C-class TBMs, he could still be in the game, the very second Aristillus landed.

But he didn't have TBMs. Damn it. He clenched a fist. He needed working capital. If only the Revolution had come a year later - or five! He'd have the D-class TBMs up and running.

He scowled and turned away from the stage. Darcy was right - he wasn't at all cut out for writing his memoirs or playing chess. He wanted to *do* something. He wanted -

"Mike?"

Mike blinked and looked down at the small Nigerian girl next to him.

"Hi...uh." She was familiar. How did he know her? "Wait, don't tell me, it's..."

"It's Ewoma! You used to eat at my family's restaurant, Benue River."

Of course! "Ah, sorry, Ewoma, I didn't recognize you."

"It might be my new haircut."

He looked at her hair. It was in pigtails now. "Did it used to be loose?"

"Yes." She smiled, as if happy that he'd remembered.

He didn't have the heart to tell her that he'd been guessing.

She continued, "I tried it a couple different ways over the last week, and my tips are highest when I've got pigtails." As if it was an explanation she added, "A/B testing."

Mike shook his head - retail would always be a mystery to him. "A lot has happened since I last saw you. How have you been?"

"I've been great. I got a dog!"

"Congratulations!"

"Thanks. But I think you've had more excitement than I have."

"Yeah, you could say that -"

"It was really awesome the way you didn't crack when the PKs captured you."

"Uh - thanks. I guess." Mike furrowed his brow. "But how did you -"

"Oh, I watched the docudrama. Although I don't think they should have had Jim Lawson play you. He's too Bollywood for my taste."

"Docu - wait - what?"

"Never mind. So, anyway, do you want a snack?"

Mike realized Ewoma was standing next to something - an improvised food cart? It was an equipment pallet with a few boxes strapped to it, a heating unit tack welded in place, and several large slabs of what looked like steel decking planks to ballast the whole thing in the light gravity.

Improvisation everywhere. It reminded him of the jury-rigged equipment they'd used in the first tunnels. He approved.

"Actually, I *am* sort of hungry. What've you got?"

"For kebabs, we've got onion-and-pepper, chicken, and goat. For side dishes, we've also got boiled yam and grilled yam. And to drink we've got water or beer."

Mike was about to blindly order the goat kebabs before remembering how crazy prices had been recently.

"How much for goat kebabs?"

She looked offended. "Whatever you want is on the house!"

"I'll pay. So how much?"

"Prices are marked on the side, there."

Mike saw the price list and raised his eyebrows.

Ewoma smiled mischievously. "If you're feeling poor, I recommend the boiled yams. Or I could treat you to -"

"I'm not so poor I'm going to eat yams." He paused. "Not yet, at least." He looked at the menu. Pricey, but not that bad. "Give me two chicken skewers, and a beer."

Ewoma made change, handed Mike the skewers and the bottle of Mineshaft Ten, and then said her goodbyes and moved on through the crowd. Up on the stage the guitarist was still posing and doing licks, but the audience was growing impatient.

He was getting impatient too, and was thinking about leaving when Ewoma came back into view a few minutes later. "Hey, Ewoma!"

She looked up. "More chicken?"

"No." He gestured with his full hands, showing that he still had plenty. "I just realized I should ask - did your family, and your restaurant come through all this -" he gestured around "- OK ?"

"The family is fine, but the restaurant was destroyed in the fighting."

"I'm happy about the family, and - but, wait, how are you serving food? Are you working for someone else?"

Ewoma took a moment to sell beer and skewers to two other revelers and then turned back to Mike. "No, we had enough of that back on Earth. Mom and Dad are renting half of a Mexican restaurant's kitchen until we get done rebuilding."

"And you're the mobile arm, eh?"

Ewoma smiled again. She was good at that - her bright white teeth lit up her face. "No, I'm on my own. I buy food from mom and dad and sell it at a mark-up at the music festival every night." Another two customers walked up to her and she smiled apologetically. "Talk more later!"

Mike nodded. Smart kid. She was avoiding all the overhead of manufacturing, and just arbitraging prices between two locations.

He thought it over for a moment. *Really* smart kid. She didn't have to deal with any of the bullshit around supplies, labor, or equipment break-down. The headaches he'd had from operating the TBMs alone...

Mike froze midstep.

What had Darren said a while back? Something about trade with Earth?

The idea hit him all at once.

One of the chicken skewers fell from his hand.

Behind him the band launched into their song - some sort of metal ballad - but Mike didn't hear it.

He'd been thinking small.

If he was going to arbitrage goods, he was going to need a ship. A big one.

The transfer orbit from Mars to Earth and back took long enough that they'd probably have to grow their own food as they went, with some sort of hydroponics setup. Could Amber's Grains or Wong Farms run that for him? How much space was that going to take? As the plans exploded in his head he realized that the word "ship" was too small for what he needed.

The lead singer growled out the lyrics. "There's atmosphere and topsoil here but water's all too rare." The crowd recognized the song and a cheer went up. Mike looked around distractedly and started walking to the edge of the crowd.

No, not a ship, per se.

His model shouldn't be the old ocean-going ships that they'd repurposed for the Earth–Moon run; his model should be the city of Aristillus, as it was today. A big chunk of rock, with tunnels inside for living space and cargo.

An asteroid maybe. Or - hm - a chunk of Phobos or Deimos. A god-damned flying mountain.

Questions and ideas started bubbling up faster and faster.

"There's atmosphere and topsoil here, water's all too rare."

He'd need solar farms for power - he could reuse the "solar wings" idea that the people of Aristillus were building now.

How to build it? Could he rent some of his old TBMs from Darren or one of the other new owners?

Would his old employees follow him?

Gamma wasn't going to need the batteries and AG drive units that had launched Aristillus - could he get those on the cheap?

The band's guitars wailed. "Hard land, Moon or Mars. Hard land, among the stars."

Where was he going to get financing for all of this? He needed to talk to someone who'd made a lot of money recently. Darren, maybe? Or could he get a better deal elsewhere?

Mike walked for a moment and then pulled out his phone and dialed. On the third ring it was answered.

He covered his other ear with one hand and shouted into the phone. "Blue?"

Chapter 185

2064: Justa Gym, Aristillus, 7.2 million km from Earth

Mike grunted as he pushed the barbell up against the strain of the elastic bands. He reached lockout on his final rep, lowered the bar into the cage's J-hooks, and then sat up and wiped sweat from his forehead. "So capital punishment is entirely forbidden?"

Father Alex shook his head. "Well, not *entirely*. The Church doesn't like it, but it is within the purview of the legitimate state."

"Well, I don't think that there is such a thing as a legitimate state."

Father Alex sighed. "Yes, Mike. You've made that very clear. And in turn I've been clear that I'm sympathetic to your view. Most states that you and I have seen in our lives have not been legitimate - "

"Saying that to me is fine, but why don't you say that somewhere more public?"

"I'm not here in Aristillus to help you with PR for your libertarian society, Mike. I'm here to research the Dogs and Gamma."

Mike shrugged. "Your loss." He pointed to the bar. "Want to work in a set?"

Father Alex shook his head. "I swam earlier. I'm good."

Mike shrugged. "So the good news is that capital punishment can be legitimate."

Father Alex scowled. "*Good* news?" He shook his head. "Forget the question of legitimacy. Can you honestly tell me that you want these men dead, Mike?"

"They locked me in a cage for six months during the CEO Trials, and they would have gladly kept me there for life. Then they tried to do it again during our revolution. If they don't care about my life or freedom, why should I care about theirs?"

"So your argument is that you intend to live down to their standard?"

Mike took a sip from his water bottle. "This isn't about me. The point is that they came *here*, to a place that we built with our own hands. *They* attacked *us*. Just to steal some gold to prop up their filthy little regime - for what? Another year? Another six months? And look at the results. How many people did they kill? How many lives' worth of construction and building did they casually destroy?"

Father Alex sat down on a nearby bench and leaned forward, elbows on knees. "I asked you if you wanted to live down to their standard, and that's your answer? Just a longer version of 'yes'?"

Mike scowled. "Even if I accepted your worldview - and I'm not saying I do - even in your framework, there's a place for justice. Prisons, executions under some circumstances, right? It sounds like you're trying to construct a higher standard for me than you are for everyone else."

"Did you read the document I mailed you?"

"Yes."

Father Alex raised an eyebrow. "Really?"

Mike shrugged. "I skimmed it."

"Skimmed it?! Mike, I didn't send you the entire catechism. I didn't even send you all of Section One. I just gave you one article. One! Given that you asked me for advice I'd have thought you'd be interested in the advice I gave."

Mike looked away in chagrin.

Father Alex shook his head. "Here's the important part." He closed his eyes and recited from memory.

"Authority does not derive its moral legitimacy from itself. It must not behave in a despotic manner, but must act for the common good as a moral force based on freedom and a sense of responsibility."

He opened his eyes and stared at Mike. "Do you at the very least agree with that?"

Mike pursed his lips and said "Maybe." He looked at the clock. It had been two minutes; he leaned back against the bench and grabbed the bar for another set.

Father Alex sighed again. "The next paragraph is relevant. I don't have 1903 memorized but it's something like 'Authority is exercised legitimately only when it seeks the common good of - I think it's 'the people' - and if it employs morally..." he stumbled, then recovered "...morally licit means to attain it.'"

Mike took his hands off the bar "What does that last part, about 'morally licit means' mean?"

"Would you chop a child's hand off if you caught him stealing from an apple cart?"

"Of course not."

"Glad to hear it. What if it was an adult?"

Mike hedged. "There aren't any legal service provider contracts that specify -"

Father Alex blew air out between his lips in exasperation. "Oh, stop spouting your crazy anarchocapitalism for a minute and forget the phrase 'legal service providers.' Let's say you're both the owner of the apple cart and the one in charge of making legal decisions. Do you chop the adult's hand off for stealing an apple?"

Mike took his hands off the bar and sat up, the set of lifting forgotten. "No, hang on. If you had two legal service providers, the second one would try to negotiate the punishment -"

"Damn it, Mike, this is a moral question, not a read-the-fine-print question. Is it legitimate - MORALLY LEGITIMATE - to chop off someone's hand for stealing an apple, even if he signed a document agreeing to that punishment for that crime? Yes or no!"

Mike grimaced. These theoretical questions were bullshit.

Father Alex rubbed his chin, then started again, more softly this time. "Mike, I think your hard-line stance is as much performance art as it is actual politics. So, just the two of us here. Real world - you own the apple cart. You own an axe. Would you *actually* cut someone's hand off?"

"Performance art, huh?" Mike felt a hint of a smile touch his face. No wonder Darcy liked Father Alex so much - the man had his number. He sighed. "OK, maybe I wouldn't actually cut the guy's hand off."

Father Alex arched one eyebrow. "Good. Why not?" He leaned forward. "Come on, play Devil's Advocate. Generate all the possible reasons for not cutting his hand off despite a signed contract. I know you're smart enough to defend any position, so come on, give it your all."

Mike shrugged. "Well, maybe he had reasons to steal the apple that made it less bad."

"Good. What else?"

"Maybe we're not 100% sure he did it."

"Despite the video evidence?"

"Who knows what the video shows. Maybe the video was edited."

"What else?"

"Cutting his hand off is barbaric - it's what they do in the Caliphate."

Father Alex shot his hand forward and pointed. "Ah-ha! Yes. It's barbaric! That is what I was looking for. Mutilation is an affront to human dignity. If you set yourself up to carve up human bodies, you are disrespecting the integrity of the human form, you are setting yourself up as an ultimate authority instead of just a provisional temporal authority." He paused. "And."

"And?"

"And, most importantly, you can't take it back!"

Mike sat in silence a moment. "You're arguing that capital punishment - even for people who tried to steal from us, enslave us, and kill us - is like cutting off a hand?"

"No. I'm arguing that it's worse."

Mike looked away. "Pfft."

"No. Don't 'pfft' me. Enough of your performance art. It's worse, and you know it. Why?"

Mike reluctantly answered, "Because instead of destroying a hand, you're destroying a life."

Father Alex shrugged, as if to say, "The words are coming out of your mouth, not mine."

Mike shook his head to try to clear it of the unwelcome idea. Leroy, these PKs - they'd killed people. Friends of his. They deserved to die. Father Alex's point was valid, in its own little context, but it ignored the bigger context. "That's bullshit, Father. Fournier and the PKs violated laws of war. Thousands of people died because of them."

"You've already convinced me that cutting off someone's hand is barbaric, Mike. How does telling me that there are other barbarians out there refute your initial argument?"

Mike grimaced. This was bullshit all the way down. It was unfair that these people could invade Aristillus, destroy so many lives, and get away with it. He was sick of this conversation. He looked at the clock. "Damn it. I've cooled down. I might as well bag the last set of bench and move on to squats." He pulled the bench out of the cage and began to loop more elastic bands around one end of the bar.

Father Alex moved to the other end. "What weight?"

"100 kilos."

Alex nodded and looped four bands around the far end of the bar.

Mike stepped into the squat cage, started to duck under the bar, and then stopped and turned. "On the other hand, you do realize that keeping them locked up and feeding them costs thousands of grams a month. I don't have the money for that." Mike turned and slipped under the bar, and then stood straight. The weight on his shoulders felt good.

Father Alex furrowed his brow. "Mike, you realize that you can't kill the PKs because it's convenient."

Mike lowered himself toward the floor and concentrated on keeping his back straight.

"Mike, you realize that, don't you?"

Mike grunted as he pushed himself upright against the force.

"Mike?"

Chapter 186

2066: Johnson Clinic Health Center, Aristillus, 7.5 million km from Earth

Samir listened as the doctor directed him through a series of steps. "Raise both arms from your sides until they're horizontal...now move your arms forward. Good. Now touch your hands in front of you."

His son stood in a corner of the small office and translated. Step by step Samir followed the instructions.

The young doctor appraised Samir's movements and raise one eyebrow. "Well, I'm impressed. You've got full mobility back in the shoulders, and -" he gestured to the wall screen "- your blood work looks great. You can put your shirt back on. You can cancel your last appointments - we don't need to see you again." Again Samir's son translated.

Samir listened, nodded, and reached for his shirt. As he shrugged it on, he saw the puckered scars on his torso from the PK bullets and knives stretching and tugging as he moved his arms.

Samir's son asked, "Are there any instructions my dad has to follow?"

"Yeah - tell him to slow down. No more gun battles - he needs to retire. Enjoy his golden years."

The son nodded.

Samir turned to him. "What did he say?" The son relayed it.

Samir surged to his feet and crossed his arms. "Tell the doctor that he is crazy! Tell him that there's a big world down there -" He gestured down through the floor of the hospital, toward Mars "- and I'm only eighty-two years old!"

"Dad, maybe the doctor's right - maybe you should let some younger people do the dangerous stuff for a change?"

Samir barked a laugh.

Chapter 187

2066: Northern Logistics Office, Aristillus, 7.7 million km from Earth

Colonel Lemmons rolled over on the cheap foam mattress, scratched his lower back, and clicked on his tablet to bring up the next page of the new president's speech. He scanned it and started to click to the next page, but realized he'd reached the end. Vague statements, promises that boiled down to nothing. The usual. He put the slate down with a sigh and looked at where Colonel Loomis was sitting at a desk playing chess against Leroy Fournier.

Thank God Fournier shut up when he was playing chess. A dozen times over the months Lemmons had decided that if the man didn't stop his bragging and insane self-regarding pronouncements that he'd beat him into silence. Thankfully he'd managed to restrain himself every time so far, but if he was locked up with him much longer, he swore, he was going to hurt the man.

What did it say about the situation here that the person he hated most was - or, he guessed, had been – his ally?

He shook his head. Say what you will about the rebels, but they had some honor. They shouldn't have rebelled against legitimate government, but he had to admit that they'd fought for what they believed in. Fournier, though - the man was a snake.

Lemmons let his eyes drift up to the ceiling tiles of the conference room the colonels had staked out for their quarters.

Major Saltner, two mattresses over, put down his book - an actual hard-copy one he'd gotten from somewhere. "Bored?"

Lemmons raised his eyebrows theatrically. "Yeah. Don't know why - there's so much to do."

Major Saltner ignored the well-worn joke and tilted his head toward Lemmons' discarded slate. "Anything interesting going on in the world?"

Lemmons shook his head. "No." He paused. "You know, the first few weeks we were locked up, the news blackout kept me optimistic. If the expats wouldn't let us read anything, it must be for a reason. The rescue mission must be on its way, right? Or the expats were running into some problem they couldn't handle, and maybe they'd have to ask our help, treat us as equals. You know what I mean? But then -"

Saltner nodded. "But then they gave us slates."

"Exactly." Lemmons sighed, then fell silent.

After a long pause Saltner and Lemmons fell into desultory conversation about the relative merits of the Yankees and the Cardinals, aiming to kill the hour until lunch was delivered. They'd just gotten around to discussing pitchers when a private knocked on the conference room door.

Lemmons sat up. "Enter."

The door opened. "Colonel! The expats are conducting exit interviews!"

"Exit interviews? What does that mean?"

* * *

Lemmons' stomach rumbled. It was almost 4pm and there hadn't been lunch today.

The expats were processing them in order of rank, and had started with the privates. The Northern logistics office the expats were using as an interim prison had gotten emptier and emptier over the last few hours, background chatter dying down to a level Lemmons usually only heard at night.

Now there was no sound except for the slow swish of the environmental fans and the directionless hum of electronic equipment somewhere.

Lemmons looked around at the four other colonels. It was down to just the five of them.

Then the expats called his name.

* * *

"You've seen the video, and you've had a chance to read the manual - do you have any questions?"

Lemmons scowled. "You honestly expect me to sign away my loyalty to the US and the United Nations?"

The ADF interviewer shook his head. "You don't have to sign away your citizenship or indicate any disloyalty. You just have to state that you're resigning from the military and swear that you won't harm people or property in Aristillus -"

"I'm not going to sign away my rights."

The interviewer looked perplexed. "We don't want you to sign away your rights; you'll be entirely free to speak your mind, argue against anyone you want -"

"Will I be free to vote?"

The interviewer blinked. "Ah - there's not really a government here, so I don't-"

"So no right to vote then."

The interviewer turned up his hand. "Uh - I guess not. No."

Colonel Lemmons straightened in his chair and recited, "If I am captured, I will continue to resist by all means available. I will accept neither parole nor special favors from the enemy."

The interviewer fixed him with a gaze for a few seconds, and then shrugged and turned off his slate. "OK, fine. You can join the others who decided against the offer. Hopefully we'll find a way to repatriate you in the next few years." He pointed with his chin to the two doors that led out of the room. "Left one."

Lemmons stood up crisply, refusing to nod or speak to his captor, and walked to the indicated door, opened it, and stepped through. On the far side a man in the uniform of the Aristillus Defense Force pointed down the corridor. Lemmons marched as formally as he could in the ultra-low gravity, and then finally gave up and reverted to the lazy loping movement they'd all adopted over the past few months. At the end of the corridor he opened the door and let himself into another conference room.

In the room were two colonels, three majors, and a smattering of lower- ranked troops.

Lemmons looked around, confused. "Where's everyone else?"

Colonel Loomis shook his head sadly. "This is everyone, Lem. All the loyal troops."

Lemmons looked around. "Where's Fournier? Don't tell me that they let HIM out of prison?"

Loomis shrugged. "No idea."

"Well, at least we don't have to listen to his shit anymore."

Chapter 188

2066: Gargoyle Engineering office, Aristillus, Areostationary Mars Orbit

Mike leaned back in his office chair and ran one hand over the battered arm. It was one of the few things he'd salvaged from the Morlock office, probably because the bank had thought that it was worthless.

They weren't wrong.

Still, he liked it.

The wallscreen showed video shot by a rover parked on the rim of the new crater. A long line of automated dump trucks climbed the spiral roadbed from the bottom, carting rubble to the east. At the bottom of the crater, hundreds of bulldozers and loaders worked to load Martian rock, fragmented by gravel boat orbital bombardment, into the never-ending procession of empty trucks.

Mike smiled. It had taken him years to get over the incongruity of watching yellow machines from the heartland of North America carting dusty gray lunar regolith. No sooner had that started to seem pedestrian than he was watching them haul slabs of rusty Martian rock under an alien yellow sky.

Another three months and Aristillus would have a new home, gray rock nestling up against red, sealed in place by millions of kilograms of cement that was even now being prepared in vast kilns to the south of the landing site.

A timer alarm went off and Mike looked away from the video. Twenty minutes until dinner with Darcy - and this was a schedule even more important than the construction project down below.

Nineteen minutes later he was in the lobby of the Topside Cafe. He craned his head and looked around. He'd read the reviews and viewed pictures online, but it was more impressive in person. The Crystal-Palace-like structure vaulting overhead, the huge windows, the view of Mars - wow. He looked more closely at the beams of the dome. Huh. That was a clever hack - they way the lip on each one cradled the vacuum-resistant glass sheets -

His reverie was interrupted by someone clearing a throat. He looked down, and then coughed, embarrassed. "Oh, hey, Darce."

"You were admiring my dress, right?"

Mike grinned, knowing he was busted, but decided to play it for effect. "Babe, your dress is absolutely the most stunning thing in this entire place." He paused. "Right after the extruded aluminum -"

Darcy gave him a faux reproachful look and he put up his hands in surrender. "The dress would look good on most women, but on you, it looks amazing."

Darcy beamed and accepted his kiss before the maitre d'hotel greeted them and escorted them to a table.

* * *

Mike cut the last piece of the torte in half with his fork. He left one bite for Darcy and speared the other, swallowed, smiled in appreciation. Darcy took her last bite and in unplanned unison they each leaned back in their chairs. Overhead Mars loomed large. A few minutes passed in companionable silence as they watched the clouds of dust roll in over the western end of Valles Marineris.

Mike shifted in his seat. He was procrastinating. He steeled himself, and then looked down from the dome and spoke. "You know Father Alex convinced me on the PK pardons."

"It's been all over the news. And I think I might have heard about it once or twice from a certain someone."

"Yeah, well, my point isn't about that decision. My point is that I thought I could finally get Father Alex out of my hair by agreeing to all of his Just War stuff..."

"And?"

"Didn't work."

Darcy looked surprised. "Really? What's he bothering you about now?"

"So, apparently the catechism isn't *just* about when you're allowed to kill your enemies." He fidgeted. "Turns out that there's *also* a chapter in there about marriage -"

Darcy started to grin, then forced it off her face.

Mike paused. "You put him up to this, didn't you?"

Darcy tried hard to look innocent, and then admitted, "After the Nan Garde experience Javier told me I needed to talk to someone."

"So Javier and you conspired against me." Mike narrowed his eyes. "Just like the good old days."

Darcy's smile slipped back onto her face.

Mike shifted in his seat again. "So anyway. We're getting married." He paused again. "You and me, I mean. Not me and Father Alex."

Darcy's smile got wider. "Mike Martin, that is the most romantic proposal I have ever heard."

Mike shrugged and smiled deviously. "Could be that I'll get better with practice. You know, Father Alex isn't the only spiritual adviser in Aristillus. Mark Soldner's group may not believe in plural marriage, but there are some LDS fundamentalists in Aristillus. Maybe my technique'll be better by the time I get to sister wife three or four -"

His teasing was interrupted by Darcy's hard punch to his left shoulder. Mike grinned wider and laughed and Darcy dropped her arm and placed her hand back in her lap, resuming her ladylike posture. She grew serious. "There's one condition, though."

Mike blinked. "Condition? Condition on what?"

"On me saying yes."

"On you - wait. I thought - OK. What's your condition?"

"Mark Soldner and his folks are talking about 'populating the new land', and the Puppies are all over the news. And -" She looked at Mike and raised her eyebrows "- Father Alex and I agree that the whole solar system shouldn't get filled up with just Dogs and Mormons."

Mike coughed, and took a sip of his water to play for time. "Are you saying what I think you're saying?"

"If you think I'm saying 'you've got to promise me kids,' then yes."

Mike thought for a moment. "How many?"

"Four." She paused. "At least."

Mike took a second sip then spoke. "One condition back at you."

"And that is?"

"No more navigation runs into hostile territory. Ever."

"Done."

Mike realized he was smiling like an idiot. He'd gotten the better side of the deal.

He saw that Darcy had the same silly smile plastered on her face and realized that she was probably thinking the same thing.

He reached out and took her hand and, still smiling, looked up through the dome.

The sun coming up over the edge of Aristillus made the stars invisible. The sky was black and Mars hung overhead. Mike smiled in satisfaction - soon a city would glow there, turning a dark planet bright.

THE END

...which is to say, a beginning...

Chapter 189

2064: Florence ADX, Fremont County, Colorado

General Restivo flipped through the real estate listings on the slate. This one - he liked it. Sixty two acres, partially wooded, a small stream, and room enough next to the old barn to put in a goat pen and a chicken coop.

He nodded, thinking about the goats. Two of them - maybe three. Enough so that they never felt lonely. He definitely wanted milk goats, but should he also have a meat goat? Would that be too weird, to cheerfully greet some of your goats every morning of retirement, but know that that *other* goat was destined for the stew pot?

Hm.

No, he didn't like that. No meat goats - just a few for milk. And chickens, of course. He pictured himself standing near the barn. He closed his eyes and imagined the scene. In his mind he turned to his left to look up the path that led past the pump to the farmhouse, and then turned to the right to look at the mountains. He could smell the pine trees and picture the sun peeking out over the white of the snowcaps.

He smiled and enjoyed the sight for a long moment, savoring the morning light, the sound of the rooster's call, the chill in the air that would soon be driven off.

Then he opened his eyes and looked at the concrete wall of the cell.

He tapped the screen of the slate, turning it off. He only had the slate because his lawyer had finally gotten permission to see some of the charges filed against him, and then - through several more petitions - had gotten permission to show Restivo the same documents. Or, at least, heavily redacted versions of them. He still wasn't precisely sure what it was he was being accused of. Was the stuff about violating procurement and staffing rules the actual charge against him, or were those just background details for some conspiracy charge?

With all of the blacked-out sections it was hard to tell.

He sighed. Even if the legal documents were worthless, the real estate listings that his lawyer had tucked into a subfolder were a nice Easter Egg that had brought him a few hours of - if not joy - then at least distraction.

He closed his eyes briefly.

Thank you, God, for Julie McKenzie. She's a good lawyer - and a great human being.

He opened his eyes again. The concrete walls hadn't changed.

He didn't expect they ever would.

Chapter 190

2066: PK Detention Facility, Midway Atoll

There was banging. Loud banging. John woke.

He'd been sleeping a lot recently. Too much, he knew.

He tried to open his eyes. The right was still swollen from the most recent beating and wouldn't open, but the left showed the bright cell. Always bright. Never a break from the damn blue-white glare. After a few days here he'd tried to smash the lights, but they were too far above him. And even if he could jump that high - oh, to be back in lunar gravity - the chain didn't have that much slack.

The banging grew closer - one of the guards was using his truncheon to whack each cell door. It must be the one he thought of as Mustache. Not the best - that was Curry, who never spoke, but also never taunted - but also not the worst. Garlic and Tattoo - those were the two he hated the most. The ones who amused themselves with random beatings or buckets of cold water.

Even the thought of cold water made John wrap his arms around himself for extra warmth. Where was he, anyway? The flight that brought him here had been interminable - at least 12 hours, maybe more. He'd had a hood on the whole time, but as they'd hustled him across the runway he smelled salt air and tropical trees. The asphalt had been hot under his bare feet.

Twelve hours from the Caribbean - where did that put them? Africa? An island in the Pacific? Somewhere near the Indian Ocean?

For the thousandth time he wondered how it could be so cool here in his cell if the facility was in the tropics. Were they air conditioning this place just to make it miserable, or was it some quirk of construction?

His hands ached as he hugged himself. He looked at them. Unlike his arms and legs, they had no obvious bruises, but the joints still hurt. Some days he just wanted the aches and pains to end. Well. Not some days. All days.

The banging of the truncheon stopped and John looked up with his one good eye. The guard 'Mustache' was standing on the far side of the door, his face visible through the wire-reinforced glass window. The slot in the door opened and Mustache pushed his meal tray through onto the attached shelf.

Normally Mustache just turned and left after the tray was down, but today he spoke. "You're never getting a trial, you know. No one ever comes out of Level Three."

John glared at Mustache through the window, and fought to control himself. A passive face - put on a passive face.

Apparently he succeeded.

Mustache pursed his lips. "Don't you care about that? You're here forever. Until you die." Mustache raised one eyebrow at him, looking for a sign of reaction.

John started to speak. He damned himself for it even as he started, but couldn't stop himself. He did, at least, force himself to mumble. "They'll come for me."

"What?"

He raised his chin and said it louder. "They'll come for me!"

Mustache shook his head and smiled. "No, my friend. No one knows you're here. No one knows your name. No one cares. And besides- they're all gone."

In a final humiliation Mustache gave the food tray a shove, sending it sliding over the edge of the shelf and tumbling to the floor. He laughed slightly and then turned and walked away, his truncheon banging against the empty cells as he went.

'All gone'? What did that mean? Had the PKs assaulted Aristillus? Or nuked the colony?

John fought it, but within minutes he was sobbing.

An hour later, after he'd calmed himself down and the hunger pangs started to war with the aches, John crawled towards the door, dragging his chain behind him. Then he used his fingers to scoop the flavorless pasta and jello off the floor and into his mouth.

Chapter 191

2066: The Den, Aristillus, Areostationary Mars Orbit

Blue sat behind the low table at the front of the room and looked to his left at Duncan and Max. Duncan was looking around the room wide-eyed and grinning, but Max was concentrating on his slate. Blue shook his head. The fact that he and Max were here made a lot of sense - they'd always been two of the leading voices in the Dog community. Duncan, though - Duncan had always had a reputation as a bit of a goof.

A few months ago no one - least of all Blue - would have ever expected him to be sitting up here, helping to decide policy...but in recent weeks the story about the role Duncan's LARP mode had played in the second invasion had spread. And at some point Blue had told the story about how Duncan and Rex had saved them all by reprogramming the mules on Farside to kick at PKs faceplates. And then Max had given more details on Duncan and his "Age of Gothis" idea for evolved rover combat tactics...and before they'd quite realized it, Duncan had status as high as Blue and Max did.

Blue shook his head. Maybe higher.

Blue turned away from Duncan and looked at the audience. The converted warehouse held every Dog in Aristillus. Which meant, really, every Dog that existed. Blue thought - not for the first time - how small and precarious his species' toehold was. Just over 500 of them. 504 when they reached the moon, 503 after Lancy died from a stroke three years ago, 502 after Kuparr was crushed in that industrial accident, and then 501 after the PKs killed Rex. Blue turned his eye to the hundreds of expecting mothers in the crowd. The population would climb soon enough. Ultrasound showed that the average litter was almost three pups, with some mothers carrying up to six. In a few short months there'd be well north of a thousand! Still, the species was far too small, and far too precarious. Longer term, they needed -

He was snapped from his reverie when Duncan whispered to him. "Almost time."

Blue nodded. "Right, sorry." Blue looked down at his slate and reached for his glasses, fumbling as he put them in place. He still wasn't used to the damned things. As soon as trade was reestablished they'd DEFINITELY have to get a laser eye surgery machine.

He scanned his notes, and then looked up and cleared his throat. The din quieted. Blue raised his voice so that the entire room could hear him.

"Everyone. Everyone. Let's call this meeting to order. First, do we have any corrections to the minutes? No? OK, reports of the standing committees. Alphabetically that's...Architectural committee, please."

Spartacus - although Blue still thought of him as 'Spot', his name until he'd changed it after the Revolution - stood. "The architectural committee has concluded that the D-class tunnel boring machines are unlikely to come on line in the next two years, so we've made plans for town development based around C-class tunnels. There's also a minority proposal that we investigate some of the existing properties that have come on the market. There are a few unique choices which we're in a position to afford at current market rates, although-"

The architectural report was still going strong twenty minutes later. Blue caught Duncan's eye and tipped his head, indicating his destination, and slipped out to use the restroom. A few minutes later he was wiping his still-damp paws on his jumpsuit and approaching the warehouse when he heard yelling. He pushed through and heard and saw the full tumult. The audience was yelling, barking, and slapping paws on the floor while Max stood on his rear legs and shouted. What the hell was going on?

Max pounded the table with a paw. "We need to find the John and the other survivors of the Nan Garde mission and rescue them. ...but mere rescue is not enough! We need vengeance."

Blue barked. "Max - Max!"

Max looked at him. "I have the floor. Wait your turn."

The barks of approval and the boos of dissent from the audience grew louder.

"As chairman, I'm taking the floor back."

"I don't relinquish it."

Blue licked his lips, and then turned and scanned the audience for support. Half the Dogs avoided his gaze and the other half looked indecisive. He wasn't going to get help from any of them. He turned back to Max, who was pounding on the table for attention. If Blue wanted to get this meeting under control, he was going to have to do it himself. Blue raised his voice. "Max! We've already discussed this. We don't even know if there ARE any survivors. First we need to -"

Max raised his voice, pitching it for the audience. "We can't wait. *John and the other prisoners* can't wait."

"Can't wait? What are you- "

Max stabbed the air with one paw. "You're right - we can't attack today. But we *can* start planning - and practicing!"

"Wait! Wait! We don't even know if there are prisoners. The UN and US claim that there aren't, and that's consistent with the last images from Deladrier's cameras. Even if there are, we can talk to Father Alex and see what help -"

"Help? Help from humans?" Max turned to the audience. Both of his ears - even the mangled left one -

were pricked to full height with focus and anger. "We don't need help. But we do need to act. We - all of us in this room - are alive today because John assembled The Team and saved us as pups from BuSuR's euthanasia squads. John is a pack-mate. A brother. And we're not going to spare an expense - any expense - to save John -"

Blue shook his head and yelled to be heard over the noise. "No one's talking about money. My point is that we don't even know if he's alive! We have to research it, then if he's alive we negotiate. *if* that fails, *then* we assemble a surgical -"

"The Team saved a lot of us from the Cambridge Lab. John saved those of us in Palo Alto personally. But there weren't enough of them to save the Dogs in Glasgow. And because of that, they are dead. *Dead*. All of us have lost brothers and sisters because The Team didn't have more resources."

Blue tried to yelled over Max. "We don't disagree about any of this, but -"

Max was louder. "We have the resources. We're smarter, we're better at planning. Thanks to your trading and our investments, we've got billions. And now is the time to use it. We're going to rescue John!"

There was a cheer. Max climbed onto his chair.

"We're going to rescue the others!"

Another cheer.

"And we're going to strike down our enemies. Every one of them. What should we do with the PKs guarding John and the other prisoners?" He answered his own question. "Kill them! And what should we do about the people on the Euthanasia Squads?"

A good fraction of the audience took up his response. "Kill them!"

...but there was also dissent.

"What should we do about the Bureau of Sustainable Research?"

More barking, howling, and paw pounding, but also shouts of "No!"

"What should we do about the lab administrators who allowed the Euthanasia?"

More yelling. More outrage. More conflict. A few Dogs pushing and shoving each other.

Blue, eyes wide, looked over the audience. The five hundred Dogs were moving across the carpeted floor, partitioning themselves into two groups.

"What should we do about the legislators who voted to kill us, to wipe out our entire kind?"

Blue looked at Duncan. Duncan had his eyebrows raised in shock and incomprehension. He shook his head and leaned in to yell over the noise. "Don't look at me. I'm good at games and coding. But this? You're the organized one."

Blue nodded. He took a deep breath, climbed onto his chair, and took off his glasses. "Point of order, Mr. Speaker!"

Chapter 192

2066: Zhukovskiy Crater, Lunar Farside

Sean Jay, the Chief Electronic Forensic Archaeologist, stood on the observation platform and looked out through his spacesuit's helmet at his dig site. It looked good - clean, organized. Exactly as he'd planned it.

Greg Knock, one of his section chiefs, stood next to him. "Chief, I think we should move on from grid C-12 to -"

Sean shook his head, and then remembered that the motion wouldn't show in the spacesuit. "No, we'll stick with C-12 for a while longer. The density of fiber-optic bundles looks promising."

"We thought that about A-25, but that was just a signal processing node. I think that C-12 is another signal -"

They were interrupted by a shout over the shared channel. "Chief, you've got to come see this - I think we might have found it."

"Be right there." Sean turned away from Greg and climbed down the ladder. The modular observation platform had been assembled in one of the grid squares, near but not in one of the lanes the bulldozers had cleared through the wreckage of Gamma's Zhukovskiy facility. Sean stepped into the nearest lane and walked purposefully toward square C-25, stepping around the occasional piece of sharp-edged material that the equipment hadn't entirely cleared away. The younger man hurried to catch up, succeeded, and tried awkwardly to make conversation. "It's a shame we had to cut these lanes - so many artifacts were destroyed."

"If we had more time we could take more care. But we don't. Blame Washington, if you want." Sean hoped

---

that his tone made it clear that he didn't want to hear any whining.

The younger man was silent for a few minutes as they walked. "Still, these artifacts are priceless - if we could have obeyed the normal protocols -"

Jesus. This kid. Sean let a precisely calibrated bit of annoyance creep into his voice. "The other Gamma sites are pristine; we can get any anything we need from them - except the cognition banks. And since we know from those sites that the artifacts we want are underground, my decision to plow the lanes was a good one." He let a little more edge slip into his voice. "Don't you agree?"

The section chief was duly chastised. "Yes, of course, Chief."

Only partially mollified, Sean continued, "Watch your tone, Greg - you sound almost like one of those technology-worshiping start-up nerds from fifty years ago. This junk isn't 'priceless', or 'fascinating,' as I've also heard you call it. The Bureau of Sustainable Research sent us here to help prevent Gamma and the expats from starting a Singularity, not to jump-start one ourselves."

Greg nodded. "I'm sorry. You're right, Chief." He paused. "Still, it is kind of ironic that we're planning on fighting Gamma by resurrecting him."

"Not Gamma. Just a copy of Gamma. *Our* copy. And only after we modify it for loyalty."

They turned a corner and Sean saw two space-suited figures - Jones and Ivory - standing and operating one of the scanners. A dozen other team members stood in a circle, watching them. Red cables snaked from the device into an open hatch in the ground.

They'd reached grid square C-25.

The Chief Archaeologist turned away from his section chief to the workers. "What do we know?"

Jones turned away from the console. "It's awesome, chief. Awesome." Sean could hear the smile in his voice. "*Hodie natus est radici frater.*"

"What?"

Jones shook his head. "Old joke. Anyway, this is it. The jackpot. When the nuke went off, it sheared all of the data lines and control lines, but the brain is down there, and it's all intact. We've got it captured like a farm animal in a cage."

The Chief Archaeologist shook his head. "A bad analogy, gentlemen. Farm animals have rights."

Colophon

This book was created with FSF Emacs, Apache OpenOffice, Ubuntu Linux, and various open source fonts, scripts and other tools.

My thanks to all of the hackers who help create and maintain these tools.

Afterword

Picasso noted that "good artists copy but great artists steal".

Amateur artists also steal - there's no getting around the fact that there's a lot of theft in this novel (or, as I prefer to call it: "homage").

References to fiction and literature

The similarity to Heinlein's "The Moon is a Harsh Mistress" is obvious and intentional; reading it was a formative experience for me and helped establish my awareness of and interest in rational anarchism / anarcho capitalism / mutualism / voluntaryism. There are dozens of hat-tips in the text. Readers may note that the Hazel Stone analogue is somewhat darker skinned in my version. And while Ewoma is home-schooled Mike suggests at one point that she might want to attend Meade Prep.

Tom Godwin's "The Cold Equations" is referenced in Darcy's predicament with an overloaded ship. In that same scene, when Darcy whispers to herself "priceless eggs in variable gravity", she's referencing a Moatie line from the Niven and Pournelle's "The Mote in God's Eye" and it's a parallel to a line spoken by Joss Whedon's character Wash in the movie Serenity as he deals with a similar test of his piloting skill.

The name of the ship Deladrier is a small Heinlein in-joke. As is the "RMR" Highway network.

Several ships are named in tribute to the Ships of Ian Banks' Culture universe, except for the retrofitted Liquified Natural Gas tanker "Grace Under Pressure", which is named after a Rush album.

Speaking of Rush leads me to progressive rock, and I note that the minor character Michael Stuart-Test is "listening to EagleGust on his ear-buds" - a small reference to Hawkwind.

John Ross' "Unintended Consequences" certainly inspired a scene or two, including John sniping lumbering PK ninjas from his perch atop a crater wall.

The Dogs owe a debt to Vernor Vinge's "Tines" and to David Brin's "Uplift" series.

As a teen, I stumbled into L Neil Smith's "The Probability Broach". The story didn't make much sense at the time, and I disliked the swipes he took at William F Buckley. It is perhaps understatement to say that my opinions have changed a bit since then.

The scene where the Dogs decide to evolve a set of tactics algorithms for the armed rovers was based on ideas I first encountered when reading about Douglas Lenat and his awesome hack of the Traveller RPG competition "Trillion Credit Squadron" in 1981 and 1982 and encountered again when reading "Genetic Programming: On the Programming of Computers by Means of Natural Selection" by John R. Koza.

It wasn't until I had one character speaking and referring to the influx of refugees from the Earth as "the Exodus" that I realized that much the novel was influenced by Leon Uris' novel of the same title...although I had, at that point, consciously fashioned John and the Dogs' adventures on lunar farside after Moses and the Jews wandering in the desert after leaving Egypt.

The climax of the story, of course, is stolen lock stock and barrel from James Blish. His "Cities in Flight" novels are a bit dated, but still a fun read...ideally with some Boston albums playing in the background.

The scene with Mike eating a peach and concluding that he'll fight and win the war is inspired loosely -

very loosely! - by the poem "This Is Just To Say" by William Carlos Williams.

Mike lifts once or twice at "Justa Gym", which aside from the obvious cheesy pun, is also a passing reference to Steve Justa, author of "Rock Iron Steel: The Book of Strength".

While my story was not directly inspired by them, I would be remiss not to note some similarities in plot device to "The Getaway Special" by Jerry Oltion and "Gilpins Space" by Reginald Bretnor.

The college kid journalists thread owes some debt of inspiration to "Ecotopia: The Notebooks and Reports of William Weston" by Ernest Callenbach.

Political influences

The political philosophy of the book (which is to say, my political philosophy) was influenced strongly by several pieces of writing.

- Robert Heinlein's "The Moon is a Harsh Mistress" (again).
- Robert Nozick's "Anarchy, State, and Utopia".
- Robert Nozick's essay "Why Do Intellectuals Oppose Capitalism?"
- David Friedman's "Machinery of Freedom".
- David Friedman's "Law's Order".
- Bryan Caplan's "The Myth of the Rational Voter".
- James C Scott's "The Art of Not Being Governed" and "Seeing Like a State"
- Albert O Hirschman's "Exit, Voice, and Loyalty".
- "The Catechism of the Catholic Church".

Other writers that have influenced both my opinions and the plot of the novel include:

- Nick Szabo, Timothy C May and Jim Bell from the early days of the "cypherpunks" mailing list
- Neal Stephenson, particularly the "HEAP" project from "Cryptonomicon", which, in fact, led me to form my first corporation, SmartFlix.com.
- Eric S Raymond, particularly his essay "The Cathedral and the Bazaar"
- Thomas Jefferson, particularly the first draft of the Declaration of Independence (and also the watered down second draft that was actually signed).
- Claude Frederic Bastiat
- Alexis de Tocqueville's "Democracy in America", which is a stunning portrait of a free people in a young, risk-taking, participatory culture.
- Robin Hanson, whose writing has informed my thinking on lots of topics around rationality, the singularity, and AIs. While I didn't realize it as I was writing, looking back afterwards there is a lot of subtle stuff around AIs and competition which I larded in through these two novels as a foundation for more developments later in the universe, and much of this bears Hansonian fingerprints.
- Mencius Moldbug, who has expressed well and in public many thoughts on the deficiencies and un-advisability of Democracy that I have only expressed poorly and in private. The scene where Hugh Haig manipulates the futures markets to feed the ADF forces bad information took some inspiration from the debate between Moldbug and Robert Hanson. http://vimeo.com/9262193 http://www.overcomingbias.com/2010/01/my-moldbug-debate.html http://unqualified-

reservations.blogspot.com/2010/01/hanson-moldbug-debate.html

- Radley Balko for documenting the thuggish brutality with which typical American "civil servants" treat the citizens who pay their salaries. Read a handful of his "puppycide" posts and you'll understand the genesis of debates between Blue and Rex in act 3.

- Tyler Cowen. As someone interested in both food and economics, I love everything he writes. In the novel the "Cowen Wiki" - a yelp-like food review website mentioned in passing - is a hat tip.

- Alex Tabarrok

- Reason magazine, which I've subscribed to for around a quarter of a century.

- Barbara Fairchild's "The Bon Appetit Cookbook".

- The "StrategyPage" blog, including this post http://www.strategypage.com/htmw/htproc/articl es/20120606.aspx

- The Moral Foundations Theory of Jonathan Haidt inspired the scene where Mike and Mark Soldner debate law and morality

- At one point the Dogs reference Steven Pinker.

References to historical personages

- In Dewitt's speech to the boardroom group when he says "We will to wage this war, tunnel by tunnel, with all our might and with all the strength that God can give us. We're going to wage war against a tyranny. What is our aim? Two words. Victory. Victory and freedom. Victory and freedom, however long and hard the road may be" he is paraphrasing Churchill's speech to House of Commons on May 13, 1940.

- Dewitt's refusal of the title of 'General' after the Revolution and his reference to "learning how to plow" is a reference to Lucius Quinctius Cincinnatus (520 BC – 430 BC).
- The minor character Samir Akthr Abyd is based on Samuel Whittemore. For five years I walked daily past a monument marking the site where he stood up against government gun-grabbers. The monument reads

  > Near this spot, Samuel Whittemore, then 80 years old, killed three British soldiers, April 19, 1775. He was shot, bayoneted, beaten and left for dead, but recovered and lived to be 98 years of age.

Any man who shot and killed three government gun-grabbers in broad daylight is truly an American hero.

References to historical events

Where Heinlein's "The Moon is a Harsh Mistress" was written to parallel, in many ways, the American Revolution, this novel was inspired by the period of Icelandic Settlement.

The final climactic battle takes inspiration both from the running battles of April 19th, 1775, and - a bit - from Operation Market Garden in WWII.

References to real-world technology

There is a passing reference to the Wookiee and the other ships using "Draco" thrusters. The suggestion here is that Elon Musk's Space X firm at some point in the future open sources the real-world thruster of that name.

Snippets of source code bear more than a passing relationship to the Ruby programming language. Many thanks to Yukihiro Matsumoto who has made my life more pleasant than it would otherwise be.

"Abrash mode" in the VR helmets is a nod to software pioneer Michael Abrash.

Random historical footnotes

The Cathedral of Saint Joseph of Cupertino is named after the patron saint of astronauts.

Further Reading

If the economics concepts of the novel intrigued you, you might want to search Wikipedia, Amazon, and the blogosphere for more about:

- comparative advantage
- regulatory capture
- public choice theory
- principle / agent theory
- anarchocapitalism
- creative destruction
- immigration
- futarchy
- genetic algorithms
- private defense agencies and the Roman concept of "liturgies" ("contributions made by rich citizens for specific defense purposes").

About the Author

Travis J I Corcoran is a Catholic anarcho-capitalist software-engineer business-owner. He is an amateur at wood turning, blacksmithing, guitar playing, gourmet cooking, throwing ceramic pots, and a few other things.

He lives on a 50 acre farm in New Hampshire with his wife, dogs, livestock, and a variety of lathes and milling machines.

Travis has had non-fiction articles published in several national magazines including Dragon, Make, and Fine Homebuilding.

"Causes of Separation" is his second novel.

Please help me write more SF novels

There are three ways you can help me bring you more great science fiction stories:

- Go to Amazon.com right now (no, seriously, RIGHT NOW) and leave a review of this book (even really short like "loved it").
- Go to http://morlockpublishing.com/email-signup and sign up for very very infrequent emails when new books are written.
- Follow me on twitter at @morlockp

Made in the USA
Monee, IL
12 August 2022